D0994419

# Where I Belong

## Willow Woods

ISBN-13: 978-1-9993097-0-1

Aiséirí Publishing

# DEDICATION

Thank you to my awesome husband Nick who has been supportive throughout the whole writing process and offering unending encouragement.

To Lucy, Carrie, Kyri, Roz, Richard, Jon, Rachael, Andy and James for either reading drafts, offering advice and shoulders to cry on!

And of course, my parents!

Thank you!

(And Rumplestiltskin for not destroying all my notebooks)

To my Nanny Power who I miss every day

# Chapter One

The air was thick and dry. Each time the young woman tried to draw in a breath, she found herself choking. *Try not to panic. Open your eyes.* The voice was commanding but she couldn't follow the simple instructions; her eyes felt as if they had been sewn shut. Instead, she tried to focus on her surroundings, she could hear the crashing of waves close by, she could feel them lapping at her waist. Her clothes were soaked and weighed heavily on her back, pushing her further down into the sinking ground.

'Over here!' Alexandra heard a frantic voice shouting, followed by several pairs of hands pulling her.

'Miss? Miss, can you hear me?' Warm fingers pressed against the pulse in her throat and wrists. 'She has a pulse but its low,' something tugged at Alexandra's eyelids, and a bright light blinded her.

'What's wrong?'

'Her eyes...there's no pupil dilation but...*look.*' *Wake up!* The commanding voice was growing ever more urgent; *you must go now. He will find you!* She tried to ask the voice who 'he' was but there was no recollection of anyone. The light in her eye mercifully went out but hands around her persisted in their prodding. 'How long has she been like this?'

'We don't know, we found her here and called you straight away. We've been with her since...maybe twenty minutes?'

1

'Her body temperature is dangerously low,' Alexandra felt herself lifted from the sinking ground and placed on something long and thin.

'Will she be alright?' *Me?* She asked herself, *why would I not be?* She tried to reassure the faceless voices that she would be fine, that she *was* fine. There was the sound of banging followed by an unfamiliar rumbling sound as whatever she lay on began vibrating roughly. Something sharp stabbed into the skin on the back of her hand, and she bit back a cry. *He found me…what did I do wrong?* Mercifully she succumbed to a dark blanket, away from the painful pokes and stabs of the prying hands.

When Alexandra awoke she found herself in a bright room; the walls were a fresh white and the floor a pale blue. On either side of her were empty beds which looked oddly threatening. *Where am I?* This was not where she was supposed to be, but she didn't know where she was meant to be. Looking down she studied herself; she was wearing a thin paper-like gown the same blue shade as the floor, her arms were covered in bruises, and strange tubes protruded from the back of her right hand. She tried to pull at the tubes wanting them out of her skin, yelping at the sharp pain which shot up her arm.

'Oh no dearie,' Alexandra looked up at the sound of footsteps to see a kindly woman shaking her head.

'Where am I? What is going on?' Her voice was hoarse and painful; she suddenly realised she was thirsty and accepted a cup of water from the woman. She stared at the unfamiliar clear object, her eyebrows drawing together in a frown.

'The doctor will come see you soon. Try to relax; you were given a sedative.'

'Sedative?' The woman smiled at her but remained silent, bustling around her and feeling the pulse at her wrists before prodding a strange object into her ears. She flinched backwards and looked at the woman nervously.

'I know it is a bit disorienting dear but try to relax,' Alexandra nodded and gritted her teeth as the woman gently pushed the object into her ear once more.

'What does it do?' She asked as it beeped, and the woman pulled back.

'Takes your temperature…' The woman studied her curiously. As their eyes met, she frowned, and Alexandra felt her cheeks warm up; was there something wrong with her appearance? Tentatively she touched her fingertips to her cheeks and nose but could find nothing unusual. *Why will she not stop looking at my eyes?* The woman seemed on the brink of asking a question, but the sound of footsteps cut her off. A younger woman, perhaps in her mid- to late-twenties smiled warmly and approached the bedside.

'Hello, I'm Dr Williams. How are you feeling?' She asked picking up a clipboard from the end of the bed and scanning it.

'I...' Alexandra could only shrug helplessly as she looked at the doctor.

'Don't worry,' Dr Williams smiled reassuringly. 'I just have a few questions for you; firstly, can you tell me your name?' Alexandra frowned and shook her head but caught herself.

'I – I think it is Alexandra...I am not sure,' she closed her eyes as she felt a tugging sensation at the back of her head. She could almost hear someone calling her, a man's deep voice sounding frantic. Was she imagining it? 'Yes...Alexandra.'

'And your last name?' Alexandra's eyes were still closed as she fought to try and remember something, *anything*.

'I am sorry, but I do not know.' She opened her eyes and looked at Dr Williams. The doctor's deep brown eyes were reassuring and warm.

'Alexandra don't worry; you are most likely suffering from retrograde amnesia. You have suffered trauma, hopefully, over time your memories should return. Now can you tell me the date and where you are?' Again, Alexandra tried to think of the answer, but she couldn't. Her mind was thick and dark. The doctor frowned ever so slightly, but Alexandra caught the flicker of concern. As if to distract herself Dr Williams reached into her pocket and pulled out a cylindrical object which shone brightly from one end. 'Just look over my shoulder,' Alexandra nodded and focused her gaze on a chipped piece of paint on the wall.

'I – Is something wrong?' Alexandra asked noticing the woman pull back slightly.

'No, your eyes...I'm sorry I don't mean to be rude...' Seemingly embarrassed the doctor distracted Alexandra from further questions by having her follow her light with her eyes. 'Do you remember how you came to be here?'

'No…I – I remember I was hot but cold. I felt like I was sinking…' Dr Williams sat in a worn plastic chair beside her bed and took a pen from the pocket of her deep blue scrubs.

'Alexandra you were found lying face down not too far from the pier. You had obviously been there for a while as you were soaked from the tide, the sinking feeling I imagine would be the sand beneath you. As for being hot and cold…well you were soaked from the shoulders down. Are you sure you don't remember anything?' Alexandra shook her head feeling sick; what would have happened if she had drowned? How had she gotten there? 'Do you think you could manage a short walk?' Alexandra nodded eager to stand up; the doctor helped to detach her from various machines and offered her an arm to lean on.

'Dr Williams, where am I?' Alexandra asked wearily as she followed the woman through various corridors. Her bare feet pattered against the hard-shiny floor. The air had a funny scent and her nose wrinkled at the mixture of overcooked cabbage and disinfectant. Everything was unfamiliar, and she couldn't help the tendrils of fear snaking through her veins.

'Royal Bournemouth Hospital – you were brought here three days ago, you've been asleep since then. You are quite lucky. When you were brought in you were close to hypothermia. You must have been in the water for quite some time Alexandra; you are lucky it is the middle of summer – had it been winter I doubt you would be walking with me now.' Alexandra appreciated the doctor's blunt truth. She had almost died. Why? What had she been doing? Dr Williams led her into a large room filled with lockers; she looked at the objects in fascination and stroked her fingertips against the cool metal. *Why does none of this look familiar? Why do I not know what any of this is?* 'Alexandra, when you were brought to us…you were very unusual attire.' The doctor opened a locker taller than herself and pulled out a garment in a long polythene bag. She pulled the plastic covering up and held the garment out to her. 'Do you recognise this?' Alexandra took the dress and studied it. It would have been a beautiful garment once, but it must have been destroyed when she was in the water. The delicate fabric was stiff and ripped in several places; it had undoubtedly once been a pure white gown but was now grey with patches of stubborn sand staining it. The skirt of the dress glittered with beautiful jewels, and she ran her hand over them, hoping to learn their secrets.

'This is what I was wearing?'

'Yes…do you recognise it?' Alexandra turned to stare back at the garment intently but could decipher nothing from it.

'I am sorry…but…it looks like a wedding dress.' Everything she had seen so far felt unfamiliar and frightening, the dress she held felt the total opposite, and she hugged it close burying her face into the destroyed fabric. Tears fell down her cheeks and blended with the salt of the ocean. Was she supposed to be getting married? What had happened? Were her family safe? Her husband? *Do I have a husband?* A sob wrenched itself free and she found herself embraced by the doctor.

'Ssh, I am sorry this is distressing. I hoped that seeing this would trigger a memory…give it time Alexandra. Let me take you back to the ward; I'm sure you're starving. The dress is ruined, but I will keep it locked here to protect it for you…' The doctor's eyes glanced down to the jewel-ridden skirt. 'With a dress like this, I am sure there are people desperately searching for you. Don't worry; we'll get you home.'

After a few days, Alexandra was discharged from the hospital with nothing but her ruined wedding dress and a scrap of paper with an address on it. After being interviewed by the police and several medical professionals she was still no closer to discovering who she was. Her auburn hair was swept back into a long ponytail and she rubbed the back of her neck nervously as she stepped out onto the scalding tarmac of the hospital car park. The air was suffocating and beads of sweat formed on her forehead and back of her neck. She was dressed unflatteringly in a baggy pair of jeans and an old t-shirt that someone had kindly donated to her.

*Where do I go?* She thought biting back blind panic and looking around. None of her surroundings were familiar; nothing made sense. She looked down at the scrap of paper in her hand and shouldered the bag carrying her dress. Dr Williams had assured her that the address wasn't too far from the hospital. She followed the instructions scribbled underneath paying close attention to the signs. As she approached a main road she looked around; strange metal vehicles rushed past causing her ponytail to whip around. They broke through the suffocating heat but left Alexandra choking on a thick chemical taste.

The hostel was a dilapidated building that Alexandra was surprised was still standing. Steeling her nerves, she knocked on the door and stepped back as a blurred figure appeared behind the frosted glass. *Do not be nervous, they are expecting you after all.* The hospital had called on her behalf to arrange a room for her to stay in.

'Alex?' A curt man with an egg-shaped head and balding face peered at her through thick glasses suspiciously.

'Alexandra,' she replied standing straight and raising her chin. 'I believe the hospital called?'

'C'min,' the man stepped back, and Alexandra smiled as she stepped out of the heat into the sticky air of the hallway. Her nose wrinkled at an acrid smell of burning and something rotten. 'The hospital didn't say much about you.'

'There is not much to tell,' Alexandra shrugged, 'I was found on the seafront a week ago. I do not remember anything...' She could see the man disapprove as he frowned, and she could tell he was concerned about her appearance. 'I assure you that I will not be a problem. I hope to remember something soon, and in the meantime I am sure my family are looking for me.' *I can only pray they are.*

'Well regardless the rent is due every Friday. Forty quid a week, food and essentials are your own cost, so I suggest you get a job – if you don't already have one.' Alexandra nodded although she was clueless to what he was talking about; rent? And what were essentials?

'Of course...I shall go out and try to find one straight away.'

'Let me show you to your room.' The man gestured for her to follow him up a rickety staircase; from somewhere above, she heard the steady beat of music making the ceiling vibrate. 'We have strict rules here, break any and you're out.' Alexandra nodded as she listened to the list of rules – half of which she barely understood but she made the occasional noise to show she was listening. 'This is your room,' a wooden door was unlocked, and Alexandra was surprised at how nice the room was. The walls were a freshly painted cream with a new carpet to match; thin pale orange curtains framed the small window which looked out on to an alley below. 'Clean it yourself and mind you don't damage anything – if there's damage to the walls or furniture you'll be charged when you leave.'

'Thank you,' Alexandra accepted the key and blinked back tears. She felt stupid for crying all of a sudden and ducked her head to hide them from the strange man.

'I've seen a bit about you on the news,' the man's voice was gruff but his manner was somewhat gentler. 'I'm sure you'll remember who you are and as you say your family will be looking for you. In the meantime find yourself a job – I would hate to have to kick you out, but we have rules to follow. There's some shops close to the seafront; they'll be hiring as it's the tourist season. You shouldn't find it too hard to get something.' Alexandra smiled gratefully and closed the door behind her as the man departed. The room was sparsely furnished; an unmade bed with a duvet and pillow, a cheap bedside cabinet, desk, chair and sink were all that were there. Setting the bag on the bed she opened it and looked down at the destroyed dress, the jewels glimmering up at her. Biting back a fresh wave of tears she forced herself to pluck three from the dress and slip them in the pocket of her jeans. Dr Williams had told her she might be able to sell them, although it pained her to think of doing so what choice did she have?

When Alexandra returned to the hostel that evening she took the wad of notes from her jeans pocket and looked around for a place to put them. She had known from the moment she'd stepped in to the shop that the man behind the counter was ripping her off, but she could hardly refuse. She had used some of the money to buy clothes that would fit and taken the advice of the man who'd shown her to her room of finding a job.

After spending several hours being asked if she had a 'cv' Alexandra finally secured herself a job in a small coffee shop. The money from the jewels would tide her over for emergencies, but at least she didn't have to worry about being kicked out for not paying rent. Unable to find a secure hiding place Alexandra folded the notes and stashed them under the mattress.

Exhausted by the day Alexandra set about making the bed, staring at the sheets in confusion as she unwrapped them. *I must know how to do this, surely?* After several attempts, she managed to stuff the duvet into one of the covers although it remained lumpy and uneven no matter how many times she shook it out. Extracting one of the bath towels from a bag, she locked the door to her room and sought out the bathroom. It was small but pleasant with white tiles along the floor and walls giving it a bright and fresh feeling. Catching her reflection in the mirror, she stared at herself for a few moments before cautiously approaching. She had not seen her appearance since waking up in the hospital; it had never even occurred to her what she might look like. Would she recognise herself?

An oval-shaped face with an almond shaped eyes stared back at her. She ran a hand through her long auburn hair testing the soft texture before touching her fingertips to the smooth skin on her nose. She thought back to the reaction of each of the people she had met, everyone had been shocked by something about her appearance but what was it? She frowned as she leant closer into the mirror. Her eyes were a bright forest green; she was about to give up when she caught sight of what startled everyone. The black of her pupils spiralled out giving an unusual pattern. *Why does this alarm everyone? Surely it cannot be unusual?* Knowing there was no point in worrying about it she pushed the pattern of her eyes to the back of her mind.

# *Chapter Two*

Gradually Alexandra began to fall into a pattern as she settled in the hostel. Each morning she would wake up, shower and leave for work shortly before six. The walk from the hostel to the coffee shop was pleasant, and she would often leave earlier than she needed so that she could enjoy a quick stroll along the seafront. She partly walked along the shore as she enjoyed the view of the sunrise against the ocean, but secretly she hoped it would trigger a memory. Despite the days having now melted into weeks, she was still not close to finding out who she was.

'Have you ever thought about hypnotherapy?' Matt, the hostel owner, asked her one sunny morning as he picked up his coffee from the counter. Alexandra shook her head and remained silent; she was sick of appearing ignorant and did not want to have to ask what hypnotherapy was. 'Personally I don't believe in that stuff, I'd rather not have people poking around in my head. But you never know – it could work, and what do you have to lose?'

'Do you know of anyone?' Alexandra asked wiping the counter down.

'A friend of mine has recently been seeing someone to quit smoking. I'll get their number for you; it's up to you whether you call or not. I don't want to push you into anything.'

'Thank you, Matt,' Alexandra smiled warmly, 'I appreciate it.' She glanced around to make sure Paul didn't see her placing a slice of coffee cake on a plate and sliding it to Matt with a wink.

'Don't go getting yourself in trouble.'

'I will not,' Alexandra reassured him moving from behind the counter so that she could begin clearing tables. After Matt left, she found herself wondering how much hypnotherapy would cost. She had forced herself to pick the jewels from her what she could only assume really was her wedding dress, it was beyond repair and she had no choice but to discard it although it pained her to do so. She had hidden the jewels in a small pouch she had bought in a charity shop which was tucked safely beneath her bed in the fold of the sheet.

When Alexandra arrived back at the hostel she found several of the residents seated in the dining area eating out of plastic microwavable containers. She had been slender, to begin with, but even she could tell that she was losing a ridiculous amount of weight. The food seemed so unappetising and on several occasions, she had been ill.

'Matt left this for you,' a boy with baggy jeans and a tattoo on his neck handed her a sealed envelope.

'Thank you,' Alexandra smiled and took the envelope from him. She could feel the business card inside but was thankful Matt had put it out of sight from prying eyes.

Two weeks had passed before Alexandra finally plucked up the courage to call the number on the business card. She found herself standing in a nondescript cul-de-sac knocking on a door with a frosted diamond panel, a young man only a few years older with piercing blue eyes opened answered and smiled warmly at her.

'Alexandra?' She nodded and smiled stepping into the house at his gesture. 'I'm Henry; it's a pleasure to meet you.' She followed him through the house into a back room which was painted a cream colour with a matching carpet. There was a small bookcase against one wall, a desk with a computer, chocolate brown settee and matching armchair. Henry gestured for Alexandra to take a seat and she tentatively sat down on the settee, glancing nervously around her. When she finally forced herself to meet Henry's gaze, she regretted it instantly for she saw his blue eyes fixate on the spiral pattern of her pupils.

'I'm sorry Alexandra, you are probably sick of people commenting on your eyes.' He smiled sheepishly, and Alexandra felt herself relax.

'A little,' she nodded unable to help grinning at him. Suddenly he seemed more human, less imposing.

'You said over the phone you were hoping to regain some memories, could you elaborate a little more?' Henry settled back into his chair, and Alexandra looked down at her hands folded neatly in her lap as she thought over what to say.

'Not really,' she finally admitted. 'I'm sorry – this may be a complete waste of your time. I woke up in hospital about a month ago; I barely knew who I was. All I know is my name, everything else is completely gone.'

'There was nothing to indicate how you had gotten there?' Alexandra felt reassured by his question; as if he did not think she was a complete lost cause.

'No. Apparently I was wearing a wedding dress,' tears stung her eyes as she thought of the destroyed dress.

'It is unusual to have no memories at all...I haven't encountered this before. But that isn't to say you are a lost cause,' Henry held up his hand as he saw Alexandra's face fall. 'It may be difficult, and you might not get anything from your first session. But what do you have to lose?' Alexandra smiled slightly as she remembered Matt had said the same thing. She didn't have anything to lose, other than the expensive fee. *I have the diamonds...if this helps me get my memory back then surely selling them is the best solution* At Henry's instructions she made herself comfortable on the settee, lying down and closing her eyes. She found herself compelled to listen to Henry's voice as his tone took on a soothing note. 'Picture yourself in a corridor, and in this corridor, there are many doors.' Feeling self-conscious Alexandra pictured a corridor with several doors. *This is not going to work!* She pushed the voice to the back of her head and drew in a deep breath as Henry instructed.

Gradually she felt herself coaxed into the trance; she found herself walking through the corridor pausing at each door. Calmly she walked down the dark corridor, her hands resting against each door as she passed it. *Not this one,* she nodded to the voice and calmly strode away. The sound of rustling pricked her ears, and she glanced down at her clothes, no longer was she in jeans and a fitted t-shirt. She wore a floor-length dress with a sweeping skirt, bell sleeves and a fitted bodice. Frowning Alexandra studied the velvet fabric; was she dreaming? Had she fallen asleep rather than going into a trance? Pushing the thought to the back of her head she carried on walking down the corridor, finally settling on a door that she knew she needed to open. Her hand hesitated above the polished brass doorknob; what if she didn't like the answers that lay behind it? Steeling her nerves, she forced herself to open the door.

She was struck by the odd sensation of watching herself from a distance. She was dressed in a similar gown to the one she wore now, her long hair tied back in an elegant plait which was draped over her right shoulder. She was standing up and pacing a room lined with bookcases and old scrolls, even from a distance she could tell that she was distressed. *This cannot be real,* Alexandra thought to herself frowning. She turned as she watched her other-self do so. She caught a split-second glance of a tall man entering the room before she could attempt to focus on his features Henry's voice broke through the scene.

'Why are you angry?'

'I…' Alexandra shook her head, and her eyes flew open. 'I was not…was I?' Dazed she looked around surprised to find herself in Henry's brightly lit room rather than the candlelit study. She could see Henry was looking at her thoughtfully and she swallowed her nerves.

'Do you remember seeing anything?'

'Yes…were you asking me questions the whole time?' Henry nodded, and Alexandra rubbed her head feeling the beginning throb of a headache. 'What does any of this mean?'

'It is positive in some ways; you do have memories which can be found. However…you seem to have buried them quite deep. The scene and clothes you describe are not a lifestyle you would find yourself in. Obviously we already knew you were dealing with some form of trauma, but I suspect it may be deeper than first thought. Alexandra, I want you to think long and hard about whether this is a treatment you wish to continue.'

'I cannot continue as I am now,' Alexandra pointed out, 'I cannot stay in the hostel forever. And what of my family? I need to know who I am.' Henry nodded gravely and led Alexandra to the door.

'I understand, but please do think on this.'

Over the next several nights Alexandra slept fitfully. Her dreams were plagued with sporadic flashes, none of which she could focus on. She caught glimpses of rich and elegant clothes, crowds of people dancing and feasts that looked like they belonged in fairy tales. But not once could she capture a face or a snatch of conversation.

'I think you may be reading too much into this Alexandra,' Henry tried to reason on her third session. 'The human mind is complicated, memories we believe to be true can be in fact false. These images you are seeing are false; you have clearly suffered a traumatic event that your subconscious is trying to suppress.'

'But what if I am not?' Alexandra protested, 'What if these are real memories?' Henry arched an eyebrow and Alexandra bit back a frustrated sigh.

'These images you are seeing, where would they be from Alexandra? The only places you would see clothes and events such as the ones you describe would be in history books, art galleries and novels – children's' fairy tales!' Alexandra studied Henry as he paused to take off his glasses and clean them. *These are not false,* Alexandra told herself, *I know these are real. But how can I make Henry understand?*

'What if these are false memories, but what if they help me to remember? *Please* Henry I know these mean something, they are not just hallucinations and dreams.' Henry sighed but slowly nodded.

'Very well, but Alexandra I ask you again to think carefully on this.'

'Of course,' Alexandra nodded and stood up.

*'You should not have to go through with this!' Alexandra turned to face a dark-skinned woman with short black cropped hair and eyes like melted chocolate. 'Mathe is distraught and I know you are –'*

*'I am no such thing. I am doing my duty.'*

*'Why are you lying?' Angrily Alexandra stood up and slammed the book she had been reading shut. 'You will have to live with this for the rest of your life; there will be no turning back if you go through with it.'*

*'I am not a fool Krista,' Alexandra snapped. 'I have made my decision, I have given my word, and I will not go back on it.'*

*'We can find another way.' Alexandra smiled sadly and shook her head.*

*'No. We cannot.'*

# Chapter Three

Krista, the dark skinned woman, was never far from Alexandra's mind. She was careful not to mention her to Henry, nor to anyone who enquired how her search was going. The dreams had resumed to their sporadic flashes, but now she was able to recognise Krista and begin to make out people who stood close to her. Deep down she knew that the memories were not false, that Henry was wrong. But she still had no clue as to who she was, where she came from or even how to get home.

Closing her eyes, she inhaled a breath of the salty sea breeze and stretched her arms over the edge of the pier. *Maybe I should just give up;* she thought to herself opening her eyes and watching the sun sink lower in the sky. Grey clouds loomed overhead ominously, and fat drops of rain splattered against her face. *I have a job; I could sell some more of the diamonds and get out of the hostel. Settle down…start afresh.* Tears stung her eyes at the thought, and she wiped them away only for fresh ones to follow. Could she really give up? Several months had passed and she was still no closer to discovering anything about herself. The dreams were progress, but they only created fresh questions and rarely any answers.

Zipping her fleece up higher Alexandra shoved her hands into her pockets and turned to walk back along the pier towards the hostel. Perhaps she should never have waited this long to settle in, to find her own way. But she had been sure she would be home by now, wherever that was. She stopped at a newsagent to pick up the local paper followed by the fish and chip shop to get herself some dinner. Pulling out the property section she set the greasy food on top of the rest of the paper and sat on the bedroom floor as she pored over the properties for rent.

*Who are you, Krista?* She asked herself as she circled a one-bedroom flat close to the seafront. The name felt strange yet somehow familiar; it comforted her as she said it aloud to herself. Glancing at the mattress she tapped the pen against the floor; she hated the thought of selling the diamonds, but she needed to make a choice. She could not stay in the hostel much longer, and others were more in need of the room than her. She could only hope that if they were sewn on to a dress, they were not some kind of family heirloom. Biting back a yawn she scrunched up the empty fish wrapper and gathered up the greasy newspaper. She would sell a few more; hopefully, her family would forgive her.

*Alexandra walked down a grassy path; hedges towered over her on either side and on several occasions, she ran into a dead end which forced her to turn back on herself. Glancing down she saw that she wore an elegant green velvet gown with bell sleeves and a flared floor length skirt. Another dream? She asked herself as she turned back once more and took a left turn. Somewhere in the distance she could hear trickling water, blocking out all other sounds she focused on the water and found her way to the centre of a maze. In the centre stood a fountain carved from a mixture of white marble and black onyx in the shape of an elegant woman draped in elegant fabrics.*

*'Alexandra?' At the sound of a deep voice, she turned her back on the fountain and found herself staring at a tall figure. He stepped closer to her and Alexandra craned her neck to get a better look at the man. He was exceptionally tall with golden blonde hair and deep blue eyes, relief flooded through her as she noticed the same spiral pattern in his irises that she herself had. Her relief was short-lived when she realised there was something almost chilly about his appearance and she found herself suppressing a shudder.*

*'I – I'm sorry but...do I know you?' Alexandra frowned; there was something vaguely familiar about this man. 'Wait,' she cut him off before he could answer. 'You know who I am? You're from my home?'*

*'You do not recognise me?' Alexandra shrugged helplessly suddenly embarrassed. 'Oh, Alexandra what have you done? Do you know where you are?'*

'Bournemouth,' Alexandra answered quickly, but the confused look on the man's face only disheartened her further. 'Please can you tell me what happened? Why am I here? Who are you?' She caught something flickering across the man's face but couldn't distinguish what it was.

'I am afraid I am not able to answer all of your questions Alexandra, I do not know why you are there – or where Bournemouth is. I have not heard of this kingdom…'

'Kingdom?' Alexandra frowned but even as she said the word she felt it was oddly familiar. 'Who are you?' She asked with a sigh, too exhausted to be polite. 'I'm sorry but I don't understand what is going on. I woke up in a hospital to be told I was found on the seafront in a wedding dress, please if you can – tell me what happened?'

'My name is Carlyle,' he bowed deeply as he spoke and the overwhelming urge to curtsey took hold of Alexandra. She fought it back and craned her neck as Carlyle stepped closer to her. Gently he placed his hands on either side of her face, keeping her eyes captive with his own. 'You truly do not remember me?' His thumb traced the outline of her lower lip and Alexandra stepped back feeling uncomfortable. 'You should not fear me, Alexandra; I would never harm you. I have been searching for you ever since you vanished; all I want is to bring you home.'

'And where is home?' Alexandra asked taking an uneasy step back, 'How do I know this is not all a dream?'

'This is a dream, it is the only way I could contact you – and even that has been challenging. I want to bring you home, but it may be a while before I can cross over to you.'

'Cross over? Where are you?'

'It does not matter.' Cold lips touched her forehead, and Alexandra stepped back.

'Carlyle –'

'Soon Alexandra. I just needed to know you were safe.'

'Wait! Please…tell me who you are at least? How do I know you?'

'We are betrothed. On the day of our wedding, I arrived at the temple to find your mother distraught, you had disappeared.'

'This wasn't a dream Henry this was real.'

'Alexandra please think rationally; do you really believe this man is from another world? That *you* are from another world?' Alexandra moved to argue but quickly settled back in the chair, rubbing her eyes as she adjusted awakening from the hypnosis.

'No of course not.'

'Alexandra I strongly suggest you take a break. I will refer you to a counsellor – someone who can talk through this with you more in depth, but I don't think it's appropriate for that person to be me, or for you to continue hypnosis.'

Accepting a business card, Alexandra smiled weakly at Henry and thanked him for his help. She blinked back tears as she walked towards the coast and her new flat. Inside it was stiflingly quiet; there was no shouting or thudding of feet against her ceiling. Slumping against the door, she slid to the floor no longer fighting back the tears. She had taken a short-term lease of only six months, but it was beginning to now dawn on her that she would never return home. She was sure her dreams were real, that Carlyle was real, but she had not dreamt of him since the first one three days ago. *Accept it;* she told herself, *you are not going to go home ever. This home now…is it that bad?*

# *Chapter Four*

Rain pounded against the window, Alexandra sat on the windowsill with her back against the wall and her feet propped up on a footstool. Her head rested against the cool glass of the window, and she watched as the rain splattered on the ground below, the ocean was rough and barely distinguishable from the deep grey skill. Her dreams had stopped completely, no more did she dream of Krista, Carlyle or even the brief glimpses of various people. She still had the number of the counsellor from Henry after their final meeting almost three weeks ago, but she had not given them a call. What was the point? She had grown to accept that her dreams were nothing more than dreams; her meeting with Carlyle had clearly been her imagination reaching a breaking point. Readjusting the duvet wrapped around her shoulders, Alexandra settled back so that she could slide down the wall and was half-lying, half-sitting on the windowsill. The sound of the torrential downpour outside was comforting, the howling wind made her feel sleepy, and she closed her eyes planning to rest them just for a few minutes.

She slept deeply, not a single dream broke through her subconscious, and she awoke the next morning she felt restless. *Whatever those dreams meant, this is my home now.* She thought showering, as she brushed her teeth as she stared at her reflection. She was fixated with the spiral pattern of her eyes, what did it mean? Was it merely a birth defect or was it a sign that she was different? *It doesn't matter anymore*, she told herself, *and it's just the way you are – stop trying to make something of it.* As she dressed for work, she wondered what had made her assume that she was from another world. The clothes Carlyle had worn had seemed straight from a fantasy film; richly embroidered tunics and full-sleeved shirts. His language too had suggested there was something otherworldly about him. She had not heard anyone mention 'kingdoms' and 'temples' since she was found on the seafront. *Focus on today;* she told herself pulling her orange t-shirt with the *Coffee Chum!* logo splashed on the back.

'How goes the search for your hidden past?' Alexandra fought back a scowl as she closed the till and handed a customer their change. Only once they had left did she turn around to look at the manager, Paul.

'Over.' She answered honestly, 'that hypnotherapist I was seeing, Henry, thought perhaps it was doing more harm than good. If my family want to find me then I am sure they will. But let's face it – it's been four months and there has been nothing. No sign of anyone looking for me.' She tried to smile and sound cheery about it, but she could see from Paul's expression she was failing miserably. 'What is the point of upheaving my life and going into the unknown? I've moved out of the hospital and have the flat now; I'm happy here. So…you're stuck with me. If that's ok?'

'I'm glad – I hate having to recruit new team members.' Alexandra rolled her eyes but couldn't help smiling. She was still uncertain of Paul, she knew there were certain legal issues around her employment, but she didn't dare raise them in case she was kicked out. But despite his business ethics, he was a fun boss, and good to be around sometimes. She set about clearing tables as the last few customers left. 'Why don't you come out for a drink tonight? To celebrate you staying.'

'Celebrate not going home and losing my family?' *Losing my fiancé who I apparently jilted?* She said the last part to herself; she had not mentioned to anyone the dreams – how would she explain them? She blushed at the look on Paul's face and cleared her throat nervously. 'I'm sorry Paul, drinks would be great.' She tried to alleviate her guilt by telling herself that she wasn't married. She'd never made it to the wedding. *Carlyle is not even real;* a firm voice tried to dissuade the doubts in her mind.

Dressed in a pair of fitted jeans and a polo-neck jumper Alexandra slipped through the pub doors and smiled as Paul waved her over to a table. In front of him was a half-drunk pint glass and a glass of wine which he pushed towards Alexandra as she took a seat. As she sipped at the wine, her eyes darted around the pub trying to locate the rest of the team members from *Coffee Chum!*

'I wanted a chance to talk to you alone. Outside of work.' Paul answered her questioning look. 'I've been thinking for a while now about something, but I didn't want to bring it up. I didn't want you feel pressured into staying.' Alexandra felt tendrils of unease creeping up her spine as Paul rested a hand on her knee. 'If you're serious about staying I'd like you to become Assistant Manager, I've been thinking of hiring for a while now. You'd be perfect; you're reliable, a hard worker and you get on with the customers.' *Not to mention I'm cheap labour,* she thought slightly bitterly. She had learnt early on that Paul was paying her less than he was legally obligated, but she had no choice. She still didn't. As far as the system was concerned she didn't exist; there was no record of her anywhere. She had no National Insurance number, no passport or even birth certificate. She might as well not exist, and it was hard to argue for fair pay when you didn't exist in the eyes of the law. The diamonds were never far from her mind, but she knew it would be too risky to sell them. It would raise questions about where she had obtained them. Besides they were part of her past, while she knew they were worth a fortune she couldn't bear to part with them. Pushing the thoughts to the back of her head she forced a grateful smile and gulped down the rest of her wine.

'That would be great,' she answered forcing a grin, 'are you sure I would not be stepping on anyone's toes though? I've been here the least amount of time.' She barely listened to his answer. Instead, she smiled and nodded in what she hoped were the right places. Somehow, she endured the evening, slowing down on her drinking and switching to soft drinks when she realised Paul would not relent in his 'celebration' of her promotion.

'I like you Alexandra, you were stuck up when we met – but lately…we should get to know each other better.' Paul's words were slightly slurred, and Alexandra could smell the beer on his breath even as she tried to lean back. Blind panic settled over Alexandra, how had she gotten into this situation?

'I should go home, it's getting late and we've got work tomorrow.' As if to emphasise her point a bell at the bar rang.

'One more, we might as well stay for last orders.' Paul grinned seeming completely unphased by her avoidance of the subject. He didn't even wait for her to decline the offer as he pushed his seat back, scraping it across the worn wooden floor and elbowing his way over to the bar. Sighing Alexandra leant back in her chair, exhaustion was sweeping over her, and she feared she would fall asleep then and there at the pub table. *One more drink,* she told herself, *just get through this one last drink and then sleep.* Out of the corner of her eye, she saw Paul making his way through the crush of people, holding the two glasses above his head. She was dismayed to see he held a pint of beer and yet another wine glass for her.

'I – I really should get going,' she stammered not sure her liver could take one more glass of wine that night. She pulled her jacket on as she stood up, but Paul swung his arms around her shoulder keeping her in place.

'It's one more drink Alex –'

'Alexandra,' she snapped blushing immediately. 'It's late Paul, and we do both have work tomorrow. How will it look for the soon-to-be Assistant Manager to turn up to work drunk?' With one arm still around her shoulders, Paul picked up the pint glass and gulped it back at an alarming rate. Slamming it on the table, he picked up the wine glass and held it out for Alexandra, grinning drunkenly. 'Down in one.' Alexandra looked down at the glass shaking her head. Part of her wanted to take the glass from him and throw it in his face, but she knew she would lose her job – not to mention it would be an overreaction. Her eyes focused on the glass as if Paul held out an angry cobra. She reached out to take it planning to spill it somehow. Her hand frozen when she saw the glass begin to shake in his hand, sending the wine spilling out.

'What –' The question died on her lips as the glass shattered in Paul's hand. Covering her face with her hands as fragments of glass sprayed over them. 'Are you alright?' She could see the glass embedded in Paul's hand and when she looked up, she could see his face had turned a sickly pale. 'Sit down,' her voice took on a commanding tone which felt strangely natural as if she was used to giving commands. 'Paul, I need you to sit down,' behind her she could hear voices talking in hushed whispers. 'We should get you to A and E; you look like you might need stitches.' She gently eased a shard of glass from his palm and set it on a napkin. Blood poured from the wound and she bit her lip feeling nauseous at the sight of blood.

'It's fine,' Paul croaked, and Alexandra glared at him.

'Come on, let's find a taxi.' Pressing a wad of napkins around his hand Alexandra led him outside the pub and to a line of taxis. The hospital was crowded with a mixture of late night drinkers, crying children and people with various ailments. Exhaustion continued to pull at Alexandra as she plonked down on an uncomfortable plastic chair. Biting back a yawn she blinked rapidly trying to clear her bleary eyes.

'Here,' Alexandra wrinkled her nose as the smell of cheap coffee jolted her awake. She took the paper cup and smiled weakly at Paul. 'You should go home.' *I've been telling you that for hours now,* Alexandra thought dryly but shook her head. She couldn't leave him to wait this out on his own, who knew how long it could be before he was seen? 'I'm sorry I kept you out…I should have stopped drinking…' His words were still slurred, but she could see the shock of the accident had sobered him up somewhat.

'It's fine,' Alexandra shrugged, 'you can make it up to me by giving me a Sunday off.'

'Deal, how about next Sunday? It's bonfire night on Saturday. Come to the fireworks with me; we can get dinner after.' Alexandra bit her lip uncertainly, wasn't she technically engaged? Did it still stand if she had jilted her fiancé? If she had crossed worlds to get away from him? *What makes you think it was Carlyle you're running away from?* She thought suddenly but pushed it to the back of her mind; there was no point in dwelling on it. She was done with her past, or whatever those dreams were. Besides Paul knew nothing about her circumstances, she had never told him or any of her teammates about the wedding dress. There was no jewellery to suggest she was betrothed, so why mention it at all? She was so consumed by her thoughts she didn't realise Paul had leant over, not until she felt his wet lips against hers and the taste of beer on his breath. 'Just give me a chance?' Suppressing a grimace Alexandra nodded and smiled in what she hoped was a demure manner.

'Sure. One chance,' she teased taking a deep swig of coffee to wash the taste of beer from her mouth. *Maybe I should start looking for a job.*

The taxi dropped her home in the early hours of the morning. Knowing she would only get a few hours of sleep before she had to be awake again Alexandra rested her forehead against the front door of her flat. Was there point in going to bed or should she try to persevere and just stay up? *Sleep!* She screamed at herself. Exhaustion was tugging at her, pulling her like waves pulling her out to sea. She felt as if she was drowning from the exhaustion and longed to give in and let sleep embrace her. Somehow, she managed to fight it off long enough to brush her teeth and shed her clothes before finally slipping under the deliciously cosy duvet.

*Alexandra found herself standing beside the fountain in the maze from her last dream. Carlyle stood in the entryway of the centre looking slightly annoyed.*

*'I have been trying to contact you for several hours, why have you been fighting me?'*

*'I haven't...I think.'* Alexandra shrugged *pacing around the fountain. 'Besides how could I fight a figment of my imagination? You're not here; you're not even real.'* She dipped her hand into the fountain and withdrew it quickly when she felt the icy temperature of the water.

*'Alexandra I can assure you I am quite real. I have been searching for you –'*

*'Then where are you? Why am I still in Bournemouth with no idea of who I am?'*

*'Because I am yet to find a way to reach you – to cross worlds.'* Alexandra froze and stared at Carlyle blankly over her shoulder. So it was true? Was she from another world? Impossible, *she told herself,* this is a dream! *'Perhaps I should have told you this when I first found you.'* Carlyle closed the distance between them, his long legs covering the distance quickly. Gently he lowered Alexandra, so she was sitting on the edge of the fountain; she was still dazed and shook her head numbly. *'Alexandra you are a Princess of Karstares – soon to been Queen of Saphyre.'*

*'Where? What?'* Alexandra shook her head unable to shake the dazed feeling. *This is not real. I make* coffee *for a living. I scrub tables and clean toilets. I can't be a princess. This is just a dream.'* She said the last part more to herself, trying to reinforce that she was dreaming and not losing her mind. What had happened to her in her past to make her dream up Carlyle?

*'Alexandra please calm down.'* Carlyle tried to pull her into his arms, but she pushed him away. Jumping up she began frantically pacing back and forth. *'I can prove it to you –'*

*'No please. Wake up,'* she closed her eyes trying to steady her breathing. When she opened her eyes Carlyle was holding out a golden locket; he flipped it open to reveal two miniature portraits on the inside. The left image looked exactly like her in a medieval forest green gown, her thick hair hung in loose ringlets, and a golden circlet rested on top of her head. The right image was clearly Carlyle; he stood regally with his right hand clasping a sword belted around his hips. He wore a delicately embroidered blue tunic lined in silver over a silver shirt with full sleeves.

*'I presented this to you when our betrothal was formally announced. The locket was my mother's. The morning of our wedding this was presented to me…you had left it behind.'* Carlyle's face darkened at the memory and Alexandra gulped back a lump of fear at his expression. Ignoring her protests, he unclasped the locked and fitted it around her neck. *'You are a Princess, Alexandra. You do not belong in the world you are in now, not if you are doing the work of servants. Please give me time. I will find you.'* Alexandra closed her eyes and shook her head; this was a dream. He wasn't real. *'I promise I will find you.'*

When Alexandra woke up, she was curled up in the foetal position. Sitting up she stretched her arms above her head, flinching as her hands moved behind her neck and brushed something cool at her throat. A feeling of dread tugged at her stomach as she pulled the locket over her head. Flipping it open she stared down at the miniature portraits of herself and Carlyle.

# Chapter Five

Alexandra sat up in bed holding the locket and staring at it intently. Was she going insane? Checking her alarm she saw she had only a few minutes until it would go off. Carefully she placed the locket in the bedside cabinet; the pouch of diamonds tucked safely in the back of the draw and got up to shower. She tried to tell herself there was no point in dwelling over the locket, that it didn't mean anything. But deep down she knew she was lying to herself, that she was just too plain scared to face the truth. She had either lost her mind, or Carlyle was real and telling the truth. She wasn't quite sure which option was the preferable one. *It was bad enough discovering I had run out on my wedding;* she thought turning the shower on and yelping as the cold water hit her. Had she really run from a kingdom? Guilt tugged at her, what kind of person would run away from their responsibilities like that? *There is no way I am a princess!* Panic bubble in her stomach and she tried to push the thoughts from her mind. *Concentrate on today*, she reasoned with herself; *even if Carlyle is real, he isn't here.*

Alexandra wasn't surprised to find Paul absent from work that day. Rumours of his visit to the accident and emergency the previous night had spread like wildfire among the team, but luckily none of them thought to question Alexandra over the events. She thought of the glass he had been holding, how had it just exploded? Paul hadn't appeared to be holding the glass too tightly, so what happened?

By the time she had closed the shop and cashed up the sky had turned pitch black and rain hammered against the pavement outside. *Great,* Alexandra sighed flipping up the hood of her coat. As she walked quickly to her flat, her mind turned over the events from the previous night, both the shattering glass and the dream with Carlyle. She had been lost in thought about them all day, questions turning over in her head, but she hadn't been able to answer one of them. It wasn't until she was in the kitchen of her flat cooking dinner that she moved on from mulling over past events to debating her future. Would Carlyle ever find a way to bring her home? *I need to call Paul…I can hardly go out with him on Saturday knowing I have a fiancé.* But did she? *Maybe I should call Henry…surely, he would be able to give me some kind of advice?* But she dismissed the thought almost instantly; what if he thought she was crazy? Could he have her sectioned? *Just keep your head down, don't get close to anyone.* Sitting on the futon, she surveyed the small living room of her flat and bit back a sigh. Could she really live the rest of her life like this? Completely alone and shut-off from everyone?

The intercom to her flat emitted a shriek making Alexandra jump. She rarely had visitors and had forgotten the cursed thing even existed. Carefully setting her plate on the coffee table, she stood up and pressed the 'speak' button.

'Forgive me, but I believe there is a young lady in flat seven that I am seeking.' Alexandra felt her mouth go dry at the voice, could she ignore it?

'W – Who is this?' She finally asked dreading the answer. *Why are you dreading it? You've wanted answers for so long – they might finally be here. What is wrong with you?* But she couldn't explain her fear or doubt to herself, surely she should be happy? Elated even?

'My name is Carlyle, I –' Cutting him off Alexandra pressed the button to buzz him up, her mind swimming. Was Carlyle really here? She stood by the door to her flat listening for the sound of approaching footsteps. Bracing herself she took a deep breath and opened the door. Carlyle towered over her, his deep blue eyes with their spiral pattern looking sombre. Alexandra opened her mouth, but her words were cut-off as Carlyle enveloped her in a bone-crushing embrace.

'I feared I would not see you again,' he pressed his lips to the top of her head still holding her close. Finding herself completely lost for words Alexandra buried her face into Carlyle's shoulder, his scent was familiar and pulled at something in the back of her mind, but she couldn't tug it forward. 'Are you pleased to see me?'

'O – Of course I am,' she smiled weakly and stepped from his embrace gesturing for him to step inside. 'I'm sorry I just…I wasn't expecting you to find me…' She moved her head from side to side and walked into the kitchen, pouring herself a glass of water and draining it instantly. Her throat was painfully dry; even the second glass did little to quench her sudden thirst. 'I wasn't sure if you were real or not,' she murmured staring out of the small kitchen window; she could see Carlyle's reflection in the window watching her just as intently. 'Would you like a drink?' She asked turning to look at him. It felt like a stupid question, but she could think of nothing else to ask.

'No. Alexandra I would like nothing more than to take you home and leave this forsaken world. Now.'

'You want to take me back…now?' Alexandra repeated.

'I have a kingdom to run Alexandra. *We* have a kingdom to run.' Carlyle crossed the room and gripped her hand, squeezing it reassuringly. 'You have nothing to fear Alexandra.'

'I – I have a job though, I can't just leave.' Alexandra replied weakly, 'please Carlyle I just need a few days – a week at the most.' She could see he wanted to refuse her request and she stared down at their entwined hands. There was something almost unnatural about the gesture, frowning slightly she looked back up at him. 'You can't force me to go back – unless you are going to drag me back to our world. That is hardly a good start to a marriage.'

'I see you have not forgotten your stubbornness.' *Why do I get the feeling we disagree a lot?* Alexandra decided to try and change tactics, to learn more about why she had jilted Carlyle and fled her life. Leading him to the sitting room she glanced down at her discarded dinner, suddenly she was no longer hungry, and she quickly disposed of it in the kitchen. She stared at the discarded food in the bin, her mind turning over the hundreds of questions she wanted to bombard Carlyle with. *Start at the beginning;* she told herself heading back to the sitting room.

'What happened? Why did I run away? There must have been a reason; I don't want to return home only to find out that I had good reason to run away.' Carlyle sat back on the futon, even in jeans and a leather jacket over a jumper he looked foreboding.

'There were rumours about a rebel group in Saphyre; you caught wind of these rumours. It was suggested you would be in danger.' With nowhere else to sit Alexandra sat beside Carlyle, he took her left hand and stared at her bare ring finger forlornly. 'I had hoped we would be preparing for the arrival of our son by now.' Pulling her hand free Alexandra brushed it through her hair nervously. 'Please come home with me. The people of Saphyre are eagerly awaiting your arrival; they are eager to meet their new queen.'

'I need time, *please.*' She knew she would not get more from Carlyle, that he was hiding something. 'Who are Krista and Mathe?'

'I thought you did not remember anything?' Carlyle asked sharply.

'I don't…I had a dream – or a memory…I was talking to a girl named Krista.' Alexandra shrugged as her unease grew, 'Carlyle don't you see – I'm not ready to go home just yet. I don't know anything, who are my parents? What is Karstares like?' She could see that she was beginning to persuade Carlyle. 'Please – just one week. Help me remember who I am before we return and let me tie up loose ends here.' Carlyle held her gaze, his eyes moving side to side as he searched her face for signs of deceit.

'Very well. One week.'

Alexandra unfolded the futon for Carlyle to sleep on. She could see he was not happy at the prospect of sleeping on the floor, but she was not prepared to offer him her bed. She had assumed he would cross back to their world until he revealed it was a dangerous piece of sorcery.

'Is that how I ended up here? Did I practice sorcery and…mess up?' Alexandra asked feeling guilt stab at her, if it was dangerous had she endangered anyone?

'You would not have done this alone Alexandra. You…do not possess the Source I am afraid.' *So how did I end up here?* She asked herself as she climbed into her own bed and slowly drifted off to sleep.

'What do you do all day?' Carlyle's lip was curled in disdain as he looked out of the sitting room window at the dismal weather beyond.

'Work normally.' Alexandra shrugged popping two pieces of bread in the toaster. 'Do you want some?' She gestured to the loaf of bread; she smiled at his confused face. She hadn't known what a toaster or even a kettle was, the first time she had seen them. She was caught completely off-guard by his next question.

'You cook?' He looked utterly horrified at the thought, 'Alexandra this is far beneath your station.'

'Making toast?' She arched an eyebrow at Carlyle as she set a plate with two buttered slices in front of him. 'Tell me about our world. Who are my parents? What is their kingdom like?' Alexandra sat opposite Carlyle as she listened to him about her family. She was fascinated to learn her family had ruled Karstares for over a thousand years, and that her mother was a powerful sorceress. She had felt disappointment the previous night at being told she did not possess the Source, upon learning that her mother was a powerful sorceress she felt utterly disheartened.

'These things can happen Alexandra,' Carlyle tried to soothe her. 'Any sons we have would be bound to inherit the Source; you should not feel disheartened.'

'What about Saphyre how far away is it from Karstares?' She asked in an attempt to change the subject. She wasn't comfortable at the prospect of children; surely she was too young? The thought made her sit up straight as she realised she didn't know the most basic of things about herself, let alone her kingdom. 'Carlyle…how old am I?'

'Surely you remember that much at least?'

'No…when I was found I could only remember my name.' Watching his face darken she switched the conversation back to Saphyre. The capital, Evany, was a coastal city with the castle situated atop a cliff overlooking the city. Once they had finished their breakfast, Alexandra took the cups and plates, as she washed up she stared out at the continuing rain. She suddenly felt penned in and needed fresh air but knew suggesting a walk in the torrential downpour would not go down well. *IT's going to be a long day;* she thought biting back a sigh and turning to face Carlyle with a bright smile.

'How was your day off?' Alexandra smiled at the question and shrugged nonchalantly.

'The usual – sleeping in late and cleaning. Any news on Paul?'

'He'll be off till next week; he left you a note on his desk.' Thankful to be out of the flat Alexandra shoved her coat and bag into her locker before retrieving the note from Paul. It mentioned nothing about the evening they had gone out together, and Alexandra was thankful, she was eager to forget the evening had ever happened. Instead, he asked her to run the store in his absence. *He'll be off till next week.'* The words rang in her mind, and Alexandra swore under her breath, she was going to have to tell Paul about her leaving over the phone. What would she tell him? The truth? Or the partial truth at least? *Think about it later;* she told herself pocketing the note. For now, she would keep the news of her imminent departure silent.

As Alexandra closed the front door to her flat, she could hear the deep rumble of Carlyle's voice coming from the sitting room.

'Not yet. She is weak, it may be best to resume her studies when we reach Saphyre, but I fear we may have to start afresh.'

'Even if she has forgotten everything, I am confident once she begins again it will feel natural to her. It will not take her long to master –' The voice became distorted and Alexandra frowned. Stepping in the doorway to the sitting room she found Carlyle sitting cross-legged on the unfolded futon, a crystal ball floating in mid-air in front of him. Alexandra could just make out a woman with dark hair and felt as if she had been punched in the stomach.

'M – Mother?' Alexandra gripped the edge of the doorframe fighting to keep her breathing steady. The image in the crystal ball evaporated, and Alexandra felt her throat tighten painfully as if someone was squeezing the life from her. Carlyle looked up as he carefully set the crystal down on the futon.

'I was reassuring her that you were safe…I thought it would be too upsetting for you to speak to her like this. Once we are wed, we will arrange for your mother at least to come to Saphyre for a diplomatic visit.'

'Won't I see her when we go home?' Alexandra asked feeling confused. She sat beside Carlyle and picked up the crystal ball, no longer could she see the dark-haired woman but only the palm of her hand.

'Alexandra when we go home we will be going to Saphyre. The journey from Karstares to Saphyre would take half a moon at least.' *So?* Alexandra wanted to ask, *why do we need to rush back?* 'I have a kingdom to run; *we* have a kingdom to run. We are neglecting our people, our responsibilities, by being here. I am sorry you do not remember your family or your past, but perhaps that is for the best. After our marriage, we will begin planning for your coronation. Once you are crowned, you will no longer be a Princess of Karstares but the Queen of Saphyre, you will not be able to leave the kingdom. Especially to visit distant family...I am sorry for my harshness Alexandra; I would do anything to save you from hurt which is *why* I think it is best for us to go straight to Saphyre. You have already undertaken the journey from Karstares to Saphyre once; it drained you emotionally. I am not going to put you through that again,' Carlyle pulled her close wrapping his arms around her and pressing his lips to her temple. 'I love you Alexandra, and I will do anything in my power to protect you.'

Taking a deep breath Alexandra locked the office door and picked up the phone. She had put off calling Paul but knew the longer she left it, the worse the situation would become. Dialling Paul's number she took a deep breath and nervously waited for him to answer. Why did she care so much about what he thought? In three days' time, she would never see Paul again, let alone hear from him.

'Hello?' Paul's voice was groggy suggesting that he had not spent much of his time resting.

'Paul hi...it's Alexandra. How's your head?' She winced at the overly bright tone of her voice.

'It's fine, are you ok?'

'Yes. Of course. Fine.' Shaking her head Alexandra took a deep breath, 'Paul I'm sorry to call you while you're off but...this can't exactly wait.'

'What is it Alexandra?' Paul's impatient tone snapped her back to reality.

'I'm leaving,' she said without thinking, the tone of his voice snapping something within her. 'Someone from my past turned up a few days ago…my fiancé. I wanted to tell you in person –'

'How do you know this person is from your past and not just lying to you?' The question caught Alexandra off-guard. 'Don't be an idiot Alex; this person could be tricking you! Do you really want to throw this opportunity away? If this person turns out to be fake…well, don't come crying to me. I'm not keeping your job open for you.' Alexandra bit down on her tongue; he made it sound as if he had done her a favour – that he had offered her the world! 'Forget about Saturday too; I'll ask Danielle if she wants to go with me.' *I'll be leaving then anyway;* she wanted to say but thought better of retaliating.

'Thanks for everything Paul,' she forced herself to be polite – he was still technically her boss.

'Alex –'

'Alexandra,' she snapped. She had let the first one slide but knew now he was just being spiteful.

'Whatever. Leave your keys in the safe after you close up tonight. Don't bother coming back.' Hanging up Alexandra placed the phone back in its cradle, staring at it miserably. *Don't tell Carlyle,* she warned herself; *he'll only use this as an excuse to go home now.* She didn't dare let herself ponder on why that would be bad; she didn't want to dwell on why she was terrified to return home. Instead, she took a deep breath as she tried to compose herself before heading back to the shop floor.

Lugging the heavy black bag to the bins outside Alexandra heaved the rubbish up and opened the lid, choking back nausea as the smell of rotten food hit her nose. *At least I won't have to deal with this anymore;* she thought wiping her hands on her apron. She looked up at the moon, the rain had finally cleared, and she frowned as she stared up at the moon. Something was tugging at the back of her mind, but she couldn't quite place what it was.

'Alexandra,' she turned to see Carlyle standing in the mouth of the alley, holding a glittering object in his right hand. Frowning Alexandra walked up to Carlyle and took hold of the locket in his outstretched hands.

'I am not allowed to wear jewellery at work,' she looked up at him with a furious scowl. 'How dare you go through my belongings?' Carlyle opened his mouth, but Alexandra cut him off, 'no. We are not married yet – and either if we were, you would still have no right to go through my personal belongings.

King or not,' she added sensing that he would use his status as an argument. Handing him back the locket she strode past him and back to the shop, switching off the lights and locking the door behind them. Rage boiled deep within, starting in her belly and spreading through to the tips of her fingers and down to her feet. Somehow, she resisted the urge to bang the coins on the counter as she began cashing up the day's takings.

'I apologise,' Carlyle murmured taking a seat opposite the counter. Alexandra slammed the till shut and looked up at him. 'I noticed you were not wearing it. I could not help myself.' Alexandra took a deep breath before forcing herself to reply.

'Why are we marrying?' She managed to force the question that had plagued her mind since Carlyle had told her of their failed wedding. 'Is it a political marriage?'

'Partly yes,' Carlyle nodded. 'But we are also marrying for love.' *But I don't love you*, Alexandra felt ashamed at the thought but deep down knew it to be true. 'I understand that you may be confused. The age gap concerned you when we were first introduced. But over time you adjusted, you allowed me to court you.' Carlyle took her hand and squeezed it gently, 'I wish I could give you the time you need, but unfortunately we do not have that.'

'Do you love me?'

'Yes.' Carlyle answered instantaneously pulling Alexandra close as she emerged from behind the counter. 'From the moment I heard you had disappeared I have not felt complete. I spent every night fearing the worst – that you had been killed or were suffering somewhere.' Alexandra was surprised to see Carlyle's eyes suddenly bright with tears.

'I'm sorry,' she murmured guilt-stricken, 'I wish I knew why I did what I did, or how. But I don't…' She shrugged and gestured to the till in her hands. 'I need to lock this up; I'll just be five minutes.' Taking the till down to the office Alexandra locked the till in the safe along with her till keys. As she set the combination on the safe, she sat back and looked around the office one final time. Picking up a pen she scribbled *I'm sorry!* on a sticky note and stuck it to the monitor of Paul's computer. She couldn't lock her keys in the safe like he had asked but decided she would drop them off in the morning. She was adamant she would keep her recent unemployment from Carlyle; she would simply go out each morning as if she was going to work.

Upstairs she found Carlyle standing beside the door and looking out at the deserted streets.

'We do not have time to begin our courting relationship anew,' he picked up her hand and brushed his lips across her knuckles gently. 'But we can at least become reacquainted, allow me to take you to dinner?' Alexandra smiled at him a small blush creeping upon her cheeks.

'Of course – your majesty,' she said in a half-joking tone. 'Let's go home first so I can change into something a bit nicer.'

Three courses and a half-bottle of wine later Alexandra half-stumbled, half-fell through the front door of her flat. Pulling her heels off she dropped them by the door, leaning against Carlyle for support as she tried to put the lock on.

'Was I always such a lightweight?' She joked embarrassed as she realised she was slurring her words. She couldn't help the burst of laughter as she caught the confused expression on his face. 'Unable to drink much alcohol?' Carlyle lifted her in his arms and carried her to her bedroom, his expression thoughtful.

'This was a poor imitation of the wine we have back home,' he finally answered. 'This was as pleasant as drinking vinegar,' Alexandra giggled as he settled her on her bed. Carlyle sat beside her; nervously Alexandra met his deep blue eyes. She was mesmerised by the spiral pattern, exactly the same as her own. The pattern seemed to move in a clockwise motion, and she felt sleep beginning to pull her down into its warm depths. 'I love you Alexandra,' he refused to break the contact as he rested his forehead against hers. His hands cupped her cheeks, his thumbs lightly stroking her skin. Tilting her head back Alexandra expected to feel his lips brush against her own; she was surprised instead when she felt his lips caressing her cheek. 'It would be inappropriate. I do not want to take advantage of you, especially when you are not able to think clearly.' Kissing her cheek once more he tucked the duvet around her before leaving her to fall into a deep sleep.

The day of Alexandra's departure arrived all too quickly. On Saturday morning, she laid in bed staring at the ceiling and fiddling with the locket at her throat. *Am I ready?* She kept asking herself before finally answering it with, *does it matter?* Carlyle would be taking her home tonight regardless of whether she felt she was ready or not. And how could she argue with him that she should remain here? She didn't belong in Bournemouth; it wasn't her world. She had nothing keeping her there, not even a job was tying her down. Sighing she put on a dressing gown and padded into the kitchen so that she could put the kettle on.

'Carlyle?' She poked her head into the sitting room blushing as she caught him sitting shirtless amongst the duvets. 'Sorry, I…erm…' She silently cursed herself for blushing and losing the ability to speak coherently. What must he be thinking of her? *He's amused;* a voice snickered in answer as she caught him smirking. 'Do you want some breakfast?'

'No. I think we should go now.' Alexandra felt her throat tighten and she gripped the door handle feeling it grow slick under her sweaty hand. *I'm not ready.*

'Tonight,' she said firmly. 'Unless you intend on dragging me back home?' Carlyle smiled, but she could see the anger flickering beneath his eyes.

'Of course not. Tonight.'

Alexandra slipped out soon after breakfast for a final walk along the seafront. She slipped the pouch of diamonds deep into her pocket afraid that Carlyle would snoop amongst her belongings once more. The wind was strong almost knocking her backward several times as she walked; she noticed the red flags across the shore warning people away from the sea's violent waves. She turned to face the sea head-on, despite the crashing waves she felt soothed watching the ocean. *I don't want to go back,* she thought feeling tears sting her eyes. *I ran for a reason and I don't even know what that is…what if I've just made everything worse?* She reached into her pocket and squeezed the pouch of diamonds as if trying to seek some kind of reassurance from them. She didn't stop to think why she wanted to keep them from Carlyle, but she felt the urge to keep them hidden from him. who knew if she might need them back home?

Gradually the sky darkened, and rain began to spatter Alexandra in fat droplets. She moved under the pier seeking shelter, sitting on the sand and staring at the wooden panels above. Despite the rain, crowds were already beginning to gather for the fireworks display due to take place in a few hours' time. footsteps thundered overhead, and she laid back on the sand, so she could watch the footsteps passing above. *I need to run,* she thought suddenly, *until I know why I left then I will not go back.* She stood up and brushed the sand from her jeans. A hand grabbed her arm as she turned to head out back towards the rain and for a second, she feared it was Carlyle; had he guessed she would try to run away again? Would he be angry?

'Paul!' She gasped, 'You startled me.' She had not spoken to him since their phone conversation earlier that week. Out of the corner of her eye, she saw Carlyle approaching them and she pulled her arm free from Paul's grip.

'Don't go,' Alexandra froze as she stared at him. 'Please. I know you said that your fiancé had found you but...' Above them, a firework went off with a deafening *bang!* The crowds on the pier began to cheer and Alexandra jumped backward in fright.

'Paul I'm sorry but I – I can't do this,' turning Alexandra ran out from beneath the pier, pushing her way through the crowds which had gathered along the seafront. Fireworks lit the sky, deafening Alexandra as she ran. Panic swelled up with each explosion, was this normal? At the back of her mind she was aware of people mentioning these fireworks, of the colourful explosions and displays, but nothing this deafening could be good surely?

'Alexandra stop!' Running faster Alexandra bent her head, as her lungs began to burn she fought back the urge to stop and rest for a moment. 'Alexandra!' Her lungs felt as if they were about to burst but still she continued to run. '*Stop!*' Her feet froze on the spot and Alexandra almost toppled forwards, only managing to regain her balance at the last moment before she fell flat on her face. 'Were you running away again?' Carlyle stepped around her; his face was pale and thunderous as he grabbed her by her upper arms roughly. 'Why must you continue to run from your responsibilities?' He yellowed over the explosion of fireworks. Alexandra looked up at the sky in fear, she half-expected it to come crashing down on them at any moment. 'You have a duty to our people, to *me* –'

'I'm *scared*,' Alexandra cried feeling the tears break free and pour down her cheeks. 'Carlyle I was running from something and I have no idea what. You have power,' she gestured to her frozen feet realizing that it was Carlyle's magic which kept her pinned in place. 'What do I have?' She watched in horror as a hole in the ground opened up behind Carlyle. She stared into the dark depths, flinching as bolts of blue lightning swirled across the portal. '*Please* Carlyle,' she begged. 'Don't make me go back – I'm not ready!'

'I will protect you, Alexandra. You do not need the Source, you will have me and that is all you will ever need.' Alexandra shook her head choking back a sob.

'You know why I ran away, you are hiding something from me – I know you are.' Carlyle tightened his grip on her arms, his face creasing in anger.

'I do not have time for this. We are going home, *now*.' Moving so he could sweep an arm around her waist Alexandra felt her feet move forwards. *Please, Goddess,* she thought desperately, *let me go home.* She had no idea where the prayer had come from, but she clung to it as she forced her mind to focus on Karstares. She felt a surge of power which sent her flying forwards into the swirling portal.

# *Chapter Six*

The wind was knocked from Alexandra's lungs as she landed ungracefully on a hard surface. Blinking through black spots, she fought the room to stop spinning and sat up. When everything finally came to a halt she surveyed her surroundings feeling the tug of familiarity pulling at the back of her mind. Her eyes rested on a diamond-shaped field with an emerald green field and golden border. In the center was a crescent-shaped moon over a sword, a small owl sitting on the edge of the moon. *I'm home*, she thought, looking around stunned. Beside her stood Carlyle, a less than pleased expression on his face. Ahead of them, a large door opened, and an elegant woman draped in silks and velvets with dark hair falling in ringlets stepped through. Still sitting on the floor Alexandra stared at the woman in stunned fascination.

'Alexandra!' The dark-haired woman stopped in her tracks, almost dropping the scroll she had been reading. 'I – I thought...' the woman's gaze flicked over to Carlyle, 'I thought we agreed it would be best for you both to travel to Saphyre?' Alexandra accepted Carlyle's hand as he held her to her feet, unsure of what was happening she continued to stare between the two monarchs. *Mother*, she fought back the urge to run into her mother's arms sensing that it would be deemed inappropriate.

'I will be honest your majesty, that is what I had intended.' Carlyle bowed, and Alexandra froze. Running to embrace her mother might be wrong, but was she meant to curtsey? She looked down at her torn and loose-fitting jeans wondering on earth she was supposed to curtsey in such a ragged outfit.

'Must we be so formal,' the Queen smiled and embraced Alexandra tightly, kissing both her cheeks. 'I feared I would never see you again. The Goddess is truly kind,' Alexandra was ashamed to see her mother's green eyes bright with tears, ashamed that she was the reason for them. 'Thank you, Carlyle. Karstares will forever be in your debt.' Inwardly Alexandra flinched, wishing her mother had not said those simple words. She didn't want her family, or Karstares, in Carlyle's debt – why? 'Come, your father has just left the council. I am sure this will brighten his day.' Alexandra felt herself pulled forwards, but she could only stare helplessly at her mother, her feet fixed to the floor.

'I...' She trailed off, how could she explain she didn't remember what her father looked like let alone where he was most likely to be?

'Ismenya...I am afraid I have been unable to help Alexandra regain her memory.' The sadness in Ismenya's eyes deepened and Alexandra looked away as a fresh wave of shame jolted through her. 'She remembers nothing about herself or us...'

'No,' Alexandra protested although Carlyle was telling the truth. 'That's not...I – I know you're my mother. I...' She cut herself off; she could see from Ismenya's expression that she didn't quite believe her daughter.

'Your memories will come back, just give yourself time.' Ismenya smiled sadly as she reached out to squeeze Alexandra's hand. With Carlyle walking slightly behind Alexandra followed her mother down hallways filled with torches and decorated with rich velvet tapestries. 'We did not expect you home, there are no vessels prepared to take you to Saphyre. I will send a message to Visaye in the morning, I am sure they will be able to prepare vessels for your journey.'

'Can we not stay for a little while before plans are made for our departure?'

'No Alexandra,' she was shocked and hurt slightly to hear her mother speak so sharply. 'You have a duty to your people, to *Carlyle.*'

'Perhaps we could leave the day after tomorrow? It will take us a day to reach Visaye; this will give them more time to prepare the vessels.' Carlyle rested a hand on Alexandra's shoulder as they walked. 'The wedding dress was destroyed, I'm sure it could be made on board but perhaps it could be started tomorrow. I imagine the crossing will be a bit unpleasant for standing still.'

'Of course I would prefer you to stay Alexandra – do not think for a moment that neither I nor your father want you here...but Karstares is no longer your home. You belong in Saphyre,' Alexandra blinked back tears before meeting her mother's gaze. 'I am not trying to be cruel Alexandra. Far from it. Your father, Carlyle and I discussed what would be best for you if, when,' she corrected herself, 'you were found. I accompanied you on your voyage to Saphyre, you were distraught – none of us wanted to put you through that again.' A boy dressed in green leggings and a long tunic bowed low as they approached a large door. The page's eyes widened as he looked at Alexandra and he almost toppled forwards as he bowed low once more, a large grin on his face.

'Welcome home your highness! We have all prayed for your safe return.' Alexandra couldn't help returning his grin as she thanked the page; she glanced at her mother and found her smiling tearfully. Only Carlyle seemed indignant at the page's welcome. Remembering where he was the page sprang to attention and opened the door, announcing first Carlyle, then her mother and finally Alexandra; there were only two people in the room, a man a year or two older than Alexandra and a second just over middle-age with auburn hair sprinkled with grey. Both bore a striking resemblance to Alexandra; auburn hair and straight noses, there was even a similar mischievous glint in the younger man's eyes that Alexandra had. Although his eyes were a pale grey rather than her own forest green. Ismenya released Alexandra's hand and moved to her husband's side, squeezing his arm and whispering in his ear.

'Father...' Alexandra shifted uneasily beside the door unsure of what to do or say. She had never allowed herself to think of what her homecoming would be like, but when she had it had certainly been nothing like this; stiff and awkward. She realized how ridiculous she must appear in baggy jeans and a hooded jumper. Even Carlyle was better dressed than her in black jeans, a shirt, and fitted jacket. She didn't ask herself how he had gotten such fine clothes.

'Do not speak,' her father's voice was low, and Alexandra blinked stunned. She had prepared herself for an onslaught of pent-up rage. She was surprised instead when her father clasped her arms and gazed at her in disbelief. 'Praise the Goddess,' he embraced Alexandra tightly and she fought back a fresh wave of tears as she hugged him back.

'I am sorry father,' she spoke formally, surprised at how natural the tone felt. 'I never meant to cause grief.'

'It is in the past,' his response surprised her even more; she had expected some sort of scolding at least. 'I thought I would never look upon you again.' Stepping back he held her once more at arm's length, 'you are as beautiful as ever. But thin...and your clothing...' Alexandra smiled weakly studying her father's own strange clothing; robes of fine silk and velvet trousers. 'Many of your possessions are in Saphyre, I am afraid you might find your old chambers a bit bare. But hopefully, it will be familiar,' the mention of Saphyre seemed to pull the king back to the present. 'I hope you will join us for supper, tomorrow we will have a feast. But tonight I am sure our citizens will not begrudge us a private supper.'

'Of course,' Alexandra smiled and turned to watch the king leave with her mother and Carlyle. She felt a spark of bitterness as she realized they were to discuss her future, without her. Was she granted no say in what happened next? She turned to look at the remaining figure, sizing the man up apprehensively. He had remained silent throughout the whole exchange.

'Brother.'

'Sister.' Her greeting was returned solemnly, and Alexandra felt the flicker of a smile cross her face. 'Your clothes truly are hideous.'

'Thank you Giric,' Alexandra scowled and followed him out from the council chambers.

'So, tell me about your adventures. Where have you been?'

'It was hardly an adventure,' Alexandra looked at him seriously. 'This was never a game Giric...I don't even remember why I left. I don't know where I am now.' Giric grabbed her hand and squeezed it gently.

'All I know is that you ran away because you were scared of your future; there were rumours about a rebel movement in Saphyre. But you should not be afraid of them Alexandra, Carlyle loves you – he would protect you with his dying breath.' Alexandra remained silent as she followed Giric, she couldn't shake the feeling that she was more afraid of Carlyle than a rebel movement.

The dinner was not the celebratory occasion Alexandra had imagined it to be, even if it was just to be a private affair. She had thought it would be joyous, that there would be plenty of laughter and telling of tales. Instead, it was an awkward affair, stiff and uncomfortable. Alexandra could barely sit through the main course before she grew tired of everyone staring at her as if they were waiting for her to run away once more. Unable to take the tense atmosphere she made her apologies feigning a migraine, so she could depart for her own chambers, Ismenya accompanying her.

'We will begin your dress first thing in the morning,' her mother spoke in an attempt to make conversation. But the thought of her impending marriage did little to life Alexandra's spirits. Once more she could only wonder what was wrong with her. 'I have arranged for some servants to go to the market at dawn, they will come back with some fabric for you to select.'

'Perhaps we could go?' Alexandra winced at the hopeful tone of her voice. 'It would be nice to spend some time with you before...' She trailed off wondering what she had said that was so wrong.

'Alexandra it is not appropriate. We cannot just walk into the city as everyday citizens, it is not safe.' Ismenya kissed her cheek, smoothing her hair back from her face. Alexandra bit her tongue; she had grown so accustomed to doing as she pleased the past few months. If she had woken at sunrise she had thought nothing about dressing early and walking along the shore before her shift began. She realized with a jolt what a difference her two lives had been, and she could not remember anything about her real life. 'It must have been a traumatic time for you, get some rest. I am loathed to say goodbye to you, but you have a duty to Carlyle and your people.' *What about me?* She thought selfishly but didn't dare voice it.

Curled up in bed Alexandra could not shake her mother's words from her head. Would this be her life from now on? A duty to her husband? Not once had she heard anyone mention his duty to her, why? *We are not even married yet and already they sound like I am his,* she was surprised at the bitterness and resentment she felt. What was wrong with her? Surely, she should be overwhelmed by love? Or if she didn't love him surely, she should like him at least? So why did she feel distrust and fear? The thoughts plagued her, even after she had fallen asleep. She was plagued by dreams of colourful explosions and what people meant by duty.

It was still dark when Alexandra awoke. Her hand fumbled beneath the pillow for her alarm clock, but her fingers scraped only sheets. Bolting upright Alexandra looked around in confusion at the strange surroundings, a mixture of familiar yet completely alien. She was no longer in the cramped room of her flat, but a room the size of her flat combined. *I'm home,* she reminded herself. Knowing that she was unlikely to sleep again she pushed back the blankets, shivering in the chilly air. The stone floor was freezing beneath her bare feet and she almost sprinted towards the dressing chamber her mother had shown her. It was sparsely filled; some of her dresses had been shipped to Saphyre while others had been donated to the poor. The few that remained she discarded, they were full of layers and lacings that would make it impossible to dress herself. Instead, she threw on a robe followed by a thick fur-lined cape.

The hallways were almost empty, only a few servants were up. They curtsied as Alexandra passed and greeted her warmly, although she saw the suspicious glint in their eyes and knew they were watching her for any suspicious behaviour. The hearths had not yet been lit and the fur cape did little to warm her against the freezing cold. Wistfully Alexandra thought back to the small electric heater in her flat.

'Her Majesty said that Alexandra arrived late last night. She does not know anything; she remembers nothing about why she ran away, about Carlyle…or us.'

'Then we tell her,' the second voice was a male and Alexandra pressed herself into a wall sconce peered around the corner. It was too dark to make out the speaker, but she could see the silhouettes of three people.

'No.' The first voice, a woman's, spoke sharply. 'She is better off not knowing. You want her to be happy do you not? And safe? This way perhaps she can be both.' Alexandra's chest tightened, safe? She fought back the urge to step out of the wall sconce and confront the three. Half of her didn't want to get them in trouble, the other half wanted to remain blissfully ignorant of whatever was happening. If she was in danger, then perhaps it would be best to remain ignorant until she knew more about herself. The voices faded, and Alexandra followed them, she didn't want to confront them but there was something achingly familiar about the three. *Krista!* The face of the dark-skinned woman filled her vision and she almost sprinted towards the three.

'Promise me you will do nothing foolish. She is going to Saphyre, we cannot stop the marriage. We tried once and failed if we try again…' Krista trailed off and Alexandra desperately fought the fog in her mind trying to place the names of the other two. *Mariah,* she thought staring at the second female. A vision of a raven-haired beauty with deep green eyes filled her memory, a stab of bitter jealousy quickly followed and Alexandra bit back a sigh. 'We have put her in enough danger already. Carlyle can manipulate her now, although if she truly believes she is in love with him then perhaps he will leave her be.'

'Of course he will not,' Alexandra's heart twisted at the male's voice. 'She would never love him…' The voices faded but Alexandra paused not wanting to hear anymore, already she wished she had stayed in her chambers. *I can't marry him, I don't love him, and it must have been Carlyle I was fleeing not some rebellion.* She returned to her chambers blinking back tears. A servant had lit the fire and she grabbed a blanket from her bed, so she could wrap herself in it and sit before the hearth. What had she done? If she didn't love Carlyle, then why had she agreed to a marriage with him in the first place? Why did her heart melt at the sound of that man's voice? Why was she jealous of Mariah? Too many questions buzzed in her head making Alexandra wish she had never come home. She should never have sought out the answers; she should have left well enough alone. *Too late now,* she thought bitterly rubbing her head as she felt the pounding of a migraine begin.

'Alexandra, what in the name of the Goddess are you doing sitting on the floor?' Alexandra looked up surprised to see her mother and a middle-aged woman beside her. 'Stand up.' Alexandra obeyed and tossed the blanket on the bed, she was surprised when the woman took her cloak and the robe from her. She almost protested until she caught sight of the ribbon in the woman's hands, it was long and had notches and symbols across the length. As the woman wrapped the ribbon around her she fought back the urge to hurtle questions at her mother. *Later*, she promised herself.

The speed at which the dress had taken shape startled Alexandra. The material had been brought up from the market soon after she had broken her fast and immediately cut to the measurements. The day had barely broken noon and she was already pinned beneath layers of white shimmering silks, satins and pale icy blue brocades. Each time she moved the pins would scratch against her skin, reminding her to hold still. She kept telling herself that she had time to speak to her mother, to put a stop to the marriage. But the swift creation of the dress jolted her to reality. She would be leaving the next morning. *If I don't do it now, then I will never do it.* Looking up at the ceiling Alexandra sent a silent prayer to the Goddess, trying to ignore the twinge of guilt that she knew nothing about the deity but hoping she would help anyway.

'Could you please give us a moment?' She asked the dressmaker and her apprentices. The dressmaker turned to look at the Queen, her mouth full of pins as she took up the front of Alexandra's gown.

'Alexandra, we do not have time to waste.'

'Please mother, it's important.' Ismenya studied Alexandra and for a moment she feared her mother would refuse. Finally, she nodded and gestured for the other women to leave, closing the door to her dressing chamber behind them. 'I do not want to leave for Saphyre; I do not want to marry Carlyle.' She blurted out. 'Please let him return alone, let me stay home.' She expected her mother to be angry and was surprised by the sadness in her eyes.

'This is why we decided you should go straight to Saphyre. I understand you are frightened, but this rebellion…it is only rumours.'

'I am not frightened of the rebellion! It is Carlyle, I don't love him! Please –'

'No.' Ismenya's voice suddenly hardened and Alexandra knew she would not win this argument. 'I will not tolerate this again Alexandra. You had a choice in your marriage; your father and I were generous like that. You told us you loved Carlyle, that you wished to marry him. What do you think this will achieve? Do you think that by backing out on your word you will be able to marry Mathe?' *Mathe*, Alexandra flinched at the name and she realized who the voice had belonged to the previous night.

'You will be seen as dishonourable – no one will want to marry you. How could anyone trust you? Treaties are drawn up; these things take time Alexandra. Is this the kind of queen you want to be? One who will go back on her word with each breath that she draws?' Alexandra blinked back tears of shame and looked down at the floor. How could she explain to her mother why she couldn't marry Carlyle when she didn't even understand herself? Ismenya's tone softened and she took hold of Alexandra's hands, squeezing them lightly. 'Enough is enough Alexandra. Tomorrow we will leave for Saphyre and you will marry Carlyle. Once you are wed and crowned queen you will realise your silly fears are no more than wedding jitters.' Alexandra could only nod; she remained silent for the rest of the afternoon as the wedding gown was pinned and hemmed against her.

Despite the feast, there was a subdued feeling in the atmosphere. Below the dais where Alexandra sat with her family and Carlyle, noble men and women reveled in the sumptuous food, wine, and music that was on offer. Alexandra sat at the end of the table with Carlyle by her side, across the grand hall she could feel a pair of eyes watching her, but it was hard to see who they belonged to through the crowded hall. She looked over towards the door and felt her breath catch in her throat. The man stood too far away for her to make out his features, but she recognized the way his hair flopped into his eyes making him constantly push it back. *Mathe*, she thought longingly.

'I have spoken to the King and Queen,' Carlyle's voice was soft, and he rested his hand over her own. 'We thought that perhaps it would be best for you to ride with me tomorrow. A litter would slow us down too much, nor do I wish to risk you falling and injuring yourself if you were to ride alone.'

Alexandra nodded without really listening to what he was saying. Her eyes were transfixed on the man by the door. A dark-skinned woman with cropped black hair walked over to him and leaned in close. Snapping to attention the man slipped through the door and the woman took up his position.

'Krista,' Alexandra whispered recognizing her instantly. She moved to stand up, but Carlyle's fingers tightened ever-so-slightly around her wrist. 'I want to talk to my friends.'

'Your parents have advised them against speaking with you. It would not be appropriate after all that has come to pass. Now sit down.' Alexandra pushed her chair back and stood up, snatching her wrist free from Carlyle. She was shocked when the room fell deathly silent and each of the revelers and entertainers dropped into bows and curtseys.

'Alexandra sit down.' She looked over to see her mother and father glaring suspiciously at her. Giric was half-standing as if to follow her, his face full of concern.

'Please forgive me, but I find I have no appetite. We have a long journey tomorrow and I wish to be well rested.' She turned to face the people below and forced herself to smile warmly. 'I thank you all for your kind welcoming; please enjoy the rest of the evening.' Her eyes were fixated on Krista as she strode from the dais, picking up her pace as Krista slipped from the hall. 'Krista – wait!' She called as the door shut behind her and she found herself in an empty hallway. Her eyes swept up and down but there was no sign of Krista or Mathe. Lifting the skirts of her pale satin dress Alexandra hurtled through the torch-lit hallways; she didn't know where she was running too but followed on instinct.

A strong wind whipped through her and Alexandra blinked trying to let her eyesight adjust to the darkness. Looking up at the sky she drew in a startled breath at what the sight before her. Two moons peaked through the clouds; one was the pale silvery colour that she recognized from Bournemouth, but the second moon was slightly larger and pale green in colour. Pulling herself back to the present Alexandra tore her gaze away from the sky and to the castle grounds spread before her. She could make out very little in the darkness, but immediately recognized the distinctive silhouette of the maze. Without pausing to think she made her way into the maze, her skirts soaking up the moisture from the rain-soaked grass making her legs freeze. It wasn't long before she realized she was lost in the maze and she came to a halt as she tried to fight back the bubble of panic threatening to burst. *You know the way,* she told herself. She had walked this maze countless times; she knew it better than anyone in her family and had often hidden in it as a child. She forced herself to move on before she got too cold. She was still adjusting to the fashion of Karstares, so different from that of Bournemouth. The full-length dresses with their corsets were a far cry from the baggy jeans, jumpers, and t-shirts she had grown so accustomed too. Nor were they half as comfortable. Clouds covered both moons plunging Alexandra into total darkness. But while her mind fretted over the way she let her feet walk automatically. *Why did I come here?* She had been seeking out Krista, but there was no way the other woman had come out to the maze. Not in this freezing weather. No one in their right mind would be outside tonight.

She was unsurprised to find the center of the maze empty; all that she found was the marble carved fountain. It was so cold that even the water spraying out had frozen solid. It shimmered and glowed like jade beneath the moonlight whenever the moons emerged from the clouds. Alexandra sat on the fountain lip, clicking her fingernails against the frozen surface. What was she going to do? By this time tomorrow, she would be on a ship to Saphyre. She wondered if she could run away again if she could find the spell that had enabled her to flee the first time. Who had done it for her? *Mariah,* she realized. Was this why she had felt the bitter stab of jealousy? Her friend had the Source while she did not? *Surely, I am not that petty?* But she pushed all thoughts of the Source from her mind; she could not run away again. What had she achieved running the first time? She didn't know why she had fled, or who from. Although from the snatches of conversation she had overhead she was beginning to get an idea. *I've made everything worse,* she thought as she tested the strength of the ice beneath her. It was completely frozen through and she scooted back so that she could sit with her back against the marble sculpture in the center. As the clouds cleared once more she stared up at the jade moon, losing herself in thought.

*'Alexandra please do not agree to this. We will think of a way to protect you.' Warm hands rested on Alexandra's shoulders and she felt her back rest against something solid and strong. 'You promised me –'*

*'I have promised you nothing. How can I when we both know this is impossible? My parents suspect about us. We cannot go on like this. I love you but...' Alexandra was turned around, so she could face her companion. Deep grey eyes met hers; soft strands of hair falling across them, she resisted the urge to brush the strands free as she tilted her head up but pulled away before his lips could graze hers. 'Mathe, no.'*

Alexandra's eyes snapped open and she looked around in confusion. Mathe. The man Krista had been whispering too, the man she had overheard earlier that morning. He had been adamant she did not love Carlyle, that she would never love him. But if Mathe loved her...if it was mutual then why had he not sought her out? Why had none of her friends made contact? *'Your parents have advised them against speaking with you. It would not be appropriate after all that has come to pass.'* Carlyle's words rang tauntingly through her ears. Hazily she began to make sense of what had happened on that ship. The escape had been her idea, but Krista and Mariah had been with her. They had helped and subsequently punished. Her ears pricked at the sound of voices and Alexandra slid off the fountain looking for somewhere to hide.

'Your Highness!' Three figures stood stiffly in the entrance to the center of the maze and Alexandra shifted awkwardly. 'Forgive us, we did not mean to intrude.'

'Wait,' Alexandra pleaded as the three retreated. 'I know who you are...what you did for me.' She stared between the three; Mathe, Krista, and Mariah. They stared back at her just as apprehensively. 'I'm so sorry,' her voice thickened, and she blinked back tears determined not to cry. 'I must have caused you so much trouble, for nothing.'

'No.' Krista shook her head and met Alexandra's eyes, a small smile on her lips. 'Not for nothing. It worked, for a while at least.' She stepped forward and hugged Alexandra tightly; she was shocked at how solid the woman was. As she stepped back from Krista she turned to Mariah and embraced her, before finally coming to rest in Mathe's arms. He stiffened slightly as if he was holding back, but she couldn't bring herself to question what was wrong.

'Alexandra there you are!' She jumped away from Mathe guiltily and self-consciously hugged herself as if she was trying to get warm. She couldn't see Carlyle being best pleased if he found her in the arms of another man – especially Mathe. She looked at Carlyle to see his eyes glancing around the group and saw a flash of pure hatred as they rested upon Mathe. 'Have you three not been forbidden to be in the Princess's company unchaperoned? Have you not caused enough damage?' He roared. 'GO! *Now!*'

'Mathe please,' Alexandra hissed as she saw him open his mouth to refuse.

'I am not leaving you alone with him.' Mathe spat on the ground at Carlyle's feet. His eyes burned with equal hatred, but unlike Carlyle, there were the tell-tale signs of fear in his eyes.

'How dare you, you insolent –'

'Stop it!' Alexandra cried, 'Mathe, all of you, please just go.' She swallowed a lump in her throat seeing what she had to do. 'My lord, Carlyle,' she said in what she hoped was the right mix of submission and adoration, 'forgive him – it is my fault, I am just so confused...' She stepped closer to him and rested her hand on his forearm. 'I need help; I cannot bear this not remembering. I remembered this place from my dreams, my friends found me here by accident. They have done no wrong, but I was hoping they could help me remember...' Carlyle reached out to embrace her, one hand enveloping her waist and the other tenderly stroking her hair. Alexandra fought back the urge to shudder and rested her head against his tunic. She heard Mathe splutter in disbelief but before he could protest Krista and Mariah shooed him off. She caught the look of hurt and disbelief as she glanced over her shoulder, what had the point in all this been? She'd been asking the question more and more but instead of answers all she gained was more questions.

Carlyle hugged her tighter, his grip becoming possessive. 'You are freezing, come back into the castle and have a drink. Just you and I.' Alexandra could tell this was not an offer to be refused; forcing a smile she nodded and allowed him to guide her back inside, the hand gripping her waist making her all too aware that deep down he was angry.

# *Chapter Seven*

The courtyard was filled with a mixture of servants and nobles to bid Alexandra and her small traveling party farewell. Mathe, Krista, and Mariah stood to the one side with a handful of soldiers who would accompany them on the journey to Visaye. She had managed to convince Carlyle to allow her friends to travel with her, that they would help her to remember. She had promised him that she would do nothing to prevent the wedding; she had somehow managed to convince him that she was looking forward to it. Her face was expressionless as she bid her father farewell, curtseying deeply. Tears pricked her eyes as she leaned forward to kiss his cheek. This would be the last time she saw her father, and she still remembered nothing about him. *Why are they so eager for me to be gone? Surely, they would want me to remember them?* She asked herself as she stepped towards the cluster of horses. She eyed them apprehensively; she didn't know the first thing about herself let alone horse riding. Was she really expected to ride? Strong hands gripped her waist and she jumped around startled.

'I apologize, I did not mean to startle you.' Carlyle smiled down at her half-wolfishly and half-mischievously. 'I thought you would like a hand up, I told you last night we would ride together.'

'Yes of course,' Alexandra nodded remembering the feast the previous night. She glanced at the speckled chestnut and grey horse apprehensively; would it really take the weight of both of them?

'Your father and mother assured me that he is a gentle beast, and strong. He should carry the two of us with ease.' The fingers on her waist squeezed her gently and Alexandra smiled in relief up at him. 'You were quite the accomplished rider, once you are settled in Saphyre than we go riding together. Nothing would give me greater pleasure than teaching you.' Carlyle's lips grazed her cheek and Alexandra felt herself blushing faintly. He lifted her up and into the saddle with ease, gracefully pulling himself up behind her. She turned to look at Mathe, wishing she could talk to him privately. Out of the corner of her eye, she saw Carlyle follow her gaze. 'I hope that foolish girl can undo what she did on your first journey.'

'Which one?' Alexandra asked looking up at Carlyle, 'I still don't understand what happened.'

'Mariah. She was your mother's protégée, quite the powerful sorceress. Almost as powerful as...' Alexandra frowned and looked up at Carlyle. 'As your mother,' he finished his sentence and smiled down at Alexandra. 'She was the one who conjured the portal, where she found the strength...'

'You think there is a spell that will help me remember?'

'Not to my knowledge and you are all forbidden to meddle with the Source. She has caused enough damage. Once we are married we will work on getting your memories back,' Carlyle tried to console her. 'But you will be beginning a new life; we will create plenty of new memories.' His hand rested on her belly, stroking it gently. Blushing Alexandra looked back towards the castle, swallowing a lump which had formed in her throat. As the horse broke into a gentle trot she gripped the saddle from fright. 'Do not worry; I will not let you fall.'

'How are you feeling?' Ismenya rode beside Carlyle and smiled sadly at Alexandra. 'I hope you do not mind that no fuss was made, we thought a quick and quiet farewell would be best for you.' Alexandra nodded but couldn't find the words she needed to speak. She wasn't sure how she felt; she didn't feel sad – she remembered nothing of her life; nothing of her childhood or family. She felt empty. 'Perhaps it is for the best,' Ismenya comforted her, 'it was upsetting the first time. I am sure no one wants to relive what has come to pass.'

'Surely I would have been happy? If I was leaving to marry the man I love?' Alexandra asked bluntly, forgetting that Carlyle was right behind her. His arms stiffened around her and Ismenya frowned in warning.

'You were leaving your home Alexandra – of course, you would have been upset.' Alexandra glanced back towards her friends at the back of the traveling party, all were stony-faced and silent. *Maybe it is better that I don't remember,* Alexandra thought bitterly as she bit her tongue to stop herself replying.

The ship rocked steadily as waves lapped against it, Alexandra stood on deck her gaze alternating between the moons, sails, and pitch-black water. Only the eerie green and silver glow from the moons was visible upon the water's surface. The thought of standing on a ship once more had plagued her with night sweats when she'd first clapped eyes upon it two days ago. Now that her feet were back on the godforsaken thing she felt no better – in fact, she felt far worse. Her mind flickered back to Earth and constantly settled upon the wrecked Mary-Rose. She had visited the wreckage one weekend, hoping that visiting different places would jolt her memory. There's something familiar about the wreckage that had sent a wave of longing and homesickness coursing through her veins. That was now replaced with a sickening terror. From land the ship had looked beautiful; the wood smooth and polished, the sails bright and full with the wind puffing them out. Her mind seemed to have romanticised the vision of the ship, ignoring the raging wind that sent waves battering against the sides. Now she was on board it was no longer a romantic idea.

'Alexandra?' Startled at the sound of her name Alexandra's head snapped round to look over her shoulder. 'Dear daughter you should be sleeping, or at least below the deck it is not safe here.' Ismenya squeezed her daughter's arm gently. 'What is wrong?' Alexandra shook her head and blinked back tears rapidly if she voiced her feelings she had no doubt it would just result in another argument and she was desperate to avoid this. 'I remember when I left my father's kingdom, it was terrifying. I knew nothing of your father nor his kingdom. I did not even speak the language. All I knew were simple words and phrases, it took the patience and kindness of your father to teach me over the years – I was barely fluent when Giric was born.' Alexandra turned to look at her mother and studied her more intently, somewhere deep in her mind she'd known her mother was a foreign bride, Carlyle had reminded her on several occasions, but only now did the revelation of their shared position truly sink in. Ismenya was bundled up in layer upon layer of furs; her hair was loose and framed her face in an attempt to keep some of the winter chills off her face. 'As you can tell I have never quite acclimatized to the temperature up here either.' Her forest green eyes flickered mischievously but upon a deeper inspection, Alexandra could see the grief that being a foreign bride had brought her mother and the fact that her daughter was about to go through the same ordeal.

Alexandra willed herself to smile, her behaviour now seemed suddenly selfish, the whole year seemed incredibly selfish and she desperately wished she could turn back time. She should have spent yesterday reassuring her that her ordeal wouldn't be so bad, not pleading with her to call the wedding off. She had probably only worsened her mother's fears by now.

'I...' She shook her head unsure of what to say, could she really lie and say she thought she was lucky? Could she lie? Knowing that she had no choice she hugged her tightly. How could she let her mother fear for her? 'I know I am an extremely lucky mother, Carlyle loves me. And at least I have met him, I agreed to marry him of my own free will...and of course, we share a language....do we not?' It suddenly occurred to her she wasn't sure if Carlyle's kingdom did share her language. Laughing Ismenya nodded and kissed her cheek.

'Yes, my daughter you do, although Carlyle can teach you languages along with your other studies. He will be a good teacher; his power far surpasses mine.' Alexandra looked confused but didn't have a chance to question this as her mother carried on with her train of thought, she seemed to be speaking to comfort herself now. 'You know each other too, the climate is not too drastic either – his winters can be quite harsh, but the summer moons will be similar to those in Karstares. Besides you always did favour the winter, and the elements hardly pose a problem for you.' Her mother looked at Alexandra fondly and stroked her cheek, tears welling up in her eyes. 'I am so proud of you my daughter. You are beautiful, kind and so talented...' She bit her lip and looked into the water before turning to look back up at Alexandra. 'Come, we should return below deck where it is warmer and safer.' Knowing it was more for her mother's comfort than her own; Alexandra nodded and followed her below deck and into her mother's regal cabin. Despite the terror of being on the deck, she'd enjoyed the cool crisp air and the rare chance at being alone. But she would hopefully have plenty of that in Carlyle's kingdom, once the wedding was over she would hardly see her mother, if ever again. She would not refuse time with her mother now.

For the rest of the night, she listened to her mother reminisce about her home kingdom. The eternal heat, exotic fashion including shimmering paints, glittering jewelry worn on ankles, upper arms and foreheads. But the memories she most enjoyed of her mother's was the ones involving magic; the rituals, lessons, and potions. Although magic in this world was more common than Earth to Alexandra it still seemed mythical and exotic. As she fell asleep in her mother's arms feeling like a small child once more, she found herself wishing that she too had been gifted with the Source.

***

The days were short but felt as if they lasted a lifetime, there wasn't much to do cooped up on a ship all day long. The men travelled on a separate vessel as it was deemed improper to travel aboard the same one and although Alexandra liked and enjoyed the company of the women around her they were all too...girly. All they could talk about was the marriage ceremony; who would be wearing what and what eligible men would be there. Only two women besides the Queen brought Alexandra constant relief; Mariah and Krista. Although not forgiven Ismenya and Carlyle had seemed there would be no problem in allowing them to partake in the ceremony as originally planned, they had after all been Alexandra's ladies-in-waiting as well as her closest friends. Carlyle had even allowed Mathe to attend the ceremony, he was to represent the Karstare's elite guards and escort her on her journey to the temple. Alexandra couldn't help but think this was more punishment than forgiveness; Mathe would be the one to walk with her to the temple from the ship and officially deliver her to Carlyle and her new life. The thought for her was unbearable, but Mathe was alone on a ship full of Carlyle and his men – god only knew how they tormented him with this image. Her romantic interest in Mathe had not been a secret, and although no improper actions had gone on she knew Carlyle harboured a grudge at what he deemed an embarrassment.

'Are you nervous?' Krista asked adjusting Alexandra's footwork as they practiced hand-to-hand combat. Although officially a lady-in-waiting Krista had spent most of her time with the pages and squires when they were children and if she had been born a boy would most certainly have been knighted by now. Ismenya had appointed her as a lady-in-waiting thinking it would be good for Alexandra to have some sort of protection at all times, she had also begrudgingly consented to Krista teaching Alexandra some tricks providing no weapons were used.

'Carlyle has been patient enough with your unconventional antics, I hardly expect him to have to endure yet more!' She had scolded when she found them sparring below deck one morning. At first, Alexandra had thought Krista merely wanted something to do, but now she could tell there was a hidden motive to the lessons.

'Of course, I am.' Alexandra bit back a yelp as she brought her right hand up to block a strike, only to find she'd protected the wrong side of her face. 'I know there is more to this mess than people let on; I know I do not love Carlyle.' She couldn't help smirk as she blocked a punch and retaliated by curving her hand and bringing it round to strike Krista on the side of her head. She couldn't bring herself to mention she had overheard the three of them talking the night of her arrival.

'Perhaps we should stop for the day,' Krista grumbled shaking her head and trying to regain the sense of hearing. 'No one is trying to fool you Alexandra; we are just...looking out for you.'

'By lying?' Krista remained silent and Alexandra stamped her foot in frustration.

'Do not start Alexandra. We are *protecting* you – trust me.' Alexandra didn't bother asking how; no-one would tell her the truth. 'Just accept this...it is for the best.'

\*\*\*

The winds were harsh and raged against the ship. The ocean-battered the sides yet Alexandra remained on deck, although her face was calm and impassive her hands gripped the ship's railing, splinters pushed into her palms and her knuckles blanched as she clenched it in terror; whether from the storm or from what lay ahead of her she wasn't sure.

'What are you doing up here? Are you trying to get yourself *killed?*' Rough hands tore Alexandra away from the ship's edge, she realized rain had begun to pelt down and her dark hair was plastered to her face and her clothes clung to her in sopping heaps. *I thought that was just the ocean's spray.* She thought vaguely. '*Alexandra!*' She looked up to see Carlyle glaring down at her, a livid expression on his face.

'I thought you could not be on the same ship?' She asked her voice void of any emotion; the cold had numbed her body which in turn had spread inside of her and numbed her mind making it impossible to think coherently. Carlyle swore and gripped her arm propelling her quickly down below deck and into her private cabin. He locked the door behind him and spoke in a lowered voice to avoid being detected.

'Do you realize we are to be married today?' He hissed at her.

'*Today?*'

'We will dock in the next few hours; the temple is not too far from the shore – barely even an hour's journey. Of course, that would be for a normal person a normal day. There will be a parade of people all vying to see their long awaited queen.'

'I – I did not expect it to be so soon...'

'Soon? Alexandra this should have happened long ago! We should be on the way to celebrating our first anniversary with a prince on the way!' Carlyle stared at her intently, numbly Alexandra felt him rest one hand on her abdomen whilst he brushed a strand of hair from her eyes with the other.

'What are you doing here Carlyle?' She asked sitting on the edge of the bed and accepting a sheet from him, so she could dry her hair and face. A small voice nagged in the back of her mind, she should get out of her sopping clothes, but she wasn't prepared to change with Carlyle standing there. At the unsure expression on his face, she frowned. 'You wanted to make sure I was still here. A good start to the marriage, you do not even trust me.' *And I do not love you,* but she dared not voice that thought aloud. Carlyle arched an eyebrow at her but Alexandra merely shrugged refusing to take the bait. 'I am done apologizing for something I do not even remember.' Carlyle reached out so that he could turn her to face him, his hand gently cupping her cheek.

'I will admit I came to ensure you were still here. But I wanted to see how you fared, the crossing has been a rough one and I know you are concerned about our future.' Alexandra shrugged refusing to show how she felt; it would do no good. No matter what she said Carlyle would only answer with lies, of that she was sure. 'I should go...as you pointed out I should not be here.' He bowed low to her formally and turned to leave; he was halfway out the door when he seemed to have a second thought and came back towards her. 'I love you.' He whispered into her ear, kissing her cheek softly as he paused to study her reaction before finally turning to leave. Alexandra snapped back to attention and quickly bolted the door shut before he could come back in again. Slumping to the floor a cold, burning rage filtered through her limbs making her shiver. Angrily she wiped at the spot on her cheek where Carlyle had kissed; how could everyone have neglected to tell her that after only a day with her family and a two-week treacherous voyage across the ocean she would be expected to marry barely an hour after stepping on land? It was ludicrous! She was in half a mind to go and question her mother but knew it would be pointless. Why would Carlyle lie? He gained nothing from it, not only that but if she heard one more word about running away she would scream. *You were not even meant to return to Karstares*, she reminded herself. *I was meant to come straight to Saphyre. Would he have expected us to marry as soon as we arrived then?* Keeping the door bolted Alexandra moved onto the cabin bed and curling up hugged a pillow tightly to her chest. She didn't expect to get any sleep, yet she closed her eyes in the vain hope it would come to her.

# Chapter Eight

A frantic knocking tugged Alexandra from her light slumber, she jumped up alert fearing the worst. Had the ship struck rocks?

'Why was your door locked?' Ismenya's eyes were wide, her cheeks pale and her nostrils flared. Alexandra resisted rolling her eyes as she stepped aside to allow her mother in, shocked when a barrage of women filed in behind her.

'I wanted privacy,' Alexandra shrugged trying not to sound too offended. 'Have we arrived?'

'We docked just before dawn. Carlyle should already be at the temple,' Ismenya gestured for Alexandra to step behind a small partition. 'We do not have time to dawdle.' *She thinks I am going to try and run away again.* Unable to think of anything to say to comfort her mother Alexandra remained silent and did as she was bid. She was bathed styled, primped and dressed as if she was a doll for everyone's amusement. Not once did someone consults her to see what she thought, but Alexandra remained silent throughout. She didn't care how she looked; she just wanted the day over with. When Ismenya stepped back her green eyes were bright with unshed tears, her lips quivering. 'Your father would be so proud of you.' Alexandra blinked back her own tears and looked away; would he? What had she done to make him proud of her? She turned to face the full-length mirror, so she could inspect herself, but she felt nothing as she looked upon her reflection.

Her gown was shoulderless, revealing her slender shoulders and neck. At her throat rested the locket Carlyle had given her, and she brushed polished fingernails against it. The sleeves were made from a sheer fabric which had been slashed just above her elbows and revealed her arms as she moved them. The bodice of the dress was fitted and had been laced up so tightly that Alexandra could barely breathe. She rested a hand on the diamond encrusted pattern of her family emblem; the crescent moon over a sword with an owl on the tip. Each had been painstakingly sewn on during the voyage, and Alexandra felt a twinge of guilt as she remembered the diamonds from her original dress. There were no diamonds sewn to the skirts of this gown, instead, it was layers of white satin slashed to reveal icy blue silk, reminding her of rippling water as she moved. She felt the eyes of the women who had created the dress upon her, and she realised in horror she was looking far from overjoyed.

'It is beautiful,' she whispered turning to face them and forcing herself to smile. 'I...thank you all so much. I hope you can forgive me for...' She trailed off unsure of how she could ever apologise for the beautiful creation she had destroyed. *They must think me such a brat* she thought with horror.

'Your Highness it is in the past,' Alexandra smiled gratefully but still could not shake off the guilt.

'There is just one more item,' Ismenya turned to take a small wooden box from one of the women. They curtsied to her as they departed, the door shutting behind them. Ismenya opened the box to reveal a delicate circlet of twisted gold. 'I did not...I was not able to give this to you the last time.' She set the wooden box on a cabinet and took the twisted circlet from its velvet bed. 'My mother gave this to me on the day I married your father, and her mother to her...it has been passed down to the firstborn daughter for generations.' Alexandra bowed her head as Ismenya placed the circlet on her auburn ringlets. 'One day you will pass this on to your daughter, and you will understand how proud I am now.' Desperate not to cry Alexandra embraced her mother tightly. How could her parents say they were proud of her?

'I am sorry for all the grief and suffering I have caused you, all of you.' Her voice was thick, and she coughed in an attempt to stop the tears from flowing. Turning to give herself time to blink away tears she reached under her pillow to pull out the pouch of diamonds. 'I could not save the dress, but I managed to save these, they were my only connection home.' She didn't mention how she had sold some in order to live; she had never talked about her life in Bournemouth. She didn't want to make things harder for her parents.

'Keep them,' Ismenya kissed both Alexandra's cheeks. 'You saved them for a reason. The Goddess has plans for you, Alexandra, let her guide you.' Alexandra was shocked by the unusual comment, nodding obediently she set the pouch in the empty box which had contained the circlet. Turning to the mirror, she tugged at one of her curls and bit her lip nervously. *I can't do this,* but she knew it was too late. She had run away once and failed. 'We should not keep His Majesty waiting.'

'Of course not,' the numbness returned, and Alexandra felt herself shut down. *I can't run forever,* she followed Ismenya to the top deck and smiled as she was greeted by Krista and Mariah. Both were dressed elegantly in the green and gold colours of Karstares, they were swathed in thick cloaks, and Alexandra eyed them wishfully. Storm clouds hung overhead threateningly, but patches of golden sunlight managed to break through the clouds although it offered no warmth. The ground below was wet, and Alexandra glanced at several deep puddles nervously. Her mother had assured her that her gown and shoes were protected by strong spells which would resist dirt, but she still did not want to risk spoiling the beautiful gown. Not again.

'Your Highness you look stunning.' Mathe bowed formally as he greeted Alexandra and the women on the docks. Alexandra smiled weakly, turning to Giric she resisted the urge to laugh at him.

'If it was not blasphemous then I would say your beauty rivals that of the Goddess.' He embraced Alexandra and kissed her lightly on both cheeks. 'You truly are beautiful sister.'

'Thank you Giric,' she watched as Giric bowed to their mother and led her ahead of the party. Accepting Mathe's offered arm she turned to see Krista and Mariah preparing to follow them. Krista looked uncomfortable surrounded by the crowds of people, her hands twitching on the hilt of the sword strapped to her waist. When she turned to face forwards again, she was shocked to see five men dressed head to toe in black, their tunics bordered with silver.

'The Castle Guards,' Mathe explained, 'they will escort us to the temple. Carlyle prefers his Castle Sorcerers but keeps them hidden in crowds to ensure there is no unrest; they make useful spies.' Alexandra flinched as a man with chestnut hair turned to look at her, even from a distance she could see the loathing in his eyes. The man turned back to Ismenya and bowed stiffly before leading her away.

'He *prefers* his Castle Sorcerers?' Alexandra asked confused.

'Carlyle favours those with the Source; he deems those without it unworthy.' Mathe's tone was overwhelmingly bitter and Alexandra flinched. Did Carlyle see her as unworthy? *Mother has power; he is adamant our children will inherit the Source.* A strong wind tore through the air and Alexandra shivered, wishing she had asked for a cloak to wear. No one had seemed to think to offer her one, and she had not dared voice her concern at the cold. As they walked through Evany's streets, she looked at the crowds who cheered and called out blessings. Very few people were dressed adequately for the freezing weather. Alexandra studied the people as she forced herself to smile at them through her nerves. They weren't just inadequately dressed; many were dressed in rags and looked haggard.

'These people are starving,' she whispered horrified.

'Every city has no slums, it is normal.' Mathe shrugged, and Alexandra looked at him disgusted; how could he be so callous?

'Tell me about Carlyle,' she said in an attempt to change the subject. She wanted to keep her eyes forward; she couldn't bear looking at these people dressed in their rags while they swept by in so much finery. *What must they think of me?* She thought as she smiled at a child who threw small flowers at the royal party. These were her people now, and she had abandoned them.

'Alexandra you are about to marry the man, you will learn all about him soon enough.' Mathe said no more and Alexandra didn't press the subject, the atmosphere between them was just as frosty as the winter air and she prayed for their walk to be over. They reached the bottom of the temple steps, Alexandra's eyes swept up the towering stairs, and she drew in a sharp breath. There seemed to be hundreds and her legs trembled at the thought of walking up so many.

'Mathe I'm sorry,' she whispered looking at him, but he remained silent his jaw clenching. 'Why are you being so childish?'

'What would you like me to say? That this is not your fault? You *agreed* to marry Carlyle; we tried our best to save you and failed. I can do nothing. I would like nothing more than to promise you that I will find a way to bring you home, to marry you.'

'I don't want you to promise anything; I just want you to tell me the *truth*. Why do I hate the man everyone else believes I love?' But she gained no answers. 'I never wanted to hurt you, Mathe; I do not know why I ran away or *how* yet you seem to think I have done this to hurt you intentionally.' As they reached the top of the temple steps she saw that the large wooden doors were open and that the temple was full to bursting with people. Her mother and Giric stood in the doorway, Alexandra panicked at the sombre expressions upon their faces until she saw Giric's eyes dancing with laughter. *He never could take formal occasions seriously;* the thought came from nowhere and Alexandra bit back a smile as the image of Giric greeting a foreign king several years ago came to the front of her mind. He had looked impressive in his crown, but he had been unable to stop grinning. *Father had been furious with him.*

'It has been an honour serving you,' Mathe bowed stiffly, and Alexandra met his eyes coldly.

'May the Goddess protect you,' Mariah stepped forward curtseying. Alexandra glanced at Krista, but the woman could only bow her dark eyes misty.

'Thank you all,' it took every ounce of willpower for Alexandra to turn from her friends and face her mother and brother.

'Are you ready to do your duty as Princess of Karstares? To form an allegiance with the King of Saphyre, to give him heirs and ensure our two kingdoms live in peace.' Giric's deep voice resonated through the temple and Alexandra glanced at Carlyle at the top beside the altar.

'I am,' she said ignoring the fear and loathing sweeping through her belly. The thought of bearing Carlyle's children was not a happy one and she shoved it to the back of her mind. One thing at a time.

As both Ismenya and Giric turned to walk up the temple aisle Alexandra glanced behind. Mathe, Krista, and Mariah stood in the crowd watching her, their faces expressionless masks. Keeping her hands at her side, resisting the urge to clasp them nervously, Alexandra followed her mother and brother. The inside of the temple was brightly lit, the floors, walls, ceilings and even columns were made from a dazzling white marble. Hundreds of eyes followed her progress towards Carlyle, all the time her mind screamed at her to turn around and run. What if she didn't use a spell this time but simply made herself anonymous? She could live in exile from both Karstares and Saphyre. *Carlyle found me in a different world; I'm sure finding me here will be no problem.* She scolded herself. She almost walked into her mother not realising they had come to a halt at the head of the temple. She curtsied deeply as she was left to stand beside Carlyle in front of the temple priest.

The priest spoke in a monotone voice to which Alexandra could barely bring herself to listen too; only when Carlyle squeezed her hand did she snap to attention and try to force emotion into her voice.

'With your blood, I bind you both as one,' Alexandra's blood ran cold as the priest produced a knife which he cut across her right palm. She stared in horror as blood seeped from the wound, dripping on to the floor. As Carlyle clasped her hand she could feel his blood joining with hers; her right arm tingled as she felt a power begin to flow through her veins and as she looked up at him to see what he was feeling she found herself overcome with the urge to kill him. The urge to summon a bolt of lightning or blanket of fire, or even to every sharp object within the temple and hurl them towards him. The thoughts and images that filled her mind terrified her and she felt her knees beginning to buckle, with his uncut hand Carlyle quickly caught her and supported her weight before she could fall to the floor.

'It is almost over,' he promised her with a surprising gentleness to his voice. 'The worst part is over,' Alexandra nodded and forced her knees to straighten so that she could support herself. Why had no one mentioned there would be blood?

'The blood of your two kingdoms forms an unbreakable alliance. May the kingdoms of Saphyre and Karstares forever reign in peace.' The priest continued, but he looked at Alexandra with a slightly concerned look. *Does he expect me to bolt once more?* She couldn't blame him – she was thinking about it after all. Unaware that the priest was even still speaking or about anything going on around her she suddenly felt Carlyle pull her close with his uninjured hand, tilted her face up and slowly brushed his lips against hers, the hand under her chin moved to behind her neck holding her firmly in place as he softly deepened the kiss.

*'I will not marry you!' Alexandra cried pulling away, 'it is Mathe I love – not you!'*

*'He is a knight; he is worse than that he is an orphan brat risen through the ranks. He is nothing, less than a commoner. You are a princess of blood it is not even lawful for you to wed him, has he filled your head with empty promises? Will the two of you run away together, start a life where you can live peacefully out of public eye?' Carlyle laughed cruelly and shook his head, 'you will be my bride – my queen. You have no say in the matter really.'*

*'Then why do you continue to ask me as if I do?' Alexandra hissed spinning on her heels and walking towards the exit of the maze. 'Why not just take me and have done with it?' She turned to glare at him over her shoulder but was surprised to find him gone, feeling a stab of fear she turned to leave once more, a scream escaping her lips when she turned to find him barring her path.*

*'I want to preserve the illusions everyone has of me. I want our marriage to be a happy occasion –'*

*'It will never happen! I would rather* die *than marry a tyrant such as yourself!'*

*'Like your grandmother?' Alexandra froze, too shocked to retort and Carlyle took the opportunity to place a soft kiss on her lips. 'You will be mine. Or your friends will go the same way; everyone will. Your hand in marriage for their lives is hardly unfair now is it?' He asked moving in to kiss her once more. 'So, Princess Alexandra – will you do me the honour of being my bride and Queen of Saphyre?' Alexandra looked into his sapphire eyes and could see he was serious, he had killed once before, and he would do it again. Blinking back tears she nodded.*

*'Yes.'*

Alexandra froze as the scene disappeared and she found herself back in the temple. She snapped her head away from Carlyle, her eyes scanning his face as if searching for the truth. When she finally met his gaze, she was surprised to see them full of sorrow.

'I was hoping you would not remember…I feared a kiss would do something to make you remember.' *That's why he was so careful never to kiss me,* Alexandra realised and kicked herself for being so foolish. Carlyle kept his head close to hers, so they could speak quietly, to the crowd in the pews it looked as if they shared nothing more than words of bliss.

'You monster!' She hissed but before she could break free from Carlyle's grasp the hand which gripped the back of her neck squeezed in a painful warning.

'If I were you I would think *very* carefully before you say or do anything rash. I have your mother here, your brother. Not to mention your precious knight.' Alexandra searched his eyes praying he was lying, but she could see in them he was deadly serious, she nodded and licked her lips, her mouth felt as if it had been stuffed with cotton balls. 'Now smile and curtsey to your people.' Unsure of how she managed to do so, Alexandra smiled and obeyed, turning towards the crowd and dipping into a deep curtsey.

Cheers erupted all around the temple, but Alexandra studied the faces of Carlyle's people as she passed them, her blood chilled as she now noticed the same forced joyful expressions on their faces and the fear that constantly flickered in their eyes, was she imagining it – or was Carlyle truly a tyrannical king? *No good king would let his people live in such poverty;* she reminded herself of the people who had crowded outside on the freezing streets. *Goddess what have I gotten myself in to?*

The wedding feast seemed to be course after course and Alexandra was grateful she was permitted only a dainty forkful of each dish, despite being given a platter full of each course. To her left Carlyle proposed a constant stream of toasts; of new beginnings and happy years to follow. Alexandra took a careful sip of wine from her goblet; it was taking all her self-control not to consume every drop of wine, to lose herself in a drunken oblivion.

'Enough of this gluttony!' Carlyle called lifting his own golden goblet encrusted with an obscene number of jewels into the air. 'I would like to dance with my new wife!' Instantly the musicians struck up a slow romantic waltz, and Carlyle led Alexandra into the centre of the room. 'Stop sulking,' he murmured in her ear, 'I will not have a bitter wife who constantly sulks. Now smile, or someone will die.'

'*Stop it.*' Alexandra cried pulling away from him. 'I will not spend the rest of my life being blackmailed by you. I will not tolerate you using death as a way to manipulate me.' Her voice rose to an almost hysterical pitch and she blushed realising that the music had ceased and that everyone was staring at her in horror. Alexandra looked over at her mother, she could see Ismenya's eyes blazing angrily, and she quickly walked back to the head table. 'Your Majesty, *mother*, please I beg you not to leave me here!' She dropped to her knees, clinging desperately to Ismenya's hands.

'Alexandra rise! You are making a scene!' She had never heard her mother sound so outraged.

'I do not care; this man is a monster!'

'That is nonsense, His Majesty –'

'He killed grandmother!' Alexandra shrieked rising to her feet; she was a sorry sight to behold; her eyes shone with tears, and her whole body trembled. 'She saw Carlyle for what he truly is a monster. *That* is why I agreed to this marriage, to protect you!'

'Queen Ismenya,' a young man stepped forward from the terrified court and bowed deeply, his whole body clearing trembling. He had the look of a man facing death, but his voice was steady as he spoke. 'The Princess is right, King Carlyle is –' but the man never got the opportunity to finish his sentence, a high-pitched shriek filled the grand hall and the smell of burning flesh filled Alexandra's nostrils as before her eyes the man was consumed in flames. Within seconds he was nothing more than a charred spot and a pile of ashes upon the marble floor. The room was enveloped in a horrified silence, too terrified to even faint Alexandra clung to her mother. Ismenya rose to her feet and held her daughter close while Carlyle's court stared down at their shoes hoping he wouldn't target one of them next. Carlyle's footsteps clicked loudly against the marble as he strode forth to stand beside Alexandra and her mother.

'I am afraid Alexandra is right, and I apologise. I had no intentions of harming anyone when I arrived in Karstares, but the King's Mother did not believe I had Alexandra's best interests at heart. She came to my chambers one evening and threatened me, what else could I do?' No one dared to answer Carlyle, and he reached out to take hold of Alexandra, but she stepped out of his reach and eyed him wearily. 'It is only out of the love I have for my wife, and the respect I hold for you, that I will allow you and your party to leave Saphyre. But only if you leave *now*.'

'I will not go without my daughter.' Alexandra felt tears course down her cheeks as she watched the horror and pain dawn on her mother's face. She followed Ismenya's gaze over to Mathe and Krista who stood with swords drawn and pointed at Carlyle's own Castle Guards who looked ready to strike. Mariah stood slightly behind them; her head bowed but a look of deep concentration visible on her face. Giric too stood with his sword drawn, but it was a half-hearted gesture as he seemed to know it would be a futile battle.

'Your daughter belongs to me now; we are bound by blood – a bond which as you know is impossible to break.' Alexandra looked up sickened by the look of intense pleasure on his face. 'Go. Now.' Carlyle repeated, the room filled with a suffocating mist and Alexandra cried out as she felt her mother's presence disappear. When the mist had cleared only Carlyle's people remained.

'Mother!' She cried running forwards, but Carlyle grabbed her arm before she could flee. 'Please, let me say goodbye!'

'You had a chance to say goodbye and you ignored it. That is no fault of mine.' Carlyle turned to look at the remaining courtiers and growled. 'This is not a funeral! *Dance*!' The music began once more, and the crowd moved towards the dance floor, avoiding the ashes of the unfortunate man who'd been foolish enough to speak badly of their king. With a nod of his head what Alexandra assumed to be a servant moved forwards to sweep the pile up. Carlyle led Alexandra back towards the dais half supporting her as she walked. Motioning with his hand two women walked towards them, their heads bowed obediently. 'These...women will prepare you for the bathing ceremony.' He said looking Alexandra up and down coldly as if she were a horse he considered purchasing. He tilted her chin up, his eyes bored into her own as he pressed his lips against hers. 'And I hope for your sake you are free from another's touch.'

The two women accompanied led Alexandra through a series of underground tunnels. She followed in silence thankful that neither offered her words of encouragement, reassurance or any words for that matter. She had spent most of her energy dreading the ceremony that she had given little thought for what would come after. Until this moment she had remained blissfully ignorant of what would be expected of her next. She followed the two women down a twisting tunnel which opened into a cavernous room. The room was unadorned, the only decoration on the red clay walls were candles which flickered gloomily. A large pool with steam rising from it was the only feature of the room and Alexandra looked at it in confusion.

'It is the final ritual of the night,' the priest from earlier stepped into the room, and Alexandra looked at him blankly. 'You must be bathed; your sins washed away so that you can be purely received into the king's bed.' *What of his own sins?* She wanted to ask but couldn't find her voice. Instead she nodded simply and looked back at the pool. It looked big enough for at least three dozen people. Rose petals floated along the surface and the scent filled Alexandra's nostrils overwhelming her. Too tired and frightened to protest Alexandra let the women undress her and lead her into the water. Although not scalding it was unpleasantly warm and made her feel weak, sick and drowsy. Her cheeks burned with humiliation as the two women began to wash her, rubbing petals over her bare skin and pouring the scented water over her head. The priest stood at the edge of the pool, murmuring in a language Alexandra neither recognised nor understood. Squeezing her eyes tightly shut she tried stifle the sobs which threaten to consume her. All she wanted to do was sink beneath the surface of the water, to let it embrace her. As the rose petals brushed against her skin, she tried to focus on their scent, to try and trigger a memory that would bring her some sense of relief. But she found no comfort, all she could do was pray for the night to be over.

The women led her from the water, patted her dry and slipped a thin silk robe over her naked form; they secured it with a belt of the same fabric leaving her bare beneath the thin material. Wordlessly she was led from the cavernous room and through a second set of tunnels, all the time her heart pounded in fear. What if someone should see her in such a vulnerable state? And what was Carlyle likely to do with her? She knew the answer to the latter, it was obvious – but it was how he would do it that terrified her. He was evil. A tear slipped down her cheek, and she hurriedly wiped it away, pushing the thoughts to the back of her mind. She wasn't naive to relationships, after her experience on Earth she had no doubt she knew more than would be deemed appropriate. She didn't fear Carlyle's threat – she'd been far too occupied trying to discover her past than dally in any sort of relationship. Only Paul had tried to get close, and even then, she had managed to keep him somewhat at bay. But Carlyle was obviously a cruel man – who knew what tastes would satisfy his sexual appetite. One of the women knocked on a door, Alexandra had been so lost in thought she'd not even noticed the transition from dingy tunnel to elaborate hallway.

'Leave.' The women obeyed as Carlyle opened the door and pulled Alexandra in. Her eyes swept around the large room once, but she saw nothing except the magnificently carved bed. White silk sheets adorned the bed and golden veils hung from the ceiling offering some shield of privacy. *Run, run, run,* a voice in Alexandra's mind pleaded with her but she couldn't move her head let alone her legs. She could feel her mind shutting down in defeat; it was too late to run. She was married to Carlyle, at least now she knew why she had agreed to this marriage. She flinched as she felt Carlyle's hands resting on her shoulders; pulling her close and tilting her head up so that he could kiss her mouth. His touch was gentle and surprisingly tender, but it did nothing to alleviate her nerves. Especially when his hand slipped beneath her robe, his fingertips stroking her bare skin. A small gasp escaped from Alexandra's lips, and she broke away from the kiss trying to move free from his grip. His hand moved down to her waist, holding her firmly in place. 'Look at me,' he commanded forcing her eyes to lock gaze with his. 'I will never harm you; I was not lying when I told you that I love you. Allow yourself some pleasure at least.' Alexandra couldn't break free from his gaze, her mind too cloudy to respond. All she could do was blush as he slipped his other hand into her robe, slowly caressing her before pushing the robe down to her elbows revealing her; still, she couldn't break free of his gaze. As she felt the knot at her waist released and the robe pool to her feet Carlyle bent his head to kiss her, she watched in fascination as the spiral pattern in his eyes began to move clockwise, and the black of his pupils enveloped her as she fell into darkness.

# Chapter Nine

A stifling darkness filled the chamber, a pounding noise drummed against Alexandra's skull and she pressed a hand to her head. Massaging her forehead to try and stem the pain. It took her a moment to realise that the pounding wasn't just from the pain of a migraine but the sound of Carlyle's strong heartbeat. Squeezing her eyes tightly shut she tried to block out the previous day. But try as she might she could not block out the tortured screams of the man consumed by flames, her mother disappearing within the mist nor the cavernous tunnels. But she was mortified when she realised her memory stopped short. She saw herself walking to Carlyle's chambers, remembered the touch of his fingertips brushing against her bare skin as he disrobed her. But after that she remembered nothing, her memory was a blank slate. Alexandra bolted upright wincing as her body roared in protest. Every muscle ached, and it didn't take her long to realise why.

'Good morning,' Carlyle gently clasped her hand, pressing her palm to his warm lips. 'It is still early; breakfast will not be brought up for some time.' *What time is it?* Alexandra couldn't help asking herself, she had not adjusted to having no way to tell the passing of time. A bell had rung each hour in her father's castle, but between the hours of midnight and six it had remained dormant.

'I'm not hungry.' Alexandra mumbled pulling her hand free. She blinked as candles on the wall and the hearth flared to life. A comforting warmth radiated almost immediately from the hearth and Alexandra closed her eyes, focusing on the crackling of the logs. 'Why can I not remember last night?' her voice was surprisingly empty; why was she not angry? When she eventually opened her eyes she kept her gaze fixated on the hearth, listening as Carlyle moved from the bed and poured something.

'It is just water.' Alexandra stared down at the clear liquid suspiciously. 'Alexandra what reason would I have to harm you? You are my wife; soon you will be my queen.'

'What reason would you have to manipulate me, so I don't remember something? Why would you not want me to remember the night of our marriage?' Alexandra shot back at him holding one of the many layers of blankets tightly to herself. '*Why* do I not remember last night?' She repeated the question finally forcing herself to look at Carlyle. She was surprised at how vulnerable he looked; his blonde hair was dishevelled and falling in to his deep blue eyes which were bleary with sleep. As she met his gaze she remembered how the spiral pattern had twisted in a clockwise motion and she quickly looked away.

'You were terrified; the day had been an emotional one for you. I wanted you to relax, to enjoy some pleasure at least.'

'You had no right,' Alexandra hissed clenching her fists. '*You* of all people know how difficult it has been not knowing anything, not even the most basic things about myself. Having no memories – yet you saw fit to take more from me?' Sweeping one of the fur blankets around her shoulders Alexandra stood up and wandered over to the window. She unlatched the shutter and pulled it open, wincing as a strong wind gusted through the chamber almost blowing the candles out. Quickly she closed the shutter and rested her forehead against it.

'I apologise. Truly I was just trying to help you, we had a duty to do…I did not want you to suffer more.' There was nothing she could say in reply, nothing she *wanted* to say, and so she remained silent. 'I did not think you would be up so early, your ladies will not be up for some time yet.'

'I just want to be alone.' Alexandra murmured, 'is there somewhere I can bathe? Alone.' She wanted to wash all traces of Carlyle from her person. She followed him through a door and down a spiralling staircase, conscious that she was still only clothed in the fur blanket. The further down they walked the warmer the temperature grew and there was the sound of rushing water. Two waterfalls crashed through the ceiling and into a large pool, steam rising from the water. Towels and robes were folded in a carved alcove beside the entrance.

'Evany was chosen as the capital for its natural springs. The water strengthens those with the Source, my great-grandfather discovered there was a spring close by and built this chamber to utilise it.' Alexandra remained silent, sidestepping as Carlyle tried to tilt her chin up. 'Alexandra —'

'Please just leave me alone.' She whispered still refusing to look up at him. At the sound of retreating footsteps she shed blanket in a corner of the room and slid beneath the water. The water was pleasant against her skin and she found a ledge carved in the pool which she could sit on while resting her head against the wall. For a while she sat listening to the waterfall, her eyes closed.

*I will get my memories back,* she told herself. *I just need to find out what triggers them.* Briefly she wondered if hypnosis would work but quickly dismissed the thought. She doubted hypnosis existed in this world, or if she would want someone to overhear her memories. She knew now that any of Carlyle would not show him in the way he desired. She took her time bathing and washing her hair, enjoying her first bath where she had absolute and privacy and wasn't on a ship lurching from side to side. When she finally returned to Carlyle's chambers, she found two women setting up breakfast on a table tucked into the corner of the room.

'These are you ladies,' the two women dropped in too deep curtsies as Alexandra glanced over at them. 'They will dress you, run your errands and accompany you around the castle.' Both women remained silent and in their curtsies, neither daring to look up as Alexandra took a seat opposite Carlyle. 'The Captain of the Castle Guard will be up soon; he will be responsible for your visible safety.'

'Visible safety?'

'Castle Sorcerers will be around you, but discreetly so. I use the Castle Guard as a visible warning to any who think it would be wise to attempt to harm either myself or you.'

'I will *not* have my every move watched Carlyle,' Alexandra knew that these Castle Sorcerers would report anything and everything back to him. She would be lucky if she had a moment of privacy to herself ever again.

'It is for your safety,' Alexandra glared at him across the table making it clear that she knew what he really meant.

'Would you please help me dress?' She turned to the two women desperate to put more space between herself and Carlyle. Obediently they leapt up and led her into a dressing chamber. The two women moved to curtsey once more, but Alexandra held up a hand. 'Please don't, you don't have to curtsey every time you see me.' Had she really lived like this before? People curtseying and bowing to her without thought? She studied the two women as they straightened. They were the complete opposite of each other; one was a stunning blonde with a lithe body that Alexandra could only stare enviously at. The second was a petite woman with plain features and mousey brown hair.

'It is an honour to serve you, Your Highness.' The petite woman spoke in a voice barely above a whisper. 'Many of the dresses are from your kingdom if you would like we can have new gowns made up in Saphyre's fashion.'

'Thank you, but my old dresses will be perfectly fine,' she looked between the two women waiting for them to introduce themselves. 'What are your names?' She finally asked unable to take the silence that filled the room. The two women exchanged glances with each other and Alexandra wondered what she had asked that was so wrong.

'Roisin,' the petite woman answered.

'Helena,' they looked terrified as they whispered their names that Alexandra felt fear creeping into her stomach; what kind of king was Carlyle that people were terrified to reveal their names? Seeing that questions would only frighten them, more Alexandra decided to remain quiet. She picked out a warm looking green velvet gown with a fitted bodice and full skirt. Once both women had helped her to dress Roisin sat her in front of a mirror where she proceeded to style Alexandra's hair, Helena gestured to the array of make-up on the table, but Alexandra shook her head. 'His Majesty would prefer if you were appropriately made up, you must look pleasing.'

'I will speak to His Majesty about that,' Alexandra promised seeing the fear in Helena's eyes. 'I will ensure you are not blamed.' She was not prepared to be dressed as a doll just to please a man she loathed.

Carlyle rose to Kiss Alexandra's cheeks as she emerged from the dressing chamber. He frowned slightly at her unmade face, but Alexandra scowled at him, saved from speaking by a knock at the door. She turned as a tall man with chestnut hair bowed low, instantly recognising him as one of the Castle Guards from the previous day.

'Well?' Carlyle's voice was impatient as he waited for the man to rise.

'Queen Ismenya departed last night, peacefully. One of the women aboard her vessel asked for this to be delivered to you.' He held out a wax-sealed scroll which Carlyle quickly scanned.

'No,' shaking his head he handed the scroll back. 'Send a hawk with my reply. I do not want her in my kingdom.' Alexandra arched an eyebrow, but Carlyle left the subject. 'Alexandra this is the Captain of the Castle Guards, Captain Xander.' Xander turned steel grey eyes to Alexander as he bowed stiffly once more.

'I will defend you with my life, Your Highness.'

'Thank you, Captain,' Alexandra kept her voice neutral as she replied. She could see the Captain wanted nothing to do with her, was it just because she was married to Carlyle or was there something else? *You have never met this man before,* a voice in the back of her mind spoke. She knew it to be true; there was nothing remotely familiar about this man. So why did he look so loathing?

Shortly after dismissing Xander, Carlyle rested a hand on her waist and led her from the chambers. Alexandra was convinced within minutes that she would never learn her way around the behemoth-sized castle. Laughter and chatter filled the hallways and rooms but as soon as people caught sight of Carlyle a hushed silence would descend. Helena and Roisin followed close behind, looking like silent shadows in their black gowns. Outside rain lashed against the castle and Alexandra felt her stomach churn as she thought of her mother and friends on the ship returning to Karstares.

'Your mother will be fine,' Carlyle tried to comfort her, but Alexandra only glared at him in reply. Had her mother truly had no idea of Carlyle? About the fear in his kingdom? As they wandered, Carlyle explained that the castle was built atop of a cliff giving them a clear view of Evany and the ocean below. 'The Sorcerers' Tower is the second highest in the castle. My study is the highest; the view is breathtaking.' Alexandra rolled her eyes; did he think he would win her over by bragging about views? 'Wait here.' He commanded Helena and Roisin before leading Alexandra down a spiral staircase which felt as if it went down several floors. She was sure by the time they reached the bottom they were deep underground. Putting her loathing aside Alexandra kept close to Carlyle's side as he led her through a labyrinth of tunnels. The walls were bare of torches; the only Source of light was that which Carlyle summoned. 'These tunnels lead to our chambers, no one knows of them so should you ever find yourself in danger these will lead you to safety.'

'If I can ever find them,' Alexandra muttered and halted as they came to a fork. Gently Carlyle unclasped her locket and held it in front of her, slowly it began to glow, and as she touched it she found it was warm to the touch.

'I would never risk something happening to you,' she slipped the locket back over her head. 'If ever you get lost this will show you the way back.' He guided her down the left fork, but Alexandra paused and looked towards the right.

'What's down here?' She asked peeling away from his grip and following the tunnel down.

'The dungeons. Alexandra come back, you do not need to see them.' Ignoring him, she continued down the twisting tunnel. An overpowering stanching hit her nostrils making her retch, but she refused to turn back. 'Alexandra –'

'Surely if I am to be queen I should know *all* of the castles' secrets?' The dungeons were swallowed in darkness. The floors and walls were damp and slippery with slime. 'These can't be the dungeons,' Alexandra's eyes swept up and down the hallway; there was no evidence of cells, guards or even prisoners. Her ears pricked at a muffled noise but no matter how hard she squinted in the darkness she could not see where it came from. She turned to face Carlyle and watched in fascination as he pressed his glowing hand against the wall. Faint markings outlining a door appeared, and Alexandra let out a strangled cry as the section of wall disappeared to reveal the cell within. It was small and cramped, barely tall enough even for her to stand upright in. There was no room to stretch out or even lie down.

'It is a dungeon – people are brought down here for committing crimes. Alexandra –' Unable to breathe and suddenly aware of where the muffled noise was coming from, Alexandra turned and fled back through the tunnels to the ground floor. She desperately needed air. The bodice of her dress felt too tight and the air around her was stiflingly hot. Beautifully carved oak doors stood between her and fresh air, ignoring the surprised looks from courtiers Alexandra sprinted for the doors. They were extremely heavy, and Alexandra pulled with all her strength to open just one, the door groaned as it moved slowly on its hinges. Windswept through her hair, sending the long skirt of her dress billowing out. Taking a deep breath she felt the panic within her stomach subside and she stepped outside, only to find her path blocked. Confused Alexandra stepped backwards looking the doorway up and down. There was nothing in her way, yet when she tried to step over the threshold, she found her path blocked by what felt like a pane of glass.

'Surprised?' Carlyle's face was blank as he walked towards her, the light from his hand extinguished completely.

'I just need fresh air.'

'No. I am not going to risk you fleeing once more.' His voice was low as he closed the door and steered Alexandra away.

'Excuse me?' Alexandra's eyes blazed as she halted in her tracks, the grand hallway quickly emptying of courtiers. Only Helena and Roisin remained, standing as far away as they could.

'You have fled once; I will not risk you fleeing for a second time.' Carlyle repeated slowly as if he spoke to a child, 'you are not to leave the castle, not unless *I* am with you.'

'Do you truly think you can keep me locked away for the rest of my life? I am so lucky to have a husband such as you,' she couldn't stop the biting sarcasm. 'I see why you have waited so long in life to marry. You could not trick someone in to loving you, even someone who had no memory of you. Instead you have to resort to blackmail and sordid trickery –'

'Enough. You are forbidden to leave the castle only until your coronation. Once you are Queen of Saphyre, you can leave the castle as and when you please – within reason.'

'Why after my coronation?' Her stomach clenched knowing she would not like the answer.

'The crown will bind you to Saphyre…it has been a tradition of the kingdom for over five-hundred years.' Alexandra searched Carlyle's eyes, looking for any hint that he may be joking. Even if it was a cruel joke.

'Bind me…what does that mean?'

'Once you are crowned queen you will not be able to leave Saphyre.'

'But Karstares is my home, how will I see my family?'

'Saphyre is your home now, and *I* am your family.' Carlyle stroked her cheek gently, but Alexandra flinched away from his touch. 'This is the weight all foreign princesses must bear, leaving their kingdoms to start anew. Even your mother underwent this ordeal.'

'My mother is not married to a tyrant intent on keeping her prisoner.' Alexandra pointed out pushing past him; she glared at him as he grabbed her hand to spin her around.

'I am not trying to keep you prisoner Alexandra I am trying to keep you *safe*. You have shown me you do not think rationally if this is what it takes to protect you then I will do it. I *love* you; you will see that one day.'

'You don't know how to love,' freeing her hand from his grasp she turned and calmly walked up the staircase.

Sitting at the intimate table in Carlyle's private dining chamber Alexandra pushed the food around on her plate absently. She had managed to avoid Carlyle for the day, retreating to an empty tower where she had set on the window ledge staring at the city below. Her fear for her mother and friends had not been eased as she'd watched the torrential rain and battering winds. Her mind wandered back to the previous day and the people who had lined the streets dressed in rags. How many of them would see the winter through?

'You need to eat something; you have not eaten since the feast yesterday.'

'I'm not hungry,' she looked over at Helena and Roisin who stood with their eyes downcast as they waited for orders. 'Do you not dine publicly?' Faint images of dining with her family pulled at her mind; they had always dined in the great hall with the courtiers, their families and those who worked in the castle but were off-duty.

'If the occasion calls for it. I like my privacy.' The silence between the two resumed, and Alexandra set her cutlery down. 'Go,' Carlyle dismissed the two women. 'I will help Her Highness prepare for the evening,' *I can prepare myself*, but somehow Alexandra remained silent and followed Carlyle to their chambers. Gritting her teeth as she thought about what she would have to endure.

Alexandra spent the next few days in a similar pattern to the first. Each morning she would wake up and wash vigorously, Carlyle did not try to blank her memory as he had their first night together. And while she was thankful for this, she now had to live with the memory of lying with him every night. He was surprisingly gentle, tender and loving. But she couldn't shake the horror that he was a tyrant, that had killed a man in cold blood at their wedding. That he had murdered her own grandmother. She had not questioned him about this, too afraid of the answer.

On the morning of her fourth day in the castle, Alexandra awoke early to a dull pain. Quietly she slid from the bed and drew a chemise over her head; knocking on the door of the dressing chamber she let herself in with an apologetic look to Helena and Roisin. Both women slept on pallets on the floor but jumped to their feet at Alexandra's appearance.

'I'm sorry for waking you both,' she whispered. 'I…' She felt her cheeks warm up. She knew what the dull ache meant, but she knew paracetamol wouldn't be the answer she wanted. Helena took one look at Alexandra's face and smiled sympathetically.

'I will fetch a potion from the healers.' Alexandra smiled in relief and nodded, as Helena walked past she rested a hand on Alexandra's shoulder. 'Forgive me Your Highness but…His Majesty will not be pleased; you should break this to him gently.' Alexandra frowned as she turned Helena's words over in her head.

Alexandra broke the news to Carlyle as they broke their fast that morning. She was surprised at how cold he suddenly became. Rising from his seat, he tossed his half-eaten piece of toasted bread on his wooden plate and stormed to the door.

'Your ladies will show you to your private chamber.' He said without looking at her, before slamming the door to their chambers shut. Alexandra gaped at the door, looking over to Helena and Roisin nervously. Helena had warned her that Carlyle would not be happy with her news, yet she had not expected that reaction.

'You failed to conceive; His Majesty needs a son and heir to secure his succession.' Alexandra shook her head refusing to believe that could be the reason for his sudden mood swing. Gesturing to the food on the table she invited the two to join her, biting her tongue as they sat on the floor. *I will talk to him later*, she told herself. *Let him calm down first.* She had not yet seen Carlyle lose his temper wholly and it was something she was desperate to avoid. He had seemed calm when he had murdered the man at their wedding; if that was what he could do when he had his temper…she shuddered and pushed the thought from her mind.

Her private chamber was a single room in a tower, the door to which was at the end of the hallway of the chambers she shared with Carlyle. The room was circular and sparsely furnished with only a bed, chest and wooden tub for bathing. A door led up to a privy chamber, but other than that there was nothing there.

'His Majesty commands that you are to sleep here only during your bleeding when you are deemed unclean to share his bed.' Helena explained as Alexandra surveyed her new surroundings. 'We will both continue to sleep in your dressing chamber and will come up each morning to prepare you to break your fast with His Majesty.' Alexandra nodded barely listening as she turned to look out the window. Having spent much of the day fretting over Carlyle's temper, she found herself exhausted and wanted nothing more than to curl up and sleep.

'Thank you both,' she said biting back a yawn. 'Would you please mind leaving me for the night? I think I am ready to retire for the evening.' She'd barely pulled the covers up to her chin when she felt herself pulled into a deep, unbreakable sleep.

*'Alexandra! Thank the Goddess!' Alexandra let out a grunt of surprise as a pair of arms enveloped her in a tight embrace. Blinking she moved her head backwards and found herself staring at her mother's soft oval face. She looked around recognising her mother's cabin on the ship.*

*'What…how did I get here?' Hope flared in her belly, had her mother somehow found a way to break Carlyle's spell? Was she truly in her home?*

*'It is only a dream I am afraid,' her mother's voice was apologetic, and Alexandra remembered the brief dreams which Carlyle had used to find her. 'Alexandra –'*

*'Please don't apologise,'* Alexandra begged, *'Carlyle had us all under a spell. I'm not sure why it didn't work on Krista and Mariah...'* She didn't mention Mathe; she was willing to gamble that even had the spell worked on him, his jealousy would have overpowered it.

*'We should have detected it,'* Ismenya sighed. *'How is he treating you?'* Alexandra stood up and shrugged her shoulders as she looked around her mother's cabin.

*'He has not harmed me; he has been...kind,'* she pulled a face at the word, but it was true at least. She decided against telling her mother about being trapped in the castle, why make her feel worse than she already must? *'Please, will you come back for me?'*

*'I am afraid I cannot Alexandra, as much as I wish I could. You are married, it is an unbreakable bond, and yours was sealed by blood. While Carlyle lives, we cannot bring you home.'* Alexandra nodded, she had expected the answer. While Carlyle lives, *she repeated the words to herself. If something happened to him would she be free?* It would have to be before my coronation, *but she quashed that train of thought quickly. She was not a killer, she would not kill Carlyle just to escape her marriage. Besides, she could not kill Saphyre's King and leave the kingdom. Who would rule? 'Be strong Alexandra; remember you are a Saorsa, one of the most ancient royal families in Jadeus.'* Ismenya kissed Alexandra's cheeks and she felt herself beginning to stir. *'This spell does not last for long. I wanted to ensure you were safe; this is the first time I have managed to make contact. Study hard and regain your strength, I will speak with you soon.'*

Before she could question what she was meant to be studying Alexandra's eyes snapped open. She found herself staring up at the dark ceiling of her bedchamber. Raw grief screamed through her veins, and for the first time since her wedding, she allowed herself to succumb to the tears she had fought so long to hold back.

'His Majesty has requested you dine with him,' Roisin broke the news to Alexandra the evening after her bleeding had stopped. Alexandra nodded swallowing a lump of fear. She had avoided Carlyle for much of the week; the few occasions their paths had crossed he had been cold and distant towards her. She couldn't believe his change in attitude over something she had no control over. She was just beginning to settle into her life in Saphyre, but she couldn't shake the fear of what it would be like for Carlyle to become so cold every moon. She stood up from the window ledge and followed Roisin down to the chambers she shared with Carlyle. Roisin knocked on the door; muffled voices from the other side fell silent. Alexandra frowned; she did not think Carlyle liked to hold meetings in their chambers so why was he doing so now? Helena opened the door and curtsied low.

'His Majesty is just preparing for dinner Your Highness,' she said as Alexandra stepped over the threshold. Carlyle emerged finely dressed; he stared coldly at Alexandra as he offered her his arm.

'I cannot help but feel I have offended you somehow.' Alexandra said as they walked to his private dining chamber, for once she found she was unable to stomach the silence between them. Carlyle refused to answer until they were seated, instantly dismissing Helena and Roisin once the food had been served.

'You have refused to give me a son.' Alexandra looked at him stunned; Helena and Roisin had said this was why he was so cold, but she hadn't truly believed them. 'I have lain with you every night –'

'Carlyle we had been married for less than a week when…' Alexandra blushed a deep crimson not wishing to discuss her body with him. 'Do you really want a family so soon?'

'Do not be such a fool Alexandra; I do not care for families. I am a King – I need a son. An heir.' Alexandra blinked and looked away. Scalding rage tore through her veins; it took every ounce of willpower she could must not to throw her goblet of wine in his face. He told her that he loved her, yet he didn't care for a family? *The man makes no sense;* she seethed to herself as she fought to keep her temper under control before finally speaking.

'I – I do not understand why you have gone through so much trouble of marrying me…simply for sons! Could you not have chosen any woman to do that? Surely you could have found someone who was willing, why did you have to ruin my life?'

'I chose you for three reasons. Firstly, no I could *not* just pick any woman to marry I needed a princess of the blood. Someone who has been raised from birth to run a country – who knows how things are done, although do not think the irony is lost on me, I am now not only responsible for ensuring you know my customs but also your own! Secondly, your mother is a powerful Sorceress – she could be a close match for me except she is weak on the inside, she would never be able to wield the Source as I do. She has the power, just not the ability,' he scoffed.

'But I do *not* have the Source you said so yourself, so why not find a bride who does if it is that important to you?'

'All I can do is pray that your lack of power,' he spat in disgust, 'is just a fluke and that any sons we have will inherit power not only from my side but also yours.' Alexandra closed her eyes counting to three.

'You said there were three reasons?' She asked when she was sure her voice was calm and would not betray her anger. She wished she could use the Source; perhaps if the Goddess had blessed her with it, then she would have some form of protection against Carlyle. Perhaps she could have prevented the marriage from taking place. She was surprised when Carlyle spoke at the softness once more in his voice.

'I truly do love you. My father's councilmen suggested you as a potential bride when I was fifteen and he was seeking marriage for me. But you were far too young, even when considering betrothals took years. After his death I had little thought for marriage, I neglected my duty as a king. I was content with seducing noblewomen, part of me considered just taking the first noble born daughter that was offered to me, but my own councilmen persuaded me against it. So I asked for a list of princesses who came from families that were strong with the Source, yours was the first that was mentioned. I had portraits of you sent to me before I began travelling, I knew of your mother's power although I did not know of your lack of it at that time. Your beauty was breath-taking, and it tipped the scales and finally persuaded me to leave my kingdom and bring home a queen. When I met you, you proved different from other princesses; you were kind, intelligent and you had a sense of humour. You proved to be a breath of fresh air. And when I realised you were not under my spell, that you had somehow eluded it and begun to shy away from me...you posed me a challenge I could not refuse.' Alexandra sat back in her seat, her anger evaporated. She had never thought to ask Carlyle how he had come to travel to Karstares.

'So you *had* cast a spell? To make sure nobody would see you for who you are?' Carlyle simply nodded but this only confused Alexandra further, how could she who had no power eluded his spell? She looked at Carlyle deeply unsure of what to say, gone was his own fury from his eyes and in their place was a tender loving expression that filled her with fear. Was someone as cruel as Carlyle really capable of love? 'Carlyle…' She shook her head unsure of what to say. Eventually she settled on the truth. 'I am not going to live my life in fear. I cannot control how quickly I conceive and worrying about this every moon will not help.' Carlyle chewed a mouthful of food, a thoughtful expression on his face.

'You are right of course,' he sighed. 'I apologise for the way I have behaved. I will admit part of me thought you had deliberately prevented yourself from conceiving.' *Would that be possible?* Alexandra asked herself but decided it would be too risky to try. Goddess only knew the rage he would unleash if she purposefully kept herself from conceiving. 'I have spent much of the week in discussion with my councilmen; we have decided to hold your coronation within six moons.' Alexandra sipped her wine unsure of how she felt. *Six moons trapped within the castle, but after that, I will never be allowed to leave the kingdom.* She had to find a way to break the spell he had placed upon her, but could she stop the coronation? She was married to him, and she was not prepared to murder to free herself from a blood bond. *I am going to be queen,* she told herself. *I had best accept it now.*

# *Chapter Ten*

Tears splashed on to the scroll clasped in Alexandra's hand. It was battered from the treacherous weather, but it had brought her the first piece of relief since her two weeks of marriage. The ship carrying her mother, brother, and friends back to Karstares had arrived safely back home. *Home*, Alexandra turned the word over in her miserably and felt the relief begin to fade.

'I had hoped this news would bring you cheer,' Carlyle kissed her cheek and pulled her back down on the bed. His fingertips brushed along her shoulders and Alexandra suppressed a shudder, inching forward ever so slightly to escape his touch. She had already sent her reply back to her mother; she had told Ismenya that Carlyle had been kind to her and it was true. While he was cold and cruel to those around him, to Alexandra, he had shown nothing but a gentle tenderness. *Except for my bleeding,* she reminded herself.

'It does, but I miss her. I miss them all.' Carlyle remained silent and Alexandra stood up. 'I want to be alone.' She desperately wanted to go for a walk in the castle grounds, but she was sick of arguing with Carlyle about being let outside. Instead, she settled for a walk around the castle on her own. She was beginning to enjoy exploring the castle by herself, without her ladies or Carlyle was she was obvious and could often observe the courtiers without their noticing. On the surface many seemed happy, they would walk past Alexandra oblivious to her as they smiled and laughed together. But the closer she looked, the more she noticed the strain buried deep within their eyes and the tightness of their jaws.

'Your Highness,' a man gasped dropping into a low bow. 'Forgive me; I did not realise you had graced us with your presence.' Alexandra blushed deeply as those around the man followed suit. Did they fear her as much as Carlyle? Unable to stand the fearful gazes Alexandra turned and quickly walked away, almost breaking into a sprint to escape. She made her way up to the abandoned tower knowing that she would not incite fear there. In the two weeks, she had lived within the castle she had yet to cross another person within the tower. She never noticed the lone figure standing to the side of the door as she walked in. it wasn't until a hand rested on her shoulder and something wet was pressed against her nose and mouth that she realised she wasn't alone. Before she could push the figure away, she had already fallen into darkness.

'This is a foolish idea – how can we trust her? Even *he* does not trust her; she cannot leave the castle.' Alexandra held her breath at the sound of the familiar voice. She kept perfectly still as she tried to work out where she was. She was sitting up against something solid, her hands bound firmly rested in her lap, and a blindfold covered her eyes.

'How can we trust anyone?' A second voice answered, just as familiar as the first.

'Carlyle?' For a split second she had feared the rebels had snatched her, but why would Carlyle be involved with them?

'Not quite.' The second voice was almost sheepish, and Alexandra frowned. 'Your Highness, please forgive me for having you brought like this but unfortunately trust is a luxury I am too poor to take for granted.' A cup was pressed to her lips, and Alexandra shook her head trying to move away, pursing her lips tightly together. 'This will not harm you; it is just a truth potion. But I must be sure it works before I can unbind you.' *There is no point in fighting,* Alexandra reasoned as the cup found her lips once more. She gulped the potion, almost choking on the bitter herbs. 'What is your name?'

'Alexandra Saorsa.'

'How old are you?' Alexandra froze at the question and shook her head slowly.

'I – I don't know…I don't remember…'

'I told you she would be of no use to us. Not to mention she is the *wife* of our enemy.' *Enemy?* Pain began to thud at the back of Alexandra's head, spreading to the front as she tried to realise what was happening.

'*Enough*,' Alexandra frowned. There was no mistaking that voice. 'Your Highness do you know why you agreed to marry Carlyle?'

'Yes, he killed my grandmother.' Tears stung Alexandra's eyes, and she felt her throat tighten as she thought back to the day of their wedding. 'I had no choice; if I didn't marry him, then he would have killed more people I loved. I wanted no blood on my hands.'

'Do you love your husband?'

'Of course not!' The venom in her voice surprised even Alexandra.

'You saw the events unfold at the wedding, you know she was not willing to marry. We can trust her.' Alexandra held her breath while the two debated, she couldn't push the thought that this was a trap from her mind. 'If I take the blindfold off will you stay calm?'

'Of course,' Alexandra nodded although her voice didn't sound as sure as she hoped it would. She felt the bonds at her wrist loosened first, and she reached up to pull the blindfold off. The room was windowless and dimly lit, only two candles on a crate provided light. Turning to look at the man kneeling beside her Alexandra jumped up and almost tripped as she tried to put space between herself and Carlyle.

'I told you, you should have warned her first.' Xander clasped Alexandra's shoulder and led her over to a barrel where she sat down. 'This is not your husband; surely you would recognise the man with who you share a bed?' Alexandra blushed and faced the second man as he sat opposite her. There was a sheepish smile on his familiar face, but as she studied him closely, she realised there were some subtle differences. His hair was a slightly darker almost dirty blonde, and there was a faint shadow of stubble across his face. His clothes were of a poor quality than Carlyle's and wrinkled as if he had worn the same shirt for more than a day.

'Who are you? Why do you look so much like Carlyle?' Carlyle rarely spoke of his family, but he had never mentioned any living relatives, especially any who bore such a striking resemblance to him.

'Do I truly resemble him?' Alexandra nodded, 'I am not sure if this could be used to my advantage or not…' The man sighed and rubbed a hand across his stubble covered chin. 'My name is Caleb. As for explaining my resemblance to your husband…that is a long story.' Alexandra's eyes darted around the cramped room trying to find a door should she need to make a quick escape, but much of the room was plunged in shadows. 'You do not need to be frightened of us; I have no intentions of harming you. We had to bring you here unconscious to be sure that you would not run away, and the potion…I needed to be sure that I can trust you. That you will not betray us to your husband.'

'I would never do that,' the potion answered instinctively, but even without it Alexandra's answer would have been the same. She had just met Caleb, but there was something about him that told her she could trust him. 'You did not need to bring me here; I want no part of Carlyle's reign.'

'Unfortunately, Your Highness whether you want to be a part of his reign or not, is not something you have a choice in.'

'Please, just call me Alexandra.' She pleaded wearily rubbing her forehead. 'Carlyle told me the reason I ran away was because I was frightened of a rebellion group. Is this true? Did I flee from you?'

'We are *not* a rebellion group,' Caleb's voice was waspish. 'Your husband is not a King – not a *true* King of Saphyre. His ancestors stole the throne over five hundred years ago and have held on to it by brute force ever since then.' Alexandra rested her elbows on the crate in front of her, burying her face into her hands. *All I wanted was to go home, to remember who I was…perhaps I should have left well enough alone. I could have had a quiet life in Bournemouth.* 'Forgive me; I did not mean to sound harsh.' Caleb apologised, 'but it is true. Carlyle and I are distantly related…' Alexandra looked up at as Xander took a seat.

'I don't understand.'

'Then listen,' Xander snapped before addressing Caleb. 'We do not have much time; it will not be long before her absence is noted.'

'Very well,' Caleb nodded. 'The last true King of Saphyre reigned over five hundred years ago. He was a good king, although I am sure he had his faults. The king had a twin brother, one who harboured jealousy for his brother's elevated position. They had been born only minutes apart, and the brother was sure that it was he who was meant to be king. Mixing them at birth would have been an easy mistake to make, and he grew to believe his own falsehood. Eventually, his jealousy consumed him, and he had his brother and the queen murdered in their sleep. But slaves saved the king's son and hid him away.'

'And you are a descendant of this prince?' Alexandra's voice was sceptical although she had to admit his striking resemblance to Carlyle did give the story a ring of truth. 'But if this is true…how has it taken you so long to get the throne back? Five hundred years…that seems like a long time to fight.'

'What am I meant to do? What should my father and ancestors have done? Just given in? Would you rather the people of Saphyre were left to suffer under this tyranny for another five hundred years?' Alexandra looked away guiltily. 'Your Highness…Alexandra, the Goddess has brought you here for a reason. It is your destiny to help me release Saphyre from the tyranny they have suffered for so long. Please, help me.'

'How can I help?' Alexandra asked without thinking.

'Our greatest weakness, one that I am loathe to admit, is that we can never match the power that Carlyle harvests. Nor can we get close to him; if you help us, we will finally achieve peace. I am sure of it.' Alexandra was silent as she turned over his request in her head. Finally, she shook her head and looked at him sadly.

'I'm not sure I will be of much help to you. I certainly could never match Carlyle in power – I'm not sure how you could even think such a thing.'

'You are just as powerful as Carlyle, but more importantly you are the closest person to him. Forgive me for speaking boldly, but you share a bedchamber with him. None of us could ever hope to get as close to him as you can.' Alexandra found herself blushing and she looked away. As much as she hated it his words were true, physically she would be the closest person to Carlyle but that was where the closeness ended. Although she would become his queen he had not invited her to join in discussions on state matters, in fact, she knew nothing of how he ran his kingdom; she would not be able to divulge information like that to them if that's what they hoped for. 'We do not expect you to be able to change things overnight; this could take moons...even years. But we have already been fighting for centuries; we are patient. And I am confident that with your help we can finally overthrow Carlyle and end the tyranny that Saphyre has endured.'

'If I joined...once Carlyle was overthrown, could I go home?' She rubbed her wrists self-consciously and looked at Caleb nervously.

'I am afraid not Alexandra. Not unless you could help us overthrow him before your coronation. Once that crown touches your head you will be bound to this kingdom. In Saphyre, when someone is crowned a monarch, only death can undo it.' Alexandra nodded feeling her throat tighten, deep down she had known he would be unable to help her, but it was still a blow. At the sound of a door opening and closing softly Alexandra jumped to her feet with Caleb and Xander. She was surprised at how weary the two looked; did they really trust no one? *How can Xander be a part of this? He is Captain of the Castle Guards; surely he would not betray Carlyle like this?*

'Vanya what are you doing here?'

'His Majesty is in a rage,' a heavily accented voice spoke from the shadows. 'Her Highness's absence has been noticed; he is tearing the castle apart looking for her,' Caleb swore and kicked the barrel he had been sitting on aside. 'Would you like me to escort her back?'

'No, thank you. Return to the kitchens; I do not want you putting yourself in danger unnecessarily.' Alexandra squinted through the darkness, but the person stayed in the shadows. 'Vanya is one of the kitchen staff; she is vital in hearing things that others would tend to ignore.' Caleb bent down to pick the blindfold from the floor, 'forgive me Alexandra, but I must do this for your own protection. If you do not know where we are then you cannot be forced to reveal our location.'

'Very well,' Alexandra nodded, but she could see Caleb was hesitant about blind folding her once more. He twisted the fabric around his hand, a sad look in his eyes.

'I know it is a lot to ask and that I have no right to ask this of you. Why should you help us when this is none of your concern? You could simply wear the crown, bow to Carlyle's every whim and turn a blind eye to his tyranny. But the true queen of Saphyre would never do such a thing.'

'And you believe me to be the true queen?' Alexandra scoffed, 'I do not even know how old I am –'

'Age is of no concern, and gradually your memories will come back. To be honest Alexandra we have no idea if you *are* our true queen, we know nothing about you. But your decisions and actions will tell us whether you are or are not.' She decided not to press the issue; she wasn't sure she wanted to know what would happen if she wasn't Saphyre's true Queen...or if she was. She thought about her words carefully and forced herself to speak as she was expected too. 'Will you join us? I am sure you have noticed Carlyle's arrogance, he would never suspect you of aligning yourself with us.'

'I – I don't know if I can.' She whispered, 'I'm sorry but...Carlyle has already killed someone I love.' Caleb nodded sadly.

'At least think about it. Five hundred years is a long time to fight; I would like my people to live without fear.' Alexandra nodded but could think of nothing to say as Caleb tied the blindfold around her head once more. 'I will take you back, but first I need to be sure the potion has worn off - try and lie to me.' Alexandra's mouth moved to form a lie, to tell a fake name, but nothing came out. 'We will go slowly, whenever I ask you a question, please try to lie to me.' She nodded, blushing as he gently held her by her upper arms to move her forward. It was disconcerting not knowing which way she was going, she had to trust that Caleb wouldn't walk her into a wall, but every so often she couldn't help but flinch backwards when she felt darkness looming towards her. She could almost feel the air solidify into a wall, but it was just her paranoia. 'How did you get to Saphyre?'

'By ship. Sorry.' Whatever potion he had given her was quite strong before she even had a chance to think about lying her mouth had answered for her. They walked in silence for a few minutes, every so often Caleb would spin her around leaving her disorientated and unable to guess which way they were going. The sensation that she was about to walk into a wall filled her once more and she flinched backwards, Caleb continued forwards. 'Caleb, please stop.' But before he could register the genuine fear in her voice she hit something cool, smooth and solid. Caleb's hands left her arms and she heard him cry out startled, she pulled the blindfold from her face startled to see him standing only three feet directly in front of her.

'What...' The question died on his lips and he looked at Alexandra in disbelief.

'It is Carlyle. He put some sort of spell on me.' Alexandra raised her hands and pressed them against what should have been thin air but instead felt like glass. 'I can't leave the castle; I can't even open a window.' Her voice was bitter, and tears of frustration blurred her eyes, she kicked at the solid air in frustration. The pain that shot through her ankle gave way to the anger, forcing back tears she looked at Caleb.

'Xander said you could not leave the castle but I did not realise he meant literally.' A wave of bitter anger swept through Alexandra.

'He says he cannot trust me to not run away again, that he will keep me locked in the castle until the coronation.' She fought back the urge to strike the barrier once more, 'where are we?'

'This passage runs under the gardens, we must be where the castle and gardens meet.' Gently Caleb took the blindfold from her, squeezing her hand firmly. 'Alexandra...I know you have no reason to trust me but –'

'You're right. I don't have a reason to trust you,' Alexandra said quietly. 'Caleb all I want is to go home. I will help you, but if you win your fight against Carlyle before my coronation then promise you will let me go home?' Caleb was silent, 'you said it yourself five hundred years is a long time – surely you must be prepared to finally take the battle to Carlyle?'

'When is your coronation?'

'Six Moons...please, Caleb.' Alexandra pleaded, 'Saphyre is your home, *your* kingdom but it is not mine. I do not belong here.'

'Very well,' Caleb sighed. '*If* we can defeat Carlyle before your coronation then I give my word to send you home. But Alexandra if you are crowned before Carlyle is overthrown – there is nothing I can do. You will be bound to Saphyre.'

'I understand,' Six moons, surely that was plenty of time to help Caleb and his rebellion? *If they have been fighting for over five hundred years, what makes you think you can help in six moons?* Alexandra pushed the sneering voice to the back of her mind, at least she had hope.

'We must hurry, I do not want to put you at harm.'
Alexandra nodded and followed Caleb down a labyrinth of
tunnels, thankful that he no longer saw the blindfold necessary.

'Can you take me back to the tower I was in? I don't think
anyone realises that's where I go.' Caleb nodded, and Alexandra
stayed close to him as they made their way through the darkness.
Did he live under the castle? Was he safe living so close to
Carlyle? 'Surely Carlyle knows of these tunnels?' Alexandra asked
as they rushed up a staircase, 'he has shown me one which leads
to his chambers – what if he is looking for me here?'

'These are ones that have been made since the throne was
stolen. We have ensured they are kept secret, not even all of
those loyal to me know of some.' This did little to alleviate
Alexandra's fears that they would be discovered but she kept
silent. Eventually, they reached a cramped dead-end, Alexandra
watched as Caleb placed his palms on the wall in front of him
and it slid open. 'We have been lucky to recruit some Castle
Sorcerers, I hope with your help we can recruit more.' Alexandra
didn't reply, she wasn't sure how she would be able to convince
the Castle Sorcerers to defy their king, why would they listen to
her? 'I am sorry if I frightened you earlier, I hope you can
understand our need for secrecy.'

'Of course.' Alexandra smiled weakly. Once Caleb was sure
that the potion had worn off he left Alexandra alone in the
tower. The shutters were closed and she could hear the rain
pounding once more. Carefully she opened the shutter and
stared out at the dismal weather, the sky was a deep cry and it
was difficult to tell where the sky and ocean met. She could
make out a few ships docked and sent a silent prayer thanking
the Goddess that her mother and friends had reached Karstares
safely. *What have I gotten myself in to?* She asked herself as she
secured the shutters once more. Pushing Caleb and his rebellion
to the back of her mind she turned and made her way down
from the tower. She had no idea where Carlyle was, but she
doubted he would be difficult to find given her noted absence.

'Where have you been?' Carlyle's embrace was tight, but his
voice was cold and Alexandra caught the anger flaring in his
gaze.

'I wanted to be alone; I told you this.' Alexandra shrugged
glancing nervously at the four men stood around the circular

table. She had been brought to the council chamber where Carlyle had been mid-meeting. At Carlyle's gesture, the four men bowed and departed.

'*Where* were you?' Alexandra scowled, she didn't want to reveal the tower, but she couldn't think of a lie quick enough.

'There is a tower I discovered; I'm not sure if it has been forgotten or if it is just not of interest to anyone.' She shrugged, 'I went up there to be alone, to think. I did not realise how much time had passed.'

'Surely you heard the bell ring?' Alexandra shook her head thankful that at least that wasn't a lie. 'Alexandra it is not safe for you to wander alone –'

'Why?' Alexandra quickly cut him off, 'you have made sure I cannot leave the castle. Even if someone should attempt to abduct me they will hardly get far will they?' Carlyle's grip on her tightened and Alexandra pushed him away gently. 'Carlyle, we have spoken of this. I am not going to have my every move watched.'

'I worry for your safety.' Carlyle said, 'I know that no one can take you from the castle, but they can still try to harm you, Alexandra. I would never forgive myself if anything happened to you.' Alexandra looked away, her eyes catching sight of the parchments scattered across the table. 'Plans for your coronation,' Carlyle explained, and Alexandra felt her curiosity peaked. She knew very little about Carlyle's family other than his mother had died when he was young; Saphyre had not had a queen for over twenty years. Alexandra looked up to see something strange flicker across Carlyle's eyes, was this just as strange for him? The Saphyre he had grown up had only ever had a king, would it be strange for him to have a queen alongside him? He in would not have to rule alone, if he allowed her then Alexandra could help share the burden. Could it be his cold and evil manner was simply down to being lonely? Alexandra probably could have tricked herself into believing that, it would certainly make life easier, if only it had not been for Caleb earlier that morning. The kingdom of Saphyre had suffered tyranny for five hundred years. Perhaps a more likely explanation towards his cold and evil manner was that it was carried through his bloodline. Alexandra pressed a hand to her abdomen feeling sick; she couldn't bear the thought of people loathing her children and living in fear of them, let alone the thought that they could harbour the same hatred and cruelness that Carlyle did. Carlyle noticed her action and rubbed her shoulders gently.

'We will have sons soon enough,' Alexandra nodded tightly but said nothing, instead she felt her heart twist with longing as she thought she would much rather share Mathe's bed. She was sure he wouldn't care whether she bore him sons or daughters first. Caleb's words flickered back into her mind. Once she was crowned queen she would be well and truly trapped, but if she helped Caleb achieve his goal, then he would help her return home. She had no reason to doubt Caleb, Saphyre would have no need of her, and surely he would want to choose his own queen. *Mother and father must let me choose my next husband, perhaps they would let Mathe and I marry?* She was sure her parents would not force her into another royal marriage considering how disastrous and cruel this one had been? Hope began to blossom within her – she would persuade Caleb that the quicker they acted the better. Carlyle would be distracted organising the coronation, and it must be taking up quite a bit of his Source keeping her bound to the castle. What better time to strike?

'You look deep in thought; is something wrong?' Alexandra blinked realising she had been staring in to space.

'No...' Alexandra shook her head and took a sip of the wine in front of her. 'Carlyle how long have your family ruled Saphyre?'

'Centuries,' he shrugged, 'my bloodline is almost as old as yours.' Alexandra closed her eyes as she tried to think back to her own family; she must have learnt how old her own bloodline was. *A thousand years,* the answer came to her suddenly, and Alexandra blinked in shock. How was that possible? She pushed the questions to the back of her mind; she did not want to think how her family had held on to the throne for so long. If there had been any foul play, then she would make up for it in Saphyre. 'As long as sons are provided then there is no reason that a kingdom should not be ruled by more than one family.' Alexandra bit her tongue at the cutting remark and instead glared at Carlyle across the table.

'Who ruled before your ancestors?'

'I am not sure. Saphyre was on the brink of civil war when my ancestors took the throne. They held it together; it is my duty to ensure their legacy continues. The past is of no consequence Alexandra – it cannot be changed.'

\*\*\*

Caleb was never far from Alexandra's mind, nor was Xander. Was he truly on side with Caleb or was he secretly working for Carlyle? Surely it would be his duty as the Captain to report suspicious activity back to Carlyle, what better way to find out how the rebellion operated than by infiltrating it? *Why do I care?* She constantly asked herself. She had met Caleb once, why should it matter to her if he was betrayed or not? She had mentioned her meeting with Caleb to no one, who could she tell? Her mother had not visited her since the first dream, and she had no friends in Saphyre.

'You have been staring at the same page for an hour now,' Helena's voice teased gently and Alexandra looked up from the book she had been studying. 'Are you alright?' *No,* Alexandra thought, but she could hardly answer with the truth. She looked down at the massive volume and pushed it across Carlyle's desk.

'These laws are nonsense,' she eventually shrugged. 'A woman cannot reject an offer of marriage? It is barbaric!'

'It is the way Saphyre has worked for centuries, besides most women are not propositioned. It is mostly dealt through the men; a father wants his daughter to marry well to rise his social position. Surely it would have been similar in Karstares?' Alexandra remained silent as she thought back to a conversation with her mother. Hadn't she been told she would not be able to marry for love? She'd had a choice in who she married; she could have refused to marry Carlyle – but what then? How many marriage proposals would her parents have allowed her to reject?

'At least you can marry. As slaves, we cannot even take lovers...or at least not ones of our choosing.' Helena spoke so casually Alexandra almost thought she had misheard her.

'Slaves?' She looked at Helena and Roisin, who was quietly kneeling on the floor mending a dress. 'You are both *slaves?*' *How could I not know this?* 'Are there many slaves in Saphyre?' *But slaves saved the king's son and hid him away.*

'It has always been this way,' Helena shrugged, and Roisin nodded not taking her eyes off her task.

'Before or after Carlyle's ancestors stole the throne?'

'Before,' Roisin shrugged. She dropped her needle in horror and looked at Alexandra with wide, fearful eyes. 'Forgive me Your Highness I did not mean to speak out of turn. His Majesty's ancestors did not steal the throne…where would you get such an idea?'

'Nowhere,' Alexandra lied eyeing Roisin up curiously.

'You should be careful what you say,' Helena warned, 'the walls have ears.' She seemed to direct this more at Roisin.

'I never realised,' Alexandra said feeling guilt pull at her. 'I –'

'Please do not feel sorry for us,' Helena's voice turned waspish. 'This is the lot the Goddess has bestowed upon us, and both Roisin and I are better off than most. We are ladies to the future *queen*. We have food, luxurious clothes, somewhere to sleep – and our beds are our own.' The door to the study opened and Alexandra looked up to see Carlyle with a boy carrying a food-laden tray behind him. Alexandra couldn't take her eyes off the boy, was he a slave too? Was Xander? At Carlyle's gesture, Helena and Roisin followed the boy out, closing the door to the study behind them.

'You missed dinner.'

'I didn't realise it was that late.' Alexandra looked up to see that the sky was completely black 'Sorry…I must have lost track of time.' She cleared Carlyle's desk so that he could spread the food out and helped herself to a generous piece of bread and cheese. For a while she sat in silence, staring down at one of the books which lay pushed to the side on the desk. The writing was too small to read without pressing her face to the pages, and she closed it.

'You have been studying hard; I knew you were the perfect choice to be my queen.' Alexandra arched an eyebrow at him in question, her mouth too full of food to ask him what he meant. 'If ever I am called away on foreign affairs, or have to travel abroad for war, you would be my regent.'

'You would trust me to run your kingdom? You do not even trust me to go outside for fresh air.' She could see from his expression he didn't see the funny side and she sat up straight like a scolded child. 'Carlyle, why did you not tell me that my ladies are slaves?'

'I assumed you knew,' he shrugged as if it was nothing of importance. 'I apologise, I thought that on your journey your

Willow Woods

mother or companions would have mentioned the slavery within
Saphyre. That is the one thing your father, and I never agreed on
in our diplomatic discussions. Karstares ruled out slavery over
two centuries ago.'

'I don't want slaves – can we not set them free? Employ
them as servants?' Carlyle choked on a piece of meat and took a
deep gulp of wine; it took Alexandra a moment to realise that he
was choking with laughter. 'Carlyle –'

'Alexandra of course I would trust you to rule my kingdom
in my absence – you would not be able to leave once you are
queen. But you should get rid of such foolish notions; you do
not understand slavery. Not yet. But give it a few years, and you
will see what good it does Saphyre; it has saved our economy
from bankrupt more than once. Servants cost money; they are
*lazy.*' Alexandra opened her mouth but quickly shut it as Carlyle
held up his hand. 'Not everyone working in the castle is a slave,
we do have some servants.' *Then why can we not abolish slavery? The
economy would adjust.* Alexandra wanted to argue but knew to save
it for another time; she didn't know enough to argue against
Carlyle – to make him see why he was wrong. Carlyle stood up
and slipped several books back into their places. Alexandra
looked at one of the torches fixed to the wall, lost in thought.
Slowly she began to feel a tingling sensation trickling through
her arms and down to her fingertips, she couldn't tear her gaze
away from the flame, and she watched in fascination as it grew
brighter and brighter. 'Alexandra!' The flame blew out as if a
heavy wind had blown past it and Alexandra looked at it in
stunned confusion. The tingling sensation stopped, and she
forced herself to look at Carlyle; his face was twisted in a mask
of annoyance and fear. *You're imagining things;* she told herself
feeling her hands shake slightly. 'Enough studying for one night,
come and bathe.'

# Chapter Eleven

Alexandra heard nothing from Caleb after their first meeting, nor did Xander reference it. She never truly expected him too, but each time she crossed paths with him her stomach would clench painfully. What if he told Carlyle that there was a possibility she would become embroiled in the rebellion – especially if it meant she could return to Karstares. What would Carlyle do to her? Would he execute her? The thought made her feel nauseous and she tried to push the thoughts from her mind, but guilt tugged at her making it impossible to ignore what she was doing. Carlyle gradually began acting strangely over the next few days. He would smile in a secretive manner, making it obvious that he was plotting something. But as to what it was Alexandra was completely clueless. She tried asking him what was going on, but his answer had been to grin mysteriously.

'Alexandra wake up,' she felt her body moving from side to side, and she feared she was back on the ship being tossed around in a storm. She forced one eyelid open and stared up at Carlyle, glowering at him from beneath the nest of blankets. She was lying on her stomach, her arms wrapped around the pillows. Only the skin on her arms was exposed to the air but she could feel the bitter cold, and she snapped her eye back shut and burrowed beneath the blankets. 'Alexandra get up.' Carlyle yanked the blankets away, and Alexandra let out a yelp as her body was doused in the frigid air. Still half-asleep she glanced over to the window, the shutters were open, and she could see the moons were still visible. Dawn had not even begun yet. She didn't resist as Carlyle gathered her into his arms and carried her into the dressing chamber, she was too tired to protest, and she leant against the wall too tired to undress. Most mornings she was dressed by Helena and Roisin, but on occasion, Carlyle seemed to relish the task. Alexandra had never grown used to anyone other than herself dressing her; she missed being able to dress herself. She missed the privacy.

'Are these not yours?' She asked in confusion as Carlyle handed her a pair of breeches, shirt, and tunic.

'I think they might be a bit small on me,' Carlyle's tone was sarcastic, but he was smiling nonetheless. Alexandra shook out the shirt and indeed saw that it was not made for Carlyle's broad six foot frame. She looked at Carlyle expectantly, pointing her eyes to the door. 'Surely you are not shy of me seeing you bare?' He smiled wolfishly and pulled her close, leaning his head down so he could trail butterfly-light kisses along her throat.

'*I* don't like seeing me bare,' Alexandra sighed hating how her body responded to his touch, even as hatred surged through her. 'I hardly need your help dressing in these. Please Carlyle, I did not need anyone looking after me in Bournemouth. I know that is not the life I grew up in, but I liked it. I miss doing things for myself.' Carlyle straightened, his hand still cupping her lower back.

'Very well,' he tilted her head up to kiss her lips softly. 'But do not take long; I have plans for the day.' Alexandra rolled her eyes as Carlyle departed. She slipped on the breeches, relishing the warmth of the sheepskin lining followed by the shirt and tunic. They were fitted to flatter her feminine form, but for the first time since she had left Bournemouth she was in something comfortable. 'Here, we do not have time to break our fast.' Carlyle handed her an oatcake. Alexandra quickly wolfed it down suddenly feeling ravenous. She wished he had not mentioned breakfast, she hadn't noticed she was hungry until then. Carlyle picked up three wrapped packages and Alexandra took them confused.

'What is going on?' She finally asked. She could not understand why Carlyle was acting strangely. He had never let her wear breeches before, nor could she understand why they were up so early.

'You still do not remember?' Alexandra shook her head impatiently, 'today is your twenty-second life-day.' *Life-day?* Alexandra thought to herself but was too embarrassed to ask. 'The anniversary of your birth,' Carlyle stroked her cheek gently. 'These things will come back to you naturally, I am sure of it.' Alexandra smiled; she was touched that Carlyle would acknowledge the day. She had often wondered how old she was but had never thought too much about the actual day of her birth. She had just assumed it would pass by unnoticed. 'Open your gifts,' Carlyle urged and Alexandra sat on the edge of the bed so she could unwrap them tentatively. She found she was oddly nervous at what she might find; Carlyle had tried to be sweet and tender but there had always been an underlying threat to everything he did.

The first gift was a thick emerald green velvet cloak lined with fur and fastened with a golden clasp engraved with Carlyle's emblem; a crown over a burning five pointed star. A pair of boots and gloves, both lined with sheepskin, followed. Tears pricked Alexandra's eyes, was he mocking her? When she had dressed, she had thought nothing of the warm clothes. But now she was growing uncomfortably hot; why was she dressed for the cold?

'Put them on.'

'Why?' Bitterness flashed in her eyes as she glanced up at Carlyle. She bit back a sigh as he winked and gestured for her to follow him from the chambers. She was so angry she didn't notice that he was dressed in thick winter clothes. Furiously she swept the cloak on and fastened it with shaking hands; stuffing her feet in to the boots she picked up the gloves and followed Carlyle. Most of the torches along the walls had been extinguished leaving only the eerie glow from the moons to light their way. The hallways were freezing, and Alexandra burrowed deeper into the cloak, stroking her cheek against the fur lining. They finally came to a stop beside a small door; it was made from a heavy looking wood and was smaller than Carlyle. 'Carlyle what are you doing?' Alexandra sighed; she was grumpy at his plans to torment her and wanted nothing more than to return to bed. Carlyle opened the door and Alexandra watched him glumly as he stepped out into the crisp night air. How far would he go just to torment her? *His cruelty has no bounds,* she thought.

'I have something to show you,' Carlyle turned and held out his hand for Alexandra to take.

'You know I can't go out,' Alexandra hissed at him crossing her arms over her chest. She remembered how she had run into the barrier when Caleb had tried to bring her back; she was not about to fall for Carlyle's trick. *Why would he have you walk into the barrier?* She asked herself but didn't have an answer.

'Alexandra, will you please do as I say just *once*? Can you not trust me even a little?' Carlyle flicked his wrist, his eyes darkening as she glowered at him. 'I wanted to make today special for you. I know this has not been easy on you and I want to do something to show you how much I care.' Alexandra stared at his outstretched hand with mistrust; hesitantly she put her own gloved hand in his and allowed him to pull her forwards gently. She flinched backwards as she passed over the threshold, half-expecting to feel herself hitting the invisible wall. A bitter breeze whipped through her hair and Alexandra let out a yelp, but rather than burrowing into her cloak she fought back the urge to throw it off. She had not felt fresh air in weeks. Letting go of Carlyle's hands she stretched her arms out, enjoying the sensation of the wind buffering against her. Carlyle smiled and shook his head, gesturing for Alexandra to follow him down a path. Frost kissed the grass and Alexandra tore her boots off enjoying the cold sensation as the grass crunched beneath her stockinged feet. 'You will catch a cold!' Carlyle said, his voice exasperated as he caught sight of Alexandra walking practically barefoot.

'Then perhaps you should let me outside more, let my body adapt to the chill.' Alexandra smiled, but her voice was just as cold. Carlyle sighed and wrapped an arm around Alexandra's waist, holding her close. He lit the way using his Source, but Alexandra could barely make anything out in the darkness, but while her eyes didn't work her nose worked perfectly fine. The scent of manure, hay, and horse was overwhelming, and Alexandra pushed herself away from Carlyle to brace herself against a stone wall. Images were pulled from the depths of her mind, flashing too quickly for her to make sense off. *Concentrate, breath.* She told herself taking deep breath.

*'Someone will find us!' The worry was real, but Alexandra's tone was light and giggly as someone pulled her into the stables. Her back pushed*

*a wooden stable door shut as she fell against Mathe still laughing as his lips began caressing hers.*

'Alexandra,' a hand squeezed her arm firmly and Alexandra shook her head trying to clear the assaulting images. Her heart twisted painfully at the thought of Mathe and she blinked back tears. 'Do you get many memories?'

'No…not really.' Alexandra paused and wiped her eyes, 'they come too quickly – too many.'

'What did you see?'

'Nothing,' Alexandra lied, 'there were too many to make sense off.' Pushing herself away from the wall she followed Carlyle into the stables and looked wistfully at the horses. Despite the early hour the stable boys were already up and mucking out stalls, they paused in their work to bow deeply as Carlyle passed. Alexandra walked slowly, observing each of the horses as she passed. A dazzling white mare tossed her head over her stall and whinnied as she saw Alexandra. Smiling Alexandra approached the horse, holding out her hand in greeting. The mare's coat was a brilliant snow white, her mane a glorious onyx black. 'Hello beautiful,' Alexandra cooed and boots and gloves on the ground so she could caress the silky mane. She smiled as the mare butted her hand affectionately; she was so absorbed in the beauty of the creature that she didn't hear Carlyle returning.

'The slaves will not return to their work until we are gone,' he whispered in her ear teasingly. Alexandra looked over her shoulder, shocked to see the stable boys still bowing deeply. *Do they see me as a tyrant as well?* She already knew the answer to that, each time she walked past someone they stared at her with as much fear as they would Carlyle. Sadly, Alexandra put her boots and gloves back on, following Carlyle from the stall.

'Do you remember how to ride?' Alexandra looked at him fearfully as she saw the large chestnut he led towards her. Her head barely reached the horse's chest and she shook her head staring at the beast with wide eyes. 'For now you will ride with me.' Carlyle lifted her in to the saddle before swinging himself up with ease. Alexandra found herself relaxing once she was in the saddle, it felt familiar and she almost reached out to take the reins. 'Later,' Carlyle's voice held a note of promise.

The horse gently trotted out the castle grounds. She expected them to go down to the city, but Carlyle took them in the opposite direction behind the castle. Neither spoke, Alexandra spent as much time as possible avoiding Carlyle. It felt strange to be this close to him; she could hear his heart beating through the fabric of his clothes. *I share a bed with him and yet this I find strange?* Alexandra bit back a bubble of hysterical laughter, but a small giggle still managed to escape.

'What do you find so amusing?'

'*This,*' she laughed. 'We are never this close – only…' She blushed not wishing to discuss their sleeping arrangements.

'Is it strange we should be this close?' As if to emphasise his point Carlyle readjusted the reins so he held them in one hand, using his free hand to pull Alexandra's hair to the side he kissed her neck teasingly.

'Carlyle –' Alexandra moved her head, but it was difficult to put herself out of reach when she was wrapped in his arms.

'We are married Alexandra, there is nothing wrong with showing affection.' *Except I feel none.* Gradually the sky began to lighten, and Alexandra relaxed as she lost herself watching the sunrise. The horse moved so fluidly that Alexandra felt herself being lulled into relaxation. *Keep awake, don't fall off.* Carlyle's arms were around her, but she still feared slipping from the horse. As the sky turned from a deep blue to a dusky pink Alexandra spotted a forest looming ahead.

'Carlyle where are we going?'

'You will see,' the air became muffled as they entered the forest. Carlyle placed the reins in her hands and squeezed them gently. 'You will not fall off. You learnt to ride as soon as you learnt to walk.' His voice was encouraging, and Alexandra took a deep breath as she readjusted her grip. 'We went riding together in Karstares; when I first arrived, I joined you on a hunting trip.' Alexandra's eyes briefly closed as she saw a flickering memory, she could see herself on horseback with a bow notched and ready. Remembering that she was riding, she snapped her eyes back open.

'I used to love riding,' she smiled as the familiar feeling crept down her arms and she controlled the horse without coaxing from Carlyle. 'I used to go out in the summer with…' She trailed off knowing it would be unwise to finish her sentence. Mathe's name hung between them; an unspoken tension neither wanted to mention. *I miss him,* Alexandra thought blinking back tears.

'Stop here,' Carlyle instructed, and Alexandra pulled on the reins gently. She climbed from the saddle and stroked the mare's nose gently.

'I always pictured you on a warhorse, not a gentle stallion.' Alexandra said suddenly; the calm and gentle manner of the horse certainly didn't reflect Carlyle's personality.

'I have a warhorse. But Ríoga is far gentler; she suits crowds better – I prefer to use my warhorse for occasions that call for it.' Alexandra looked at Ríoga and smiled at the mare as she led her into a clearing. Alexandra's eyes widened at the breath-taking sight; she had never seen anywhere so tranquil before. To the left of the clearing's entrance was a rocky wall with water cascading down into a small spring. 'My mother was quite powerful, but she was much like yours and did not use her powers for anything that could be perceived as...dark. She created this place so she could come here and think, before it was just an overgrown forest. Dark and cold, there were no flowers and the trees were menacing. My mother cultivated this forest with her Source and made it a tranquil environment where she could come and contemplate.' Alexandra's eyes swept over the scene as Carlyle spoke, it was clear that his mother's Source still fuelled the beauty of the area. The grass was free from frost, green and lush. The air was thick with the scent of the bright coloured flowers, and Alexandra knelt beside a thick cluster so she could bury her nose in their welcoming petals. 'I have never brought anyone here.'

'What about your father? Did he not come here also?' Alexandra slipped off her cloak finding the air slightly warmer. She set it on the grass and sat down, watching as Carlyle pulled out an assortment of food and lit a fire using his Source. A pang of envy twisted her stomach and she helped herself to a piece of fruit to keep her mind from wishing.

'My father did not know of this place; I do not believe he accepted how powerful my mother truly was. The fact that she is dead, yet her Source still lingers here is a triumph few can achieve. Once he discovered that she was taking me out of the castle he put a stop to it...' His voice grew thick and Alexandra looked at him shocked. There was something in his eyes, an almost tear-like glimmer, but when she blinked there was no trace and his eyes were cold once more. 'I was six by the time he eventually found out, old enough to travel by myself.'

'You were only six…how could you possibly have thought you were old enough to come all this way by yourself?' Alexandra whispered horrified, 'you could have been *killed*!' For a fleeting moment she wondered what her life would have been like had he been killed. She certainly wouldn't be here now. Perhaps Caleb would be sitting on the throne; the country saved from a bloody civil war. Quickly she pushed the thoughts from her mind; she couldn't bring herself to hate the young Carlyle. Perhaps if his mother had been around, he wouldn't have grown up to be as cruel as he was now.

'My father and I were never close; he did not acknowledge me until I came of age at eighteen. He died two years later…'

'Was he old?' Alexandra found herself being drawn into the conversation with him. Rarely had they spoken about personal matters, and never about his childhood. Had she known these things before she had run away? Or was she finding out new information about him?

'He was sixty-three; my mother was his second wife. His first had died in childbirth, the daughter with her.' He shrugged callously as if the death of his half-sister was of no importance and Alexandra suppressed a shudder. Would he think so callously of their own daughter if she bore him one? But there was something hidden in the tone of his voice as if the death of his half-sister was not just an unfortunate tragedy. 'When my father remarried he hoped for an army of sons to ensure his line was continued. My mother gave him two before me. The first was born strong and lusty; I was told that my father had never been seen to smile until the birth of his first son. The second was stillborn three years later, six moons after that the first died of the Fever.'

'The Fever?'

'An illness which burns you up from the inside, it can come on suddenly, and within a day you can be dead. When my mother eventually bore me, my father would not acknowledge me for fear I would soon die.' Alexandra felt a twinge of pity for Carlyle; she was beginning to understand his bitterness and warped sense of love. 'Mother was my only companion other than my tutors. I was not permitted to socialise with the other boys my own age; father deemed them unworthy even though they would one day sit on my council.' She had not even noticed that Carlyle had cooked them a large breakfast over the fire as he had talked. Silently she took a plate made from stale bread and filled with bacon, sausage, toasted bread, and fruit. 'My mother had only a daughter after me, but she too soon died. After that she was banished from my father's bed, he thought her unworthy to share a king's bed and took a mistress instead. My mother spent more and more time with me, bringing me here so I could watch her create this beautiful scene. I promised myself I would bring my own wife here, and our sons...we would picnic together and doze off...' Alexandra looked at Carlyle feeling shocked; who was this man? The scene he described was one of a loving family; it was certainly not a picture that Alexandra could imagine.

'What happened to your mother?'

'She was executed shortly before my ninth birthing day.' Alexandra's face twisted into a mask of pity and horror. How could his own father do such a thing? Would her father ever be so callous? 'To this day I do not know why he did it. He never took a third wife; he just shut himself away with his councilmen.' Through his horrifying tale Carlyle had still polished off his own breakfast and he set the plate of stale bread on the ground for the birds to pick at. 'I have wanted to bring you here for so long. I knew you despised me and I planned to bring you up here the day after our wedding – before you fled.' Alexandra surprised herself by reaching over and slipping her hand in Carlyle's. She wished she could say something to relieve the tension between them; but there was nothing she could say. She couldn't apologise for despising him, not after everything he had done.

'Thank you for bringing me here today,' Alexandra squeezed his hand smiling weakly at him. 'It is a beautiful place. Your mother...she must have been a wonderful woman to create such beauty.' *Could Carlyle create anything like this? Or is his Source so tainted by darkness that it would decay?* Alexandra couldn't help but wonder. 'I wish I could create something as beautiful,' she sighed wistfully.

'You can,' Carlyle laid down on the cloak spread beneath them, pulling Alexandra with him. 'Your needlework is exquisite.'

'I hardly believe that – I do not know the first thing about sewing.' Alexandra laughed hitting Carlyle lightly on the chest.

'Nonsense. I still have the tunic you made me when I arrived in Karstares; you presented it to me at my welcoming ball.' Alexandra blushed and closed her eyes; she could just about recall the memory. Mathe had glared at her the entire evening as he had circled the room with a tray of drinks. It had been the first time Alexandra had seen Carlyle, and she had been well aware of her parents' hopes that she would marry the visiting king. They would not pressure her, but the expectation had at least been there. They had encouraged her to prepare a gift for Carlyle and to present it to him at the ball thrown in his honour. She remembered the moment she had first glimpsed Carlyle; she had stood with Giric slightly behind their parents' thrones. Carlyle had been dressed head to toe in a deep royal blue velvet; she had thought him extremely handsome and had shared a small smile with him. *I wanted to annoy Mathe,* she suddenly remembered. She had flirted with Carlyle after their formal introduction after she had given him the tunic and he had graciously thanked her for it.

'We dined together that evening,' Alexandra whispered, 'you complimented the pattern I had done and said not even your castle tailor could have matched it.' She felt guilt wash over her as she remembered purposefully trying to make Mathe jealous. What kind of person was she? She had flirted with this monster to get back at Mathe, but why? They must have argued over something trivial. *I did not know then that he was a monster – none of us knew.* She tried to alleviate her guilt, but it didn't work. Why should it matter if she had known or not what Carlyle was truly like? She had been cruel to Mathe, was she any different to Carlyle?

'I had heard rumours that you were dallying with a useless knight. But I could see you found me attractive when we first met,' Carlyle's voice was a whisper as he bent his head closer to hers and brushed his lips against her cheek. She felt his hands slip down to the hem of her tunic and begin pulling it upwards.

'What are you doing?' She cried shocked, she pulled away and looked around, but it was only the two of them.

'No one will disturb us.' She wanted to argue that someone might discover them, but Carlyle had said he'd brought no one to the clearing, it was his secret. Swiftly he removed her tunic, but she stopped him as he tried to relieve her of her shirt. 'Alexandra, I have seen you bare plenty of times,' he sighed as he began stripping off his own clothes. She watched him in horror as he leapt into the water completely bare.

'Yes, but we were alone and *inside*.' She kept glancing around as if expecting a crowd of people to burst through the trees. Nervously Alexandra looked around once more before finally closing her eyes and shedding her clothes. She quickly stepped into the water letting out a yelp as the warm water caressed her skin. It was not hot, but she had expected it to be almost ice cold, not a gentle warm. 'During the summer moons the water is quite cool,' Carlyle swam beside her, and she felt his fingers twist into her auburn hair, tilting her head back, so she was forced to look at him. 'Tomorrow there will be an official dinner with the court, but for today I wanted it to be just the two of us.' Carlyle's fingers grazed her back as he held her close.

It was nightfall when they began the journey back to the castle. Alexandra put up no resistance as Carlyle tucked her cloak around her like a blanket. She was exhausted and couldn't help but rest her head against him as she dozed, no longer frightened that she would fall off Ríoga. Despite having spent every minute of the day with Carlyle, it had been her most enjoyable in Saphyre. *Hardly surprising when I have spent every day hiding in a tower,* she thought glumly blinking back tears.

The following day greatly differed from the previous. Alexandra had woken up early, the thick velvet drapes had been pulled back and although the sun was beginning its ascent the room was still quite dark. Someone, she guessed Carlyle, had lit a few of the candles but as to where he actually was she couldn't guess. Sitting up she wrapped the duvet firmly around herself and debated whether she should rise or if she could go back to sleep for another hour. It was rare that she got to enjoy the bed to herself; she might even be able to stretch out and take advantage of the space. Her ears twitched at the sound of footsteps emerging from the staircase, and she looked over to see Carlyle emerge drying his hair.

'I had thought to wake you but decided perhaps you would appreciate a lie-in after yesterday.' He leant down to kiss her in greeting, his lips were surprisingly warm, and Alexandra saw that his eyes and skin were still flushed from the heat of the bathing chamber. 'You,' he pointed to Helena, 'dress me. You can dress your mistress.' Roisin curtsied and held out a robe for Alexandra to slip on.

'Did you enjoy your life-day yesterday, Your Highness?' She asked shyly as she held out fresh stockings for Alexandra.

'Yes...almost.' She smiled wryly, the spring had been beautiful, and it had been bliss to escape the castle and be outside once more. But the day had been rather marred spending it with Carlyle and no other soul. She slipped into the tight-fitting shoulderless gown that Roisin presented her with. It was made from a beautiful blue satin and shimmered as the light hit it, reminding her of lazy summer days spent sprawled on warm golden sand while staring at the ocean. She pulled her hair aside as Roisin began lacing the back of the dress up and watched the door apprehensively expecting Carlyle to burst in just to glimpse her dressing. When Roisin tapped her back gently, and Alexandra sat in front of her dresser so that her face and hair could be styled. She glanced at her reflection in the looking glass and winced; she did not envy Roisin's task. Her skin had always been pale, but now it was deathly so. It looked drawn and tight across her skull; her eyes had deep purple markings making her sockets look further back into her head than they were.

'You are looking at yourself too harshly,' Roisin scolded her; 'you are beautiful.'

'I have seen better-looking skulls than I,' Alexandra smiled wryly, and she thought for a fleeting second that Roisin shared her smile. Helena was the more outspoken of the two and she had almost developed a friendship with the other woman, but Roisin kept to herself and was more guarded. She watched Roisin in the mirror as she ran a brush through her hair deftly braiding it. She closed her eyes so Roisin could dab some coloured powder on her lids. She found the silence comforting and she allowed her mind to wander. If she had married Mathe would this have been her daily routine? *No...I wouldn't have had slaves dress me; I wouldn't have slaves...but Mathe would help me.* No matter how hard she tried she could not free her mind from Mathe. She could not stop wandering what marriage with Mathe would be like. She was burning with desperation to get Caleb on the throne, so she could go home. When she opened her eyes, she looked at her reflection startled.

'Do you not like it?' Roisin asked nervously; she twisted her hands before catching herself and standing straight.

Alexandra looked at her silver painted lips; her eyes were a dark blue in the corners which faded to a lighter shade mixed with silver as it moved upwards.

'It is outstanding,' She smiled at Roisin, 'I love it. Thank you.' She glanced at her reflection once more; there was something mysterious about the way Roisin had applied it. Checking her appearance once more she led Roisin from the dressing room to find Carlyle patiently waiting for her. He wore a black linen shirt beneath a tunic which finished just above his knees and was belted at the waist. The fabric was a deep royal blue, and he wore velvet trousers of the same shade. Alexandra studied the deep gold thread and the intricate pattern it created; she smiled and shook her head at him. 'New tunic?' Carlyle opened his mouth, but Alexandra laughed at him, 'I recognise it.' She reached out to stroke the smooth satin fabric, her fingertips tracing the intricate pattern. 'I really made this?' Carlyle placed his hand over hers, pressing it to his chest so she could feel his heart beating.

'Yes Alexandra, you made this.' After a few moments, he stepped back and looked her up and down critically. 'You did well slave,' he nodded to Roisin, 'my wife looks exquisite. But there is something missing...' Out of the corner of her eye, Alexandra saw Roisin twitch in suppressed fear

'Roisin has not missed anything,' Alexandra protested frightened that Roisin would be in trouble.

'I did not say *she* had,' Carlyle said sharply, and Alexandra blushed. He stepped over to a small writing desk and picked up a glittering rope-like object. 'I had thought to present you this on your coronation day, but I think now would be the perfect time.' He held the length of rope for Alexandra to inspect, it wasn't rope but in fact, a belt intricately woven from white gold and studded with deep blue sapphires and diamonds, twinkling in the rising sunlight. He draped it loosely around her slender waist where it settled on her hips. She caught the flicker of annoyance in Carlyle's patterned blue eyes and she quickly forced herself to smile and kiss him softly.

'It is beautiful Carlyle. Thank you.'

The day began quiet enough; Carlyle led her to their small private dining room so they could break their fast on a light meal of lightly toasted bread, eggs, and fruit. Helena, Roisin and a squire of Carlyle's stood in a corner of the room waiting to be summoned to refill a goblet or plate. When the meal was over Carlyle led Alexandra to the throne room, a circular room with two thrones up set up a small staircase, so the two monarchs were raised above everyone else. At first glance, the two thrones looked as if they were placed in the same position, side by side, but Alexandra had found the one she sat in was set slightly further back so that she was seated just behind Carlyle. Her hand resting lightly on Carlyle's, Alexandra followed him up the staircase and sunk into a deep curtsy as he took his seat before taking her own. She moved to fold her hands elegantly in her lap, as Helena and Roisin had shown her, but Carlyle took hold of it once more and stroked her palm lightly.

The throne room was filled with a sea of people who, one by one, took it in turns to present Alexandra with gifts. Representatives of each city guild presented her with an item of their wares; exquisite items carved from gold, bolts of luxurious fabric, wines and books. As the day wore on she grew weary of trying to smile reassuringly at people, what would she have to do to convince everyone that she was nothing like Carlyle?

'Your Highness, those of us in the kitchen would like to present you with this cake.' Alexandra recognised the heavily accented voice and she fought to keep her face neutral as she came face to face with Vanya. The woman had thick dark hair and even darker eyes. There was no warmth to them and Alexandra flinched at the cold loathing. *She does not trust me either;* she realised biting back a sigh. Was Caleb the only one to trust her? If so was there any point in her aiding him? Vanya stood to the side as two women stepped forward, between them they held a giant cake which Alexandra was sure could feed everyone in the room with a generous serving and still have some left over.

'Thank you. It looks delicious; I hope everyone here will share this cake with His Majesty and I.' Alexandra thanked Vanya with what she hoped was a regal nod. Out of the corner of her eye, she could see Carlyle studying her, was he wondering if she would do anything irrational? *Like what?* She asked herself; *I only spoke out at the wedding in hopes I could go home. Who would help me here?*

# Chapter Twelve

Alexandra inched away from Carlyle when she was certain he was in a deep sleep. Sharing his bed each night had not gotten any easier, and she longed for the day when Caleb assumed the throne and sent her home. She twisted the locket at her throat, just over three moons remained until her coronation and Caleb seemed no closer to taking the throne than when she had first met him. He needed resources that she couldn't get. Carlyle rarely discussed council matters in their chambers and never after they had coupled. *How can I convince him to let me sit on his council?* The thought had pestered her for a while now, she could think of no other way to get close to Carlyle's councilmen. But she was rarely in their presence. Biting back a sigh Alexandra carefully sat up trying not to disturb Carlyle. She poured herself a drink from a pewter jug and gulped it greedily. She needed to go outside, to go for a walk so the crisp air could clear her head. Being cooped up inside for almost three moons had done her little good.

'Alexandra come back to bed,' Carlyle's voice was muffled as he nestled against the pillows.

'I cannot sleep. Please, Carlyle, will you let me go outside for a walk? Just for an hour – I need fresh air.' Carlyle ignored her, but Alexandra knew he had not gone back to sleep. Unable to stop herself she slammed the cup she had been drinking from down beside the jug. 'Carlyle I cannot live like this for three more moons! I need to be able to go outside; I want to come and go as I please –'

'Why do you not admit what you really want?' Carlyle roared flinging the blankets aside as he leapt to his feet, light flaring around him as he summoned his Source. 'You wish to return to Karstares; you would rather be that knight's whore than a queen!' Alexandra's cheeks flushed with anger and she glared at him through the darkness. She could feel hot anger bubbling in her stomach, causing her arms to shake and her palms grow slick with sweat. 'Alexandra, do you truly believe that even if you had discovered a way to return to Karstares you would be able to marry Mathe?' Alexandra felt her stomach drop; did he know that she had found a way to return to Karstares? Even if it was a slim chance, she still clung to it. *No, he would never keep quiet about such a betrayal. If he suspected me in the rebellion, he would not hesitate to confront me about it.* She opened her mouth to argue with him, but no sound came out. She felt as if an elastic band had been tied around her throat, she could still breathe easily but her voice felt as if it had been constricted. She glared at Carlyle, disgusted that he would use his Source on her in such a degrading manner. 'Even if your parents were foolish enough to agree to such a lowly marriage, even they cannot reverse what has been done.' Fury was replaced with fear and Alexandra gripped the sides of the table. Had something happened to Mathe? She assumed her friends were all safe and well, surely she would hear otherwise. But why would she? Karstares was no longer her home; it was in her past. Her parents were less than happy at her relationship with Mathe, and she received no communications from any of her former friends. It was as if she had been forgotten. 'Mathe has married my beloved,' it was as if he had punched her in the stomach. All the air had been knocked from her and Alexandra fell back against the wall weakly, struggling to gulp in a lungful of air. Weakly she shook her head, trying to shake his words from her mind. Carlyle stepped towards her, his grin was now one of pure malice and Alexandra watched in horror as an image appeared between them.

Mathe was standing beside a red-headed woman in a modest temple. Alexandra could only watch in a stunned silence as Mathe's lips moved but no sound came from him. Slowly he drew the woman into his arms and placed a tender kiss on her lips; she could almost feel the butterfly-light kiss against her own lips and tears snaked down her cheeks. The image began to fade away, only to be replaced by one of Mathe and the same woman, but this time rather than a temple they were in a small bedchamber. Alexandra willed her eyes to shut but they wouldn't obey, she felt as if someone were holding her eyelids open and she looked at Carlyle pleadingly. She couldn't watch this, she tried to turn her head away, but her neck was twisted so that she was forced to watch the soul destroying image of Mathe and the woman slowly undressing each other, each savouring the moment. Their bodies began to writhe as they tumbled into a bed and –

'*STOP!*' Alexandra cried finding the strength to throw her arms up and cover her eyes to block the vision. A hurricane seemed to tear through the room, knocking Carlyle backwards into the wall. Alexandra stared at him in distraught bewilderment, and he stared back as if he might strike. Composing himself Carlyle stood up, the malicious glint fading from his dark eyes.

'There is nothing for you back in Karstares – there never was. Mathe had been seeing that wench before you even returned, even now she is heavy with child.' he softened his tone and drew her close. 'You cannot return to Karstares; you do not belong there. You never have, as a princess, it was always your duty to rule as queen in a foreign kingdom. Saphyre is where you belong.' Alexandra didn't hear his words though; her mind was shattered by Carlyle's revelation. Mathe's wife was pregnant. How long had he started seeing her after Alexandra had disappeared? Or had he been seeing the woman at the same time as her? Alexandra let out an anguished cry and buried her face into the front of Carlyle's robes.

'I still do not trust her,' Xander hissed waspishly, 'she is the wife of our enemy – she is one of *them!*'

'One of *whom* exactly?' Alexandra shot back angrily slamming her palm on the barrel-cum-table in front of her. She winced as everyone shot her a furious warning glare; they were only a few feet under the dungeons and had to be careful that no prisoners were alerted to their unwelcome presence. *Even if they did hear, who would they tell?* Alexandra thought repressing a shudder as she remembered the dungeon cells. Confined in a stone cage, unable to sit or even stand properly. She prayed that no one was actually held in those cells.

'Someone who wields the Source.' Alexandra turned to glare at Caleb, and she could see him biting back a sigh. *Surely he does not mean me?* 'Carlyle only keeps those who possess the Source close to him.'

'Well, I am the unfortunate exception to the rule. I do not have the Source.' Alexandra shook her head unable to understand why they would think she had such powers. 'Carlyle told me about the source when I lived in Bournemouth; I asked him if he had it and he said no. I have no memory of wielding such power, and there is nothing to suggest I have it.' Alexandra decided not to mention the hurricane-like wind which had torn through the bedchamber during the early hours that morning.

'*Carlyle* told you this? And you *believed* him?' Xander scoffed and Alexandra felt her cheeks warm up as she blushed furiously. 'Open up your eyes Your Highness; he lied to you. Your mother is one of the most powerful Sorceresses in this world; all of the women in her family have the Source – why should you be any different?' Alexandra shrugged having no response. She ran a hand through her hair as she thought over Xander's words. Was he right; did she possess the Source? But why would Carlyle lie? If the Source was as important to him as he claimed then surely he would want her to be at her full potential? *Caleb is clinging to a false hope; maybe he thinks I could use the Source to help him.*

'I'm sorry, but you are both wrong,' guilt pulled at her as she saw the disappointment in Caleb's eyes. 'Carlyle would have no reason to lie to me. He is a powerful Sorcerer; I could never rival him.'

'I apologise, we just assumed because of your mother's power that you would have inherited the ability.' There was no denying the disappointment in Caleb's eyes and Alexandra felt hurt. Was he just as bad as Carlyle, did he prize the Source for the power it would bring? 'But be careful. I have heard of sorcerers draining their enemies, using them as a way to top up their own Source. Who is to say Carlyle has lied to you, so he can use you in this way?

'My coronation is just over three moons away, are you any closer to being ready?' Alexandra asked hopefully in an attempt to change the subject. The thought of Carlyle secretly draining her of her power was not an appealing thought. *He can't be doing that. I don't have any power for him to steal.*

'No. I am trying Alexandra, but we cannot rush this. I understand you want to return to Karstares, but have you really thought about what your life will be like back there?'

'You will be seen as an outcast,' Vanya spoke up. 'A woman who runs away – abandoning her betrothed. A woman who betrays her husband, who abandons those who need her.' Alexandra felt her cheeks flame, and she looked at the dark-haired woman.

'If you had the choice to return to your home kingdom, would you not take it?' Alexandra asked quietly.

'I am not a slave.' Vanya's tone darkened, 'I am free to leave whenever I choose. But Saphyre is my home; His Majesty employed me when nobody else would.'

'Alexandra…would you not consider remaining in Saphyre?' At Caleb's voice, Alexandra turned to look at him. *Is there anything for me to go home too?* She thought of Mathe and his wife, had he ever cared for her? *Vanya is right, no one will trust me. I would be a burden on my parents.* Blinking back tears she shook her head.

'I can't,' she whispered thickly. 'I don't belong here.' She couldn't bring herself to meet Caleb's eyes. 'I should go back; I do not want Carlyle to notice I am missing.'

Lying on her back in the pool-sized bath Alexandra stared blankly at the ceiling. She had hoped a bath would help her to relax, to put the past twenty-four hours out of her mind. But she couldn't rid herself of the vision of Mathe and the red-haired woman. How could he? *I am married*, she scolded herself. *Does this not make me as bad as Mathe – or worse?* She had not cheated on Carlyle, nor would she. She was not a fool, and she had no interest in taking a lover on the side. But did fantasising about Mathe make her just as guilty? *Carlyle knows I do not love him; he tried to make me believe I did.* What would it be like to fall in love with Carlyle? Could she do it? *It would make life so much easier,* she thought with a sigh. But she knew it was impossible. She had never been able to forget the man Carlyle had obliterated at their wedding. *He killed grandmother; he would not have hesitated to kill others that I loved.* With a groan, Alexandra swam to the edge of the bath and pulled herself out.

'I was beginning to worry you may have fallen asleep down there.' Carlyle was seated at his desk, almost buried beneath a towering pile of books, scrolls and loose pieces of parchments. Alexandra shrugged in reply; she had barely spoken to Carlyle all day. When he had spoken to her over dinner, she had kept her replies brief. She picked up a piece of parchment from the desk, surprised to see it was nothing more than a list of names.

'What are you doing?' She finally broke the silence, 'I thought you did not like bringing work into the bedchamber?' She realised how tired Carlyle looked and set the parchment back on the table.

'These are plans for your coronation; I have been working on them for much of the day.'

'The coronation isn't for moons, why don't you take a break?' She saw Carlyle's quill pause for a split second, and she frowned. Setting the quill down Carlyle rose from his desk, cricking his neck as he stretched.

'There has been a change.' Taking Alexandra's hand, Carlyle led her over to the window seat by the window. He pushed the shutters open, and Alexandra shivered as she looked out at the city beneath them buried under layers of snow. 'Saphyre has been without a queen too long, and the people of Evany have not seen you since our marriage. The winter has been hard, many have lost their lives. Our people need a reason to celebrate.' Alexandra could feel her stomach clenching. 'There is no reason to delay your coronation, why wait three more moons when we can do it sooner?'

'I – I haven't learnt the laws yet – I can't serve the people of Saphyre as their queen. I couldn't do them justice. I still talk like I did in Bournemouth!' Alexandra protested.

'But every so often you remember yourself,' Carlyle reassured her. 'Alexandra…there have been threats made against you. You are my wife, but you are still just a princess – a foreigner. Once you are queen you will almost be my equal.' Alexandra rolled her eyes and leant her head against the wall. 'I am moving your coronation forwards. I have discussed with the council, and they agree it is for the best.' *Do they ever disagree with you?* Alexandra thought with disdain, on the few occasions she had met his councilmen they had reminded her of nothing but snivelling cowards. Even the ones who were clearly in Carlyle's favour.

'When?'

'One week,' Alexandra's head snapped up, and she glared at Carlyle. *Caleb would never be ready in a week – he barely acts like he would be ready in three moons.* Alexandra shook her head feeling bile beginning to rise, burning her throat. 'Alexandra once you are crowned you will be able to go outside – I thought this would make you happy.'

'I could go outside now if you would take off this foolish spell and just trust me.' Alexandra spat. She snatched her hand from Carlyle's grasp and threw a robe over her chemise.

'Where are you going?'

'Away from you.' She threw the door to the chamber open, surprised when she walked into an invisible wall. Closing her eyes Alexandra drew in a deep breath, would this be his tactic every time?

'Alexandra did you not hear what I said? Threats have been made against you; you are in danger. I do not want you getting hurt.' Carlyle moved to draw her close, but Alexandra pushed him away.

'You are a tyrant,' she hissed at him and gestured to the open door. '*This* is why I could never you Carlyle. You are nothing more than a murdering tyrant.'

# *Chapter Thirteen*

Gentle hands rubbed Alexandra's back as she knelt on the floor of her dressing chamber, retching in to an empty jug. She had woken up early that morning feeling nauseous. She had barely slept that night, the thought of her coronation suddenly looming made it impossible for her to relax. She could feel her nerves beginning to shatter; once she was crowned, she would be stuck with Carlyle. Even if she could leave the castle, what chance did she have of hiding from him? Not to mention she would neglecting her responsibilities. *I need to find Caleb,* she thought desperately. *Surely he must know what Carlyle is planning? Xander at least must have informed him.* She was convinced that Caleb would want her gone just as much as she longed to leave. He would want a queen of his own choosing, what would happen once she was crowned and he took the throne? Her blood ran cold at the thought – she had never paused to think what her position would be after. *What would he do to Carlyle?* Pushing the thoughts to the back of her mind Alexandra concentrated on forcing back the sickness. Surely Carlyle deserved whatever punishment Caleb deemed fit? He had murdered people...surely, he deserved no less? *Am I any better than Carlyle? I am lying to him...betraying him.* When she was sure, the sickness had passed Alexandra shakily rose and set the jug down on the dressing table.

'Should I help you dress Your Highness?' Roisin asked stepping back. Alexandra looked down at the desk, tracing a pattern along the polished wooden surface. Was she that intimidating that Roisin constantly had to refer to her by her title? *It is Carlyle she fears not me,* she tried to reassure herself. She had asked Helena if both women feared her, but Helena had found the thought merely amusing.

'No thank you Roisin, it is still quite early. I think I will just bathe for a bit.' As she turned around, she was startled to find Roisin standing closer, pressing the back of her hand against Alexandra's forehead. A look of concern passed over her plain features.

'You are pale and awfully warm, perhaps I should fetch a healer – or a potion at least?'

'It's just nerves; I'll be fine really.' Alexandra smiled in what she hoped was a reassuring manner and not a grimace. 'Why don't you and Helena go break your fast in the main hall with the others? I can spend the morning with Carlyle; perhaps you could both come back when he is due to go to council and help me study the laws a bit more?' She was hesitant referring to her ladies as slaves, loathing the word. But each time she thought about their situation she couldn't help but wonder how much could she trust them both? She liked them well enough and was thankful for their companionship. But she could never shake the thought that they had been bought by Carlyle surely their loyalties would ultimately lie with him? It was this thought which had stopped her questioning both Helena and Roisin on several occasions about Caleb and the rebellion. Did they know anything about it? Perhaps they were involved somehow? She had even yearned to ask them if they would help her, their knowledge of Saphyre would far surpass her own – surely they would be far more useful? But she had feared they would report straight back to Carlyle. *It is not their fault,* she would often tell herself. But she could not help feeling slightly resentful to her two ladies and Carlyle. Was there no one she could trust?

'If you are sure?' Alexandra nodded with a weak smile, sighing in relief when Roisin departed. Taking a deep breath, Alexandra straightened and carefully left the dressing chamber. She had managed to wake up without disturbing Carlyle; she was amazed that the sound of her sickness had not roused him. *Thank the Goddess for small graces,* she thought to herself as looked towards the bed. Carlyle was still fast asleep, a peaceful expression on his handsome face. *It's hard to believe he is a killer...a figure of terror*. She thought, her hair was slightly mussed, and his fringe almost flopped into his eyes. He laid on his side with one arm outstretched to where she normally slept beside him. He looked almost vulnerable in sleep. *Don't be fooled*; she scolded herself as she turned and made her way down to the bathing chamber.

The bath did little to alleviate her sickness, the warmth of the water seemed only to make her feel worse. Alexandra was leaning with her front against the edge of the pool-sized bath, her arms folded on the ground, her head resting on top. *Get a message to Caleb. Perhaps I could go underground with him? Surely Carlyle would not be able to find me, and even if it took years for Caleb to finally claim the throne, I would never have been crowned. I could still leave.* The heat of the water gradually began to make her feel faint, shakily Alexandra lifted her head and pulled herself from the bath. It took her longer than it should have to dry and dress in her chemise and a robe, but she kept having to pause fearing she would pass out. *Perhaps I should have asked Roisin to help me bathe,* she thought wryly. She preferred to bathe alone, never growing comfortable with others seeing her bare. As she neared the top of the staircase, she began to hear voices. Forcing her legs to stop shaking Alexandra walked into the bedchamber, acknowledging Xander with an abrupt nod.

'Good morning Your Highness.'

'Good morning Captain,' Alexandra glanced at Carlyle who was reading a torn piece of parchment and didn't appear to have noticed her. 'I assume His Majesty has informed you of his plans?' She couldn't help the pleading look in her eyes as Xander's expression remained neutral.

'Of course. Congratulations. My men and I look forward to proving our worth to both yourself and His Majesty.' Carlyle let out a grunt of disdain and Alexandra glared at him, *if he despises Xander for not having the Source then why keep him so close?*

'Perhaps you and I could discuss what your men would be doing on the day? I would like to meet the men who protect His Majesty and I.'

'That is hardly appropriate for a queen-to-be.' Carlyle scolded finally setting the letter aside. Rising he kissed Alexandra's cheek, a look of concern crossing his features. 'You do not look well. Perhaps you should rest for the day.' Alexandra remained silent, her eyes trying to meet with Xander, but the captain kept his gaze solely focused on Carlyle. 'If you hear of anything else let me know immediately.' Xander nodded, departing with a bow. As the door closed behind Xander, Carlyle turned his attention to Alexandra. 'What is wrong?' He asked pushing Alexandra's damp hair back from her face, cupping her cheek and stroking it with his thumb gently.

'Nothing. I have been feeling a bit sick, but I think it is just nerves.' Alexandra shrugged, 'I told my ladies to break their fast in the main hall. I thought perhaps I could spend the morning with you until your council meeting begins.' She put up no resistance as Carlyle kissed her softly, even as she was hit by another wave of nausea. Gripping Carlyle's arms she fought to remain upright, and she gratefully accepted his help as he led her to his desk chair.

'I have asked the dressmaker to come and take your measurements. It should not take long, but I could ask her to come this evening if you would prefer?'

'Do I have to do much?' Alexandra asked wearily.

'Not today, she will just take measurements and begin making the shape of your dress. The day after tomorrow you will need to be properly fitted so she can see what adjustments must be made.'

'I can manage today,' Alexandra nodded resisting the urge to rest her head on the surface of his desk. Carlyle brought over a platter of fruit, squeezing her shoulder gently as he picked up a pile of parchment from beside her head. Alexandra forced herself to sit upright and began picking at the fruit as she waited for the dressmaker. Her mind solely focused on the upcoming coronation. She could not remember much of the city other than the devastating poverty. Carlyle had told her how many of the citizens had not survived the winter, and it was not even over yet. Surely a celebration such as the coronation was inappropriate? *It is hardly a celebration;* Alexandra thought bitterly but shoved the thought aside. At the sound of knocking she rose to her feet, gripping the edge of the desk as dizziness swept over her. *This cannot just be nerves,* she thought, *perhaps I should see a healer.* The measuring for her dress was quicker than Alexandra expected, and she was relieved when the dressmaker promptly departed. Sweeping Alexandra into his arms Carlyle gently set her on the bed, his eyes dark with concern.

'I will fetch a healer –'

'No,' Alexandra protested shaking her head. She had kept out of the way of the Castle Sorcerers fearing that they would be much like Carlyle. 'I am fine; I just need rest.' She met Carlyle's eyes, her own growing heavy with sleep. 'Carlyle -'

'It is not what you think,' Carlyle gently held her chin in place so she could not look away. 'Please trust me. If it is nerves making you ill, then perhaps I can help you.' Alexandra stared at him apprehensively, not quite able to bring herself to meet his eyes directly. 'It will be similar to our wedding night, but I give you my word you will remember everything. I am only seeking to help you relax so that you can sleep. Please, Alexandra, trust me.' Biting the inside of her cheek Alexandra nodded, there was no point in refusing and if he could make her feel better then why refuse? The spiral pattern of Carlyle's blue eyes began to rotate slowly. Gently he stroked her face and hair, murmuring softly in a language she couldn't understand. Gradually the sickness subsided, and Alexandra rested in Carlyle's arms as she was tugged into a deep sleep.

When Alexandra woke, she was still nauseas but was relieved to find that it had greatly subsided. She could hear Carlyle snoring deeply beside her and she tentatively got out of bed. The hallways were lit with torches but their lit was sim and Alexandra struggled to see where she was going. She found she was thankful for the darkness as it meant no one would be able to recognise her should she cross paths, anyone. Pausing in the main hall Alexandra focused on the heavy doors. Would Carlyle's barrier spell still be in place even while he slept? Surely, he could not be using his powers in his sleep. *He is powerful;* she reminded herself but quickly dismissed it. She wouldn't know if she just stood there staring. Glancing around to make sure she truly was alone Alexandra silently approached the doors, but as she reached them, she knew it wouldn't matter whether or not Carlyle's spell was still in place. heavy chains were looped across both doors, making it impossible to even attempt opening. *This is not why you came down,* Alexandra reminded herself before she could grow frustrated. She needed to find Xander, or perhaps even Vanya. She needed to get a message to Caleb. *He must know,* she tried to reason with herself. *Xander must have told him.* But what if Xander had kept this from Caleb? She could never shake the distrust she felt for the captain. *I have already spoken to Xander;* she reminded herself although she had not been able to get a clear message to him. If he were going to inform Caleb he would not need Alexandra to prompt him to do so. *I have no reason to seek Xander out in the middle of the night, it would raise too much suspicion.* She reasoned with herself deciding that Vanya may be her best chance at contacting Caleb. If anyone asked what she was doing she could simply say she was hungry, it wasn't a complete lie and it would give her an excuse to visit the kitchens. She tried not to think what she would do if Vanya was not there, it would be too suspicious for her to starting enquiring on a servant's whereabouts.

It took Alexandra several attempts to find the kitchens. She was surprised to find they were already alive with activity despite the early hour. Her stomach growled at the scent of baking bread, oatcakes and something sweet she couldn't quite identify. She spotted Vanya standing beside a giant hearth with several pots simmering, giving instructions to someone Alexandra assumed was a slave. *How many people are here because they want to be?* She thought glancing around; she knew that Vanya was a servant, but she wasn't sure how many other people the castle employed. Trying to keep her head down Alexandra approached Vanya, unnerved by the scowl on the woman's face.

'Your Highness,' Vanya curtsied, and those around her copied when they realised their visitor's status. 'If you needed something I am sure your slaves would have been more than happy to fetch it for you.' Alexandra blushed as she realised she was being reprimanded, but she glared at Vanya for referring to Helena and Roisin as slaves. Surely as her ladies, they were entitled to some form of respect? *Stop lying to yourself. Carlyle chose slaves to keep a closer eye on me.* Ignoring the thought she followed Vanya through the kitchens, making sure to keep her voice low as she spoke.

'I need to get a message to Ca – him.' She cut herself off from mentioning Caleb's name barely in time. There was no one around them and the kitchens were full of noises as people went about their tasks, but Alexandra was beginning to learn she could never be too careful. 'Please.' Vanya almost slammed down the rolling pin she had picked up an incredulous look on her face.

'You –'

'I had no choice but to find you. There was no one else.' Alexandra said before Vanya could lecture her. 'Surely you do not want me here any more than I do? The longer I am here, the more I jeopardise his cause. Please – my coronation is only days away. I need help now. *Please.*' Vanya's nostrils flared as she looked Alexandra up and down. 'I just want him to know that the coronation is this week, that he needs to help me now. Once I am crowned, I cannot help him.'

'I will do my best. Now please go, your presence is suspicious, and you are making the slaves uneasy.'

'Can I take some food, please? If His Majesty is awake he will wonder where I have been, at least this way I am not lying. He should not think much of me coming to the kitchens; I was too ill yesterday.' *If he asks why I did not send either Helena or Roisin, I can tell him I needed to stretch my legs.* She added silently to herself as Vanya prepared a plate of toasted bread and porridge. Alexandra smiled when she noticed that although Vanya was still scowling, there was a glint of respect in her eyes. As she made her way back to the chambers she shared with Carlyle she thought about how Vanya had acted. The woman appeared to loathe her almost as much as Xander did. *Does anyone close to Caleb trust me?* She thought biting back a sigh. Perhaps it was for the best she return to Karstares; surely if Caleb's allies did not trust her, then she would be useless to him.

Alexandra sat beside Carlyle at the long trestle table in the great hall. Below them, courtiers ate in a stifled silence. The air was uncomfortably thick with tension and Alexandra squirmed uneasily in her seat. She found herself longing for the intimate dining room where she took her meals with only Carlyle. Carlyle had surprised her when he had informed her they would dine publicly in the great hall with the rest of the castle in the lead up to her coronation. At first the thought had exciting Alexandra, but now she could see how uncomfortable and terrified people were.

'Are you feeling ill again?' Carlyle touched her hand lightly, his eyes full of concern. 'Perhaps you should rest until your coronation; it will be an exhausting day.'

'No, I'm fine.' Alexandra smiled tightly. She had not managed to eat much of the breakfast Vanya had given her that morning and had been promptly ill once she had consumed the small amount she had been able to manage. But she was determined not to stay in bed; she had to be ready for Caleb's help.

The doors to the great hall were flung open, and Alexandra flinched at the deafening crash which filled the room. Xander strode forwards, his hands clenched by his sides. He came to a halt in front of the table where Alexandra and Carlyle sat, and although he bowed deeply he did so in a manner quicker that was normally respectful.

'Your Majesty, Your Highness, please forgive me for interrupting your meal but I bring news.' Alexandra felt her stomach clench, and she nervously clasped her hands in her lap. For a split second, she feared that Xander would reveal that Alexandra was trying to escape her coronation, to find a way home, but she quickly shoved the thought aside. What would he gain? 'My men and I have discovered that there is a threat to the Princess. They plan to strike before the coronation. Forgive me Your Highness for any distress this may cause you, but they hope to throw Saphyre into chaos. Their intentions towards you are anything but pure.'

'You must be mistaken,' Alexandra blushed at the pleading tone in her voice. Why was Xander doing this? Surely he knew Carlyle would now refuse to let her out of his sight making any rescue nigh on impossible? Carlyle mistook her tone for fear and squeezed her hand gently.

'I will not let these scum harm you,' he promised. 'Captain I want two of your men posted at all times outside our chambers.' Rising to his feet Carlyle held out his hand for Alexandra to take but she could only shake her head in disbelief.

'This is nonsense; there is no threat.' She scowled at Xander wanting to ask him why he was lying but she knew it would cause more trouble. *Why is he doing this?* 'Carlyle these are surely just rumours, we cannot rise to fear!' She flinched at the thunderous expression on Carlyle's face, and he practically dragged her to her feet.

'Carlyle is for when we are alone,' he hissed in her ear. 'In public, it is 'my lord' or 'Your Majesty'. Nor am I afraid of these rumours, but I *will* protect you. Now come.' Alexandra was surprised to find that Carlyle was leading her to the Sorcerers' Tower rather than their chambers. 'The Castle Guards will provide visible protection, but my sorcerers have better resources and can protect you more discreetly.' The Sorcerers'

Tower was almost empty except for two men, one with dull red hair and the second with a muddy brown. Both were stood over what appeared to be a bowl of water, frowns creasing their faces as they discussed the contents. At the sound of footsteps they looked up and bowed deeply.

'Your Majesty we are honoured,' the brown-haired man smiled warmly and gestured to several seats around a table, but Carlyle shook his head at the offered seats.

'I would like to discuss matters with Éibhear and Foréignean.'

'Of course, Your Majesty, I will fetch Foréignean for you.' Bowing once more the man departed. Alexandra waited in silence; she had so many questions she yearned to ask. Instead, she waited for Carlyle to snap himself from his thoughts, which he only seemed to do at the appearance of a second person. 'Allow me to formally introduce you both to my wife, the Princess Alexandra of Karstares.' Alexandra held out her hand for both men to kiss, although their touch revolted her. 'Sorcerer Foréignean is the commander of our Castle Sorcerers who specialise in combat. He trains them in warfare and strategy.' Look at Foréignean, Alexandra could see that he enjoyed this use of power and she suppressed a shudder. She would not like to come across him on a battlefield. 'I am sure you have heard the rumours that a group of troublemakers wish to cause my wife harm. Her coronation is only four days away; I want you both to ensure that it goes smoothly. Should anything happen, I will hold both of you responsible.'

'Of course, Your Majesty,' both men answered in unison.

'I have been Scrying for anything which may reveal the whereabouts of these troublemakers – but all I encounter is fog. The threat is either nothing more than a rumour, or they have a skilled Sorcerer working with them.' Éibhear scoffed at the latter, and Alexandra felt a strong sense of dislike for him surge through her. She glanced up at Carlyle to see his reaction. His face remained passive, but she could see a slight tension in his jawline as if thought was slightly more than bothersome to him.

'I put little truth to these rumours that a usurper will make a bid for my throne, nor would one be foolish enough to harm my wife. But only a fool would ignore rumours completely. Foréignean I have requested guards to stand outside my chambers, I expect at least one of them to be yours.' Alexandra looked at Carlyle in surprise; she had thought none of the Castle Guards possessed the Source. 'If you spot anyone or anything remotely suspicious then investigate immediately.'

'Of course, Your Majesty.' Foréignean bowed, his eyes were fixated on Alexandra and held a curious glimmer. His mouth had a cruel, twisted smile which made Alexandra shudder; he was definitely not a man to trust.

'I thank you both for your protection,' she forced herself to speak formally. The two men bowed once more and departed, presumably to begin their task. Alexandra fought back the urge to question Carlyle over the presence of sorcerers in the Castle Guards. Did Xander know? With his fear of the Source she found this unlikely, so why were they there? Or was he aware of them, did they act as spies against Caleb? She could hardly ask Xander, she had no way of speaking to him privately and after the risk, she had taken that morning she was not sure it would be wise to do so again. 'You cannot truly believe there is a threat?' Alexandra said resisting the urge to cry in frustration. How could Xander do this to her? Surely he wanted her gone as much as she wanted to be?

'Calm yourself,' Carlyle snapped. 'I have already said *several* times that I do not believe there is an immediate threat – especially from cowards who insist on working underground. Who may not even exist. However, it cannot hurt to be cautious.' His voice was sharp, and Alexandra wondered if he thought more of the threats than he was letting on. Two guards were already stationed outside the chamber doors, but Carlyle ignored them as he ushered Alexandra inside.

'Carlyle...send me home. I do not want to live my life in constant fear of threats. Real or not. At least let me return to Karstares until you know if there is a threat or not.'

'Enough!' Carlyle roared, and Alexandra jumped in fright as the hearth violently flared to life. Rushes on the floor close by were singed and Alexandra wrinkled her nose at the burning smell. 'When will you understand that you are my *wife*? That Saphyre is your home, that I am doing everything within my powers to make it feel as such.' Alexandra bit down on her tongue; she was smart enough to know when to pick her arguments and now was not the time. 'I am your King and husband Alexandra. I know what is best for you – for Saphyre.'

'You know nothing about me,' Alexandra spat although the irony of her words was not lost on her; did she know herself any better? 'How safe am I with you Carlyle? If the throne was truly yours then –'

'I would choose your next words *very* carefully.' Carlyle hissed reaching out and gripping her chin. 'These rumours are nothing more than that Alexandra. I have stolen nothing; I inherited my throne from my father – as he did from his father and so forth. If I were you I would think about where your loyalties lie. To suggest that I am not the king, that my ancestors stole the throne, is treason. Even a queen can be put to death Alexandra. Both my father and grandfather demonstrated this, and you are not even that high yet.' Alexandra swallowed a lump of fear, Carlyle had never outright threatened her life before. *If he executed me at least, I would be free.* She stubbornly thought. He had murdered people because of her; she would not give him the satisfaction of hearing her plead for her own life. As if he read her mind Carlyle smiled a twisted and cruel smile which turned Alexandra's blood to ice. 'I promise you Alexandra should you ever give me cause to suspect your loyalties I will make you beg for a death that will never come.' Alexandra met his eyes unflinchingly, her smile just as cold as his own.

'Then I had best not give you cause, *my lord.*'

\*\*\*

'Turn a little to your left please Your Highness.' Alexandra did as she was bid, her eyes downcast and focused sadly on the floor. From the moment she had stepped on the small podium and slipped the dress on she had been haunted by the memories of trying on her first wedding dress back in Karstares. She could see her mother's green eyes swimming with tears, hear the excited chatter of the women as they debated adjustments and accessories. Her eyes stung painfully with tears, but she refused to let them fall, she was conscious of Carlyle circling her and eyeing her critically. 'Does this meet your expectations, Your Majesty?'

'Almost,' Carlyle's fingertips brushed the inside of her wrist and Alexandra closed her eyes as a frisson of electricity shot up her arm. Since their argument a few days ago Carlyle had been increasingly tender and gentle towards her. Alexandra had even at moment been able to enjoy his touch, losing herself in pleasure when she focused on his gentle side. But afterwards she would loathe herself for giving in. She didn't care that Carlyle was her husband, that she should be able to enjoy and even crave his company. He was a murderer, and she sickened herself for giving in to him. Carlyle's hands rested on her hips teasingly and he gathered a handful of fabric on each side, slowly drawing his hands back so that he could pull the dress in. Alexandra felt her cheeks warm at the suggestiveness of his touch. 'Take the dress in a fraction more,' he instructed letting the fabric fall back in place as he stepped away. As the dressmaker stepped forwards, Alexandra touched the coronet on her head. Carlyle followed her gestured and smiled at her, a wide smile she rarely saw on his face.

'Tomorrow this will be a symbol of your past,' he said stroking her cheek fondly. 'You will no longer be Princess Alexandra of Karstares; you will be Alexandra the First; Queen of Saphyre.'

# *Chapter Fourteen*

'You must eat. You need to keep your strength up.' Carlyle's voice was gentle and persuasive, but Alexandra shook her head adamantly. She had spent much of the morning ill, over the week her stomach had continued to be volatile and she had kept barely any of her meals down. 'Please,' Carlyle coaxed spooning porridge in to a bowl. Alexandra grimace and pushed it away.

'I'm sorry,' she murmured, 'I am not trying to be difficult I am just too nervous.' Her eyes flicked to the door of their chambers. Please Caleb, but even as she silently begged she knew Caleb was not likely to come, not now. He had made no attempt to get word to her let alone prevent the coronation from taking place. She tried to reassure herself, perhaps Vanya had been unable to get word, but she knew it was useless. He must know, she told herself bitterly forcing her gaze away from the door. The whole castle has been discussing the coronation. Finally conceding defeat Carlyle ordered Helena and Roisin to prepare her for the coronation.

Alexandra followed them into the dressing room, remaining silent as the two women brushed out her hair. She bowed her head as Roisin placed her coronet atop her head and she stared at it sadly in the looking glass. She studied herself critically trying to spot flaws that Carlyle might pick up on. Her skin was pale from the lack of sunlight over the past few moons, her cheeks were flushed from the constant sickness, and there were deep circles beneath her eyes. Roisin had hidden the circles under her eyes and had even managed to make her cheeks look flushed with joy rather than illness. Praying that Carlyle would find no fault, she turned to study the dress. It was spun from cloth of gold; the neckline dipped low and scooped just above her breasts to reveal the supple curves. The sleeves were slashed from her shoulders so that her arms were almost bare, and the skirt had an elegant trail of about a foot so that she would need to raise it ever so slightly to walk. Her waist was defined further by a gem encrusted belt which Alexandra thought too gaudy, but Carlyle insisted was needed to show off her wealth.

'You look beautiful,' Carlyle said, and Alexandra looked away blushing faintly. Carlyle was dressed as finely as herself in a cloth of gold tunic, white linen shirt, and trousers. The thought of how much wealth they wore between them made Alexandra feel sick; people had not survived winter because they were too poor to keep themselves warm. How can he think it's appropriate to parade around in such wealth? 'It is a perfect day for your coronation,' Carlyle gestured to the azure blue sky and glimmering ocean below. The sun was bright but even in the warmth of the chamber, Alexandra could see there was a chill to the air. A pulled Alexandra close, and Carlyle kissed her cheek, careful, so he did not disturb Roisin's handiwork. 'You are burning up!'

'I'm fine,' Alexandra lied. She felt unbearably hot and clammy, her fitted clothes only emphasising how uncomfortable she was. It was clear from Carlyle's expression that he did not believe her, and she gratefully accepted the water he offered.

'I cannot cancel the coronation,' Alexandra was surprised at the concern in Carlyle's voice and the worry in his eyes. 'Tomorrow we will take a procession through the city. As soon as we return I will have a healer come and examine you.'

'I'm sure it's nothing.' Alexandra shrugged, 'really Carlyle it is probably just nerves. The last public event hardly went well.' Carlyle nodded thoughtfully, and Alexandra prayed that her coronation would not be a repeat of their wedding; she wanted no more lives lost. She declined the offer of a travelling cloak, and Carlyle passed it without argument to Helena.

'Inform me as soon as you begin to get a chill.' He warned her, 'it would not do for you to be struck down by the flu the day after your coronation.'

'I would welcome the cold right now.' Alexandra smiled weakly leaning against Carlyle for support as her legs began to shake. The main hall was filled with sunlight as the heavy doors were opened. Alexandra was shocked to see crowds already gathering, and she paused in the doorway. 'The barrier is gone,' Carlyle reassured her squeezing her hand. 'Do not give me doubt to put it back up.' Nodding Alexandra tentatively followed him outside, cringing as she once again expected to collide with the invisible wall. The air was refreshingly cold, and she smiled as she felt the chill in her lungs. She had not set foot outside the castle since her life-day and how not realised how stuffy the castle was. Feeling slightly better she followed Carlyle down a stone staircase and into the front courtyard. Castle Guards waited patiently by their mounts, their eyes alert for any trouble. Alexandra followed Carlyle over to his mount half-expecting him to help her into the saddle. She bit her lip and frowned, surely it was not dignified to have to ride with Carlyle? I think I would rather risk falling from the saddle. She looked up at Carlyle to question him but saw he was smiling wryly.

'I had hoped to present you with this gift after our wedding.' Touching her lower back Carlyle led her around the front of his own mare where a second stood close by. Alexandra recognised the beautiful mare she had stroked in the stables; she ran her fingers through the luxurious black mane as she greeted the horse. 'What will you call her?'

'She is for me?' She asked startled as she faced Carlyle.

'She has been waiting patiently for you. She has a gentle temperament, yet she is fast.' Carlyle helped Alexandra into the saddle, and she stroked the horse's neck smiling widely. 'She has been without a mistress and name for almost a year; such a beautiful creature enjoys both.' Alexandra brushed at the subtle scolding and gathered the reins in her hands as she looked down at the mare.

'Solas,' she said thinking back to one of the books she had flicked through in ancient Saphyrian. She hadn't understood a word of it, but the language had been intriguing, and she had yearned to ask Carlyle to teach her. She studied Carlyle to see if he approved, feeling her shoulders relax when he smiled. Closing her eyes, Alexandra tried to work up the courage to command Solas to move.

'Trust your instinct,' Carlyle encouraged her. 'You are an accomplished rider and she, Solas, is a gentle horse. She will not throw you off.' Alexandra nodded forcing herself to click her tongue, following Carlyle as he made his way down the castle path. Helena and Roisin followed on foot with two of the Castle Guard behind them and another two leading the way for Alexandra and Carlyle.

The wind was biting and helped to cool Alexandra a bit, but she was still uncomfortably hot. People cheered and waved as the royal couple rode past, Alexandra could not help noticing how their actions seemed stage and almost awkward. She wanted to ask Carlyle if he noticed anything strange, or if it was just her imagination, she decided against drawing his attention to it unsure of how he would react.

The temple had started on eye-level as they had left the castle. The deeper they travelled within the city, the higher the temple loomed, until all too soon they had reached the bottom of the temple steps. Alexandra stared up at the temple apprehensively, her mind unable to focus on the present. All she could think about was their disastrous weddding day. A hand touched her leg gently, and she snapped herself from her thoughts, glancing down to see Carlyle smiling at her reassuringly. He helped her down from Solas, offering his arm as they began the long ascent up the temple steps.

'Are you not cold?' Alexandra realised that he was not wearing a cloak.

'My Source keeps me warm. I had added some to your cloak to ensure you were warm enough.'

'Thank you,' Alexandra smiled, 'that was kind of you.' As they reached the top of the stairs, they were greeted by Xander with a deep bow. Alexandra fought to keep her face passive when she desperately wanted to throw him a look that would send him fleeing.

'Congratulations Your Highness,' Xander said as he straightened and continued without giving Alexandra a chance to reply. 'Your Majesty I have men in uniform keeping an eye on the crowds. More men are in civilian clothing within the crowds, they are armed but discreetly so as not to cause panic. I give you my word that no one shall spoil this most joyous of occassions.' Alexandra couldn't help but noticing Xander's voice was monotone as if he thought the opposite of the day. So why did he destroy my only chance of escape? She thought bitterly. Carlyle nodded his dismissal to Xander and approached the large temple doors. The temple priest greeted them with a bow, before kissing both Alexandra and Carlyle on each cheek.

'Your Highness the Goddess looks down on you favourably on this most joyous of occassions.' The priest smiled warmly at Alexandra, and she recognised him as the man who had performed the marriage ceremony. A faint blush crept on her cheek as she remembered the purifying ceremony, but she quickly pushed it to the back of her mind. The priest's eyes were sympathetic, and he squeezed Alexandra's hands in a reassuring manner. 'May the Goddess bless you and guide you through your reign.'

'I thank the Goddess for having guided me this far,' Alexandra replied returning the priest's smile. 'I pray that she will give me deem me pure of heart to rule the people of Saphyre.' As the priest led Alexandra and Carlyle into the temple, the sounds of the crowd were abruptly silenced. Unlike the day of their wedding there were no seats set out for people. Instead the circular room was filled with people standing. With every breath, Alexandra drew she felt her chest tighten and her stomach grow heavier. The neausea she had been fighting to keep at bay was suddenly too overwhelming, and she feared she would faint as she walked down the middle of the temple hall. Her hand gripping Carlyle's arm tightened, and she could feel the fabric of his shirt bunching beneath her fingers. Silently she prayed to the Goddess to help her, for Caleb to make an appearance and put a stop to the coronation. Carlyle will let nothing stop it now, she realised in horror. He has gotten me this far he will not risk something destroying it all. She tried to tell herself to get through the day, but she couldn't bring herself to fully accept what was happening. Would she truly be bound to Saphyre once the crown touched her head?

'Breathe,' Carlyle whispered in her ear. 'You are hyperventilating.' Alexandra nodded and fought to regulate her breathing. All too soon she was standing at the temple's altar, her eyes fixated on the golden crown resting on a deep blue velvet cushion.

'Princess Alexandra of Karstare's,' the priest's voice resonated through the temple with a powerful boom and snapped Alexandra from her thoughts. 'The Goddess has led you here to claim your birth right as our queen. From this day forth you shall no longer be the Princess of Karstares; your ties to the kingdom will remain in blood alone. It is your duty to look after the citizens of Saphyre, your people; young and old, rich or poor. It is your duty to put the needs of Saphyre above all else. From this day forth you will be Queen Alexandra of Saphyre; First of her name.' No ties to Karstares? Do they think I will turn my back on my kingdom? For a sickening moment, Alexandra wondered what she would do if Saphyre and Karstares were at war with each other. Do not be ridiculous – this is the point of the marriage. Political allies. 'Do you swear to put the needs of Saphyre before your own?' Alexandra looked at the priest helplessly, she could not answer without lying, but she could feel the eyes of those in the crowd on her.

'I do swear,' Alexandra's voice was steady and firm as she forced herself to meet the priest's eyes. A flicker passed between them, and she swallowed a lump in her throat, perhaps the priest would be an ally. He seems kind enough, she told herself. But she had little to do with the temple. Gently the priest pressed a thumb to her forehead, neck and the palms of her hands; Anointing her with a musky scented oil. His voice continued to resonate through the temple, but Alexandra could no longer understand what he was saying. He had switched from the common tongue to Ancient Saphyrian, leaving her to dwell on thoughts. She resisted the urge to peek over her shoulder and observe the crowd knowing it would be an unqueenly gesture.

'With this crown I bind you to the kingdom of Saphyre. From this day forth it is your duty to honour, obey and protect the citizens of Saphyre, to ensure the laws are upheld.' Alexandra could feel the muscles in her legs bunching together as she forced herself to kneel in front of the priest. Her eyes were focused on the marble floor and she rested her hands in her lap as she bowed her head demurely. Please Caleb, she begged. Help me! She still clung to the hope that the temple doors would burst open. She squeezed her eyes tightly shut as she felt the presence of the priest looming over her, the crown outstretched in his hands. Her golden coronet was lifted from her hair and Alexandra glanced up surprised. She watched in horror as Carlyle snapped the slender circlet and dropped the pieces in to her lap. She picked up the fragments and clenched them tightly in her hand. What right did he have? She thought with seething anger.

She barely noticed the crown touching her head, until a bolt of energy shot through her body making her drop the suddenly molten fragments of her coronet. The air around her began to shimmer and Alexandra bit back a cry of pain of as a searing hot pain started from the top of her and burned its way down to her toes. The pain was over in a split second, a blinding white flash returning her temperature to normal. Alexandra blinked, too frightened to move or even speak. He has spent every night preparing me for this event, from the moment we were married he told me what to expect. Why did he never mention this? A hand came in to Alexandra's vision and she looked up startled to see Carlyle waiting to help her up. Scooping up her broken coronet she accepted his hand and carefully climbed to her feet, still too stunned to register what had happened. Had she imagined the heat and the flash? But as she turned to face the crowd she could see from their stunned expressions that it had not been her imagination.

'Citizens, I present you with your new Queen; Queen Alexandra of Saphyre; First of her name.' Carlyle's voice was annoyed, and Alexandra was surprised to see a tightness to his expression. His grip on her hand was slightly too tight and she realised he was careful not to look directly at her. 'Long live the Queen!' Cries echoing Carlyle rang through the hall as people slowly began to clap. Many still looked stunned but Alexandra was surprised to see several of those within the crowd now looking jubilant, and the hum of people whispering began to overpower the cheers. Without bidding the priest farewell Carlyle began to tug Alexandra towards the back of the temple.

'What happened?' Alexandra whispered as he walked quickly down the stairs. She had to pull on his arm gently to remind him that she was walking in long skirts and could trip at any moment. In her hand, she still clasped her coronet and she passed them to Helena as they reached the bottom. She was surprised to hear the cheers seemed more genuine and she smiled shyly at a few as Carlyle lifted her back into the saddle. 'Carlyle?'

'It was nothing.' Alexandra frowned as she forced herself to try and keep pace with him as he practically galloped away. Something went wrong; she thought back fighting fear. What had happened? Had she done something wrong or had it been out of her control? Her thoughts kept her occupied that she barely registered once they had reached the castle grounds. Sliding from Solas, Alexandra touched Carlyle's arm gently. 'What happened back there? Why did you not warn me about that?'

'It is not something that we normally speak off; it would make those who are about to be crowned unnecessarily nervous. The heat, the flash, they are harmless – yet if you had known about them would you have not fretted more?' Alexandra couldn't argue with him, but she could see there was more to it than that. 'It startled me; I had hoped of course that, that would happen – but to see it once more. It was truly breath-taking.'

'What was it?' Alexandra repeated almost impatiently; she could feel the eyes of those around them upon her once more.

'It signifies that you are a true Queen of Saphyre, that I was right in choosing you to rule beside me.' If it truly means that then why does he look almost angry? 'Put it from your mind, Alexandra; it does no use dwelling on it. Come, rest for a bit before this evenings celebrations.'

At the feast that evening Carlyle seemed more relaxed and almost jubilant. Alexandra couldn't help but wonder what it was about her coronation that seemed to have put him on edge. A slave moved to pour Alexandra more wine, but she shook her head and politely declined. Her eyes met Xander's across the hall, and she could feel the mutual loathing pass between them. He is not working alongside Caleb, she thought bitterly. He would never have told Carlyle there was a threat if he had truly wanted Caleb to secure the throne. As the feast ended and the entertainment began Alexandra felt light fingers on her arm. She looked over to see Carlyle holding her coronet, no longer snapped in half.

'I thought –' she blinked back tears and accepted the coronet, holding it tightly.

'It is part of the ceremony. This coronet is a symbol of your bond to Karstares, of the duty you owe to your father's kingdom. That bond is breakable. Yes, you will always have a blood tie to your father, mother, and brother – but not to Karstares.' Alexandra nodded as if she understood, but truthfully she did not think she could ever put Saphyre before Karstares. How could she when Saphyre was not her home? 'This coronet has been passed down by the women in your family for generations; I knew you were upset when I snapped it.' Carlyle smiled fleetingly, 'I did not want you to be unhappy because of something so trivial.' Trivial? Alexandra bit her tongue and forced herself to smile.

'Thank you – I truly am grateful.' She realised she meant it as she looked down at the coronet.

'We have a long day ahead of us tomorrow; if you would like to retire early, I think our people will understand.'

'Thank you,' Alexandra bowed her head gratefully and stood up as she gestured to Helena and Roisin. The music halted abruptly, and people bowed respectfully as Alexandra walked past. She was confused but slightly pleased, to see that some of the people no longer gazed at her fearfully but with curiosity. Perhaps I can convince them I am not to be feared; she thought hopefully setting her coronet on the dressing table. She stared at it thoughtfully, was there a chance that she could convince Carlyle to change his ways? Could she grow to love him? No, she shook her head sadly. He murdered grandmother and countless others, just because he occasionally shows a glimmer of kindness does not change what he is or what he has done. Even if he repents, I can never love him.

Dressed in a sapphire blue satin gown, her hair loosely plaited, Alexandra sat aside Solas trying not to touch the crown on her head. She wasn't sure if it was her imagination or if the crown was heavier than she expected. I feel as if I am carrying the weight of Saphyre, she thought wryly. As Carlyle joined her she smiled at him in greeting, she had risen early that morning and with no appetite had decided to come down to the stables. The stable boys had not allowed her to take Solas for a ride fearing that Carlyle would accuse them of aiding her escape. I am sure soon enough Carlyle will not begrudge me going for a ride. She decided she would discuss it with him later, perhaps after the procession. Surely if this went well then, he would be in a good mood.

'You seem to be more confident in the saddle,' Carlyle complimented her as they began their procession.

'Solas is truly a gentle, and extremely patient, beast. I cannot thank you enough for such a beautiful gift.' The roads from the castle to the city were less lined in comparison to the previous day. Carlyle explained that the city had celebrated until almost dawn and that many people would remain in the city to greet them.

'How are you feeling?' Alexandra shrugged unsure of how to answer. 'Alexandra such gestures are unseemly; I will tolerate them in our chambers but perhaps in public –'

'Forgive me,' Alexandra sighed cutting him off. 'I cannot adjust to these court manners. I am...I still feel queasy,' she admitted.

'I will have a healer see you soon.' Carlyle promised, 'It may be just nerves Alexandra, but you will have to get used to being on display. Our people will need to see you, to see us.' As they entered the city people cheered, but while many were less forced than the previous day Alexandra could see that many were weary. As they rode past the temple, Alexandra glanced up at the glorious white building. Perhaps Carlyle will allow me to come and pray here – if we did it together that would keep us in the public eye. A scream pierced through the air cutting through Alexandra's chain of thought, instinctively she pressed her heels into Solas's side pulling her to a halt just in time to stop a young girl from being trampled. 'Insolent bitch!' Carlyle hissed pulling out a whip and raising his hand.

'No!' Alexandra half-stumbled and half-climbed from the saddle as she rushed to scoop the young girl into her arms. 'My lord it was an accident, she is just a child!' She realised she was barely more than a child, but rather than the chubby cheeks of toddlers she had seen in Bournemouth this girl's cheeks were gaunt and her face stained with dirt. Tears of fright slipped from her wide eyes, leaving pale streaks in their tracks. Alexandra grinned at the girl and made cooing noises, trying her best to reassure her. She is all bones! She thought horror stricken, rummaging through her saddle bag she pulled out a sticky bun and handed it to the young girl. She fought back the urge to glare at Carlyle, to scold him for being so callous towards a child. Do not start an argument, not in public where so many people can be harmed for witnessing it. Nor did she wish to anger him when she was holding a child, the girl was frightened enough. Although the sticky bun seemed to be helping allay her fears. 'Shall we find your mother?' The girl had already finished the bun and was looking around for more. Clearly her trauma forgotten. Laughing Alexandra pulled an apple from her saddlebag, looking apologetically at Solas. 'I will give you extra hay when we return to the castle,' she smiled as the mare seemed to nod her head satisfied with the exchange.

'Your M – Majesties,' an exhausted looking woman appeared at the front of the crowd. As she dropped into a clumsy curtsey, her knees hit the cobbled road and she gasped. Alexandra was horrified to see the woman was almost as thin as the child, and just as dirty and raggedly dressed. How did they survive the winter when so many others perished? Alexandra could not help herself asking, why does Carlyle not do something to end this poverty? She wanted to tell herself that, that was an unfair question. She didn't know for sure that Carlyle did nothing. 'P – Please forgive me, I took my eyes off her o – only for a second –'

'A second is all it takes wench!' Carlyle roared, and the girl in Alexandra's arms began to cry in fright. Lightly Alexandra bounced the girl in her arms and pulled faces in an attempt to stop the girl crying. She was relieved when it worked, and the girl began to giggle and clap her hands, gurgling for Alexandra to continue.

'My lord please when we have children of our own –'

'If the goddess blesses me with sons from a barren wife!' Alexandra felt as if the wind had been knocked from her and she almost dropped the child from shock. Her cheeks burning with humiliation she gently returned the child to her mother, smiling faintly. The woman's eyes were sympathetic, making Alexandra's cheeks burn hotter. Ignoring Carlyle's glare, she turned back to Solas and unclipped her saddlebag.

'You have a beautiful daughter,' she said handing the shocked woman the bag. She wished she had some coins to give the woman, but she was embarrassed to realise since returning to her own world she had held no money – she didn't even know the currency.

'May the Goddess bless you, Your Majesty.' The woman curtsied deeply, and Alexandra smiled as the child continued to watch her with unabashed curiosity. Accepting help from one of the Castle Guards she pulled herself back up into the saddle and bowed her head to the woman in thanks. She refused to acknowledge Carlyle; her eyes fixed resolutely ahead as they continued their procession.

'Long live Queen Alexandra!' Alexandra looked around in shock her eyes scanning the crowd to see who had called out, but many had joined in and the air was thick with shouts of joy. She peeked at Carlyle from the corner of her eye to study his reaction, not one person had cheered for him, and she feared his reaction. *Why would he be so cruel? He has not mentioned my lack of conceiving and we have not even been married three full moons yet.* The thought made Alexandra freeze, and she abruptly drew Solas to a halt, the mare snorted in annoyance but stood still.

'What are you doing?' Carlyle hissed stopping his own horse behind her. *No,* Alexandra prayed, *I am just ill...I have been nervous about everything happening that is all.* Her throat was suddenly painfully dry, and her head began to swim.

'P – Please my lord can we rest for a bit?' Alexandra could feel beads of sweat gathering at the back of her neck. It was a bitterly cold day, but she suddenly felt as if she had been trapped within a furnace. 'I – I feel faint.'

'You can see for yourself Alexandra there is nowhere to rest. You have worked the crowds up; we will most likely be mobbed if we stay here much longer.' *He is angry they don't cheer for him,* she realised swallowing the rising bile. Desperately she clung to the reins, but she could feel her grip slipping and her shoulders slumping. 'Sit up straight Alexandra. You are a *queen* now.' Somehow Alexandra managed to force herself to sit upright, but she could do nothing to calm the turbulent storm within her stomach. *It is nothing; perhaps I just have a fever.* She tried to calm herself, but she knew what was wrong. *How could I be so foolish?*

'Carlyle –' Pleadingly Alexandra called out to him, but it was too late. Unable to hold on to the reins any longer Alexandra felt them slip from her hands as she tumbled sideways into darkness.

*\*\*\**

'She needs rest Your Majesty she must be exhausted; she will never conceive if she is not healthy – and if she does she risks losing the babe.' *I imagined everything;* a small voice reassured Alexandra. But if she had imagined her ailment then why did she still feel so weak? Why did she have the urge to empty the contents of her stomach when she had barely eaten all week. 'She just has a fever, with rest she will be back on her feet in a matter of days.'

'Did I permit you to speak *slave*? I see that spending time with your mistress has given you a high opinion of yourself.'

'Leave her alone,' Alexandra managed to mumble as she forced herself to sit up. Glancing around she found she was in her own bedchamber; the shutters open wide despite the bitter blizzard outside. Despite the weather, her chamber was still unbearably hot, and she could feel her face was damp with sweat. 'How long have I been asleep?'

'A day,' Carlyle growled, 'How could you *humiliate* me so publicly?'

'Excuse me?' Alexandra yearned to reach out and strangle him, but she was too weak to even move from the bed. 'You know I had not been feeling well; I tried my best to continue!' Carlyle opened his mouth to argue, but Alexandra shook her head. 'Please, I am too exhausted to argue, and it is too hot in here.' She tried to stand wanting to move to the window; she needed to stick her head outside to feel the cold.

'Out,' from the corner of her eye, Alexandra saw Helena and Roisin scuttle from the chamber.

'You could be nicer to them; they are my only friends here.' *If I can call them friends,* Alexandra added to herself sadly. 'Carlyle it really is too hot, are you using your Source?' Instantly the temperature cooled, and Alexandra sighed in relief. 'Thank you.'

'They are slaves Alexandra; you should not be lowering yourself to be counting such creatures as friends. Nor should you seek friendship – you would be wise to trust no one other than myself. Many will use your position to gain advantage and favour.' Alexandra fought back the urge to point out that Carlyle had been the one to appoint slaves as her ladies-in-waiting and that they were the only people she could form a bond with in Saphyre. 'How do you feel?'

'Like death,' Alexandra sighed, 'what happened?'

'You passed out. The healers were weary of examining you while you were unconscious, now you are awake I will send for someone to come examine you this evening.'

'It is probably nothing,' Alexandra tried to shrug it off desperate to avoid being examined. She did not want what she suspected confirmed. 'Maybe it was that awful heat during the coronation?' Carlyle's face darkened, and she immediately decided to drop the subject.

'Our citizens seem to genuinely love you; you should be proud.'

'I am sure they would love you too if they saw more of you – and if you were not so quick to abuse them.' Alexandra knew it was a pointless lie for even if Carlyle miraculously changed his ways it would be too late; he had done too many awful atrocities. She barely knew what he had done, but the little she had witnessed gave her little confidence in his ruling techniques.

'Why should I change?'

'Carlyle you were going to strike a child yesterday!'

'The brat should not have wandered into our path!' Alexandra closed her eyes determined not to argue with him. 'Let us not argue,' Carlyle echoed her thoughts. 'If you feel up to it perhaps we should begin our duties.'

'Duties?' Alexandra asked opening her eyes and instantly regretting it, the room was spinning violently.

'You are queen now Alexandra, we have been married almost three moons – I need a son.' *Goddess not now please,* Alexandra begged.

'Carlyle I am *sick* I need...' She cut herself off from saying healer. She didn't want a healer; she didn't need her fears confirmed. 'I have only had *one* bleeding since we married –' She froze cutting herself off as she realised Carlyle had taken note of what she had said. He opened his mouth, but she cut him off. 'It could be nothing,' she warned, 'It could be anything!' *Please Goddess let it be anything else.* She was still berating herself for missing the signs, how could she have been so foolish? She hadn't exactly been counting the days, but she knew several weeks had gone by, and the sickness each morning...why had she not considered it? *I have been too intent on trying to find a way to stop the coronation.* An urgent knocking at the door pulled both Alexandra and Carlyle from their thoughts.

'This had better be important Captain,' Carlyle growled impatiently. Alexandra sat back and resumed her train of thoughts, not bothering to listen to Xander's reply. What did it matter? *It is just a bug;* she tried to reassure herself. She wasn't aware of Carlyle leaving until he kissed her swiftly and closed the door softly behind him. Pausing for a few moments Alexandra stared up at the ceiling, what was she going to do? Kicking the blankets aside she stood up and examined her belly; there was no bulge or evidence that something was growing inside of her. *If I was pregnant surely, I would know?* She tried to reassure herself, but she knew it was foolish. If she was pregnant it would be early days; there would be few signs. *Other than the symptoms I am already experiencing.*

'Please Goddess,' she begged aloud feeling tears prick her eyes. She had been told the Goddess was a merciful deity, but Alexandra had yet to experience the slightest bit of mercy. Deep down she had known she would fall pregnant if she could not escape Saphyre, but so soon? She had thought it would take a while to conceive, that she would have time to adjust perhaps. Lying back down she pulled the blankets over her head, desperately trying to fool herself that she was dreaming when a knock on the door pulled her back to reality. 'Come in,' she called out glumly. At the sound of footsteps, she sat up, frowning as Carlyle stood in the doorway looking sheepish. It took her a few seconds to realise that Carlyle would not wear rumpled clothing with patches of dirt on his shirt. 'Caleb, what are you doing here?' She hissed in exasperation, 'Carlyle could be back any moment!' She was surprised Carlyle had left at all with what had just been revealed to him. Anger washed over her as she realised Caleb had come to seek her out *after* her coronation. Where had he been before? 'Why are you here?' She yearned to ask him where he had been, why he had not prevented her coronation.

'I came to see how you were faring; I heard that you collapsed during the procession yesterday.'

'I'm fine,' Alexandra shrugged sitting up suddenly conscious that she was lying in bed. If Carlyle, or anyone else for that matter, were to enter now what would they think? 'Where were you? I prayed that you would stop the coronation, I *trusted* you!' Caleb stared out the window and Alexandra could see the thoughts racing through his head as he decided what he should, or should not, say. Finally, when he turned to face her, she could see the guilt in his eyes.

'Alexandra...Your Majesty -'

'*Don't* call me that, I am not a queen. Help me return to Karstares, help me go home – *please!*'

'Alexandra I am sorry, but I cannot help you return to Karstares, you *are* a queen. You are a True Queen.' Alexandra shook her head in confusion, 'I was at your coronation. I was in the temple – I had to see for myself. The flash at your coronation that is what happens when a true monarch is crowned. It is said to be a symbol of the Goddess's blessing.'

'Carlyle told me that happens.' Alexandra snapped, 'He didn't warn me of it before...of that or the heat in case, I got nervous. Surely it means nothing – if it happened at Carlyle's, then it cannot mean what you think. Otherwise, you would not think you have a claim to the throne surely?'

'Alexandra that event has not been witnessed for five hundred years; it never happened at Carlyle's coronation. He is *not* a true king; he is a usurper.' Alexandra stared at Caleb in disbelief, Carlyle's anger now made sense. Was Carlyle angry at her? *Surely he could use this against his enemies – even if he is not a true monarch his wife is.* Her eyes flicked back to Caleb as she realised he too would use her newfound status to benefit him.

'You were never going to help me return to Karstares were you? You *wanted* me crowned?' She felt as if she had been slapped; she had trusted Caleb. She had believed him when he had said he would help her return home if his movement succeeded before her coronation. *How could I have not realised nothing was happening?* Carlyle had told her to trust no one, should she take that advice?

'I had to know. I was certain that would happen, that it would be proven you are a true Queen of Saphyre I need you here, I need you to fight with me.' Blinded by anger, Alexandra stood up and marched over to Caleb, her open palm connecting with his cheek. Her hand stung it reverberated down her arm, but it felt satisfying, and she resisted slapping him again.

'You are worse than Carlyle – at least he is honest about what he wants from me. But you allowed me to believe that you would help me, you let me think that there was some chance of hope that I could return home. You had no intentions of helping me return, *ever!*'

'I am sorry Alexandra, truly I am. I wanted to help you, but I could not. I had to think of my people; I have to put them above all else.' Alexandra shook her head in disbelief. 'What would you do if you could return home? Marry another foreign king or prince? You can help us Alexandra; you can do something worthwhile here –'

'Get out.' Caleb stared at her unsure of what to do; she could see he wanted to explain further; to try and repair the damage he had inflicted on their friendship. 'Go. You should not have come here if Carlyle returns he would have you executed – and most likely me alongside you.' Anger blinded her, and she shook her head trying to clear the fog in her mind. 'You have destroyed any chance you have at claiming the throne. I'm pregnant,' the words left a bitter taste in her mouth, but she could see the effect they had on Caleb. He froze in the doorway, looking at her in shock. Alexandra stared at him in stony silence and watched as he left his expression numb.

# *Chapter Fifteen*

Alexandra was perched on the window ledge when Carlyle returned to her chambers. Still dressed in a chemise she had thrown a cloak around her shoulders and a blanket across her knees as she watched the blizzard raging below. *At least it held off,* she thought thankfully. Would Carlyle have continued with the procession yesterday if the storm had started?

'I suppose you want to tell me that along with everything else you are not ready to be a mother?' Carlyle's voice was surprisingly gentle, and he rested a hand on Alexandra's shoulder. Alexandra chose silence as her answer; did he really expect her to be? *I have been queen for only a few days, and half of it I have been asleep.* She looked down at her stomach, was there really life growing within? 'Would it surprise you if I told you that I do not feel ready to be a father?' Alexandra considered this carefully before shaking her head.

'You can want something, but when it comes to pass...you find it is not what you expected.' Alexandra bit her lip nervously, 'nothing will be the same. We will be responsible for someone...' *We already are,* she realised. *The people of Saphyre...did I not swear at my coronation to protect them? To put their needs first? Surely the needs of our child will come first.* 'What if I am a terrible mother?' She half-joked forcing a smile, and she was surprised when Carlyle returned it.

'Our people love you Alexandra, those in the city have seen you three times since your arrival. And look at how they responded to you during the procession.' *After I stopped you from beating a little girl,* but Alexandra kept the thought to herself. Would he try to harm their own child? A shadow passed over her face, and she crossed her arm over her belly as if trying to shield the child. She would never let Carlyle, or anyone for that matter, harm her child. 'We will not make any public announcements, not until you begin to show.'

'I assumed you would want to tell the whole city,' Alexandra said dryly. 'Especially after calling me barren in front of everyone.'

'I apologise...I spoke harshly and rashly. But delaying the announcement is for your safety. Captain Xander informed us of a threat against you to stop the coronation – this could have encouraged people to actively plot against us. If people would wish you harm during your coronation, then this would most likely send them into a frenzy. I will not put you, or our son, at risk.'

'Carlyle, please do not jump to any conclusions – it may be a daughter. I may not even be pregnant; I could have missed my bleeding for any number of reasons.' She was clutching at straws, but she didn't want to risk Carlyle's fury if it proved she was wrong. 'We should not get our hopes up...nor those of anyone who would wish our children harm.' She turned her face towards the window, just in time to see a brightly coloured bird caught up in the blizzard. Leaning forwards Carlyle stretched out his right hand, catching the bird with a smile. He held out his hand for Alexandra to examine the bird and she smiled in delight at the beautiful creature. It was no bigger than a sparrow, its breast a dazzling gold and back a rainbow of blues, greens and purple feathers. 'It is beautiful,' she cooed tentatively running her finger across the feathers which were surprisingly silky. The bird seemed to preen, lapping up the praise and chirping happily. It seemed to have forgotten been caught up in the blizzard. The smile on her lips died as Carlyle closed his fist, encasing the fragile bird within his tight grip. There was a sickening crunch followed by the snap of bones breaking, blood trickled from his hand and splashed on the blanket across Alexandra's lap. Alexandra was frozen to the spot, her eyes wide in horror.

'Saphyre is a beautiful kingdom,' Carlyle's voice was as hard as a stone. 'For those who please me. But for those who displease me, harm my family or plot against my reign...' He let the threat hang in the air. Opening his hand, Alexandra looked away too disgusted to bring herself to look at the mangled mess within his palm. She was surprised to hear chirping, and she forced herself to look back at Carlyle's hand. The bird looked around in confusion, standing in a pool of its own blood. It looked perfectly fine; there was nothing to suggest it had only moments ago been horrifically crushed to death. With a few nervous chirps, it ruffled its feathers and flew up into the rafters of the tower.

Alexandra lay on the bed she shared with Carlyle, her eyes staring blankly at the ceiling. Outside the blizzard continued to rage, the bird from the previous day had not yet left Alexandra's tower, and she had brought it scraps of food and fabric, so it could build a nest. She could not forget the sight of blood dripping from Carlyle's hand as he had crushed the poor creature.

A healer sat beside Alexandra, eyes closed in concentration. The woman's palms were pressed flat against Alexandra's abdomen and she could feel heat pulsating through the fabric of her chemise. Her hair was a vibrant copper shade and twisted in a loose plait which fell over her shoulder. Bright green eyes snapped open and smiled at Alexandra, but she could not bring herself to return the smile. The woman seemed kind, but she felt vulnerable lying on the bed as she was examined, Carlyle pacing backwards and forth as he awaited the healer's verdict.

'Congratulations Your Majesty,' the healer smiled. 'The Queen is indeed with child.' Those six words turned Alexandra's insides to ice, and she fought back waves of sickening fear. 'She is in the very early stages; there is evidence of a heartbeat which suggests the babe is approximately two moons...give or take a week.' the woman stood up and curtsied deeply. 'I expect within the next moon you will begin to show.'

'This is excellent news Sorceress Rhonwyn,' Carlyle smiled jubilantly. 'But I would urge you to tell this to no one – not even the other sorcerers. I am sure you understand why.'

'Of course, Your Majesty. As far as the other healers are concerned, the Queen has been suffering from a fever – she has had quite a stressful few days. I would still recommend plenty of rest; the child is young – overexertion could cause great harm.' *I am here*, Alexandra wanted to point out but bit down on her tongue.

'Perhaps she should enter confinement?'

'Too much rest can be just as bad as not enough,' Rhonwyn quickly dismissed the idea. 'Her Majesty will need plenty of fresh air; there is in no danger of going about her day as normal.' Rhonwyn hesitated as she seemed to work up the courage to say something which plagued her mind. 'Perhaps I could speak to you a moment in private Your Majesty?' Carlyle nodded and led Rhonwyn from the chambers. Sighing Alexandra stood up and threw a robe over her chemise. The temptation to see if she could eavesdrop on Carlyle was overwhelming but she restrained herself. *He killed a bird;* she thought pacing around the room. *No creature could have survived that, does this mean he has the power to raise the dead?* The thought was terrifying, and Alexandra suppressed a shudder pouring herself a goblet of wine. She stared at the crimson liquid before pouring it back into the jug. She had not been on Earth for long, but she remembered hearing the scorn against women who drank while carrying; she had no idea how women were viewed in Saphyre. *Then again the two worlds are so different*, Alexandra thought wistfully. She rarely thought of her time on Earth, it was beginning to feel like it had never happened, but every so often she would wistfully think of the conveniences. *It was never home though.* She didn't stop to let herself think that maybe it could have been home if she'd given it a chance. *It never felt like home – I didn't belong there.* When Carlyle returned his face was grave, and Alexandra watched him nervously.

'Is something wrong?' For a fleeting moment, Carlyle looked as if he was about to refuse but changed his mind.

'There is an outbreak of illness in the city. So far it has been contained in the slums, but there is the danger it could spread. I need to call a council meeting, will you please just rest?'

'What else would I do?' Alexandra asked sarcastically earning herself a withering glare.

'You are free to go outside now; I feel I need to point out that there is a blizzard raging outside.' It was Alexandra's turn to glare in response and Carlyle smiled as he kissed her cheek. 'I know you have been eager to go outside; I just wanted to make sure you realised now is not the best time. Not when you have our son to think of.' Alexandra bit her tongue; how could he be so sure they would have a son? It infuriated her, but she resisted from pointing out that she could be carrying a daughter. 'Dine without me; I may be back late.'

'Could I not help?' Carlyle looked thoughtful but shook his head. 'I am queen now – these are my people too and I have a duty just as much as you.'

'I agree,' he nodded, 'but now you need rest. We will talk about you attending meetings another time; it is not something that queens have done in the past.'

Over the next few days, Alexandra noticed a gradual change in Carlyle's mood. Despite the illness sweeping through the city he seemed relaxed as if a weight had been lifted from him. *Are children that important to him?* Alexandra would frequently ask herself, but she always had the same answer immediately; no. He only cared about sons. He needed to ensure the succession of his line. But while Carlyle seemed to relax, Xander was the complete opposite. Each time Alexandra crossed paths with him, she could see the look of cold loathing in his eyes, and each time he would glance at her stomach as if to see whether it was true or not. *Caleb must have told him...does that mean my child is in danger?* Xander's attitude left her feeling lost, she was sure he was secretly plotting against Caleb but why should her pregnancy upset him that much? *Perhaps he just truly hates me.*

A conflict raged within her; she wasn't sure whether to be pleased with her pregnancy or horrified. She felt no maternal instincts for the child growing within; she wasn't sure if she believed she was pregnant yet. Surely she would feel *something*? Questions about the child were never far from her mind; what if it was a girl? What if someone did try to harm them? But the worst thought tugging at her mind was what if the child became like Carlyle? Could she be carrying a tyrant? *I am meant to be protecting the people of Saphyre and yet I could be dooming them to centuries more of suffering.* Tossing and turning Alexandra fought to fall asleep but thoughts were swarming in her head.

'Alexandra, what is wrong?' Carlyle's voice was muffled from beneath the pillow, and she felt his hand reaching out for her.

'I can't sleep,' Alexandra sighed. 'Please, Carlyle let me sleep in my chamber.' She had hoped that now she was pregnant Carlyle would leave her in peace an allow her to sleep in her private chamber, he had quickly crushed that hope.

'Your chamber is only for when you are unpure to share our marital bed,' he mumbled. 'You are far from unpure at this moment.' Sitting up Carlyle tilted Alexandra's chin up so he could meet her eyes, his Source lighting the space between them. The spiral pattern of his eyes began to rotate and Alexandra looked away. 'It will help you sleep -'

'I don't like you using your Source on me,' Alexandra protested and flinched at the look of hurt on Carlyle's face. 'You have to admit you have abused it.'

'You need sleep,' Carlyle pressed. 'I did this once before and you were fine after were you not? Please let me help you rest.' Alexandra's eyes searched his face for any sign of deception, but what reason did he have? Nodding she settled back and clenched her hands over her stomach, unable to stop the fear she felt at giving him power over her. Carlyle knelt beside her, stroking her cheek gently as he firmly held her gaze. It didn't take Alexandra long before she succumbed to sleep.

*Alexandra smiled as the dark sky above was emblazoned with colourful bolts of light. She was lying on the grass, her head resting against a warm shoulder, arms wrapped around her. Spots of moisture hit her cheek, and she jumped up laughing wildly as rain began to lash down. Someone grabbed her hand, tugging her from the depths of the maze.*

*'Quickly before your father sends someone out looking for you!' Mathe's voice was full of laughter, and the two couldn't help giggling as they stumbled and slipped across the muddy gardens. Alexandra didn't give a thought to her gown which was becoming soaked and mud stained, all she could focus on was the warm hand strongly gripping her own.*

*The scene faded, and Alexandra found herself galloping through a forest, a bow and arrow in her hand. Scenes began to blur in to one, a colourful haze that she could barely make sense off.*

*'Alexandra concentrate!' Alexandra glanced around in confusion, recognising her mother's study. Ismenya stood on the opposite side of her desk, a candle half-burnt in front of her. 'Carlyle is an accomplished Sorcerer, but there is no reason you should not match him in power. But you must* concentrate!'

*'There is no point mother,'* she replied glumly. *'He will take my power - he will use it to strengthen his own.'* Ismenya scowled darkly at Alexandra.

*'Carlyle is not the tyrant you are making him out to be – your father and I would never match you with such a man! And it was* your *choice Alexandra; you accepted his proposal of your own free will. You cannot back out now; you will bring dishonour upon yourself – upon us. Who can trust you if you back out of such a serious vow?'* Alexandra remained silent, biting down on her tongue. Mariah was right, no one will believe us. All I can do is strengthen myself and make sure that he cannot steal my power. *Frowning at the candle Alexandra concentrated, channelling her energy into the flame so she could lift it from the wick. She guided the flame over to the fireplace where she safely deposited it, watching it dance and grow stronger.*

*The sound of gulls squawking made Alexandra's stomach knot as her mother left the small cabin. Helplessly she turned to look at Mariah and Krista, their expressions doing little to ease her panic.*

*'We have to try it,'* she said firmly. *'It is my only chance.'*

*'Neither of us are experienced enough Alexandra; something could go wrong – you could be* killed.*'*

*'Who is to say I will not be killed if I marry Carlyle? I am never going to be the obedient wife he expects; he knows I am marrying him purely to protect you all.'* Tears blurred Alexandra's eyes, and she was ashamed as they skimmed down her cheeks, smudging the cosmetics servants had only finished moments ago. *'I cannot do this. I need time...I will find a way back I give you my word.'*

*'One of us should go with you,'* Krista reasoned. *'We do not know where you could end up.'*

*'No one can know you were involved; it is bad enough they will have their suspicions. If one of you come with me then they will punish you all.'* Both Krista and Mariah opened their mouths to argue, but Alexandra shook her head. *'Please do not make me pull rank on you both,'* she half-jested. *'We do not have time to argue. Surely this is the safer option than actually marrying Carlyle?'* The two women seemed uneasy but looked as if they agreed with her. Quickly they embraced Alexandra in farewell, promising to keep everyone distracted to give her time. *'Please Goddess,'* Alexandra whispered kneeling on the floor and holding out her hands. *'Please protect them from my cowardice.'* Holding out her hands she closed her eyes and focused on her Source, pouring her energy into the ball of light deep within. She gasped as she felt it knocked from her, as if someone had reached into her and physically pulled something out. When she opened her

*eyes the room was spinning, and she almost passed out from exhaustion. She smiled when she saw the whirling portal beside her; a black hole in the ground with blue bolts spinning wildly.* I will find a way back; *she vowed groggily climbing to her feet. Her body broke out in a sweat, and she realised she was overexerting herself. Giving no time to think about what she was doing Alexandra closed her eyes and jumped into the portal.*

Alexandra sat up with a gasp, her head fuzzy from the dream. *It wasn't a dream,* she realised. She looked down at Carlyle unsure of whether she could believe what she had seen or not. What if her mind had been playing tricks on her? *Caleb thought I had the Source – he was sure of it. He even asked how I could trust Carlyle.* But why would Carlyle lie? *I used my Source to run away, that's why he used his Source to keep me here and made sure I didn't know about my own.* She wanted to say something, to confront Carlyle about his lies but how could she? If she could keep her power a secret from him then perhaps she could begin to use it again. *Who will teach me?* Standing up Alexandra poured herself some water and gulped it back, she wasn't particularly thirsty but felt she needed to give her mind something to occupy itself with. Did Carlyle suspect that she knew about her powers? *I have not used them,* she reassured herself, but she remembered the wind sweeping through the room when he had revealed Mathe's marriage. She thought back to the night she had left Bournemouth, Carlyle had been insistent that they return immediately to Saphyre. Yet they had ended up in Karstares. *Was that me? Had I subconsciously used my Source?* She couldn't remember feeling exhausted; there had been no pulling sensation when she had first summoned a portal. *But then Carlyle summoned the portal not me...did I just re-route us somehow?* As Carlyle stirred, she slid back beneath the blankets forcing herself to stay calm. Anger seared through her veins at Carlyle's betrayal; he had lied outright to her on several occasions. Had he really expected her to remain ignorant of her Source? *Whether he did or not I cannot admit to him that I know the truth, he lied about it...who is to say he will not try and take my Source away and use it to strengthen his own?* The thought hit her so suddenly she couldn't help but wonder if he was already doing that. *Tomorrow,* she promised herself. *I can do nothing for now.*

Soon after Alexandra had broken her fast, she departed for the library, managing to convince Helena and Roisin that she needed some peace after the past few days. There was a small section of scrolls and ancient tomes on the Source, but they were written in ancient Saphyrian and Alexandra knew she would have no chance of deciphering them, nor could she ask for help. *Maybe I should confront Carlyle?* She asked herself, *if he is aware that I know the truth then he would not dare to drain my Source surely?* But she couldn't bring herself to take the risk. *I need somewhere private that I can practice.* The tower she would often seek solace in felt too obvious, Carlyle would know that that was where she was most likely to be. *I cannot risk him walking in on me, but where else is there?* A blizzard still raged outside keeping her firmly within the castle walls. *Perhaps the tunnels beneath the castle?* She asked herself, it would look suspicious if she was found down there but who would find her? Deciding that this would be her safest option Alexandra made her way down to the labyrinth of tunnels below the castle.

The tunnels were dark, and there were no torches to light the way for Alexandra as she continued downwards. She had purposefully decided against bringing a torch hoping this would force her Source to come forwards. How had she kept it suppressed for so long? *I am hardly a novice; I have control over my Source.* She tried to reason with herself, although she had not had complete control over her power. When she was certain, she was far down enough to protect herself from being discovered Alexandra knelt on stone floor, wincing as the cold seeped through her skirts.

Closing her eyes she pictured the dream, trying to remember how she had summoned her Source. *'It lies deep within you, dormant until you have need for it.'* Ismenya's voice was clear in her mind as if her mother knelt beside her. *'Empty your mind.'* She tried to clear her mind but no matter how hard she tried thoughts and images kept bursting in. She could not stop thinking about Caleb; she was furious at him for having purposefully deceived her. But part of her missed him. She had felt he was someone she could trust and she missed talking to him. He had not eyed her wearily as Xander had done, nor with loathing. *Is Xander afraid of me because I have the Source?* He had made his feelings clear on the power but did anyone really think she would use hers to manipulate and threaten people as Carlyle did? *Concentrate!* She scolded herself and readjusted her position so she could sit with her back against the wall. The community board at Coffee Chum suddenly popped to the front of her mind. Many people had pinned adverts for roommates, part-time jobs and missing pets on the board but there had been the occasional class advert. One for yoga was prominent in Alexandra's memory; she remembered the conversation she'd had with the woman who'd run the class. *Focus on breathing*, she instructed herself and drew in a deep breath. Holding it, she counted to ten before exhaling, and for a few minutes, Alexandra followed this pattern before she was able to lose herself in a trance. Distantly she was aware of her ankle itching but she was able to ignore it. She had to learn the Source alone and giving in to distractions would get her nowhere. There would always be distractions; she just needed to learn with how to ignore them.

As Alexandra slowly began to fall deeper into her trance, she began to sense a power radiating deep within her consciousness. An orb of faint light flickered within, and as she focused on it, she saw that it resembled a mass of knots. She almost broke her concentration as she looked at the orb in frustration, it was such a mess how was she ever going to unravel it? Had her Source shrunk in upon itself and become a tangled mess because she had neglected it for so long? *I need mother...I can never unravel this mess by myself – I don't even know how!* Instantly the light of the orb began to waver, and she snatched her concentration back so as not to lose it. Taking a deep breath, she pushed the thoughts away and turned her attention back to the orb of her Source. Using her mind, she prodded at the orb of knots, gradually coaxing a thread of light loose. Energy flooded through her veins, she could almost see herself flooding with the light of her Source as it trickled through her, but even she could see it was weak.

When Alexandra eventually opened her eyes she let out a small cry of excitement, bobbing lazily in front of her was a tiny ball of light. It was no bigger than her thumbnail, but it was a start at least. Her joy was short lived when she tried to stand up and almost crumpled into a heap on the floor. *Get up,* a voice in Alexandra's head pleaded with her. The small ball of light was beginning to flicker, and she looked at it in a panic. No one knew she was deep in the labyrinth beneath the castle. It had seemed like a good place to practice at first. But now she could see the foolishness of her idea; no one knew where she was. If something happened to her, when she was truly alone. *Get up and get to Carlyle's chambers.* The ball of light flared brightly and began to move slowly in the direction she was sure she had come. Forcing herself to stand Alexandra hugged the wall as she followed the light which would flicker every so often. Focusing intently on it she managed to keep the ball of light alive as she followed it back up. She didn't recognise the twists and turns, but she realised she had foolishly paid little attention to how far beneath the castle she had gone. *Just get back to Carlyle's chambers,* she told herself continuing to follow the ball of light. Leaning against the wall, Alexandra fought to regain her breath, and she almost slumped to the ground once more. The ball of light hovered around the curve of a staircase, but she had no idea how far up it went. *Just keep going,* she told herself.

As she finally reached the top of the staircase, Alexandra fought back the urge to cry with joy and relief. Silently she thanked the ball of light as it flickered out plunging her into the thick darkness of the tunnel. Her hands fumbled along the door seeking out the handle, and she was dismayed to find she would have to pull it open. *Carlyle cannot find me here;* she thought fighting to pull the door open. *He will be suspicious – he may even suspect I have discovered the truth.* The thought of what Carlyle might do gave Alexandra a short burst of adrenaline, and she managed to pull the door open, almost falling backwards as she let go of the handle. Looking around Alexandra was startled to find that she was not in the main hallway as she had expected but her rather her dressing chamber. *Carlyle told me there were secret passages to his chambers, did my Source really lead me this way?* Too exhausted to dwell on the thought Alexandra shut the door and moved towards the main chamber. With each step she took exhaustion tugged at her followed by waves of dizzying sickness. With a strangled groan she fell onto the ground and curled up into a tight ball, shivering despite the warmth in the air. She tried to keep her eyes open but they cemented themselves shut and she was enveloped in a thick shroud of silent darkness.

'Alexandra!' Dimly she was aware of the urgency of the voice calling out to her in the distance, but she had no energy to open her eyes nor lift her head in answer. 'Alexandra!' *Please leave me be,* she begged. 'Alexandra open your eyes!' Strong hands gripped her arms and gently eased her in to an upright position, but still Alexandra could not open her eyes and her head lolled uselessly to the side. 'Goddess what have you been doing?'

Something cold and unpleasant splashed her and Alexandra's eyes opened from the shock of the sudden cold.

'Carlyle?'

'Ssh,' Alexandra blinked her eyes trying to clear the blurred spots. Carlyle sat beside her, one arm supporting her while his free hand pressed a cup to her lips. 'Drink this.' Most of the water streamed down her front but Alexandra managed to gulp down a few clumsy mouthfuls. She put up no resistance as Carlyle scooped her into his arms and carried her from the dressing chamber. As her feet touched the ground she swayed from side to side slightly, her hands reaching out to grip Carlyle for support. It wasn't until warm water lapped against her skin that she realised she was bare.

'What are you doing?'

'You were drenched in sweat when I found you. What in the name of the Goddess have you been doing?' Carlyle scolded lightly, but Alexandra could tell he was more frightened than angry with her.

'Nothing, I – I had gone for a walk. I thought perhaps I could dress into something nice for dinner but suddenly felt sick. I do not remember anything else.'

'Alexandra you *must* be careful. If anything should happen to you or our son I would never forgive myself. Rhonwyn believes that confinement would do you more harm than good, but I am not so sure.' Alexandra shook her head in silently protest as Carlyle gently washed her.

'I need to be able to move about Carlyle; I will be careful I give you my word.' Exhausted she leant against him, surprised at how soothing she felt his touch at that moment. *I must be ill,* she thought drily.

'It is nice you are being so compliant for a change,' Carlyle half-jested as he sat her on the edge of the bath and helped her to dry and dress. 'Alexandra I do not know what I need to do to convince you that I love you, but please be careful.' As Carlyle gathered her into his arms once more Alexandra nestled against him, feeling sleep tugging at her. She was surprised at how much the bath had helped. She was still exhausted, but the sickness had eased at least. *This is ludicrous;* she thought fighting back laughter. *We are acting as if we are a normal married couple.* 'I have work to do, but I will stay here in case you have need of me.' Alexandra felt the softness of the bed sinking beneath her weight, and the heavy warmth of blankets as Carlyle tucked them around her.

'Thank you,' she mumbled sleepily as she was absorbed into the enveloping warmth of sleep.

*'Alexandra?' When she opened her eyes, she found herself not staring into Carlyle's sapphire eyes but the bright emerald green of her mother's. 'My darling you look dreadful!' Alexandra smiled sheepishly as her mother drew her tightly into her arms.*

*'Is this a dream again?' Had it really been several moons since she had last spoken to her mother? She had received very few letters from her family and friends in Karstares, and the few she had received had been read by Carlyle before she had received them. Ismenya smiled sadly at Alexandra's question, and she felt the small flare of hope die within. She knew it was a dream, but part of her could not help hoping.* I am queen now...I am bound to Saphyre and cannot leave. *The realisation that she would most likely never see her mother again tore through Alexandra, and she choked back a sob.*

*'My darling what is wrong?' Ismenya gathered Alexandra into her arms, the warmth and smell of her mother was so real Alexandra could not bring herself to quite accept she was dreaming. 'Has he − Carlyle...has he harmed you?'*

*'No,' Alexandra shook her head. 'I loathe him but...' She shook her head not wishing to speak of her marriage; she did not want her mother to feel more guilt for Alexandra's predicament. 'Mother...I am pregnant,' she buried her face into Ismenya's shoulder too frightened to witness her reaction. 'I am so sorry!'*

*'Why in the name of the Goddess are you sorry?' Ismenya laughed pushing Alexandra back and clasping the side of her face firmly with both hands. 'My darling this is wonderful news!' Alexandra shook her head in confusion; how could carrying the child of a tyrant, one who was a powerful sorcerer who could raise a bird from the dead, be good news? 'Alexandra it is your duty as his wife, as Saphyre's Queen, to produce an heir − you are fulfilling your duty. You cannot punish yourself for that. It is I who should apologise; I should have done more to protect you. Both against Carlyle and Mathe...' Alexandra blushed faintly at the mention of Mathe. Both women sensed it was a subject too painful to discuss, Alexandra could not help feeling resentful that he had married and gotten his wife pregnant with child so quickly. Just how long had he waited until she had disappeared before he had met her?* Perhaps he had been with her while we were together, *Alexandra shoved the thoughts aside. It did not matter when*

*Mathe met his wife, nor when they had fallen in love. He was firmly in her past. Focusing on the present, she turned her attention to their surroundings and smiled at the cluttered desk littered with scrolls, books and scraps of parchments.*

*'You never did see the point in keeping your desk tidy – if you cleared it someone would add more paperwork for you to look over.'* She thought over what she wanted to say but decided that bluntness would be her best option. *'Mother...do I have the Source?'* Ismenya seemed genuinely taken aback at the question and stared at Alexandra in open confusion.

*'Of course you do, I taught you myself alongside Mariah. How could you not remember this about yourself – Carlyle promised he would help you regain your power.'* Fury glimmered in Ismenya's eyes and Alexandra stepped back nervously.

*'Carlyle told me about the Source, even when I was on Earth but he always told me I did not have it.'* Ismenya's nostrils flared. *'Surely my power is not that much of a threat he would have to lie to me?'*

*'Your Source could just as easily rival his one day, although I see now he does have an advantage. You would never use your Source to harm people, not unless you were protecting yourself or others. After what I witnessed...'* Ismenya shook her head, her nostrils continuing to flare as she breathed. *'He is frightened; he must see you as a threat otherwise he would not foolishly keep the truth from you. There is little chance your Source could break free, but it is unpredictable...how long have you known?'*

*'Today. I had a dream I remembered...leaving.'* She wanted to tell her mother about Caleb, that he had told her she had the Source, but she had scoffed at him. I owe him an apology; *she thought then remembered he had something more substantial to loathe her for. She pushed Caleb away from her mind; she could not bring herself to dwell on him.* 'I spent the day trying to practice...'

*'You have overexerted yourself,'* Ismenya reached out to stroke Alexandra's cheek. *'Oh my darling, I had feared something had happened. I have been trying to contact with you for weeks, but my Source was blocked each time I tried.'*

*'Do you think Carlyle has been preventing you?'*

*'No. I think it is your own Source; you say it was tangled?'* Alexandra nodded, *'you have been using it subconsciously and without control. You have clearly weakened yourself today and the barrier has come down. Alexandra you must be careful you could have killed yourself – or your child!'* Alexandra looked down at her stomach overridden with guilt; would it have been the worst thing if the child did not survive? *'Alexandra!'* Ismenya scolded as she guessed Alexandra's thoughts. *'This child cannot be*

*held at fault, shame on you!' Tears blurred Alexandra's eyes, and she quickly looked away. 'I know it must be terrifying –'*

*'But you don't mother. I know that you and father did not know each other, but at least father was not a cruel tyrant that his own citizens feared. Did father keep you trapped within the castle for moons? Did he constantly lie to you? Murder people in front of you?' Fury swept through Alexandra; how dare her mother judge her when she had no idea what she had gone through since her marriage. 'This child was made by Carlyle – it may be half of me, but it is also half of him. What if I am carrying a monster?' Alexandra was gathered into her mother's arms, and she sobbed helplessly into her shoulder. 'I am terrified mother – I don't know what to do!'*

*'Your child will not be evil, do not forget that while Carlyle is their father you are their mother. As long as you love them and teach them what is right and wrong, to respect the Goddess, then you will have no need to fear them.' Alexandra nodded although she could not fully share her mother's beliefs. 'Perhaps the Goddess will bless you with a daughter; I cannot see Carlyle caring too much about a daughter's upbringing, not when he will just marry her off.' Alexandra flinched at the thought that she would one day have to put her own child through this. 'I am sure you will have some say in your daughter's marriage. Do not dwell on it too much for now. Right now you must remaster your power.'*

*'How? I cannot ask Carlyle to teach me. I do not want him to realise that I know about my Source, I do not trust him.' Ismenya hesitated biting her lip as she began absently picking up scrolls from her cluttered desk.*

*'I can teach you.' She seemed hesitant, and Alexandra worried that she was a burden to her mother. 'Five nights from now, try to lower your shield, and I will begin teaching you. But you must promise me you will do no more than unravelling your Source until then.' Alexandra nodded, it was hardly a hard promise to make. She was far too frightened to attempt it on her own again.*

# *Chapter Sixteen*

'You are learning well Alexandra,' Ismenya smiled from across her desk. There were dark circles beneath her eyes, but despite this they were bright, and she smiled widely as Alexandra set a levitating rock down on the desk gently. 'How is your practice going in Saphyre?' She had been practicing on her own for almost two moons; Ismenya had practically ordered Alexandra to practice once she was awake to regain full control of her powers.

'Well I think, it has been getting warm so I have been mostly focusing on creating small breezes to keep cool. Lighting candles…I have not done anything too big. I am afraid Carlyle will notice.'

'You should have no reason to do anything big, save your strength. Your little one may even begin wreaking havoc with your Source – both you and Giric almost drained me of mine. If this happens do not worry, Carlyle will know what it is – just pretend you are ill and exhausted. I am sure he will figure out what it is and treat it discreetly; he may even admit that it is the child. It is not unheard off for an unborn babe to possess the Source to use it within their mother's belly.' Alexandra nodded, but the thought of her child using her own Source terrified her almost as much as Carlyle discovering she knew about her power. It may not happen, focus on that problem if it arises. She told herself. 'Soon you will begin to use your Source naturally, without even giving it much thought. Be cautious of doing this in front of Carlyle.' Alexandra rolled her eyes at her mother but nodded. There had been several times where she had barely stopped herself from using her Source in front of Carlyle, but she was hardly going to admit this to her mother. 'How fares the babe?'

*'Fine, I think,' Alexandra shrugged blushing faintly. She tried to think about her pregnancy as little as possible, which was quite hard considering Carlyle's excitement and her constant sickness. 'Sorceress Rhonwyn believes the child is growing strong; she says that soon they will begin stirring.' Ismenya gave Alexandra a pointed look but seemed to decide against scolding Alexandra on the lack of emotion she showed when speaking of the child. 'I am trying not to be frightened of this child mother, but I cannot help it.' She wanted to explain about Caleb, but she feared mentioning him to anyone. Would her mother approve of such a rebellion or would she scold Alexandra further?* It does not matter what mother thinks, *Alexandra told herself.* Only I can decide on my involvement with Caleb...and I must do what is best for Saphyre. *But what was best for Saphyre? Alexandra had, had no contact with Caleb since she had revealed her pregnancy to him but it did not stop her worrying over what he, or one of his followers, might do. Nor did it stop her fearing if she was damaging his cause.*

*'You will love this child Alexandra, please believe me.'*

*'Of course,' Alexandra forced herself to smile and embracing her mother.*

Alexandra's limbs were heavy when she woke up from the dream. She had found that using her Source in sleep was more exhausting than using it when she was awake. Thankfully she could put her exhaustion down to the pregnancy when Carlyle questioned her over it. As she sat up, she found that Carlyle had already departed but had left her something to break her fast and a note asking her to join him promptly in the courtyard.

'Did Your Majesty forget that you are to go on procession today?' Helena asked smiling wickedly as she helped Alexandra to quickly wash and dress. 'Roisin and I both tried to wake you, but you could not hear us over your snores.'

'Very funny,' Alexandra said drily. 'I sometimes think my husband is right. Perhaps I am too lenient with you both.' She shared Helena's grin, she was more comfortable around both her ladies and found that she could even joke with Helena. Roisin was more open with her now and would even call Alexandra by her name, providing they were alone, but she was still too serious to joke with.

As she joined Carlyle outside, he greeted her with a gentle embrace as he helped her to mount Solas. It was a bright day, and the courtyard was filled with lush, bright green grass and colourful budding flowers. Carlyle rested his hand on Alexandra's leg squeezing it gently as he turned to face the Castle Guards who stood beside their own mounts.

'We are to move at a gentle pace; no one is to come within ten feet of the queen. If there are any repeats from our last procession than I will have your heads, and that of the peasant who dares foolishly cross our path.' Alexandra flinched at Carlyle's threat and bit her tongue to stop her from pointing out his harshness. Since her pregnancy had been formally announced a few weeks ago, he had become overbearing in his protection going so far as to question both Helena and Roisin when they approached her. Turning his attention back to Alexandra Carlyle squeezed her leg gently. 'We will stick to the main road going around the perimeter of the city. If you tire or feel ill, you are to tell me immediately.'

'Of course my lord,' Alexandra nodded demurely as she resisted twitching her leg away from his grasp. 'You look beautiful,' Carlyle kissed her hand and mounted his own horse. 'Saphyre's crown truly suits you.' Alexandra felt a faint blush creep across her cheeks and she gathered Solas's reins in to her hand. She did not feel as if she was worthy to wear the crown of Saphyre, not when she could do so little to protect the kingdom's citizens. Glancing over to Xander she saw the Castle Guard's captain scowling in disgust, had he heard Carlyle's words? *Does Caleb truly trust him?* She asked herself nodding in greeting when Xander met her eyes. What would Xander think of her if Caleb did claim the throne and she continued to be queen? Would he continue to loathe her? *His opinion of me will never change…and I doubt I will ever change my mind about him.*

'Your Majesties,' Xander bowed and led his mount towards them. 'Castle Guards are stationed in the crowd. Scouts were sent out early this morning to see if there was news of any planned activities.'

'If you loathe the Castle Guard so much why do you insist on keeping them in the public eye?' Alexandra asked as they began their procession through the city. She spoke quietly so that only Carlyle could hear her; she did not want to risk offending anyone who might overhear them.

'Those who lack the Source are cowards; they feel reassured to have their own kind in their presence. I find the Castle Guard useless, which is why I have sorcerers stationed amongst them, so our protection is guaranteed. When my great-grandfather ruled he would have culled many who did not possess the Source, but the citizens began to revolt. It disgusted him to give in to their demands; why pollute the kingdom with those who are weak and useless?'

'How can you say that?' Alexandra was unable to hide her disgust. 'Have you forgotten that I do not possess the Source? Would you rather I was culled? And what of our child, what if I give you children without the Source?' Her feelings were still extremely mixed on the child she carried; she found herself more fearful than affectionate for it. But the thought Carlyle would despise their child for something out of its control sickened her. She caught Carlyle glancing at her steadily rounding belly and his expression softened slightly. *This is a dangerous subject;* she warned herself feeling an argument brewing. She was in control of her Source; no longer was it a tangled ball lying dormant within her. Her power threaded through her veins, as much a part of her as her bloodstream and she worried that Carlyle would begin to show suspicions.

'Forgive me Alexandra. Of course, I would not wish for you to be culled, I spoke in haste.' Alexandra nodded curtly knowing that she had to let the subject drop, but she was desperate to change his mind on how he viewed those without the Source. Perhaps if she could make him see that it didn't matter whether someone possessed the Source or not, then he would be more approachable. *Impossible,* she sighed inwardly. *Carlyle's ancestors have only ever married those who have the Source – he has been brought up to believe those without it are weak and useless. I will never be able to undo that.*

The crowds were just as large as when she had first toured the city, perhaps even larger. People cheered and called out blessings as Alexandra and Carlyle rode past, many cheering for the unborn babe. Even the presence of the Castle Guards mingling with the crowd did little to subdue the jubilant citizens. *They are not even trying to blend in,* Alexandra thought surprised. She could clearly pick out the Castle Guards from the citizens, their black castle uniforms sticking out amongst the brightly dressed commoners. The procession passed without any catastrophes, and Alexandra felt herself relaxing. They passed through the Temple District, Marketplace and Docks before Carlyle broke into a gallop along the shore where the crowds had decided against gathering. The tide was unpredictable, and people had preferred the safety of the main road within the city, giving Alexandra a break from the overwhelming roars of cheering.

Deciding that it was a tranquil spot for lunch, Carlyle ordered everyone to dismount and keep watch. Grabbing his saddlebag and a blanket from Alexandra's he led her away from the guards and sorcerers, spreading the blanket a few feet from where the water met the sand. The kitchen staff had packed them a variety of cold meats, fruit, bread, wine and a cordial concocted from mint, elderflower and a small amount of honey for Alexandra. As they ate their meal together, she looked over at the large crowd of slaves, grooms, and guards. They seemed to keep to their own groups; the slaves looked tired and weary as they had been walking the whole time while the Castle Guards were used to such physical exertion. Her eyes sought out Helena and Roisin who, although her ladies, were ordered to stay at the back with the rest of the slaves. They were both slumped on the ground, lying on their backs and staring at the sky.

'Perhaps we could rest, just for a little bit?' Alexandra asked stopping Carlyle from rising, he looked at her in concern, and she smiled. 'I am not tired, not much. But it is peaceful here.' She felt well enough to continue, but she wanted to give the rest of their entourage a good chance to rest, especially those on foot.

'Very well but we cannot rest for too long.' Taking her crown off Alexandra set it carefully on her lap and ran a hand through her hair, enjoying the light breeze tickling through the strands. Carlyle picked up the golden circlet, his expression suddenly heavy. *It must be strange for him to see another woman wearing it,* Alexandra had never really thought about her crown in such a way before. How did Carlyle feel about her wearing it? She touched the locket at her throat suddenly conscious of its previous owner. Placing the crown back on her head Carlyle helped Alexandra to her feet, snapping his fingers for a slave to pack up their blanket and discarded food. Alexandra was about to protest but caught sight of the slaves; they had already risen and were patiently waiting to continue the procession. The streets were just as busy, perhaps more so, as Alexandra and Carlyle made their way through the rest of the city. The sun was beginning to lower in the sky, and Alexandra sent a silent prayer to the Goddess thanking her an uneventful day as the castle loomed ahead.

'Death to the usurper!' A hushed silence immediately fell upon the crowd, and Alexandra turned to look at Carlyle nervously. His jaw was clenched, and his eyes blazed with anger. Electricity crackled across Carlyle's hands, and Alexandra moved Solas closer to his own mount so she could rest her hand over his. She could feel his Source tingling painfully against the palms of her hand, and she fought back the urge to use her own power to quell his. Mercifully the crackling energy ceased although the rage was still clear in his eyes.

'My lord if you give an order to these men there will be carnage.' She whispered urgently, 'it could spark a riot, and we will both be dragged from our mounts if they have not already thrown us off in fright.'

'Which of you is foolish enough to slander me?' Carlyle bellowed dismounting and glaring at the crowd. Those closest to him shrank back and Alexandra closed her eyes squeezing Solas's reins tightly. 'Foréignean find the fool who thinks they can speak out against their *true* king.' Alexandra looked over startled to see Foréignean emerging from the crowd; she had not even noticed the Commander of Castle Sorcerers within their entourage or the crowds. It was not long before a man was sent screaming to the front of the crowd, a wicked grin on Foréignean's face as he forced the man to his knees. Carlyle scowled down at the man, his face a mixture of open disgust and loathing. 'Captain take care of this pitiful fool.' Carlyle mounted his horse once more and glared at the terrified people below. 'I will not tolerate this nonsense; *I* am the rightful King of Saphyre. Your Queen carries *my* heir – your future king.' *Please do not bring my child into your madness,* Alexandra thought bitterly. From the corner of her eye, she saw the sunlight glint off Xander's sword as he withdrew it from his scabbard.

'Wait!' Xander paused and glanced at Alexandra, his eyes full of suspicion. Carlyle too glared at her, a warning threat in his sapphire eyes. 'My lord please - as a favour to me spare this man's life. I do not want our child born into a kingdom of fear. Let the Goddess show him the error of his ways, not the blade of a sword. He will learn nothing in death.' The silence of the crowd was deafening, and Alexandra forced her expression to stay neutral, she would not plead with Carlyle and allow him to manipulate her to look weak in front of everyone. Curtly he nodded to her before turning his attention to Xander.

'Shackle him and have him brought to the castle.' He ordered, his eyes scanning the crowd. 'Your Queen is merciful, but keep in mind *I* am not. I will not tolerate falsehoods about my reign.'

The remainder of the journey was tense, people no longer cheered and many had chosen to disperse quietly before trouble broke out. Alexandra flittered nervous glances towards Carlyle but he seemed to have reined in his temper. When they finally reached the castle, Alexandra dismounted quickly and watched as Carlyle stormed inside. Helena and Roisin appeared beside her, both looking exhausted and weary.

'Go,' she told them quietly casting a nervous glance towards the castle. 'Perhaps for tonight, you could sleep in my chamber?' She did not want to risk Carlyle taking his anger out on either of her ladies. 'I will be fine,' she reassured them catching the nervous glance they both exchanged. She found Carlyle sitting in his study, his fingers drumming angrily against the solid oak desk. 'My lord?' Carefully she approached him, resting a hand on his shoulder and squeezing it gently. She was startled to find his tunic damp with sweat. 'It was just one person.'

'It only takes *one*,' his voice was stony but he squeezed Alexandra's hand and pulled her around so she could perch on his desk and face him. 'Threats were made against you before your coronation and now peasants publicly shame me in my own capital. How long before there is a full-blown riot Alexandra? Do you know what this could do to Saphyre? To our child?'

'I realise I do not know as much as I should about Saphyre, but it sounds like there has been some sort of underground group for decades. Why should they worry you know?' Alexandra picked her words carefully so she would not reveal how much truly knew about Caleb and his organisation. 'Carlyle you have given our people little reason to love you – you murdered a man at our wedding. How many others have been killed needlessly just because they spoke against you?'

'It is *treason* –'

'Carlyle you cannot expect obedience and the love of our people when giving nothing in return.' Alexandra snapped firmly. 'Our people rarely see us outside of the castle – at least I have had the excuse of been forcibly confined to the castle walls. Why do you neglect to go out?' She could see that her Carlyle begrudgingly agreed with her as he nodded slowly. 'Our people need to see us more. Tomorrow I will go into the city and pray at the temple; perhaps you could accompany me?'

'I have council every day Alexandra; I cannot neglect my duties to go and *pray*.' Carlyle's lip curled in disgust at the thought. 'You should not be superstitious, what good can come from a day spent on your knees in prayer?'

'You are not religious?' Alexandra asked in shock. She had given little thought to religion; she had accepted the Goddess blindly having no reason to question her existence. But as she spoke about it now with Carlyle she felt fear gripping her heart; surely this was blasphemy? *I was loyal to the temples in Karstares*, she suddenly remembered. *I prayed weekly…was I truly so devoted?* 'But you often speak of the Goddess in public and give thanks to her —'

'Religion is nonsense,' Carlyle interrupted, 'it is a useful tool to keep peasants obedient to us. They believe we are chosen by the Goddess to rule.' *Then it is not working for you; people are openly speaking against you.* Alexandra wanted to argue but kept the thought to herself. 'People choose who will rule. Five hundred years ago Saphyre would have crumbled had my ancestors not taken control of the throne.'

'If that is how you feel then I shall go alone,' Alexandra insisted. 'We need to be more visible to our people. Perhaps if the citizens feel they can trust at least one of us, then it will put these rumours of a rebellion to bed.' *Or fuel the rumours and give strength to Caleb…I am not sure which would be better.* Alexandra tried not to dwell on the thought and took her crown off so she could run a hand through her hair.

'I will permit you to go and pray but not tomorrow. Give the city a few days to forget this event; I do not want the sight of you carrying my child inspiring a riot. We will arrange for you to go with your slaves and several sorcerers after next week.'

*Alexandra studied her mother's appearance with concern. There were lines on her face which hadn't been there the previous week, more threads of grey in her dark hair and the circles beneath her eyes were painfully prominent.*

'Mother are you alright?' Alexandra noted the sickly pale pallor of Ismenya's skin, shocked by how suddenly she had lost her golden glow.

'Of course darling, I am just a little exhausted. Come now, you know our time is precious.' Her mother gestured to a bowl of purple powder on the table, 'some people think the use of powders and herbs are showy. Your husband may be one,' her eyes crinkled as she smiled, 'but never underestimate these weapons. This powder will put someone into a deep sleep; if you add a bit of your Source to it, then you strengthen its properties.' Dipping her hand into the bowl Ismenya pulled out a handful of the purple powder, Alexandra watched her curiously as the powder began to glow before returning to normal. 'Your Source can be stolen,' Ismenya warned emptying the powder off her hand and into a second bowl. 'Having items such as this in reserve can be the difference between life and death.'

'Do you think Carlyle would steal my Source?' Alexandra tried not to ask herself this question frightened that the answer was blindingly obvious.

'I sometimes wonder if he would bind it to you and prevent you from using it. As long as he does not suspect you know the truth, then your Source should be safe.' Her mother gave her a warning look, and Alexandra fidgeted nervously. 'But you had best protect yourself just in case he decides he does not want you to learn the full power of your Source.' Leaning down Ismenya kissed Alexandra on both cheeks, 'be careful my daughter.'

# *Chapter Seventeen*

Carlyle fussed over Alexandra as she fought back a fresh wave of morning sickness. Rhonwyn stood over a boiling cauldron stirring it as she mixed a potion to settle Alexandra's stomach. Despite the warm weather the hearth was filled with a roaring fire, and her skin was covered in a sheen of sweat from the heat.

'Surely the sickness should have passed by now?' Carlyle rarely showed emotions in front of anyone other than Alexandra, and even that could be rare, but the concern in his voice was clear.

'Not necessarily Your Majesty,' Rhonwyn replied as she brought over the potion. 'Some women can experience the sickness close to the birth,' she shared a wry smile with Alexandra. 'I believe your own mother suffered terribly with you.' While Alexandra could see that Rhonwyn had said this to lighten the mood, it did little to alleviate her fears. *The child is already taking after Carlyle?* She thought swallowing bile. *That cannot bode well surely?* She gulped back the foul-tasting potion; she had drunk so many by now that she no longer gagged and was able to knock it back almost in one go. 'Your Majesty I know you think the Queen should stay in bed today, but I assure you that a trip to the city will do her more good. She needs fresh air and plenty of exercise.' It was a mark of how valued the sorcerers were to Carlyle that Rhonwyn felt she could speak her mind almost freely in front of him. *It is almost as if she is an ally,*

Alexandra thought wistfully, but she could still not allow herself to grow close to the Castle Sorcerers. She couldn't bring herself to trust them, especially after she had witnessed Foréignean's treatment of the man who had shouted usurper at Carlyle during the procession. *Rhonwyn does not seem like that kind of person...she is a healer, surely that means she uses her Source for good?*

'Am I too reliant on these?' She asked Rhonwyn as she handed back the cup. 'Is there any danger it could harm the baby?'

'No Your Majesty,' Rhonwyn smiled warmly. 'Councilman Lemuel's wife was reliant on these up until the day of her labour.' A dismissive grunt sounded from Carlyle's direction, and Alexandra glanced at him confused.

'Lemuel's wife bore a daughter, a child of no importance. A waste of expensive herbs,' Alexandra frowned biting her tongue to stop herself from pointing out she could be carrying a daughter. Discreetly Rhonwyn squeezed Alexandra's arm under the pretence of checking her pulse. 'Are you sure you feel well enough for the journey?'

'Yes,' Alexandra nodded her face set with determination. 'Rhonwyn's potions always work, I feel better already.' She wanted to argue that if Rhonwyn thought it was a good idea for her to go out then she should. But she feared if something went wrong then Carlyle would hold Rhonwyn responsible. While she kept her distance from the woman, she did not want something to befall her because of Alexandra's own stupidity.

'You will have a mixture of Castle Guards and Sorcerers accompanying you; Captain Xander will be your visible escort.' Carlyle rested Alexandra's hand on his arm as he led her down to the courtyard where Solas was waiting. 'If there are any signs of a disturbance you are to come straight back.'

'Of course my lord,' Alexandra nodded and watched as Xander and two of his guards mounted their own horses. The two guards reached down to help Helena and Roisin so they could ride behind, Alexandra smiled at Helena's nervous expression as the horse began to move forwards. As she was not out on a formal occasion, Alexandra was able to see the city in its natural state for the first time. Citizens of varying classes went to and fro on their daily business, barely paying attention to the group of nobles on their horses. Although Alexandra had dressed in rich fabrics, she had made sure the outfit was simple so she would be comfortable in the warm weather and she had neglected to wear her crown hoping it would distract people from looking too closely at the travelling party. Xander rode almost at her level, keeping his horse a few discreet paces just behind the head of her own. Despite her loathing for the man, Alexandra found herself yearning to question him about Caleb; how was he? *Where* was he? Did he loathe her for what she had done? *I could not stop myself falling pregnant,* Alexandra thought sadly. *I did not do this on purpose.* Somehow she managed to keep the questions down; she couldn't betray him any more than she already had. As they arrived at the mountainous steps of the temple her eyes filled with apprehension, the weather was quite warm now, and her belly was noticeably bigger. It had been hard enough walking these steps in the winter and without a child growing within.

'Your majesty should not attempt such a climb in this heat, especially in such a fragile condition.' Xander had clearly taken note of the glimmer of fear and doubt in Alexandra's eyes, but far from concern, his voice was as hard and cold as steel.

'When I would like your opinion, *captain*, I will ask for it.' Alexandra blushed at the authoritative tone to her voice and glanced over to Helena and Roisin. She was conscious that she sounded like Carlyle and she cringed inwardly. Looking back up at the mountain of stairs she swallowed a lump of bile; the air was impossibly still, and already her face was shining with perspiration. 'Oh!' She cried out as she felt a flutter in her belly, she pressed a hand to the babe and looked at her two ladies.

'Your majesty?' Roisin reached Alexandra first, gripping her elbow as Helena fished through a saddlebag for the countless potions Carlyle had insisted they bring should she grow ill once more.

'The baby – it is kicking!' Alexandra winced as the child within kicked against her once more, but she smiled nonetheless. Every day since she had discovered her pregnancy Alexandra had thought about the child from the moment she woke up to the moment she fell asleep. Even in her dreams, the child had never been far from her mind. But she had never felt any attachment to it; the child had been a phantom of fear. But as it began to move within she felt a surge of love sweep through her. *I have only ever seen this child as a threat – but how could something which has not yet taken its first breath be a threat to anyone?* Her smile widened as the child kicked her once more as if agreeing with Alexandra and scolding her for being so presumptuous. Surprising her mistress Roisin gently rested her hand over the bump and cooed as it kicked lightly against her hand. Still smiling Alexandra looked up at Xander, suddenly holding herself protectively. Whilst Helena joined Roisin in cooing over the child, the captain of the Castle Guards and confidant of the rebel leader had a dark and thunderous look etched upon his face. *He really does see my child is a threat to Caleb*. How could she help Caleb and protect her child when people like Xander obviously saw them as a threat? Helena looked up to catch the look on Xander's face, gently she tugged Alexandra forwards, and they began their long ascent up to the temple. Only a quarter of the way up Alexandra had to pause; beads of sweat were trickling down her back and between her shoulder blades.

'Your majesty perhaps we should return to the castle and pray at the temple there? It would be cooler and far more comfortable for you.'

'No. I'll be fine,' Helena had given her an idea and Alexandra smiled at the opportunity to practice her Source. She forced herself to resume the long ascent, but she cast her mind elsewhere. Casting her Source out she searched for the slightest trace of a breeze and found one not too far away in a small cluster of trees, reaching out with her Source she tugged a few threads of the breeze in the direction of the climbing group. Out of the corner of her eye, she saw Xander, Helena and Roisin glance at her momentarily. Both her ladies kept silent at the sudden coolness in the air, Xander was not so tactful.

'This is an unnatural breeze,' he shot a look at a group of travelling men behind them, and Alexandra guessed these were some of the Castle Sorcerers, Carlyle had assigned to travel with her. 'It stinks of the Source; there may be enemies about who wish to cause you harm.'

'I have no doubt of that,' Alexandra met Xander's eyes firmly forcing him to look away. 'My enemies will not harm me with magic; my lord husband could easily trace it back to them. It is just a simple breeze, captain.' The rest of the climb was far easier with the breeze, but Alexandra remained hot and uncomfortable and by the time they reached the top she was almost drenched in sweat. A Castle Guard uncorked a lambskin pouch filled with water and Alexandra accepted it with a grateful smile. With the guard's approval, she shared the water between her ladies, the three taking their time until they were rested before approaching the temple. The temple priest, the same man who had performed her marriage and coronation ceremony, greeted her with a deep bow and kissed her hand.

'Your Majesty you do us a great honour by visiting the temple. I have never had the opportunity to introduce myself; I am Father Dóchas.'

'It is a pleasure to meet you, Father,' Alexandra smiled and followed the priest into the temple. She turned to glance at Xander and the sorcerer beside him. 'I think I will be perfectly safe inside the temple, perhaps you will allow me some privacy while I pray?'

'You would be more than welcome to join me in my prayer chamber, Your Majesty if this would ease the minds of your escort?' Glancing at her ladies and the rest of the small group Alexandra could see this thought did rest better with them. *Do they really think something will happen in the temple?* Turning back to Father Dóchas she smiled warmly and nodded.

'I would be honoured to join you, Father.' Father Dóchas guided her to a small windowless room of dazzling white marble. In the ceiling was a hole filled which allowed the sun to filter in, but despite the bright sunlight, the air within the room was pleasantly cool. Alexandra knelt beside the priest in front of an altar covered in a green silk cloth, edged in gold. A statue of the goddess carved from rich jade and standing at four foot stood on top of the table; she appeared to be looking down at the two worshippers; her golden lips turned upwards in a gentle smile.

'Your majesty I would like to ask you for your forgiveness in the part I have played in your marriage.' Alexandra's head sharply turned so that she could look at the priest; trying to see if he was mocking her or luring her into a cruel trap. But there was no hint of mockery or cruelty in his lively eyes. She took in the beads of perspiration around his bald crown; he had a plump build and gave the impression of someone who was quite jolly. 'I know you follow our cause,' his voice was a low whisper and as he spoke, he turned to look back up at the statue. Alexandra followed his lead, confusion welling up within her.

'Thank you Father, but I do not hold you in any way responsible for my marriage, nor my coronation. You were simply doing your duty to our sovereign lord; I imagine it was just as hard for you.' She felt a surge of guilt as the babe kicked against her womb once more, it was beginning to grow uncomfortable, and she shifted her position ever so slightly. 'I fear I may have destroyed your cause...' She gasped at yet another kick and braced herself for more, thankfully the child seemed to grow bored and left her in peace.

'Of course the joyous news of your condition has spread throughout the kingdom by now, but I must confess that Caleb visited me after your last...encounter.' Father Dóchas paused as he seemed to turn over what he wanted to say in his head. 'May I speak frankly with you, Your Majesty?'

'Please...but I would prefer if you called me Alexandra. At least in private?' Father Dóchas bowed his head, a small smile crossing his lips.

'Should the time arise I expect both you and Caleb will be quite unconventional rulers when it comes to upholding traditions.' Alexandra blushed hoping that this was a compliment at least. She braced herself for what the priest wanted to say, not entirely sure if it was something she would be wanting to hear. But at the same time, she was sick of people telling her things that they seemed to think she *wanted* to hear. She felt as if she had spent moons living in a bubble people were too frightened to burst. She wanted the truth, not people mollycoddling her and walking around as if they stepped on eggshells. 'You understand I am sure that Caleb has great reason to loathe the child you carry. You must fear greatly for their safety?' Alexandra focused on the statue not wanting to voice her thoughts. 'Alexandra please put all thoughts that Caleb would harm your child from your mind. He cares a great deal for you and wants to protect you, *both* of you.'

'But protecting us would only jeopardise his cause. It could set him back another generation at least.' Tears of guilt burned Alexandra's eyes and she looked away wiping at them furiously. Why did she feel so guilty? She knew she could have done nothing to prevent her pregnancy, not when Carlyle insisted they lie together each night. Even now he insisted they continue coupling, although mercifully not every night.

'That is, of course, a risk; nevertheless both Caleb and I frequently pray that the Goddess blesses you with a healthy baby girl.' Alexandra grinned despite herself, she knew a daughter would make Carlyle furious, but she herself longed for a girl. *It would certainly make matters a lot simpler.* She remembered his reaction only hours ago when Rhonwyn had spoken of the wife of a councilman and how she had birthed a daughter. What would Carlyle do if she gave birth to a daughter and not the son he so obviously longed for?

'I am not sure how the king would take such news, I am sure if he could he would pass a law to make it treason to wish for a daughter over a son.' She was only half-joking but shared a small smile with the priest.

'I can assure you the king would do no such thing.' Alexandra looked up sharply at the familiar voice; her blood chilled for a split second she thought Carlyle towered over her. 'Alexandra, it is good to see you.' Caleb pulled her to her feet and enveloped her in a warm hug. The anger she had harboured at him for lying to her dissolved instantly, and she hugged him fiercely back. 'Please, can you forgive me? I should have been honest with you from the outset…'

'Yes you *should*,' Alexandra scolded him lightly and took a seat at Caleb's gesture. She didn't notice Father Dóchas slip from the room and was surprised when she turned to speak to him only to find he was not there. *Had he arranged for Caleb to come here today?* 'You should have been honest with me from the start Caleb. But I am sorry I overreacted, I just desperately wanted to return to Karstares.' Silence descended between the two and Alexandra looked down at her hands cupping her belly in an almost protective manner.

'Congratulations,' Caleb nodded towards her stomach and smiled wryly. 'Just please do not have a son.' Alexandra smiled dryly; she knew that he was only jesting but what would happen if she did have a son? Caleb picked up her hand and squeezed it tightly, when Alexandra looked at him she was surprised to see he was blushing. 'I have missed you. I was at your coronation; you looked truly beautiful…' She could see he wanted to say something else but seemed to decide against it. 'How does it feel to be the True Queen of Saphyre?' Alexandra pulled a face rolling her eyes.

'I have no more authority than when I was a Princess of Karstares,' she sighed with a small shrug. 'I was able to convince Carlyle that we should be seen more in the public, I am going to come to the temple at least once a moon to pray.' Caleb nodded in approval.

'It would be good for the people to recognise you and to see that someone is on their side.' Alexandra shifted in her seat feeling slightly uncomfortable from being in the same position for so long. 'How long until...' Caleb gestured, and Alexandra shook her head.

'Five moons I believe, but the healer who has been attending me cannot be completely sure.' Alexandra thought about Rhonwyn, how the woman seemed to be unlike any of Carlyle's other sorcerers – or at least most of the ones she had been in contact with. 'This healer...I think she may be someone who could help you but I would not know how to even approach the subject.'

'I have someone who can approach her if they think it is safe to do so. Will you tell me her name?' Alexandra bit the inside of her cheek as she thought the simple request over; what if landed Rhonwyn in trouble? Or what if she was wrong about the other woman? 'Alexandra I have spent my life dealing with these risks, I promise you my people will only approach her if it is safe to do so. Both for her and us.'

'Rhonwyn,' she breathed and flicked her eyes to the Goddess. *Please Goddess, please do not say I have just signed her death warrant.*

'Thank you,' Caleb stooped to kiss Alexandra on the cheek and she pulled back startled at the sudden intimacy between them. 'Do not think about my cause, for now, try to put it out of your mind. I give you my word that I shall do my best to ensure the safety of you and your child, you have nothing to fear from us.' At the sound of a door opening, Alexandra jumped up, frightened that someone had discovered them. Father Dóchas smiled at her in apology and gestured for her to take her seat once more when she turned to speak to Caleb she found he had already departed.

'He knows better than to stay in one place for too long,' the priest shrugged.

'I did not get to tell him that he was right,' Alexandra sighed. 'He thought I had the Source, he told me moons ago, but I did not believe him...'

'If I can be sure that the knowledge he was right about something will not go to his head then I will tell him.' Alexandra laughed and felt herself relax. 'When I heard that you would be visiting today I told Caleb, I thought he would want to be here – to see you. I hope you do not mind.'

'Of course not, I am grateful that I have had the chance to talk with him.' Looking up at the hole in the ceiling she could see that the sun was lowering in the sky, casting the room in shadows. 'I had not realised how late it was.' Alexandra stood up thanking the priest for his time.

'Please, it is a pleasure that you wish to visit us. His Majesty rarely visits the temple, even on holy days his visits are sparse.'

'I fear I will be able to do little to change his mind on this matter, but I will gladly come and pray if it will not disturb others.'

'No one will mind the disturbance but I should warn you…a crowd has already gathered.' Father Dóchas rested his hand on Alexandra's shoulder making her pause mid-step. 'Captain Xander has ordered the temple doors shut; he feared a riot might break out.'

'He had no right!' Alexandra hissed storming into the temple's hall. The temple was shrouded in darkness and her footsteps echoed through the cavernous room as she strode across the marble floor.

'The commoners have heard you are here,' Xander's face was stone, but his cold eyes revealed he was annoyed by the situation and possible threat.

'They will not harm us.' Alexandra replied firmly wondering if he knew Caleb had been present.

'You do not know that!' Xander hissed, 'these people are from the poorest slums –' Alexandra tuned out the rest of his protests and turned to see Father Dóchas talking to several monks close by, she strode over to him with Xander close by.

'Is it true?' She asked the priest, 'the people outside are from the poorest slums?'

'Yes,' Father Dóchas nodded. 'I can assure you, Your Majesty that they mean you no harm – this year has been the most they have seen of their monarchs for a long time. They are merely curious to see you for themselves without your husband close by. You have shown genuine kindness to them where His Majesty has shown them nothing of the sort.' Alexandra nodded thoughtfully and spun her wedding ring around absently. *I was lucky in Bournemouth…I had the diamonds to ensure I lived comfortably.*

*Without those, I would have had nothing…I doubt my job would have paid all the bills. Why did I not bring them with me?*

'I would like to meet them.' She said firmly.

'Do not be so *foolish*!' Xander snapped at her with blazing steel eyes, 'these people are *peasants*, they carry filth and disease –'

'Captain you will hold your tongue,' Alexandra snapped clenching her fists as she glowered at Xander. She couldn't help but feel sorry for these people. 'Please Father; will you open the door so that I may meet them?'

'Your majesty the folk will expect alms,' Roisin spoke up as she and Helena joined them from their prayers. Alexandra nodded, once again admonishing herself for not bringing the pouch of diamonds.

'Father do you have a coffer?' She asked as she drew Father Dóchas to the side with an apologetic look. 'Carl – his majesty gives me no coin, and I was not prepared for this. I simply thought to pray.' She smiled ironically as she met his eyes. 'I have some diamonds from my wedding dress…they survived the journey when I ran away. If I had been thinking sensibly, I would have thought to bring them this morning, but I fear there is no time to have them brought down now. I am sorry to ask but perhaps if you could let me distribute alms then I am sure they will more than pay off my debt?'

'We do of course have coffers, but I fear the masses would leave them empty. We regularly try to distribute money among the poor, but without support from his majesty we cannot help the poor and maintain enough to keep the temple running smoothly.' Alexandra nodded catching his hint, this at least she could change, and she was sure she could do it without too much protesting from Carlyle. She was embarrassed to see tears within the priest's eyes and she looked away unsure of how to react.

'The Goddess is truly looking down on us favourably,' he said thickly. 'I will bring a chair; you should not stand for too long.'

'No, please I will be fine standing.' Although she was exhausted, she was determined to greet these people standing so they could be on the same level. Two monks rested a chest beside her and bowed deeply. 'Thank you,' she smiled at them but they had already retreated. The heavy oak doors creaked open, and Alexandra stared down towards them, blinking at the blinding sunlight. She was horrified by the sight which confronted her. Skeletal figures with hollow cheeks and sunken eyes shuffled towards her. She gave each person an oddly shaped golden disc; no more than a millimetre in thickness it appeared smooth but when she ran a thumb over the surface she could feel the outline of a crescent shape. She realised she was examining the coin intently and blushed as she nervously placed the coin in the palm of a middle-aged woman.

'Goddess bless you,' the woman bowed deeply so she could kiss Alexandra's hand before scurrying away. The day passed in a blur; people stared at Alexandra with a mixture of apprehension and wonder. When the last person had vanished from the temple, Alexandra slumped on the floor not caring if it looked improper. She was exhausted to the bone but more than that she was sickened by what she had seen.

'The king does not have time to come and distribute alms amongst the poor and sick folk,' a young monk only a few years younger than Alexandra spoke softly, as if he were trying to comfort her. *No, he just doesn't care.* She thought glumly feeling tears sting her eyes, but she didn't dare voice the thought aloud.

'I promise I will pay off my debt to the temple and that each moon I will come and distribute alms.' The young monk helped Alexandra to her feet and she thanked him quietly saying goodbye to Father Dóchas. Helena and Roisin gently took her by the arms and helped her from the temple. 'I will be fine,' she reassured them and began the descent on her own; there were still a handful of people around the temple, and she did not want them to think her weak or pampered. Pausing, Alexandra admired the view; the sea was a deep sapphire blue and flickered with flashes of the golden sun. She could make out the outlines of ships in the distance and she wondered how many people on board were escaping and how many would return to Saphyre. *What would happen if I boarded one of those ships? Carlyle and Caleb say I am bound to Saphyre until the day I die…but surely I am free to come and go as I please? I cannot be physically bound to the kingdom.* She wanted to believe herself but remembered the spell Carlyle had used to bind her to the castle. As much as she longed to board a ship sail for Karstares, she knew that she could not abandon her citizens. Surely five centuries of suffering had to come to an end? *I have to help Caleb win his throne, even if I never see Karstares again.* She rested a hand on her stomach; *I do not want my child to grow up fearing their father.* She flinched at the thought, what was the other option? For her child to grow up not knowing their father?

'You should be careful,' a strong hand rested against her back and applied a light pressure whilst another hand gripped her wrist to prevent her from falling. Alexandra gasped and felt her heart jump; she had been so lost in thought that she had not heard someone approaching. 'It is a long tumble should you fall.'

'If I did not trust your loyalty I would think you were threatening me, Captain.' Suppressing a shudder Alexandra carefully detached herself from Xander's grip, making sure to stay close to Helena and Roisin for the rest of the descent.

Carlyle seemed genuinely relieved when Alexandra reached the castle, word of the crowd at the temple had reached the castle, and he had fretted that a riot would break out. Alexandra kissed him gently and reassured him that both she and the child were fine. Lying in bed that night, entwined in Carlyle's arms, she could not shake the images of the poverty stricken people.

'Carlyle the people of Evany, *our* people, are starving!' She told him of the people she had seen, the poverty and overwhelming sense of defeat and hopelessness. But he didn't care. *What was I expecting?* She sighed inwardly; he must have known how his people were living yet he did nothing.

'This is not something that you should be concerning yourself with Alexandra, and surely you knew about the poverty? This was not your first trip into the city.'

'I know, but every time I see it…that could easily have been me in Bournemouth. We need to do something Carlyle; we cannot ignore this!' Carlyle squeezed her gently but remained silent, Alexandra could tell he was hoping that she would drop the subject. 'I am going to the temple once a moon, I will distribute alms. Hopefully, that will show our people that we care – that we want to help somehow.'

'These people should be *working*, not standing in queues and waiting for handouts.'

'Some of these people were almost dead from starvation, how can you not care? These are *your* people.'

'You are determined to make me a soft king,' Carlyle sighed in exasperation and Alexandra fought back the urge to roll her eyes. She didn't think anything would soften Carlyle. 'Fine, but do not expect me to join you on these excursions and should I hear so much as a whisper of a threat against you or our child then I will stop this foolishness immediately.'

'Thank you,' Alexandra sighed knowing that, that was the best she could hope for. As the baby began to kick once more, she tentatively readjusted Carlyle's hand so that it rested on the swell of her belly. For a few moments he sat in stunned silence, but after the fifth kick his face broke out into a wide smile, and he pulled Alexandra into a tight embrace. His hand moved to the lacings of her nightgown, and he began to tug at them before she could stop him. 'What if we hurt the baby?' She whispered nervously, her eyes meeting his timidly. Her whole body was raw with desire, the child frequently played havoc with her hormones, but she couldn't bring herself to couple with Carlyle and enjoy it.

'We will not,' he pulled her nightgown down to her waist but Alexandra held him back.

'How can you be sure? Or do you know from experience? Do you have children I am unaware of?' *Where on earth did that come from?* She thought feeling a kick of jealousy. It would not surprise her; he made no secret to the fact that whilst she had gone to their marital bed a virgin he had long since ceased to be so innocent.

'No. I am careful not to bestow a bastard whelp upon any whore I share a bed with. My bloodline is too pure to taint with the blood of commoners.' He pulled the nightgown from her completely and stared at the small rounded swell of her belly, brushing his lips against the bump.

'Carlyle…' Alexandra relaxed when he settled back, pulling Alexandra into his arms but making no further advances. Closing her eyes, Alexandra rested her head on Carlyle's shoulder as she felt the familiar tug of a Source-induced sleep.

*As Alexandra listened to her mother's guidance, she could not help focusing on Ismenya's exhausted appearance. Her skin was drawn tightly across her face, circles were prominent under her eyes, and even her hair was greying at a rapid rate.*

*'Mother is everything alright?' Alexandra asked unable to hide the concern as Ismenya paused to rub her weary eyes. 'You look exhausted.'*

'It is nothing,' Ismenya smiled. 'There has been an outbreak of a minor pox in a small village, and I have spent much of my time training new healers. It does not appear serious, but it is better to be safe than sorry.' Alexandra nodded in understanding but could not help worrying that there was more to what her mother was telling her. 'Alexandra, please do not fret, we are all perfectly fine. You must think of yourself and your child.'

'Of course mother...' Alexandra answered but knew she would not be able to relax until she saw her mother looking more healthy. Perhaps it is just age; she tried to reassure herself. Mother is hardly young of course her hair is greying. 'Are you sure you wish to continue these lessons? I am sure we could put them on hold until you have more energy?'

'I have plenty of energy,' Ismenya snapped. 'Alexandra I am sorry, I am just a bit tired. Please, I am fine and I would rather we continue your lessons for my own peace of mind. I do not like the thought that you have been without your Source for several moons.' Alexandra managed a small and reached across the table to squeeze Ismenya's hand gratefully.

# *Chapter Eighteen*

Alexandra kept her promise to Father Dóchas and would visit the city temple once a moon to distribute alms. She would often arrive early in the morning and found that she was kept busy until well after lunch. From her third visit, she took lunch with Father Dóchas in his private prayer chamber and was glad to find that Caleb would join them on these occasions. He always enquired after her health and that of her child, ensuring that both were well enough to stay for a bit before returning to the temple. Alexandra began to quickly treasure the time she spent in the temple; neither Father Dóchas nor Caleb treated her with stiff formality and she found herself relaxing and even enjoying their company. She was also relieve when she realised that Caleb truly did not hold a grudge at her for her pregnant state, nor did he seem to loathe the child but rather genuinely interested in the babe growing within.

Her lessons with Ismenya continued at night, but it was clear her mother was struggling. Alexandra tried to insist they stop, she was almost at full-strength and was confident she would be able to protect herself should the need arise. Finally, Ismenya agreed to meet once a moon and only when Alexandra pleaded that it was tiring her. It pained her to see her mother so exhausted. *Once the pox has passed, I am sure she will be back to herself again.*

As much as Alexandra enjoyed the time she was able to spend with Ismenya both women found they had to be careful with what they discussed. Alexandra yearned to enquire after her family and friends, but any news could reveal the truth to Carlyle. He would know of things before she did, if she didn't act surprised enough then he would grow suspicious.

As Alexandra's belly began to steadily swell Carlyle threw celebration after celebration. New gowns were designed and made for the pregnant queen; all in varying colours, lengths and fabrics but all made to emphasise her growing belly. The castle seemed to absorb Carlyle's exuberant mood, only Alexandra seemed to show any signs of doubt and unease. There was always one thought which plagued the back of her mind; what if she bore him a girl? She had joked about it with Caleb and Father Dóchas often when she went to the temple to distribute alms, but while they assured her child would be safe from the rebels she was not assured of its safety from Carlyle. She could not even relieve herself of her fears with Helena and Roisin; both women would dismiss the idea of a princess being born and were adamant Alexandra carried a prince.

Despite her fears, Alexandra was pleased to see the castle joyous for a change; no longer did people look at her with fear as she passed. Now people would complement her on her healthy glow and praise the Goddess for the prince that would surely soon be delivered. During the balls, she was even able to put her fears completely out of her mind and could not help laughing as Carlyle twirled her around the Great Hall as couples danced gleefully beside them. Every so often the dance would call for a change of partners, and Carlyle would hand Alexandra into the arms of one of his trusted councilman.

'Your majesty grows more radiant with each passing hour,' one such councilman, Ywain, complimented her. 'Bearing heirs suits you; we all pray that the Goddess blesses you with many more sons.' Alexandra smiled sweetly but quickly extricated herself from his arms and slipped out into the deserted hallway for a chance to rest.

'Alexandra!' At the sound of Carlyle's voice she jumped to her feet, startled at the sharpness in his tone. 'You should not wander off; I was worried about you.' Alexandra frowned; this was not the first time she had snuck from the hall to find a moment of solace. 'I apologise, I did not mean to snap. I just…I cannot explain it but I feared for you when I looked up and saw you were no longer present.'

'I just needed to rest,' Alexandra shrugged and smiled as Carlyle slumped against the wall beside her.

'No one will see us,' he shrugged, and Alexandra realised he was using his Source to keep people away from them. Drawing her close Carlyle rested a hand on her belly smiling as the baby kicked against his hand.

'I cannot wait for this child to be born,' she sighed, 'I am *exhausted.*' She had never before considered how enduring pregnancy could be; she had not slept in weeks as the baby continuously kicked against her bladder, her back felt as if it was crumbling, her whole body was beginning to feel as if it would collapse under the added weight. She was in the final moon of her pregnancy and while she feared just how much the child would turn out like Carlyle, she was eager to hold the babe and to have her body her own again. 'Carlyle…would you mind if I retired for the evening?' She turned as Carlyle's fingertips guided her face around so he could study her features. Even beneath the flawless face paint, Roisin had applied she knew that he could see the dark circles beneath her forest green eyes and her mouth was constantly twisting as she fought off the barrage of yawns. Finally, he nodded and kissed her gently.

'Let me accompany you,' he said helping her to her feet.

'There is no need,' Alexandra protested quickly. She blushed as Carlyle looked at her in surprise. 'I really just want to rest for a little. You should enjoy the rest of the ball; I will be fine. Helena and Roisin are in my private chambers; I will ask them to keep me company until your return.'

'Go straight to our chambers,' he warned as he knelt down to kiss the swelling bump. Alexandra smiled at him as she walked quickly through the hallway. She felt ridiculous trying to run with her giant protruding belly, but she wanted to reach their chamber before someone stopped to talk about the child. *I'm sure I'm more waddling rather than running*, she thought to herself with a wry smile. When she was almost at the chambers she shared with Carlyle she slowed down to a more leisurely pace. She was lost in thought as she began walking up the polished oak staircase. Soon the child would be born; she would be mother to the future heir of Saphyre (if she did indeed carry a son) and would find out how much damage she had caused Caleb.

'Alexandra!' She heard a voice calling her from the bottom of the staircase, carefully she turned to look behind her but saw there was no one there. Turning completely she took a tentative step back down, her eyes scanning the large hall for a sign the voice who had called out.

'Hello?' She called, 'Caleb?' She wasn't sure who else would call out her name, other than Carlyle, but why would he hide from her? *It can't be Caleb, he wouldn't be so foolish as to be seen in public.* Reaching for the bannister she turned to climb back up the stairs when she felt a pair of hands shove her roughly in the small of her back. She cried out as her hand slipped and missed the bannister sending her toppling down the stairs. She felt something sharp crash into her head, stomach and back several times knocking the wind from her lungs. Instinctively she tried to curl into a tight ball, but she couldn't command her limbs. Her shoulder hit the bottom stair with a sickening *crunch.* Fighting to regain her breath, to stop the black spots bursting over vision and taking hold of her, Alexandra tried to turn, to see who was at the top of the stairs but the world was a sickening blur. The last thing she was aware of as she slipped into the darkness was the terrible sensation of her body being split asunder, and a flooding of warmth between her legs.

# Chapter Nineteen

'Your Majesty she is beginning to wake,' Alexandra felt as if she were floating, but not pleasantly. Her head was limp and spun wildly, her limbs were heavy and her stomach violently rolled from side to side as if she were back on board the ship which had brought her to Saphyre. It took her a few minutes to realise that she was not on a violently rocking ship but instead lying flat on a feather filled mattress. Her throat was painfully dry and her tongue felt as if it was too large for her mouth, causing her to panic and she feared she was about to choke. She tried to open her eyes, to ask for water, but they were sealed shut.

'Leave us,' Carlyle's voice was as hard and cold as stone. *Why is he so angry?* Alexandra asked herself, he had seemed happy enough when she had left him at the ball. What could she have possibly done to push him in to this cold anger? 'Open your eyes,' Carlyle hissed and Alexandra groggily obeyed wishing that her stomach would settle down. *What has happened?* Her mind was a blue of images but she couldn't focus on any of them, she couldn't remember what had happened and why she was in bed. She remembered leaving the ball, but after that there was nothing. Carlyle's deep blue eyes loomed over her, as cold as shards of ice. 'You spiteful bitch!' His fury was palpable and Alexandra could only stare at him in bewilderment. Her eyes slowly moved away from Carlyle's furious face and took in her surroundings. She was confused to see she was in her personal chamber rather than the ones she shared with Carlyle. *Why?* Groggily Alexandra pushed herself upright, her hand grazing her stomach as she moved. *The baby!* The thought slammed into Alexandra as if she had run into a brick wall. She looked down at her belly and let out a strangled cry, it had lost its roundness and was slack. She rested her palms against her stomach but there was no steadying kick, there was no movement at all. Desperately Alexandra looked around the room for the cradle, or any sign that her child was safe.

'Where –'

'Dead.' Alexandra looked at Carlyle horrified, she felt her throat close up and tears blur her eyes. *I can't breathe;* she thought desperately trying to suck in air. She tried to move, to stand up, but Carlyle firmly held her down pressing his hands on her shoulders.

'No…no!' Alexandra shook her head, 'NO!' She hit out at Carlyle's arms, thrashing wildly against him as he tried to pin her in place. He had to be lying, but why would he lie about such cruelty? Carlyle stepped back and Alexandra felt her body freeze in position, her back sat rigidly straight and her arms sat uselessly by her sides. Her right shoulder began to ache; closing her eyes she remembered leaving the ball. *Someone called to me…Caleb?*

'It is better this way,' Carlyle's voice was distant and Alexandra opened her eyes to look at him. 'The whelp was a girl; I will not tolerate a *daughter* Alexandra. I need a *son*, I have no time for daughters.'

'You don't mean that,' Alexandra sobbed. 'Where is she? I want to see her! *I want my daughter!*' She wailed fighting against his Source, without thinking she grabbed her own Source and forced it outwards sending Carlyle flying backwards. She didn't care about discretion; she didn't care if he realised she was in full possession of her powers, all she wanted at that moment was her daughter. 'Where is she?' She screamed at him.

'Alexandra, will you calm down and pull yourself together?' Carlyle roared gripping her arms. 'It has been disposed of.' There was no warmth in his voice, no sympathy or any sign at all that he cared. Just a cold anger that made Alexandra want to strike him. 'When you have recovered and are deemed pure enough to share my bed then we will work on conceiving another child. And you had best give me a son; *alive.*' Alexandra slumped on to the floor, burying her face into her knees. Why was Carlyle being so cruel? Why could he not see that she needed comfort right now and not blame for something out of her control?

'I cannot help if I give you a daughter, I do not *choose* –'

'But you can choose whether it lives.' Carlyle hissed coldly, and Alexandra's head snapped up to meet his gaze. '*Why* did you do it?' Alexandra shook her head at a loss as to what he meant. 'You were found at the bottom of the stairs; I wondered why you did not want me to accompany you back to our chambers. I…I never thought you were capable of such cruelty.' *This from the man who kills needlessly?* Realisation dawned on Alexandra, and she shook her head searching Carlyle's face pleadingly.

'I was *pushed*.' Alexandra cried horrified that he could think she would purposefully harm their child. 'I was going to our chambers; all I wanted to do was rest. Someone called out to me – I don't know who it was but when I turned around someone *pushed* me.' Tears cascaded from her cheeks but still, Carlyle refused to relax his thunderous expression.

'I want a son next time,' he hissed, 'or I will have yours and the whelp's heads.' He stormed from the chamber slamming the door behind him. Her limbs too heavy to move Alexandra curled up into a tight ball and allowed her sobs to flow freely. How could her child be gone? How could she feel so empty when only a short while ago she had been so content? So full of life? *How could he speak so callously of our child? What does he mean by disposed of?* Alexandra longed to follow Carlyle, to plead with him to at least let her see her daughter. What had she looked like? Who had she taken after? What colour had her eyes been?

'Your Majesty?' A hand cautiously rested on Alexandra's arm, and she lifted her head ever so slightly to glare at the speaker. Roisin knelt beside her, her face full of grief and uncertainty. 'I brought you some soup.' Alexandra shook her head and tried to curl back up, but Roisin was surprisingly stern as she coaxed Alexandra upright and back into bed.

'I am not hungry.' She protested as Roisin tried to encourage her to eat the soup.

'You must eat Your Majesty –'

'I must do no such thing,' Alexandra hissed. 'Just leave me be.' Roisin curtseyed and left silently, leaving the bowl of soup on a small stand set up beside Alexandra's bed. *I had a daughter,* fresh tears trickled down Alexandra's cheeks, and she nestled against the pillows, hugging herself tightly. Had she taken a mixture of features from Alexandra and Carlyle? Had she drawn breath? *No,* Alexandra remembered the sharp push in her lower back and the painful jolt as each step had met her with force. *Caleb promised me no harm would come to us, how could he lie like that?* The thought wouldn't leave her in peace and all Alexandra could focus on was the voice that had called out to her from the bottom of the stairs. Had it been Caleb? Had he done this to her despite his promise? Or had he been trying to warn her? *Don't be ridiculous...there was no when there when I looked. That voice had been intentional, something to distract me.* Caleb had already misled her once, allowing her to believe that there had been some slim hope of her returning to Karstares. *I cannot trust him, who is to say that if I help him claim the throne, he would not just dispose of me after?* Alexandra had never given much thought as to what would happen to her if Caleb secured his claim on the throne. She had assumed she would return home. But how could she if she was bound to Saphyre? If she was the True Queen, she was hardly going to be allowed to wander off to her home kingdom...was she? Perhaps she would be better off as Carlyle's queen, as long as she gave him sons, then her life would most likely be peaceful. *Surely he did not mean his threat?* She thought rubbing her cheek against the pillow. *Does he really feel nothing for our daughter? Did he not even hold her?* What kind of life would their children have if he could act so callously towards the death of their child? She tried to tell herself that she could raise her children with enough love just from her, but could she? Carlyle had described his own mother as kind, soft and loving and yet Carlyle himself was brutal and callous. Who was to say that Alexandra would not fail like his own mother? *Who is to say Caleb would be any better? Especially if he could murder an innocent child in cold blood, just because of their father?*

Sleep began to pull at Alexandra, but she shrugged it off. Sensing that someone was trying to use their Source to lull her into sleep she put up her shields, ignoring the voice which warned her to be careful. She could not risk Carlyle discovering she was in control of her powers, not when he was so furious with her. She realised she had used too much of her Source in the blast she had sent out earlier, already she could feel her power trickling away as she fought the sleeping spell someone was trying to put her under. *You will overexert yourself...you could die.* A voice argued with her, but Alexandra ignored it. What did it matter if she lived or died? *What do I have to live for here?* She thought bitterly, *a husband I despise.*

***

Alexandra refused to leave the sanctuary of her bed for the next several days. Each day Roisin would visit her several times with food and words of comfort, but Alexandra would simply pull the blanket over her head and burrow into the mattress and pillows. Eventually, Roisin succeeded in coaxing Alexandra to break her fast one morning and even to bathe. But the sight of her deflated belly pulled Alexandra even deeper into the depths of despair. Had she even been pregnant, to begin with? The sight of her slack belly and the stretch marks across her hips, stomach, and thighs confirmed that she had indeed carried life within her. But where was her baby? Where was her daughter? Why did the Goddess continuously torment her?

'Your Majesty *please*,' Roisin begged close to hysterical tears one evening. 'His Majesty will not tolerate your grieving for much longer. You *must* get up!'

'I do not care about Carlyle,' Alexandra spat from beneath the blankets. Roisin gasped, and Alexandra peeked from beneath the blankets expecting to see Carlyle standing in the doorway ready to reprimand her, but it was only the two of them in the room. 'Where is Helena?' She asked realising that she had not seen the other woman since the night of the ball.

'His Majesty has decided that while you are recovering, you do not need two ladies serving you. She has been given other duties,' there was something pleading in the tone of Roisin's voice, but as Alexandra tried to press the issue, she changed the subject. 'Please Your Majesty I am greatly worried about you, you have barely eaten all week – Sorceress Rhonwyn wishes to visit you, but the king will not let her while you refuse to eat or even get out of bed.'

'I do not need to be examined by a healer,' Alexandra replied stonily. 'I am fine – where was she when my daughter needed her?'

'It was Sorceress Rhonwyn who found you and your daughter; she had been going to check on you to see how you fared. She tried everything she could, but it was too late. You had been at the bottom of the staircase for quite some time...I have never seen the sorceress looking so distressed…' Alexandra tried to push back the guilt and sadness. Why should she care if Rhonwyn had been upset by what she had found? *Rhonwyn would not have harmed my daughter…she spent so much time trying to make the pregnancy comfortable for me.* 'She broke the news to the king…he almost had her arrested.' *He would do that to one of his own sorcerers?* Alexandra forced herself to sit up and could see that the small movement brought enormous relief to Roisin. She gestured for Roisin to sit beside her and sat in silence, grateful that Roisin did not try to break it. *I cannot wallow,* she told herself sternly. *Goddess knows what other duties Carlyle has assigned Helena too, the mood he is in it cannot be pleasant.*

'Will you please get me something to eat? Something small…I will see Rhonwyn if she is able to attend to me.' Left alone with her thoughts Alexandra could only think of the daughter she had never met. How could Carlyle be so callous? *Surely he must care?*

Roisin returned with a bowl of soup, bread and a potion Rhonwyn had given her with the promise that the sorceress would be up soon. A handful of slaves followed Roisin with a large wooden bath, water, and sheets to line it. Alexandra was only able to eat half of the soup that had been brought up. Setting the food aside she stood up and sat on the window ledge. The sun was beginning to sink beneath the horizon turning the sky a rich, dusky pink. *How can everything look so beautiful when she is not here?* Tears blurred her eyes and she brushed them away, gripping her belly as she felt a phantom kicking within. *This is my fault; the Goddess is surely punishing me.* She had never forgotten her uncertainty at the beginning of her pregnancy, how she had questioned whether it would have been of consequence if she had not carried the child to full-term. *How could I have thought that about my own child?* As the tears fell, she no longer tried to stem them. *I am so sorry.*

'How are you feeling Your Majesty?' Alexandra turned blurry red eyes to Rhonwyn and shrugged. As she blinked to clear her vision, she was shocked to find Rhonwyn looking unkempt. Her own eyes showed evidence of crying, and her hair was slightly tangled as if she had not brushed it in days. 'Roisin said you were the one who found…us.' Rhonwyn nodded sadly, 'thank you. I am sorry for what you must have witnessed it.' Rhonwyn reached out and squeezed Alexandra's hand; it was a gesture that Alexandra deeply needed and she stood up to embrace the sorceress tightly.

'I never got to hold her, to see her.' She whispered thickly into Rhonwyn's robes. The sorceress sniffed tearily and hugged Alexandra back.

'She was beautiful Your Majesty,' Rhonwyn assured her. *This is all I wanted from Carlyle…and he could not even give me this simple gesture.* Alexandra thought bitterly. 'I am sorry, but once the king ordered her to be taken away, …we could not disobey him. Nor did we know how long you would be unconscious for, your body went into a deep sleep to help you heal.'

'Did she suffer?'

'No Your Majesty,' Rhonwyn forced a reassuring smile on her lips. 'I promise you; the Princess never suffered at all. She is with the Goddess now.' Unsure of how to reply Alexandra remained silent and turned to stare out of the window once more. 'If you feel well enough I should examine you. His Majesty has so far refused but as you are up and have requested me yourself, I can hardly disobey an order from my Queen.' Rhonwyn smiled dryly, and Alexandra nodded in reply. Roisin left to give her some privacy, confessing that she would have to let Carlyle know that Alexandra was up and feeling well enough to be seen by a healer. 'You have healed surprisingly fast,' Rhonwyn reassured Alexandra helping her to sit up. 'There is no damage internally. His Majesty will be pleased to know that there should be no issues with you conceiving in the future.'

'He cannot expect me to go through this again?' Alexandra swallowed a solid lump in her throat. Of course, he would expect her to conceive again, and most likely quite soon.

'I am sorry Your Majesty,' Rhonwyn's said. 'The king will be expecting me to update him on your progress…you should prepare yourself. He will most likely be up soon.'

Alexandra had been surprised when Carlyle had not visited her chamber that night. She had bathed and waited for him to appear, eventually falling asleep without meaning too. When she woke up, Roisin had already brought food up for her to break her fast and she wolfed it down suddenly ravenous. She had barely finished eating when Carlyle strode into her room, ordering Roisin to leave them.

'Have you stopped this foolish sulking?' He asked sitting beside her on the bed, Alexandra could only stare at him incredulously.

'Do you truly not care at all Carlyle?' She hissed at him, 'Someone pushed me down the stairs. Someone tried to kill me; they killed our *daughter*. Are you so callous that you really feel nothing but anger towards me?' She could see her words had some effect on him as his expression softened. He reached out for her hand, but Alexandra snatched it away from him. The one time she had needed comfort and solace from him, he had denied it to her. *I will never love this man,* she vowed. *I will share his bed, but he will get no more than that from me.* 'I wish to go to the temple today, to pray for our daughter.' She met Carlyle's gaze firmly refusing to ignore the daughter she had never met.

'Tomorrow.' Alexandra decided not to argue with him and simply nodded. 'I contacted your mother shortly after…' Carlyle trailed off, and Alexandra studied him intently trying to spot any sign that he cared for the child they'd lost. 'She sends her love.'

'Can I not speak to her?'

'She will write to you I am sure.' *I should not have used my Source to deflect her,* Alexandra thought guiltily. 'Get dressed and meet me in the courtyard, if you can manage a day out bed then I will not object to you travelling into the city tomorrow.' Carlyle departed leaving Alexandra alone with her thoughts. When Roisin returned, she was carrying a green gown, but Alexandra adamantly refused to wear it.

'I am in mourning,' she argued as Roisin tried to press the gown on her.

'No…you are not.' Guilt and pain was plain on Roisin's face, but she refused to look away. 'His Majesty will not allow it…as far as he is concerned your daughter did not exist. Your pregnancy was not real…' Alexandra felt as if she had been slapped and Roisin sat her on the bed, dropping the gown in an unceremonious manner as she sat beside her mistress. 'Alexandra…I was there when you woke up. After they found you and brought you to your chamber, I stayed here waiting for you to wake. When His Majesty said that he would have the head of your next child if you bore him a girl…' Roisin trailed off, her skin paling as she recalled that evening.

'He spoke out of anger surely?' Alexandra whispered horrified, 'what kind of person would kill a child purely because of their gender?'

'Forgive me for what I am about to say, but I say it only because I love and deeply respect you.' Alexandra was shocked at Roisin's frankness and nodded dumbly. 'It is probably for the best that your daughter was not born...his majesty will not tolerate a daughter, not as his firstborn.' Alexandra stood up and retched; bracing her hands on the window ledge, she leant out and sucked in deep lungful's of air. Was she truly married to such a monster? *I know I am,* she scolded herself gripping the window ledge until her knuckles turned white.

'I am not going to ignore what happened simply because Carlyle wishes it.' She replied when she had firmly gathered her emotions under control. She could feel her Source itching in reaction to her anger, alerting her to keep her temper. 'I promise I will not let any repercussions fall on to you, I will take full responsibility but I will wear black.'

Carlyle scowled when Alexandra met him in the courtyard. She was dressed in a loose black gown with delicate silver embroidery. Roisin had not been pleased at Alexandra's insistence but had given in. She firmly met Carlyle's gaze, her eyes challenging him to comment on her attire. She hit back choice words of her own; he was dressed a royal blue tunic and trousers with a pale blue shirt. The two walked through the gardens with a slight gap between them. Alexandra stared resolutely ahead, determined not to be the first one to break the silence between them.

'Rhonwyn informed me that you are healing well and should have no issues conceiving again.'

'Is that all you care about?' Alexandra made no effort to hide the disgust and outrage as she turned to look up at Carlyle. 'I have just lost our child, our *first* child, and all you care about is how quickly I will conceive again? Did you learn no compassion from your mother?' She spat.

'Alexandra, when will you get it through that thick skull of yours?' Carlyle's grip on her arm tightened painfully as they walked. 'You failed to give me a son. The fact the whelp did not survive is of no consequence. As far as I, and our kingdom, are concerned, you were never pregnant.' Alexandra yanked her arm free from Carlyle's grip and turned to storm off, but as she spun around, she found her feet were fixed firmly upon the ground. *Do not fight it;* she warned herself, *do not give him cause to suspect.* It was hard resisting the urge to use her Source to fight back, but somehow she managed to keep it buried.

'All I wanted from you was sympathy, understanding…even just a shadow of *love.*' The pain in Alexandra's voice was prominent, and she felt her heart twist painfully. 'Don't you see Carlyle? This is why I will never love you. From the moment you found me you have done nothing but lie to me – you lied about *us.* You have been cruel, and you manipulate me at every opportunity. But when I needed you most…you had only scorn for me. You still only hold scorn. That is not love Carlyle; you are incapable of ever loving…and I pity you for that.' The force cementing her feet in place suddenly vanished, and Alexandra almost stumbled forwards. Regaining her balance, she walked off. 'I will go to the temple tomorrow. I will join you after for supper.' Looking over her shoulder, she could see that her words had, had a devastating effect on Carlyle. She forced her heart to harden and departed; he deserved no sympathy.

Seeking solace in the abandoned tower, Alexandra pushed the shutters wide open to let the room air. The final moons of her pregnancy had made stairs too much of a challenge, and she had stopped her visits. Spreading a cloak on the floor, she rested a crystal ball amongst the folds and placed several candles in the wall sconces. It was early afternoon, but she had no intentions of joining Carlyle for lunch or even supper. Sitting on the floor she doubled over in pain as cramps swept through her abdomen, she rested her forehead against the coolness of the stone floor willing them to stop. Rhonwyn had told her the cramps and the bleeding would soon cease and that she should avoid strenuous activity, but Alexandra had no intentions of staying in bed until they had ceased. She doubted Carlyle would be understanding of her ailments. As the cramps lessened to an aching dullness, she sat up and closed her eyes, drawing in a deep breath she tried her best to shut her mind from thoughts and began to meditate. She was desperate to speak with Ismenya but had not yet learnt how to command dreams; she had the nagging sensation that she had never mastered that skill. *I will master it. Eventually,* she vowed before remembering she was supposed to empty her mind. Clearing her mind, she opened her eyes and focused on the crystal resting on the cloak. Gradually she coaxed her Source into the fragile orb, trying her best to summon an image of her mother.

Ismenya's face was clear in her mind, but no matter how hard she tried she could not transfer the image from her mind into the crystal. *You are overexerting yourself,* a voice warned, but Alexandra ignored it. All she could see within the crystal was a deep grey fog, and no matter how hard she tried she could not get it to disperse. *Try harder!* Alexandra frowned; she could feel beads of sweat forming across her brow and upper lip as she poured more of her power into the crystal. Waves of sickness washed over her, pressure began to form behind her eyes and squeezed her head, but she ignored the warning signs. *I need to speak –*

'Ouch!' Alexandra yelped as something sharp bit down on her hand between thumb and index finger. Shocked she looked down to see the sparrow-sized multi-colored bird Carlyle has crushed, beady eyes staring at her furiously and beak tightly clasping the fragile skin. It bit down once more in warning before flying out the window with an angry chirp. Confused Alexandra shook her hand trying wincing as she saw tiny droplets of blood. She turned back to concentrate once more, but common sense prevailed. The crystal had emptied of fog, but as Alexandra picked it up she almost dropped it in shock; it was scalding hot. *It's glowing;* she realised picking it up with the folds of her cloak so she could study it. Just how much of her Source had she poured in? Carefully she wrapped it up within her cloak; she would ask her mother about it when she finally reached her. *Surely she will make contact soon?*

Alexandra was unsurprised to find Carlyle waiting beside Solas late the following morning. She had refused to see him again the previous day, worried that he would spot the tell-tale signs that she had exhausted herself using her Source. Ignoring his offered hand, she pulled herself into Solas's saddle.

'Are you sure this is a wise decision?' Carlyle grabbed the reins before Alexandra could set off. 'Have you recovered –'

'According to you, nothing has happened.' Alexandra cut him off waspishly. 'I visit the temple every moon. Why should I not go now?' Carlyle's jaw tightened, and he stepped back as Alexandra trotted off. Xander rode beside her with two other guards, Roisin rode side saddle behind Xander, her face clear with nerves as the horse began to walk. The journey down to the temple was peaceful; Xander did not attempt to speak with her while the two guards were weary of speaking casually with their queen.

'Your Majesty it is a great relief to see you up and about,' after greeting Alexandra formally, Father Dóchas embraced her tightly in welcome. 'I cannot tell you how sorry we are for your loss. We have held prayers for you ever night in the temple – even the taverns have been sombre with grief. Evany mourns for you, Saphyre mourns for you.' Alexandra followed the priest into his private prayer chamber and took the offered seat. She bowed her head as she faced the altar, discreetly brushing away tears. Strangers mourned for the child she had lost while her own husband refused to even acknowledge her pregnancy. 'Caleb has been here every day. He has seen the mood in the city and has been greatly affected.' Caleb's name was like a knife cutting through Alexandra and she fought to keep her face passive. 'He would like to see you –'

'No.' Alexandra said quickly. 'Not yet…please.' She debated whether, to be frank or not. *What do I have to lose?* She asked herself. She had lost her daughter, as far as she was concerned there was nothing else to lose. *I could lose Caleb;* she thought feeling her throat tighten. But if her suspicions were true…she could not go on not knowing. 'Was this because of Caleb? Did he order this?'

'Of course not!' Father Dóchas seemed genuinely horrified by the question and stared at Alexandra as if she had gone insane. 'Alexandra, please believe me, Caleb had nothing to do with this. Of course, I, nor Caleb, can rule out that someone within his organisation carried out such a soulless deed – but Caleb himself would never do such a thing. He has been wracked with grief and guilt, blaming himself for what has happened. But what could he have done? He told his followers, he reassured them countless times that your child would not be a threat to their cause – but he fears he did not do enough. He has been furious – in these moments I have never seen such a rage. I fear he matches His Majesty in that respect. It seems neither man is to be crossed.'

'That does little to ease my mind,' Alexandra cried. 'How can I be sure that I am not overthrowing one tyrant only to replace him with another?' Father Dóchas nodded thoughtfully and stood up to pour them both a drink. Alexandra almost downed the goblet of wine, her head spinning almost instantaneously. It struck her that this was her first taste of alcohol since her coronation and she sipped carefully not wanting to return to the castle drunk.

'It is true you have spent little time with Caleb but answer me this. Who would you put your trust in?' Alexandra stared at the jade statue of the Goddess, determined not to be drawn into a political discussion. Who was she to determine who should run the kingdom? She could not even protect her own child. *Remember why you came,* she told herself.

'Carlyle will expect me to share his bed again soon,' she said bluntly seeing little point in being discreet. Father Dóchas had seen her bare, he had performed the ritual to make her pure for Carlyle's bed. 'I do not want to conceive, I cannot go through this again. But I have no way to refuse him.' Father Dóchas feel in to a deep silence and Alexandra feared he was either about to refuse or tell her there was no way to prevent conception, other than praying.

'There is a spell,' Father Dóchas spoke in a hushed tone after a painfully long silence. 'But if the king suspects you and can prove his suspicious then it would be seen as treason. Not even your royal blood would protect you from the death sentence.'

'Death would release me from this loathsome marriage…it would reunite me with my daughter.' Alexandra felt fresh tears sting her eyes as she felt the phantom kicking against her belly. How could she no longer be carrying life? 'Please Father; I cannot give that man an heir – not after this.' *I could not prevent myself conceiving forever…Rhonwyn has already assured him I should conceive again one day.* She shoved the thought aside, she would deal with the consequences when they arose.

'The spell is a simple one, all I need is something you can wear when the king takes you to his bed. Something inconspicuous for you *must* be wearing it when he takes you. Women of a certain…repute often wear a small piece of jewellery that they need not take off.' Alexandra's hand flew to the locket at her throat, guilt overwhelming her. The locket had been Carlyle's mothers, the one person he seemed to truly love and cherish. The locket was precious to him; could she really taint it in such a way? *My daughter was precious to me;* she thought with resolve unclasping the delicate chain. *Please, Goddess do not judge me too harshly.* She was surprised to find herself praying not just for the Goddess's forgiveness, but also that of Carlyle's mother. Would she understand why Alexandra had to take such drastic measures? She could not help but wonder if she had made the right decision, even after leaving the temple once she had distributed alms.

Supper was a subdued affair as Alexandra and Carlyle dined with stilted conversation. Roisin was left by herself to pour drinks and clear the table between courses, her hands visibly shaking at being close to Carlyle. As soon as she was able Alexandra bid Carlyle good night and headed for her chamber. Her hand twisting the locket at her throat as she walked. She was desperate to try and contact her mother once more but forced herself to wait until Roisin had departed for the night.

Under the feather mattress was the crystal ball she had tried to use the previous day. The brightly coloured sparrow flew down from the beams, perching on the window ledge so that it could observe her suspiciously. Ignoring it, Alexandra sat cross-legged on the bed and fell into a deep meditation. But no matter how hard she tried she could not contact Ismenya.

Alexandra was discovered in her chamber one morning hunched over. She glanced up to see Roisin holding out a fresh gown for the day, but she instantly discarded it to tend to her mistress.

'I am sorry Alexandra,' Roisin tried her best to comfort Alexandra as she brought her a soothing potion. Alexandra gulped the hot liquid down, thankful for the relief..

'I had hoped…' She trailed off, what could she say without sounding foolish? Her bleeding had resumed taking away any hope that she could carry that she was still with child, that everything had been a mistake.

'You can return to His Majesties bed soon…perhaps the Goddess will bless you with a child once more.' Alexandra resisted pulling at the locket, hoping that her face did not betray the guilt that she felt.

# Chapter Twenty

'What is troubling you Alexandra?' Carlyle reached across the table to take her hand, and Alexandra looked up at him blankly. 'Is it because you failed to conceive? Rhonwyn assured me that you would again, but it may take time. You should not feel guilty.'

'No…it is not that. Carlyle…I do not want to conceive, not just yet.' Alexandra looked up at him, flushing as she saw a dark cloud cross his eyes. 'I want to be sure that our child will be safe, I do not want to risk this happening again. Please…can we just see how things go?' Carlyle settled back in his chair, his fingertips drumming against the heavy oak table.

'Of course, you are right. Although there is no way to prevent you conceiving Alexandra, if it happens then it happens.' Alexandra nodded thinking silence would be the best answer. 'If it is not this which concerns you then what is it?'

'I have heard nothing from Karstares…there have been no letters nor news. You said you told my mother what happened, then why has she not at least written? I know she could contact you, just as you contacted her from Bournemouth. I know I could speak to her like that…but there is nothing. It concerns me.' Every day Alexandra had tried to contact her mother, but she had failed miserably, and her mother had seemingly made no effort to contact her while she slept. 'Please Carlyle; will you use your Source to contact her – or at least the sorcerers back in Karstares?'

'I admit I have been concerned. I have tried to contact Queen Ismenya, but Karstares seems to be blocking outside contact.' Alexandra looked at Carlyle in alarm but he only shrugged in reply. 'It is not uncommon. If there is a sickness or threat of war, then it is a way to protect the kingdom.' *Is that the reason?* Alexandra wondered but kept the thought to herself; she could not reveal to Carlyle that she knew a pox had swept through the kingdom. She wasn't sure if he was aware of the epidemic or not. 'I am sure your parents are fine. If something had happened, we would have heard by now.' *But what if it has only just happened?* Alexandra longed to ask but knew Carlyle was trying his best to allay her fears. Carlyle rose from his seat and kissed the top of her head, resting his hands on her shoulders. He squeezed them lightly in what Alexandra assumed was meant to be a reassuring gesture. 'I will try once more to contact your mother's sorcerers if we have heard nothing by the week's end than I shall write to your mother.'

'Thank you,' Alexandra smiled, but it was forced. She could not help feeling that something terrible had happened.

'Would you like to come to the council meeting with me tomorrow? We have been married almost a year, you should be more prominent in the day-to-day running of the kingdom, and it may give you something else to focus on.'

'I would like that,' Alexandra replied, surprised at how much she meant it.

The council chamber was a large circular room; several maps were dotted along the walls, and the only furnishings was a large circular table with ten chairs seated around it. Carlyle's five councilmen were already seated when both he and Alexandra entered the room, quickly they leapt to their feet and bowed deeply to both monarchs. Alexandra felt weary as she caught the look of suspicion and disdain on Ywain's face. She glanced at the empty seats and bit back a torrent of questions. She had been introduced to Carlyle's councilmen in the past but had little interaction with them; she had been unaware that there were fewer councilmen than there should be. Carlyle claimed a throne-like chair and gestured for Ywain to vacate the seat immediately on Carlyle's right so that Alexandra was seated beside him.

'It is a pleasure to see you have recovered Your Majesty,' Jacen greeted her warmly as Alexandra took the offered chair.

'Thank you Councilmen,' Alexandra smiled tightly hoping to conceal the grief his sympathy had unearthed. Still, she was touched by the genuineness from the man, something she had never received from her own husband. As Carlyle addressed each man in turn, she made sure to pay attention, making sure she had the name matched to the correct face. Jacen seemed to be the kindest of the councilmen, every so often glancing at Alexandra and offering her what seemed to be a reassuring smile. She recognised Lemuel as the man whose wife had borne him a daughter and had incurred Carlyle's fury. Ywain was the closest of Carlyle's councilmen and she knew the man held little love for his queen. Each time she glanced in his direction she found Ywain glaring at her, his eyes full of disdain. She knew little of the remaining two councilmen, they seemed determined to remain in good graces and spoke only when he addressed them. *No one here wishes to upset Carlyle*, Alexandra realised uneasily. What would these men be like if Caleb ruled? Would they speak against him if they believed something to be wrong or would they merely keep quiet regardless of the consequences? *If they keep quiet now why would they ever speak up?* But Alexandra knew the thought was unfair, what could they do in speaking against Carlyle?

'There have been severe floods across Evany and the south of the kingdom. There is fear that many of our crops have been destroyed.' Jacen's voice pulled Alexandra from her train of thoughts, and she forced herself to focus on the present.

'Do we have reserves?' She asked ignoring Ywain's disapproving look, clearly he had expected her to just sit and observe. He looked to Carlyle as if unsure whether Alexandra's question should be taken seriously or not.

'Well, Councilman?'

'The harvest last year was poor. we have reserves but perhaps not enough to see the whole kingdom through the winter.'

'It is not just the harvest that has been affected. The city slums have also been severely flooded.' Jacen spoke up, 'with the flood comes the threat of sickness – we must act quickly to protect the city from an outbreak.'

'Seal the slums,' Carlyle ordered with a shrug and held out his hand for the sheaths of parchment Ywain shuffled. Jacen looked alarmed at the order, and his eyes darted nervously between Alexandra and Carlyle.

'But the people –'

'The loss of a few peasants is irrelevant. They are most likely already carrying whatever sickness the floods have brought in.' Ywain's voice was full of scorn and Alexandra felt her blood beginning to boil.

'Evacuate the slums. We can surely set up temporary arrangements for those who must be evacuated, once we are sure they carry no sickness we could send them to help the farms who still have crops that can be salvaged.' Out of the corner of her eyes, Alexandra could see Carlyle staring at her thoughtfully, and she was surprised to see a small smile of approval tugging at his lips.

'Does anyone object?' He asked the five men who were staring at Alexandra incredulously.

'I do! These are peasants; they do not possess the Source, why should waste our resources?'

'Why are these people of any less value than you or me Councilman Ywain?' Alexandra snapped, 'do you truly believe that those without the Source have less value? Think carefully before you answer.' In his seat, Lemuel shifted uncomfortably while Ywain's face turned an unpleasant shade of puce.

'Enough.' Carlyle barked, 'Councilman you forget yourself. Her Majesty is your *Queen* and my co-ruler. We run this kingdom together.' *Do we?* Alexandra almost arched an eyebrow but somehow managed to bury her sarcasm. 'We will evacuate the slums. My wife is right, there will be more people to work the harvest, and we can hopefully salvage some of our crops. We cannot afford another bad harvest.' The rest of the meeting seemed to drag on, by the time it had finished it was well past supper, and Alexandra was embarrassed as her stomach began to grumble. 'You did well today. I should have thought to bring you to council meetings long ago.'

'I was not ready to accept being queen, even after my coronation.' Alexandra shrugged, 'I'm not sure how much use I would have been in council meetings.'

'Are you saying you are ready to accept being queen now?' Carlyle was looking at Alexandra intently as he sat back in his throne, his long legs stretched out in front of him. *Am I?* Alexandra asked herself, *what kind of queen am I?* Her mind flickered to Caleb but she pushed the thoughts from her mind quickly, she had still not seen Caleb and was unsure of how to contact him. She wasn't even sure if she was ready to see him yet.

'I...I guess I realise I don't have a choice.' Alexandra shrugged, 'if I am the True Queen then I have a duty. I cannot neglect simply because I don't like it.' She could see it wasn't the answer Carlyle had hoped to hear, but he seemed happy enough with it.

'Come, let us get some supper. Tomorrow I would like us to leave the city and visit my mother's spring.'

'But the evacuation –'

'Jacen will ensure it begins tonight; there is really nothing more we can do Alexandra.' Seeing that he would not take no for an answer Alexandra nodded in agreement.

Alexandra was in a deep slumber when a frantic knocking on the chamber door roused her. She burrowed deeper within the cocoon of blankets; surely it was too early for a visitor? She opened her eye a crack and nodded in confirmation. Even with the thick velvet curtains pulled around the bed, she shared with Carlyle she could see that it was still pitch black. In her state of deep sleep, she turned and nestled against the figure beside her, curling up against the warmth their body emitted. Sinking back into sleep she missed the sound of footsteps and the whispered conversation; it was not until the curtains were gently pulled back at the foot of the bed that Alexandra realised she and Carlyle were not alone.

'Your Majesties I beg your forgiveness for intruding upon you at this hour,' the voice of a squire barely broken with adolescent squeaked nervously. Alexandra flicked her eyes towards the window and saw the two moons opposite; they were sinking lower beneath the gradually lightening sky. Conscious of her state of undress Alexandra pulled the blankets over her head. Carlyle was not as modest and sat up, rubbing his eyes as he waited for the boy to continue.

'Well get on with it, what do you want?'

'I – I must speak to you alone Your Majesty. I have an urgent message, but it is to be given in privacy.'

'It is too early for council business, what you have to say you can say in front of your queen.' His voice broached no argument, and Alexandra peeked from beneath the blanket towards the boy feeling a wave of pity for him. His eyes darted towards her but quickly glanced away when their gaze met.

'Your Majesty -'

'*Enough*! I am your king, are you daring to argue with me?'

'My lord please,' Alexandra tentatively rested a hand on Carlyle's thigh beneath blanket and squeezed it gently to catch his attention. He glared down at her, but she could see he was secretly pleased by the intimate gesture and Alexandra felt the courage to speak. 'No one would dare argue with you; this squire has been given his orders. He is following them; surely this proves his loyalty to you? He risks your displeasure, yet his loyalty does not waiver. Whatever he has to say is clearly important otherwise I am sure he would have waited. Please allow him to speak with you in private.' Curiosity burned within her to hear what the boy had to say but she knew it was not worth the poor boy's life!

'Go to my study,' Carlyle waved his hand in dismissal, and the boy scarpered with a bow. Helena was already waiting with a robe in hand, but Carlyle waved her away and dressed. 'When I return we shall set off,' he kissed Alexandra's forehead, 'do not go back to sleep.' Alexandra opened her mouth to protest, but Carlyle smiled at her wickedly and quickly departed.

'He truly is evil,' she sighed burying her face in the pillow and letting out a yelp as Helena pulled the blankets from her.

'But he has given you orders,' Helena chuckled handing Alexandra her dressing robe. 'Would you like me to get breakfast brought up for you?'

'Please and perhaps something for Carlyle? I'm not sure if he will think to break his fast in his study or not.' She bathed quickly, leaving the locket on the side of the bathing pool. The only time she took it off was when she bathed, frightened that the locket would become damaged. When Carlyle returned Alexandra was dressed in breeches, shirt, and tunic ready and waiting for him. She was horrified to see Carlyle's skin was a deathly shade of white and his eyes red as if he had been crying. Quickly Alexandra dismissed Helena and Roisin, dread welling up within her. What had happened to make Carlyle cry? *He did not shed a tear at the death of our daughter, at least not that I know of.* Painfully she pushed the thoughts of their daughter aside; it still tore her apart each time she brushed her flattening belly remembering how not so long ago she had been filled with the life of another. 'Carlyle?' She reached out to take his hand, but he didn't seem to register her gesture and continued to stare blankly into space. *What has happened?* Her mind tossed thoughts to and fro about what could have happened; was it the rebellion? Had something happened to Caleb? *The rebellion would not make him cry;* she thought feeling something squeeze her stomach. Her legs felt as if they were turning to jelly as she tried to rise and approach him and her body broke out in a nervous sweat. 'Carlyle, what is wrong?' She whispered; something bad had happened. She was sure of that. *Has he finally heard from Karstares? Has news of mother's silence reached him?* The smile Carlyle threw her did little to alleviate her fear. In fact, it had completely the opposite effect.

'Nothing,' Carlyle's voice was tender and he brushed a hand through her hair lovingly. 'Are you ready?'

'Of course. I had some food brought up; I was not sure if you would have broken your fast.' Carlyle shook his head at the food and instead embraced Alexandra tightly, his arms crushing the wind from her.

'I truly love you,' he whispered into her hair. 'I wish I could make you understand that.' Alexandra remained silent; too scared to speak for she knew whatever the squire had spoken of was extremely grave. *Surely he will tell me sooner or later,* Alexandra tried to reassure herself. If it was truly bad, then he could not keep it from her. 'Come, let us depart.' Throughout the journey they rode in silence, Alexandra fell a few paces behind Carlyle sensing that he needed to be alone with his thoughts. But she stayed close enough that he could not lose his temper and think she was trying give him the slip. As they reached the clearing, she followed him to the edge of the spring removed her boots and rolled the legs of her breeches up so that she could dangle her legs into the inviting water.

'Carlyle, what was the message? I am worried about you.' Carlyle remained silent as he joined her, letting his own feet sink into the water. 'I have never seen you upset – not like that. Even when you told me of our daughter –'

'There was no –'

'*You* can pretend it did not happen; *I* cannot.' Alexandra said firmly, 'I carried her for eight moons. I cannot just put that out of my mind. But my point still stands; you did not care. Yet whatever the squire told you, you do care about. You are my husband, Saphyre is my kingdom. Whatever affects you affects me just as much. Please.' But his stubborn silence was the only answer she received. Sighing in exasperation, Alexandra watched as he stood up and moved towards the horses, taking one of the saddle bags and spreading a blanket across the grass. Turning back to look ahead Alexandra focused on the waterfall, trying to let the tranquillity wash over her. But it was no use, thoughts of the previous year churned through her mind. *Has it really been almost a year?* She asked herself unable to believe how much had happened. She thought back to the solitude of her small flat in Bournemouth and smiled at the irony. All she had wanted was to know who she was, to return home. *Would I have wanted to return had I known the truth?* Her thoughts turned to her friends in Karstares. She missed Krista's wit, Mariah's sensibility, and Mathe...*How can I still miss him after all that has passed?* The thought that he was married that he was a *father*, still tore at her heart.

'You have not listened to a word I have said at all this morning, have you?' Alexandra looked up surprised to see Carlyle sitting beside her once more, 'what have you been thinking?'

'I miss my home,' she said slowly. 'Karstares. I do not have any friends here...' She trailed off biting her lip. 'You have told me several times that my safety is not guaranteed, people would be foolish to harm me, but they still could try. They *have*,' she thought of the hands shoving her in the small of the back. 'Helena and Roisin are excellent in their duties but...'

'But?'

'I would like Krista to come to Saphyre if she consents.' She met Carlyle's eyes with determination. Why had she not thought to request it before? *Why would Krista wish to come to Saphyre? She loathes Carlyle, why would she subject herself to his rule?* She was surprised to see that there was a shadow of guilt in Carlyle's eyes.

'Do you remember the morning after our wedding, I received a message?' Alexandra closed her eyes as she thought back to that morning. She remembered her fury at Carlyle upon realising that he had hypnotised her before bedding her, that he had stolen the memory of that night from her. *I do not want her in my kingdom.'* His words rang through her memory and Alexandra drew in a sharp intake of breath.

'Krista requested to stay, to serve me?'

'I have regretted my decision. Nothing you can say will make me regret it more than I already do…I was vain to think that no one would harm you simply because you are my wife. Those people would not harm you out of fear for me…I was foolish.' *How different would things have been had he just said yes?* Alexandra wondered but dismissed the thought quickly. What was the point in wondering? It would change nothing.

'May I ask her if she will serve me here?'

'She does not respect me.' *Nor do I.* But Alexandra remained silent.

'I cannot make her respect you Carlyle, but she is intelligent. She will show you respect in public, should we discuss things in private…I will not ask her to hold her tongue. I value her opinion – nor will she be a slave. She has the right to speak her mind.' Carlyle nodded, his mouth twisted in disdain. 'Please Carlyle; you cannot be with me every waking minute, and I do not appreciate having your guards and sorcerers shadowing me. You may not like Krista but you know you can trust her to protect me out of love. Please, may I write to her?'

'No…I will arrange everything.' Drawing Alexandra close Carlyle rested his chin atop of her head. 'If she consents then she should arrive before our first year is up…' Alexandra closed her eyes, the thought of being reunited with her friend making her feel content. But would Krista agree? She may have sent that request to Carlyle a year ago out of fear and desperation. Who was to say she had not moved on once she'd returned to Karstares? She surely would have been given new duties? *She may have a husband by now…perhaps even a family?*

The ride back to the castle was silent, Carlyle was once more lost deep in thought. Despite his tense mood Alexandra had found the day almost enjoyable. But every so often her mind would fear what news Carlyle had received before wondering to thoughts of her daughter. Each time she thought of her, her heart twisted painfully; where was the protruding belly which had made walking seem like a challenge? Where were the swollen hands and ankles?

'I will dine alone tonight if you wish you may take your dinner in the main dining hall with our citizens or in our private dining room with your slaves.' Carlyle snapped her from her thoughts, but before she could question him again, he had already departed.

By the time Alexandra had dined and prepared for bed Carlyle had still not returned to their chambers. She sat on the window ledge looking at the city below, envious of the lives the people there lived. They must have been simple in comparison, although she wasn't so naïve to think their lives were perfect and without their share of problems. *I have a home at least; I do not like it…but I have one. And food…*sighing she buried her face in her hands trying to block out everything from her mind. As the candles gradually began to extinguish Alexandra gave up waiting for Carlyle and decided to seek him out. Automatically her feet took her to Carlyle's study, and she knocked on the door, when she received no answer she pushed it open surprised to find it empty. He had not been there at all; the hearth was cold and empty, and none of the candles had been lit for a while. *Where is he?* He had said he would dine alone but had offered her the use of their private dining chamber. So where would he go? She searched all over the castle, even checking her own chambers to see if he had sought solace there although she had known it unlikely. Her chambers were cold, and she returned to their shared chambers feeling frightened. Knocking on the door to the dressing chamber where Helena and Roisin slept she found them bundled up in furs playing a strange game with small metal discs.

'His majesty said he was going to dine alone but has not returned to his chambers.' She tried not to let on that something was worrying her, 'I have checked his study, the throne room both our private dining room and the public one…even my own chambers but I cannot find him.'

'Perhaps his majesty does not want to be disturbed?'

'Please, if either of you know where he is I need to find him. I promise I will not divulge that it was one of you who told me of his hiding place.' Helena's eyes darted around, but it was Roisin who spoke up.

'He will be in his council chambers, but perhaps he needs peace. Whatever is plaguing him, he will tell you eventually.' But Alexandra had already turned to leave; why had she not thought of the council chambers? She was thankful for the later hour; no one was up to witness her running in her chemise and bare feet.

'Carlyle?' She knocked on the door to the councils' chambers but did not wait for a reply before pushing the heavy door open. 'Carlyle, will you *please* tell me what news arrived this morning? I am your *wife* and *queen*; how can I support you if you do not tell me what is wrong?' She hated herself for lying; she wanted to be sick. The only thing she was helping to do was push him off the throne. *I'm a horrible person;* she thought feeling tears prick her eyes; *there is no way Caleb can keep me as his queen. If I can dispose of one king and husband, surely people will think I could do it again?* Her thoughts were brought to a sharp halt as Carlyle looked up at her. His deep blue eyes were bright with tears, and he quickly looked away as he rubbed at them. She looked down at the items on the large circular council table and the scroll in his hand. It was rolled and secured with a black silk ribbon; she closed her eyes remembering when she had last seen such a scroll. *Grandmother.*

*She found herself standing in the tomb of her family. Staring at the lead lined coffin as it was placed on one of the stone shelves. Her father clasping the scroll, his face set. Alexandra turned to look at Carlyle, dressed head to toe in black and silver his face was the perfect example of a mourning king. But as he turned to look at her, his sapphire eyes glittered, and the threat was clear.*

'I am sorry Alexandra...I...' *When grandmother died, squires had written hundreds of those letters, all sealed with a black ribbon.* She thought swallowing a lump of fear; she fell into the nearest seat and shook her head. Tears stung her eyes, and she reached out her hand to take the letter. Of course, he wouldn't have unrolled it. It wasn't for him. He couldn't, it was inappropriate. But he knew. Carlyle rested the crisp white parchment in her hands, such a stark contrast against the black ribbon, but she couldn't bring herself to unravel it. She couldn't read it. *It's not true. If I don't read it then whatever is inside is not true. It has not happened.*

'Who?' She asked biting back a sob, but when he only gave her silence, she jumped up hitting his chest as he grabbed her.

'*Who is it Carlyle?*' She couldn't untie the ribbon; she couldn't bring herself to read the words for herself. She didn't want them to be true.

'Your parents.'

# Chapter Twenty-one

Tossing and turning in her bed Alexandra spent much of the night in a restless sleep. The parchment with the dreaded news was now crumpled in her hand, yet she couldn't bring herself to put it down. She kept it on her person pressed down the front of her dress and at night she slept cuddling it as if it was a teddy bear. How could her parents be dead? They were not that old. She was surprised at how empty she felt; she could feel nothing. no grief, no sadness. Just an empty black void. *A year ago I had returned home; I had parents. I had a family. Throughout this year I have had parents and a daughter. How can I be left with nothing so quickly?* Turning her head, she fixed her blank eyes upon Carlyle; he was lying on his side facing her, his hand stretched out and resting on her pillow as if to console her. But his eyes were closed, and his face had the relaxed expression of deep sleep. Carefully Alexandra slipped from the bed and tiptoed towards the dressing chamber; she paused outside the door wondering how she would get past Helena and Roisin without waking them. *I can't,* she thought in frustration. Opening the door, she slipped in and roused both of them sending them for a sleeping draught and a snack. She couldn't even feel guilty she was so void of emotion. Quickly and quietly she dressed in breeches, shirt, and tunic. She grabbed a pair of boots and a cloak as she crept from the room but did not put them on until she was at the castle door.

The stable slaves were asleep in the lofts, and Alexandra worked swiftly as she saddled Solas. She rode as quickly as she dared through the castle grounds only breaking into a gallop once she was sure she was a safe distance from the castle. She didn't pause to think how furious Carlyle would be when he woke to discover her gone; she didn't care. She wasn't running away, even if she wanted to she knew she couldn't. *What would happen if I tried to leave Saphyre?* She wondered but didn't ponder the thought too long. She just wanted to get as far away from the castle as she possibly could, just for a little while. *I am done running,* she vowed, *I ran away before, and it got me nowhere. I cannot even recall my own father's face!* She rode along the outskirts of the city and down to the shore of the ocean, the crashing waves soothing her. Looking around for some form of shelter Alexandra spotted a small cave and guided Solas towards it. She examined the sand for signs that the tide would come in this far but it seemed far enough back that there would be no danger. Removing Solas's saddle Alexandra rummaged through a bag and draped a blanket over the mare's back.

'I'm sorry,' she whispered closing her eyes and weaving her Source into the fabric to keep Solas warm. 'I know you would probably prefer to be in the warm stables, but I had to get away for a bit.' Further back in the cave she made a fire, creating a barrier with her Source to keep it in place. For a few moments, she stared at the fire thoughtfully, was this how Carlyle had kept her bound to the castle? Did she have the power to do that? *Why would I want to do that?* She asked herself, *Carlyle never leaves the castle.* But what if she could use it to bind his Source? Biting her lip Alexandra turned the thought over; he would be furious with her and even if it worked how long would it last for? Shaking her head clear of thoughts Alexandra patted Solas a final time before leaving the cave.

A line of rocks formed a path out to the ocean and Alexandra clamoured over it carefully, her cloak whipping around her in the violent wind. She ignored the voice telling her to return to the cave, that she was being foolish walking along the slippery rocks. Beneath her the sea was extraordinarily rough, each wave that crashed against the rocks sent water spraying over her but she didn't care, she barely even felt the cold biting into her. She could feel nothing at the moment, the ocean's frigid spray was at least confirmation to her that she was alive and that she could feel *something*. Closing her eyes she drew in a deep breath, holding it for several seconds before finally releasing it. Her mind cast back to Bournemouth, to the sandy beach she had been found on. She had often walked the pier and the length of the shore, even when the sea had been raging she had found it oddly soothing to listen too. *What did I do at home?* She asked herself, she remembered the maze in the castle grounds but had she sought solace there every time? Or had there been somewhere else? She tried to summon a memory of her family, of time she spent with her mother, father, and Giric. But she couldn't recall anything, only glimpses of her grandmother's funeral and the ball that had been thrown to celebrate her betrothal to Carlyle. But none of these memories were particularly heart-warming, and in each of them, her father was a shadowy figure. She could barely recall any of his features. She could recall soft grey eyes and auburn hair, but that was all. Clenching her fists, she felt the beginnings of fury boiling deep within. She directed her fury at Carlyle, barely noticing the strength picking up in the wind sending her hair whipping against her face. This was all his fault. Had he just accepted her refusal to his proposal and left her alone then she never would have had to flee her own world; she never would have lost her memory, and her parents would still be alive! *You don't know that* a small voice in the back of her head tried to reason with her. *Even if Carlyle had never journeyed to Karstares, they still could have succumbed to the illness.* Alexandra snatched the parchment from the inside of her tunic and stared down at the loathsome words. Why had her mother not told her she was ill? *She looked so pale and exhausted when we last spoke,* Alexandra thought with a pang. Her mind turned back to the last lesson with her mother, had it really been before miscarriage? *Someone tried to contact me after...what if it was mother?* Guilt replaced the rage. Had she missed a chance to speak with her mother? To hear Ismenya's comforting voice once more? She stared down at the emotionless words and phrases written on the parchment, her eyes picking them out at random; regret, grief, fever and passed within hours. She read each word over and over, but still, she could feel nothing at the loss of her parents. Just an uncontrollable rage direct at Carlyle. As she stared at the unfamiliar handwriting, her anger turned from Carlyle and towards Giric. He had not written this letter himself; it lacked any form of family affection and brotherly love. Why had he ordered a scribe to do something he should have done? As her fury got the better of her, Alexandra's hands began to tingle almost painfully. She cried out as the parchment erupted in flames and quickly dropped the scalding letter as it crumbled into ashes, leaving only the black silk ribbon unscathed.

'Who do I have now?' She asked looking up at the sky as if expecting an answer. Thick grey clouds had gathered bringing the promise of a storm, at the back of her mind Alexandra knew she should return to the castle but she ignored the thought. 'I need you mother!' *How am I to protect myself against Carlyle without you? Who will help me learn my powers?* Clutching the ribbon, Alexandra squeezed her eyes tightly shut, trying to block out the roaring of the waves and howling wind.

'What are you doing out here?' Carlyle's voice caught Alexandra by surprise, and she carefully stood up, biting back a scream as the wind almost knocked her into the ocean. She tested her grip on the rocks, surprised at how much more slippery they had become. Her hair was windswept and soaked, whether from rain or the ocean she couldn't tell. 'You *fool* Alexandra, what are you doing?' She could see Carlyle was struggling to reach her, the wind acting as a buffer against him.

'I needed to get away from the castle -'

'I did not give you permission.' Fresh rage burst through Alexandra, and she felt the soles of her boots fighting to remain on the rocks as the wind tore through her.

'I am your wife, not your prisoner!' Alexandra fought back the urge to unleash her Source, to build it into a powerful ball and hurl it at Carlyle. 'I have given you no reason to distrust me since I came to Saphyre! Not once have I tried to run away, not once have I left the castle without your permission – and why should I seek your permission? I cannot leave Saphyre Carlyle, what danger is there for me to leave the castle alone?' She would not have him use her running away as a weapon; she was sick of his distrust. She ignored the voice at the back of her mind pointing out that Carlyle did have cause to distrust her, was she not in league with those who wished to overthrow him? *I have not seen Caleb since before my pregnancy,* she thought with a pang. She pushed the thoughts away; she could not think of Caleb now or his claim to the throne. She didn't *care.* 'I have accepted I am bound to this Goddess-forsaken kingdom until I die but I will *not* accept living under your shadow, moving only when *you* permit it.' Carlyle's face softened, and he reached out for Alexandra as he grew closer, but she stepped back not caring if she plummeted into the freezing water below. Horrified she saw Carlyle's foot slip, losing what little grip he had, had on the rocks. *'Carlyle!'* Alexandra cried out as he disappeared beneath the inky depths of the ocean. *You could leave him; he would certainly die. Caleb could take the throne – this would all be over!* She dismissed the callous thought, as much as she loathed Carlyle she would never forgive herself if she just left him. Shoving the ribbon back in her tunic Alexandra shed her cloak and flattened herself against the rocks. Using her Source instinctively she bound herself to the surface of the rocks, wincing as the cold seeped through the layers of clothing. Carefully she crawled over the edge of the rocks, so she dangled almost vertically, her arms outstretched and plunged into the water. The sudden drop in temperature almost had her recoil, but she forced her hands to stay below the surface, desperately seeking Carlyle. *He won't be here;* she scolded herself. Forcing back the fear Alexandra gathered her Source and sent it pouring from her fingertips. She could feel exhaustion building up, heavy within her stomach. How much had she used? *Keep going;* she ordered herself squeezing her eyes tightly shut to block out the spinning world. Her limbs were growing heavy, her mind growing fuzzy as sleep pulled at her.

The temperature of the freezing water seeped through her Source, travelling up her arms and piercing her core. She could feel her veins beginning to freeze and her heartrate drop. *Fight it!* She scolded herself *if it is like this for me than Carlyle could be dead!* She forced her Source further beneath the surface, following her instinct and praying to the Goddess. Pressure began to squeeze her head, and Alexandra opened her eyes just in time to see a wave hurtling over her. The shock of the cold almost made her lose her grip on her Source, but somehow she kept herself pinned to the rocks. The pressure on her head increased but in her hand, she felt something tugging, almost as if she held an invisible rope.

*Pull!* Carlyle's voice broke into her mind, exhausted and faint. She could feel his exhaustion; she could feel him slipping deeper into a dark abyss. Listening to Carlyle, she pulled her Source back within her. The effort to recall her power, to pull it back within her, was excruciatingly painful. Her Source felt like small shards of ice, tearing through her as she tried to pull both her Source and Carlyle back to the surface. His gloved fingers finally clasped her own bare and frozen hands; focusing on this new physical connection, she began to pull with her body, crying out as his weight countered hers. *You're too heavy!* Her Source was wavering, and she could feel herself slipped down the rock, almost plunging them both into the icy depths.

*Focus, you are almost there!* Carlyle's voice was as clear as if he stood beside her, yet she knew there was a link connecting them subconsciously. Her boots slipped dangerously as she finally managed to haul him on to the surface of the rock.

'Get up!' She shouted over the howling wind as Carlyle curled up, his body shivering violently. She could see that his lips had turned a deep shade of blue, emphasised by the whiteness of his skin. *He'll freeze to death;* she thought fearfully and looked towards the cave. It suddenly seemed such an impossible distance, but where else could they go? Somehow she found the strength to pull him to his feet and to carefully make their way across the rocky path towards the cave. She looked around for Carlyle's own horse but could see no sign of her but pushed the thought away. Getting him warm was all that mattered now. *He would not travel without sorcerers or guards at the least.* She tried to reassure herself, but what if he had on this occasion? Relief flooded through her at the enveloping warmth of the cave and the welcoming fire which was still burning steadily.

'W – What a – a – are you d – doing?' Carlyle's teeth were still chattering violently as Alexandra began to hurriedly strip him from his soaked clothing.

'You will catch your death if you stay in these,' she knelt at his feet and impatiently motioned for him to lift each foot so she could tug off his boots. She stripped him down to his loin cloth and angrily admonished herself for leaving her cloak on the rock. *It would be soaked now;* she sighed looking around for something to keep warm. Spotting the blanket on Solas she quickly took it and draped it over Carlyle, it barely covered him, but it was all she had. Sitting beside Carlyle, she took one of his large hands in her own and began rubbing it vigorously. She ignored that her own clothes were soaked from the spray of the ocean, she was not the one who had plunged in to the icy depths.

'You helped me…why?' Carlyle broke the silence once his teeth had stopped chattering. Alexandra barely shrugged, forcing herself to keep rubbing his hands. Icy fingertips brushed her chin, and Alexandra found herself staring into Carlyle's eyes. 'I would have died…surely you want that?'

'And where would that leave me?' Alexandra snapped, loathing herself for the twinges of regret that stabbed her chest. 'I am bound to Saphyre until I die, I would rather not think about what would happen to me should I outlive you. I have no doubt that I would be a pawn to every man in this kingdom who believed he had some half-witted claim to the throne.' This was only a half-lie, she had an idea of what would happen to her if she outlived Carlyle, and she knew that she *had* to outlive him for Caleb to claim his throne? So *why* had she just saved him? Hot waves of anger swept through her but she squashed them almost as soon as they came. *I could not have let him drown.* She knew Caleb and the rebels wanted him dead, *needed* him dead, but she was beginning to question whether this would help them. There had to be another way. Surely they could imprison him? *There has to be another way…I cannot lie with this man every night and plan his death each day.* But as she thought this another voice tried to reason with her, he *had* to die. *How many lives has he taken? He killed grandfather! And you would prefer him to see his life out naturally?*

'You do not think you will outlive me?' Carlyle's voice was shocked but Alexandra merely shrugged in reply as she pulled herself from her train of thoughts. 'You are younger than me…there is nothing to suggest…'

'Your family history suggests otherwise,' Alexandra pointed out dryly. 'I am nothing like you Carlyle; I cannot let someone die. No matter how much I loathe them.' The thick silence resumed between them, the only sounds were of their breathing and the crackling fire.

'Thank you,' Carlyle reached out to pull her close but Alexandra stood up brushing him off. 'Alexandra…I am truly sorry for what has happened – that you were unable to say goodbye.' Alexandra's hands rested on Solas, she was about to pull herself up on to the mare but forced herself to face Carlyle.

'I feel *nothing*. I cannot cry, yet you…' She gestured to him and pulled a face, 'you *cried* when you found out. *Why* can I not cry? Why can I only feel anger?' Carlyle rose but the cave was too small for him to stand at full height so he sat back down, rearranging the blanket.

'You are grieving, we all react differently. Give yourself time. As for your anger…you can blame me for everything all you want Alexandra but *this* is your destiny.' Closing her eyes Alexandra rested her ran a hand through Solas's mane as she tried to keep her temper under control.

'Did you bring guards with you?' She forced herself to ask, Carlyle looked sheepish as he shook his head. 'And you call me foolish? I will send some guards and warm clothes.' She was sure his own horse would be close by, saddling Solas she led her from the cave before pulling herself in to the saddle and galloping back to the castle. She rode as low as she could in the saddle the pounding of Solas's hooves on the ground resonating throughout her. As she groomed and watered Solas, Alexandra thought about what she should tell Xander. *Tell him nothing*, she decided heading back to Carlyle's chambers. She would send either Helena or Roisin with a set of clothes to find Xander and send him to find Carlyle. *Let him decide whether Carlyle freezes to death or not*, she thought bitterly.

The main chamber had an oddly deserted feel to it as Alexandra stepped over the threshold. The hearth was unlit and the ashes from the previous night had not yet been swept away. *Where are Helena and Roisin?* Alexandra looked around worried and saw that the bed too was unmade.

'Hello?' She called out although she expected no answer. Tentatively she knocked on the dressing chamber door, pushing it open at the sound of shushing. Helena sat on the floor with her back to the door, Roisin cradling her protectively. 'W – What happened?' Alexandra asked pushing the door open and falling to her knees beside them. 'Helena?'

'What did you think would happen this morning when you fled?' Roisin's voice was surprisingly waspish and Alexandra recoiled as if she had been struck. 'His Majesty awoke before we returned, he asked us where you had gone. What could we say?' Alexandra reached out and gently turned Helena so that they were both facing, a horrified gasp escaping Alexandra's lips at the blackened eye Helena bore.

'I…I…' Alexandra trailed off looking away as she felt the guilt wash over her. Had she really thought Carlyle would not react to her disappearance? *I should have known he would be furious.*

'Helena I am truly sorry – I did not think.' Alexandra blushed under Roisin's furious gaze. 'Both of you go to my chamber and stay there for tonight.'

'If we sleep in your chamber it will just rouse His Majesty's anger further.' Roisin pointed out, but Alexandra shrugged. 'Your Majesty you cannot go on like this, you *must* think about the consequences of your actions!'

'I will deal with His Majesty. Helena…' Alexandra trailed off unsure of how she could apologise. 'I never thought he would harm you, *either* of you.' Ignoring the warning signs that she had used too much of her Source already Alexandra gently touched her fingertips to Helena's bruise and swollen eye. A pale blue light filled the skill, glowing in the dimly chamber. When Alexandra withdrew her hands the bruise had completely healed.

'But – I thought…' Roisin looked dumbfounded at what she had just witnessed.

'Just another of Carlyle's lies,' Alexandra shrugged. 'Helena please go to my chamber and rest. Roisin will you have some of Carlyle's clothes brought down to Xander? The captain will need to take some of his men and possibly Rhonwyn down to the shore; there is a cave there where Carlyle is waiting.' As both women departed Alexandra sat in the middle of the dressing chamber shivering lightly. She realised that her clothes were still damp and drying stiffly. *Carlyle will not be back for a while.* She decided to make use of the time she had alone to bathe. She was so exhausted she could feel herself drifting off into a deep sleep. *Do I tell Carlyle that I know he has been lying to me for over a year? Ever since he found me has tried to keep the truth from me…why?*

'Slaves!' The roar of Carlyle's voice snapped Alexandra from a light sleep, and she was embarrassed to find she was still in the bathing pool. Slipping the locket back on she wrapped herself in a thick sheet and made her way up to the main chamber. '*Slaves!*'

'If you mean my *ladies* they are not here.' Alexandra said quietly as she emerged from the staircase, despite the calmness of her voice her eyes blazed with molten anger. She forced herself not to lean against the wall although she was barely able to stand. 'You will *never* lay a hand upon either of them Carlyle. I swear to the Goddess if you so much as *look* at them in the wrong way I will make you pay.'

'What did the wench say?' Alexandra paid little attention to the paleness of Carlyle's skin nor the fear in his eyes, putting it down to the events of the day.

'She did not have to say anything – you blackened her eye! Did you think I would not notice?' Pushing herself away from the wall Alexandra swept from the chambers, pausing in the doorway to look at Carlyle once more. 'I am going to sleep in my chamber.'

Alexandra woke early the next morning, she longed to go for a walk in the castle grounds but neither Helena nor Roisin were awake yet, and she did not want to be the one to rouse them. *I cannot keep avoiding Caleb. Even if Carlyle did not tell Xander what happened, I'm sure he's figured it out, what if he is trying to convince Caleb I'm loyal to Carlyle?* The thought made her flinch. Surely as Carlyle's wife, she *should* be loyal to him? As Helena and Roisin began to stir Alexandra was thankful for the distraction and she broke her fast with them in her chamber, refusing to meet Carlyle. *I can't avoid him forever either;* she thought biting back a sigh. But what could she say? He had to know by now that she was in control of her powers, she wasn't sure she wanted to keep it from him anymore let alone pretend that yesterday had been a fluke.

'His Majesty has asked if you will join him for council this morning?' Roisin asked as she returned to the chamber with fresh clothes for Alexandra. She opened her mouth to reply but Roisin quickly cut her off. 'Before you refuse, please think about whether the consequences are worth it.' Alexandra blushed and looked away before nodding.

The council meeting was a stiff and awkward affair. Alexandra couldn't help noticing how pale and withdrawn Carlyle seemed. Did he feel bad for striking Helena? Or was it he feared Alexandra's reaction when she confronted him about her Source? *If,* she corrected herself. *Would it put me in a worse position to admit I know about my powers?* She was torn between what she should do, and she felt lost without her mother to give her advice. She was sure Ismenya would know what to do. As the councilmen departed Alexandra stood up to leave, but Carlyle's hand clasped her own, squeezing it lightly in gesture for her to remain seated.

'We celebrate our first year of marriage in only a few days.' Carlyle's voice was soft, and Alexandra stared ahead, fixated on a map of Saphyre on the wall. Did he really think the word celebrate was appropriate? It had hardly been a joyous year for either of them. 'I understand you are grieving for your parents, and I had hoped by now Krista would have arrived, but I would like to at least mark the occasion.'

'I will do whatever Your Majesty deems best,' Alexandra said and before Carlyle could reply she rose. 'I will be in the castle grounds should you wish to find me.' She stopped by their shared chambers to pick up a cloak, wistfully thinking of the cloak she had lost the previous day. It was still bitterly cold outside, and Alexandra had no trouble finding a secluded spot beneath a towering oak tree. Wrapping the cloak around herself, she tested her Source but could feel sickness sweeping through her. *At least it is not snowing...yet.* She thought biting back a sigh as she rested her head against the tree. Closing her eyes, she let her mind drift over the events of the past year. Why did Carlyle think it was appropriate to mark the occasion? *This marriage will never be worth celebrating.* She was surprised at the bitterness which threatened to consume her. Had she really ever believed she would marry for love? Had she and Mathe really been so foolish as to believe they could live happily ever after together? *No...but I never thought I would have to marry a tyrant, a murderer.* She could barely wait for Krista to arrive and she prayed that the journey was not too rough. *It is hard to believe this time a year ago we were making this journey together.* With that thought, her mind turned to her mother, how agitated she had seemed throughout the journey. She had barely left Alexandra alone, and never with Mariah or Krista. Had she feared they would try the same spell again? *I never even got to speak with Mariah...or Mathe. Would he have told me about his lover had he had the chance?*

*'Princess Alexandra what a pleasure it is to see you.'* Startled Alexandra whirled around to see the visiting King of Saphyre, Carlyle, in a deep bow. She smiled at the man and curtsied in reply. He was certainly handsome with a tall and broad frame, deep blue eyes and golden hair. But there was something cold about him and frighteningly so. *'I must confess I have been hoping the Goddess would bless me with the opportunity to speak privately with you.'*

*'Your Majesty I do not wish to seem disrespectful, but this is hardly appropriate, I do not have any of my ladies to act as chaperones. I cannot be*

*seen cavorting with men alone.' Alexandra said the first thing which came to her mind, desperate to get away from the king. He was handsome yes, but that did not mean she felt comfortable around him. She had not been able to figure out why but he made her nervous. Her friends and grandmother had not taken to him as the rest of the court had done, but no one could quite put their finger on what it was about the king that made them frightened.* Is frightened the right word? *Alexandra wandered before realising that yes, this king frightened her.*

*'You will not 'cavort' as you eloquently put it with a king – a man who holds status. Yet you have no issue doing so with a common knight?' Alexandra's cheeks burned with humiliation, and she scowled at the hidden undertone of the Carlyle's words.*

*'Mathe is a friend and my guardian.'* I need to get away from him; grandmother has warned me to stay away. *Her grandmother's words rang clearly in her mind.* 'There is bad blood in his family. He has the eyes of a tyrant, and we know so little of his kingdom's history. Nothing good will come from this king being here, and you would do best to make your feelings clear to your parents. Avoid this man at all costs – do not give them reason to think that you would be pleased with a betrothal between the two of you.' *Alexandra had heard rumours that she was the reason for Carlyle's visit, but she had paid them little heed. Now she was not so sure. 'Is there something I can help you with Your Majesty?' She asked deciding to try and change tactics.*

*'As I said I have been praying for an opportunity to speak with you alone. I know you fear it...inappropriate,' the Carlyle's lip curled up in a light sneer at the word. 'However I feel you agree with me that this is a matter best discussed privately.' Alexandra could feel her stomach constricting;* was she the reason for his visit? *'I have spoken with both your mother and father at great length about this subject and I am pleased that they share my sentiments – I hope that perhaps you feel the same.'*

*'About what?' Alexandra asked before she could stop herself. Only moments before she had been chilly, now she found the temperature had risen quite suddenly and uncomfortably.* His own father deemed me an inappropriate bride, and that was when I was still a babe! Surely he would not be revisiting that idea? *But if not then why had this man not yet married? He had been king for over a decade now, surely he should have married long ago and his queen produced heirs?* He is too old for me! *She knew at nineteen people considered her well over the marriageable age; her own mother had borne Giric before she was*

*Alexandra's age. But at least the age gap between her parents was only a matter of moons and not over a decade!*

*'Princess I believe you must know,' he paused and took hold of Alexandra's arm, forcing her to come to a standstill. Surprisingly soft hands brushed Alexandra's hair back from her face, and she felt her head tilted up until she was staring into a pair of deep blue eyes. The spiral pattern seemed to almost move in a clockwise direction, and Alexandra could feel herself becoming lost in them, fascinated by the spiralling movement. 'My father once thought of an alliance between our kingdoms but was too impatient to wait for you to blossom. I am glad to have been patient. Your beauty is far more radiant than the sun; you make the Goddess herself seem plain in comparison.'* You should not speak such blasphemy! *Alexandra wanted to protest but found herself unable to speak. 'Your mother is a powerful Sorceress, and your own power is surprisingly strong in one so young. You have barely finished your apprenticeship, and yet I have heard you can rival a fully-fledged Sorcerer with ease.'*

*'I –' Alexandra managed to find her voice but couldn't shake herself free from his gaze.*

*'I have proposed an alliance between my kingdom of Saphyre and the kingdom of Karstares. An unbreakable alliance which should be celebrated.' Soft lips brushed Alexandra's hand, and in that moment Carlyle broke eye contact, freeing her from his spell. Snatching her hand back Alexandra walked away briskly.*

*'I would rather die,' she spat looking over her shoulder. She had no idea where the sudden venom had come from, what had replaced fear with loathing, but she knew marrying this man was not an option. She knew nothing of his kingdom, no one did, yet there was a spark of cruelty which frightened her.* How have I never noticed this before? *She asked herself. Carlyle smiled and shrugged carelessly as if she had not just refused him marriage but simply a walk.*

*'I would not be so hasty to refuse, Your Highness.' Carlyle's voice hardened, and Alexandra suppressed a shiver turning to walk away once more. She had to get away from, to put as much distance between the two as possible.* I will tell mother and father now that I do not wish to marry this man, they will listen to me surely. *Quickening her pace, Alexandra realised she had walked into the maze of the castle gardens. Not wanting to turn around she decided to make her way to the centre, as far as she knew Carlyle did not know the way. She could hide there until he had given up, or until someone came for her. Resting on the edge of a marble fountain she glanced down at the icy surface and traced a pattern with the tip of her fingernail. 'I am not someone to be crossed lightly,' Carlyle's voice*

*pierced the stillness of the air and Alexandra glared at him.* I should never have danced with him at the ball; *she scolded herself.* Why did I have to make Mathe jealous? *She cringed inwardly at the memory; she had all but thrown herself at Carlyle just to get a reaction from Mathe.* Goddess, please forgive my immaturity! *Resting her hands in her lap, Alexandra closed her eyes and concentrated on the ice of the fountain. A cracking sound filled the air, and several jagged shards rose into the air, pointing themselves at Carlyle.*

'Nor am I to be crossed,' *Alexandra replied calmly sending the shards of ice hurtling towards Carlyle and narrowly missing him.* 'I will not marry you, and I will inform my parents of this immediately. If you wish an alliance between our kingdoms, then you can have it another way.'

'You do not have much of a choice. Your parents could force you to marry me – or anyone for that matter. Surely you do not want to make this unpleasant for them?' *There was something in his tone which suggested to Alexandra that even if she told her parents she did not want the betrothal to take place that they would not listen.* He tried to hypnotise me only moments ago; *she realised feeling her blood turn to ice.* Has he put the kingdom under such a spell? 'I ask you Princess Alexandra, and please before you refuse think carefully on the consequences, will you accept an alliance between our kingdoms? Will, you accept an offer of marriage and rule Saphyre at my side, as my queen?'

'No.' *Alexandra shook her head in firm refusal.* 'I will not become your queen, nor do I have an interest in ruling Saphyre. I refuse your offer of marriage, and all that may follow.'

'Alexandra?' Alexandra's eye's snapped open as she was torn from the memory and brought back to the present. Blinking she held her hand over her eyes trying to discern the tall figure standing over her. Seeing that it was only Carlyle she closed her eyes and settled her head back against the tree once more, she was in no mood to discuss his plans for a celebration. 'Please, Your Majesty...I know you do not want to speak with me but...' *Your Majesty?* Alexandra opened her eyes and glared at Carlyle suspiciously. He never referred to her by her title, not when they spoke privately. It wasn't until she noticed the nervous stance and tentative smile that Alexandra realised the identity of the man.

'Caleb!' Leaping to her feet, Alexandra threw her arms around Caleb, and he embraced her back just as tightly. All of the anger and accusations she had held against him in her mind over the past few moons had evaporated; Caleb would never have ordered harm upon her or her child. Remembering why they were Alexandra quickly stepped back and glanced around to ensure they were alone. 'Forgive me, that was inappropriate.' She was surprised when Caleb immediately swept her into a second bone-crushing embrace.

'Out of all that has come to pass this is hardly inappropriate,' joining Alexandra on the ground Caleb turned to face her, his eyes searching her face for something. 'Alexandra I am truly sorry for all the losses you have suffered. When I heard about...about your daughter, I went to the temple to pray. I had hoped I would see you there, but Father Dóchas told me you did not wish it.' Tears stung Alexandra's eyes at the genuine sympathy in Caleb's voice and she looked away so he wouldn't see. *How could I have ever thought Caleb was capable of such a horrified crime?* 'He said you were not ready for us to talk...'

'I was not, not back then at least. But I am now,' Alexandra smiled weakly. The events from the previous day quickly came to mind, and Alexandra's smile quickly faded. 'Caleb...' She hesitated to go on, how could she tell him what she had done? *I cannot keep this from him.* 'Yesterday I – I...saved Carlyle's life. I was down on the shore, and we argued, he slipped and fell into the ocean. I couldn't leave him...I couldn't just let him die.' Caleb sat in silence seeming to digest what Alexandra had told him. Eventually he reached out to take hold of her hand and squeezed it lightly.

'I am glad you saved him. You acted honourably – I would not expect otherwise from you.'

'But I am a continuous hazard to your cause!'

'Of course you are not!' Caleb protested and forced Alexandra to look at him. 'Alexandra please do not ever think that. None of this is your fault; you cannot help if you give Carlyle heirs – it is your duty. We will cross that bridge when we come to it.' *Father Dóchas has not told him,* Alexandra realised that Caleb did not know she was trying her best to prevent falling with child once more. *It is better this way, the less people who know than, the less people I am endangering.* 'When the time comes for me to claim the throne I must challenge Carlyle for it. I need to prove myself to our people. If Carlyle were to die in an accident, people would either be suspicious of you or say I had come to the throne through deception.'

'Surely once you claim the throne people would be suspicious of me. If I play a part in the downfall of one king who is to say I would not overthrow another?' Caleb looked deep in thought as if he had been thinking the same thing.

'I want to keep you as far away from all of this as possible. I would never ask you to help me dispose of Carlyle; I could not bring myself to put such a burden upon you.' Caleb surprised her by kissing her cheek softly sending warmth spreading across her face.

'There is more,' Alexandra said wishing her cheeks would stop burning. 'To save Carlyle I had to use my Source – I had no other choice.'

'Do you think he knows you are in control of your powers?'

'He must do,' Alexandra shrugged, 'I could hear him in my mind. But he has not said anything…not that I have given him much of a choice.'

'You should be careful Alexandra; your Source is your only protection against him –'

'And without my mother I have no one teaching me anymore.' Alexandra said looking into the distance. 'I think I should confront Carlyle. If he knows I am aware of my powers, that he has been lying to me all this time…he would not dare to try and keep my powers from me. He might even teach me – or allow me to learn from the Castle Sorcerers. Perhaps I could approach some of them –'

'Approaching the Castle Sorcerers is too risky. Many of them are close to Carlyle…we have some who have sided with us but that is all I can tell you.' Caleb rose to his feet and gently tugged Alexandra with him. 'You should go inside; you are starting to turn blue.' She could tell he was teasing, but the concern in his voice touched Alexandra. 'If you think you should confront Carlyle about your Source then perhaps you should do so. But please be careful. If anything was to happen to you…' Alexandra reached out and squeezed his arm playfully.

'I will be careful,' she promised, 'unlike you! Anyone could see us together.' Caleb grinned mischievously but Alexandra did not share the joke. 'Please Caleb you should be taking less risks than I.'

'Of course. But you should not worry about me taking risks, at least not here in the castle. I am leaving Evany for a while; I need to widen my search for people who could be loyal to my cause and who would support my claim.'

'How long will you be gone for?' Alexandra was surprised at the feeling of devastation and emptiness that his announcement left her with. She had not seen him in moons, but she had known he was there at least.

'I am not sure. A moon? A year maybe? I need to see how the people outside of the capital feel about Carlyle, how far his tyranny reaches.' Leaning down Caleb kissed Alexandra's cheek softly once more. 'Promise me you will be careful while I am gone?' Alexandra nodded and threw her arms around him once more, frightened to let him go in case she would never see him again.

The day of the celebration started off uneventfully. Alexandra bathed and dressed in a simple gown before breaking her fast with Carlyle in the small dining chamber. Every so often she would glance up at Carlyle to find his eyes glinting mischievously, the glint unsettled Alexandra, and she found herself unable to finish her meal. *What has he got planned?* Tendrils of fear gripped her stomach, was she imagining the threatening glint or was it just always there? She spent each day fearing that Carlyle would discover the locket had been charmed, what if had learnt and had something planned for her?

'I have a surprise for you,' seeing that Alexandra was not going to finish her meal Carlyle gently pulled her to her feet and led her from the dining chamber. Alexandra followed Carlyle, her hand limp in the crook of his arm and dread building within her. As they reached his study, she half-expected Xander to be waiting to arrest her. *Would Carlyle arrest me if he discovered the locket?* She wondered, *what about Caleb?* Carlyle's father and grand-father had, had no issue in executing their queens. Would Carlyle follow suit? 'Are you alright?' Carlyle gripped Alexandra's shoulders as she stumbled backwards, suddenly frightened at what awaited her. 'Alexandra?'

'I need to lie down,' she whispered trying to move away from the study, but Carlyle refused to let her go. He was smiling at her, his eyes glinting. 'Please –'

'Trust me; you will like this surprise.' Opening the door, Carlyle nudged her inside the study where a lithe woman stood with her back to them at the window. Alexandra's breath caught in her throat as she stared at the figure. Tears stung her eyes, and she looked at Carlyle to see if he was tricking her.

'Krista?' She finally managed to choke out as she stepped towards the figure. A wide grin breaking out across her face, she suddenly realised how much tension she had carried over the past year and how good it felt to smile genuinely.

'Your Majesty,' Krista turned around evidently surprised at having been caught off-guard. She bowed deeply, and Alexandra froze at the formality from her old companion, but as Krista straightened there was a wicked grin on her dark features. Stepping forwards Alexandra embraced Krista tightly, determined not to cry as she blinked back tears.

'Do not do that!' She scolded laughing, but she could hear a grunt of disapproval from Carlyle. Krista stared at him stonily and bowed, although it was considerably stiffer and less respectful than when she had greeted Alexandra. Carlyle sat behind his desk and gestured for Alexandra to sit, but she remained standing beside Krista unable to help grinning at the other woman.

'Regardless of how my wife feels you will address her as befitting her title – in pulic.' Carlyle added before Alexandra could protest. 'You are a servant here; I am employing you to keep Her Majesty safe.'

'All I have ever wanted is to protect Her Majesty,' hearing her formal title on Krista's lips was strange, and Alexandra frowned. She had always idolised her mother and had hoped to be just as good a queen as she was. *Had been,* Alexandra corrected herself and pushed thoughts of Ismenya from her mind. 'If you had let me remain in the kingdom this time a year ago I could have protected her.' Alexandra was surprised to see a shadow of regret passing over Carlyle's face. How long had the decision to refuse Krista to remain in Saphyre haunted him?

'You are to remember that you are not here as a diplomatic citizen,' Carlyle continued as if Krista had not spoken. 'If you choose to remain here then you are renouncing your loyalty to Karstares. You will be considered Saphyrian. You will follow the laws of our kingdom. break any of them, and I will ensure you are punished appropriately, do not think that a close relationship with the Queen will protect you.'

'I do not plan on getting involved in Saphyrian politics. Protecting Her Majesty is my only concern, and I will lay down my life for hers.' Alexandra gasped as she felt a rush of air punch her in the stomach. She braced her palms on Carlyle's desk and closed her eyes at the onslaught of images. She could see Krista, much younger, bowing before her father and laying a sword at his feet. *Father!* Alexandra tried to focus on his, but it was lost in shadows.

'Alexandra!' Carlyle and Krista spoke as one, and she could feel their hands on either side of her.

'It is nothing; I am fine.' Alexandra tried to reassure them, 'just a glimpse from before…another memory.'

'You *still* do not remember everything?' Krista asked incredulously.

'No,' Alexandra shrugged and eventually managed to stand up straight. 'They come back in fragments. I'm fine, really.' She turned to reassure Carlyle who was still holding her as if frightened that she might shatter at any moment.

'I will leave you two to talk,' Carlyle kissed Alexandra softly. 'Do not forget we have the feast tonight, come to our chambers to prepare before sunset.' As Carlyle departed Alexandra linked her arm through Krista's and led her through the castle.

'When did you arrive?'

'The early hours of this morning, I was shown to the barracks where a room was waiting for me. I am sorry I did not come and visit you as soon as I arrived, I thought perhaps you would be busy.' Krista was smirking, and Alexandra pulled a face punching her lightly. *At least one of us can joke about this situation.*

'When you agreed to return I was overjoyed but…Krista are you sure you wish to remain here? It is nothing like Karstares, not that I remember much about life there. Saphyre has no issue with slavery nor corruption; it seems to highly favour both.'

'Alexandra I have wanted to return ever since Carlyle the wedding. When Carlyle banished us, I begged Queen Ismenya, Goddess rest her soul, to allow me to plead with Carlyle to let me return. I loathed the thought of you all alone here, with no one but *him*. Rest assured there is nothing left for me in Karstares. Your parents tried to find a place for me in the castle, but there was little for me to do. There is no place for a woman warrior in our world, but at least by your side I had duty – I had purpose.' Alexandra smiled as her throat constricted. *It is a shame*

*Krista did not come with me to Earth, to Bournemouth…she may have fitted in easily there.* 'I am sorry for the passing of your parents,' Krista broached the subject of the overhanging cloud. 'Karstares mourns greatly for them. And Giric…I have never seen him so lost, so uncertain of himself.' Guilt struck Alexandra at that passing comment. She had been so busy focusing on how Giric had wronged her, how he had neglected to write to her with his own hand, that she had given little thought as to how he was coping. *Perhaps I should write to him…he is to be king now.*

'When is the coronation to take place?'

'Giric wishes to observe a period of mourning first. And…there is more news.' Alexandra felt her stomach twist painfully; she could not take anymore bad news. 'Giric and Mariah are betrothed. The wedding was to take place a few weeks ago but due to the death of Their Majesties they have postponed the wedding.' *But that's not fair!* Alexandra bit down on her tongue to stop herself from shouting out. She could not have married Mathe due to his low status, yet Giric was free to marry who he pleased? *Surely he should have been held to stricter rules than I?* 'Queen Ismenya was consumed by guilt when she learnt the truth about Carlyle and took a great interest in training Mariah personally. We were questioned by Their Majesties when you first disappeared but they were abrupt, when we returned to Karstares after your marriage, they wanted far more detail and were impressed with the spell you and Mariah had used. Shortly before your mother fell ill she promoted Mariah to act as her second-in-command with the Karstarian Sorcerers. Giric did not inherit the Source from your mother and it seemed like a natural match between them. Both her parents are noble-born, her father grew up with yours, and her mother was one of the Queen's ladies.'

'So it is an arranged marriage?'

'Of sorts. Although I do not think either are displeased with the decision.' Krista shrugged. *What is wrong with me? How can I be angry with Giric when he is at least marrying someone he likes if not loves? Surely I should be happy for them?* Krista squeezed Alexandra's arm comfortingly. 'I know the news may be a shock, even unfair,' she grinned as Alexandra blushed. 'Especially given your own marriage.' Krista hesitated, and Alexandra could see what was on her mind.

'He has not harmed me,' she reassured Krista. 'When I first arrived he bound me to the castle; I could not even go for a walk in the gardens. He was furious when I lost our daughter, but he has never laid a hand on me.' *Other than every night*, but Alexandra didn't want to confide that. 'He lied to me about my Source – ever since he found me he has told me I did not have it.' Krista was furious but Alexandra shushed her.

As the sky began to darken Alexandra guided Krista to the chambers, she shared with Carlyle to introduce her to Helena and Roisin. She had told Krista about saving Carlyle's life and using her Source, but she was yet to confront him about her powers. She avoided mentioning Caleb and how he thought she should remain silent, she did not want Krista involved in Caleb's cause at all. *Carlyle would not hesitate to execute her.* Although she missed Caleb, she was glad he was gone for a while, at least she did not have to worry about Krista becoming mixed up in the rebellion.

'Perhaps you should confront him,' Krista said as they neared Carlyle's chambers. 'He could teach you...and as you say if he knows that you are aware of your own powers, then he would not dare to bind it. I have heard of sorcerers draining power from others to strengthen themselves if he thinks you are ignorant he might even dare to try this on you.' Alexandra frowned, she had never thought of this. 'How did you find out?' Alexandra shrugged, she did not want to go into detail about the dreams she had shared with her mother, how Ismenya had spent much of her time teaching Alexandra to grasp her powers. *Will I really never have another lesson?* What would have happened once Alexandra was fully trained? Would her mother have continued the dreams? Or would she have ceased all contact?

Carlyle was already dressed and waiting for them when Alexandra and Krista opened the chamber door. He looked magnificent in a mixture of black velvet and golden silk. Alexandra looked down at her own black gown and shook her head; she did not feel right celebrating when she was in still in mourning. She did not feel right celebrating this marriage at all.

'You are dressed in mourning,' she realised turning to observe his rich clothing once more. 'I – I thought you did not approve of such displays?' She had never forgotten his displeasure at her insistence on mourning their child.

'I liked your parents Alexandra; I respected them. Your mother was a brilliant sorceress,' her throat tightened at the mention of her mother, and she could only nod weakly. 'I know that you wish to observe the mourning period and I want to respect your wishes which is why I have had this prepared for you,' he gestured for Alexandra to follow him into the dressing chamber where a dressmaker stood holding out a stunning golden dress. The skirt was slashed to reveal glimpses of a full-bodied black underskirt, and there was an intricate design woven in a black thread across the bodice and hem. The sleeves too were full and slashed from the shoulders to elbow to reveal a layer of black velvet. Alexandra was stunned by the surprisingly thoughtful gesture. 'I have had clothes prepared for you also,' Carlyle addressed Krista. 'Just in case you arrived in time, I hope they fit but there will be a dressmaker on hand should you need any last-minute alterations.'

'Thank you, Your Majesty.' Knowing that she had been dismissed Krista departed, leaving Alexandra with her ladies and husband to prepare for the feast. *Please do not leave me*, Alexandra wanted to call out suddenly frightened at the thought of being separated from Krista. She wasn't sure why but she felt like she needed Krista at her side at all times, more for her friend's safety than her own.

As Alexandra sat beside Carlyle at the head table, she could not help but think how different this feast was compared to that of their wedding. Despite their queen being in mourning, the people were in a joyous mood, and there were several fountains of wine placed around the great hall. Krista too seemed to be enjoying herself and was sitting with a group of Castle Guards laughing and trading stories with them. Alexandra could see Xander staring at Krista opposite him every so often, a strange look on his face. *Do not let her get involved;* a small voice reprimanded Alexandra. *Krista is here to protect me, but I need to protect her.* Yet she could not keep Krista by her side at all times; it was not fair on her. She ignored the voice scolding her, telling her that Krista was the same age as her and old enough to make her own decisions. *Should she wish to join Caleb's cause who am I to stop her?* But she ignored the thought; she would not let Krista get wrapped up in politics and risk her life.

'I know you are still furious with me,' Carlyle spoke softly so those around could not hear. 'But perhaps you could return to our chambers tonight? I have missed you.' *I cannot avoid him forever,* Alexandra reminded herself before nodding stiffly. 'Alexandra?' She turned to look at him, cautiously meeting his gaze. 'I do love you.' She looked away for a split second, guilt pulling at her.

'I cannot,' she whispered eventually. 'I cannot love you Carlyle. You know I never wanted this marriage and after all that has passed...' She shrugged and looked down at Krista who was deep in conversation with Xander.

'This is the first year of our marriage. Give it time.' *Surely this should be the best year?* Alexandra wanted to ask but remained silent. She knew her feelings would never change.

*Alexandra sat at Ismenya's desk staring at the tidy oak surface.* Mother never left her desk tidy. *She thought stroking her fingertips across the smooth wood. The air was clear, and the rushes on the floor were fresh, it smelt too clean. As if someone had scrubbed the room from top to bottom.* Of course, they would have, they need to protect the castle from the illness spreading. *But surely it was too late for that? Her mother was already her dead, her father too. Clearly disease had pierced the castle and settled in its very core. What more could be done?*

*'Alexandra?' A startled gasp broke through Alexandra's thoughts, and she looked up surprised to see Helena standing in the doorway dressed in a chemise. 'What are you doing here? You should not be here!'*

*'I – I...is this not a dream?'*

*'Yes! Which is precisely why you should not be here; do you not realise you are using your life's energy to perform this spell? Your Source could drain away in your sleep – Alexandra wake up!' Helena rushed over to her and seized Alexandra by her shoulders, shaking her violently. 'You must wake up!'*

Bolting upright Alexandra looked around startled to find herself in Carlyle's bed. The air was warm, but the hearth had burnt out, leaving only embers glowing in its place. *Was that a dream? Or was that real?* She asked herself using her Source to summon a light. Sickness washed over her, and the light was snuffed out with it. *My Source is depleted...how?* Mariah's words echoed through her mind, and she felt her blood run cold. *'Do you not realise you are using your life's energy to perform this spell?'* Was that why her mother had fallen ill? Why she had not been able to defeat the illness which had claimed not only her but her husband? *I was the reason she fell ill; she weakened herself to teach me.* Retching Alexandra stood up, her legs were shaky, and she could barely stand but she somehow managed to reach the chamber pot where she ungraciously emptied what little she had eaten at the feast.

'Your Majesty?' Helena appeared in the door of the dressing chamber looking concerned. 'Your Majesty are you ill? Roisin fetch a healer!' Alexandra shook her head but she could not speak through the helpless retching. Fearing she would suffocate she gladly accepted the cup of water Helena passed her and gulped it greedily.

'Carlyle –' she called out but was surprised to see the bed empty.

'His Majesty is not here,' Helena tried to help Alexandra back into the bed, but she shrugged her off.

'I – I need to see him.'

'You need to rest and let Sorceress Rhonwyn attend you.'

'No. I am fine; I need to speak to Carlyle.' *Where is he?* Alexandra shrugged a robe on and braced herself against the chamber door, leaning her forehead against the cool wood.

'His Majesty sometimes goes to his study if he cannot sleep,' Helena eventually confessed. 'But you should go back to bed.'

'I will after I speak with Carlyle.' Draining a second cup of water Alexandra groggily made her way down to Carlyle's study. What would she say to him? What *could* she say? *I know you have been lying to me, your deception led to my mother's death?* Could she confront him so directly? Opening the door to his study, she found him sitting back in his chair with his eyes closed.

'Alexandra, why are you not asleep?' Carlyle sat up at the sound of the door opening and lit several candles with his Source. Alexandra stared at the candles for a few moments before finally taking a seat at his desk. 'Alexandra?'

'Do I have the Source?' She asked meeting his eyes and holding them. She expected him to lie, to brush her off. Instead she was surprised when Carlyle nodded wearily, running a hand through his golden hair as if trying to brush away the past year.

'Yes,' he eventually answered.

'*Why* did you lie to me?' Alexandra finally managed to ask. She was surprised that Carlyle had not outright lied to her, so surprised that she had almost forgotten her anger. Almost. 'I asked you several times…why did you insist on lying?' Carlyle remained silent, and Alexandra looked up at him, she was angrier at herself, but she desperately wanted to lay the blame at his feet.

'You are hardly innocent,' he pointed out. 'You have lied to me –'

'Do not *dare*,' Alexandra spat, 'I had to learn my powers in secret since you did not want me using them! *Why?*'

'I was afraid you would try to run away again.' Carlyle admitted sitting forwards so he could rest his arms on the desk. 'You must know by now you are a powerful Sorceress. I did not want to have to spend every moment fearing that you would use your Source to escape your destiny.' Alexandra closed her eyes; she desperately wanted to throw something at Carlyle, to make him feel the pain she was feeling.

'I killed my mother; *I* am the reason she was too weak to stave off the illness.' Carlyle stood up and tried to pull Alexandra into an embrace, but she pushed him away, how could he think he would be able to soothe her? She loathed him at the best of times.

'Alexandra how could you think such a thing?'

'Who do you think has been teaching me to regain my powers Carlyle?' Carlyle stared at Alexandra uncomprehendingly.

'I do not understand,' he finally admitted with a shake of his head, 'Your mother has not been to Saphyre since our wedding. I would have known had she been here.' *Is he truly ignorant?* Alexandra wanted to scoff at him but somehow refrained from doing so. 'How did you even find out?'

'A dream,' Alexandra shrugged. 'Well…more a memory. It was a conversation I had with my mother; I was frightened that you would steal my power.' Carlyle looked at her in disbelief. 'Do not act as if I have offended you, you killed my grandmother and lied about my own power. Is thinking that you would steal it really that incredulous?' Carlyle had no response; he seemed to be lost in thought.

'When I found you unconscious in the dressing chamber…you had been practicing your Source?'

'Yes…and overexerted myself. I did not realise until it was too late.'

'I still do not understand how your mother comes into this.' Carlyle was now standing and pacing around the study.

Alexandra glanced at his desk horrified to see a pile of death warrants sitting there, the top emblazoned with his signature.

'She came to me in dreams. She taught me how to use my Source again.' She watched as Carlyle stiffened, his hands clenching before his shoulders slumped forward.

'I knew I should never have lied to you,' his voice was thick and Alexandra was shocked to see his body convulsing as if he were sobbing. When Carlyle finally turned to face her, he seemed to have composed himself, but his eyes were still bright with unshed tears. 'Your mother truly was a magnificent woman Alexandra. It is my greatest regret that I made an enemy of her…and caused her death.' Calmly Alexandra rose to her feet, but before she could walk out of Carlyle's study, he had grasped her shoulders lightly. 'Alexandra –'

'I blamed myself at first; I did not realise that such a spell could drain your life's energy. But you are right; I did not kill my mother. *You* did with your foolishness.' Shrugging his hands off her Alexandra left the study. Feeling utterly alone she crawled into the bed in her private chamber and finally broke down into heavy sobs for her parents.

# *Chapter Twenty-two*

Winter was in full swing making travel into Evany almost impossible. The threat of snow did not deter Alexandra from making her journey into the city to visit the temple and distribute alms, in fact it made her more determined. Thankful that she had Krista to accompany her Alexandra was able to relieve Helena and Roisin of the duty of travelling with her, leaving the two women in the warmth of the castle.

Two moons had passed since her anniversary to Carlyle, and neither had approached the subject of her Source. Alexandra began to practice alone, sometimes wondering if she could approach one of the Castle Sorcerers but finding her pride getting the better of her. Krista had begun training her in hand-to-hand and weaponry combat and while Alexandra enjoyed the way it left her feeling exhausted and too tired to care when she joined Carlyle in his chambers she couldn't help but feel she was neglecting her Source. Physical combat would not help her should the time come when she had to protect herself against Carlyle; she knew she would have to rely on her Source for that moment.

'Are you sure you should not remain in the castle?' Carlyle asked as he followed Alexandra to the stables where Krista and Xander waited for her. 'There is likely to be a blizzard tonight, what if you are trapped in the city?'

'Then we will seek shelter in the temple. I am sure Father Dóchas will not refuse us board for the night,' Alexandra replied simply refusing Carlyle's help as she swung into the saddle. Clicking her tongue, Solas walked from the stable, Xander and Krista following closely behind. Alexandra was hurt as Krista remained behind in deep conversation with Xander, leaving Alexandra to ride alone. She was uncomfortable with how close Krista and Xander had become, telling herself it was her distrust for Xander and nothing to do with jealousy. *He will only lead her in to harm*, Alexandra was convinced. But what could she say? She could not warn Xander from informing Krista of Caleb and his cause; she was sure if she did it would make him more determined to recruit Krista.

'You truly come here every moon?' Krista asked as they began their ascent up the mountainous staircase. 'Does it not remind you of your wedding day?'

'Not really,' Alexandra shrugged. 'The temple Priest, Father Dóchas, is lovely and kind. He makes me feel welcome here as if the temple is a sanctuary I can rely on.' She smiled as Krista pulled a face obviously not sharing her own sentiment. 'You and the Captain seem close, what do you two talk about?' She tried to keep the jealousy from her voice knowing that Krista would only tease her for it.

'You mostly. Xander is quite distrustful of those with the Source, although given what His Majesty is like who could blame him?' Krista's dark eyes flashed. 'I have told him that this is not what it is like with Karstares, that those with the Source are valued no more than those without it. Your father's bloodline carried the Source although it is prone to skipping generations. Karstares is not as reliant on the Source as Saphyre; they are not guaranteed a monarch who wields it. Why do you not like Xander?' Alexandra was dismayed at the first-name basis Krista was obviously on. She wanted to ask her if Xander had mentioned Caleb but was too frightened to reveal anything. If she did not know now, then she would surely want to join if Alexandra revealed anything.

'I do not trust him,' Alexandra shrugged simply. 'I believe that is a mutual feeling. Please be careful around him Krista, remember what Carlyle told you.'

'Because you listen to everything Carlyle tells you?'

'He would not execute me as easily as he would you,' although even as she said the words, Alexandra wasn't so sure. Carlyle had never raised his hand against her, but then he didn't need to, he had his Source to use against her. *But I have mine, and he knows that now.* As Alexandra distributed alms Krista remained close to her side. She could see that her friend was speechless by the poverty of the people.

'These people trust you,' Krista murmured in awe as they joined Father Dóchas for hot drinks before their departure. 'I was worried that they would be frightened given their king but...'

'Her Majesty has given the people no reason to distrust her.' Father Dóchas assured Krista, 'I think seeing His Majesty's Queen so regularly gives them hope that the Goddess will soon bless Saphyre with change.' *Please say no more,* Alexandra silently pleaded.

When they returned to the castle, Alexandra watched as Krista went with Xander to join him and the Castle Guards for supper. *Why am I so jealousy?* She thought with a sigh. It was not fair to expect Krista just to remain with her alone, but she envied how Krista could come and go as she pleased and with whom she pleased. Resigned she made her way to the small dining chamber to take her own supper with Carlyle. The atmosphere between them was still cool since Alexandra's confrontation with him about her Source. She longed for a marriage she could at least be happy with, even if she could not love her husband, but was beginning to resign herself to her fate. With Caleb out of the city, it was almost as if the resistance did not exist. What if something happened to him on his travels?

'I would like to teach you,' Carlyle suddenly broke the silence as the remnants of their first course was cleared away. 'Your Source that is...I know Queen Ismenya has most likely taught you much and that you have been practicing on your own...but I never should have neglected your studies.' *You never should have lied to me,* Alexandra wanted to point out but resisted. She was tired of the endless arguing, the endless fights.

'There is no point.' She replied shrugging her shoulders as if whether or not he taught her was of any consequence.

'You need me to teach you,' Carlyle said softly. 'I am sure your mother focused on ensuring you could protect yourself but she may have left gaps. There would not have been time to ensure you learnt all that you had known in the past.' Alexandra loathed to admit it but she knew he was right, she was at full strength, but she knew there were still large chunks of her knowledge missing. 'What can you do?' *Be careful,* she warned herself. *He knows I have my Source, but I can at least play dumb to keep him satisfied.* She was sure she knew more than he suspected, perhaps this could be used to her advantage?

'I can make light, that was the first thing I learnt to do. Weaving heat into things...'

'The blanket you gave me the day you saved my life, you had woven your Source into it then?'

'Yes. I wanted to keep Solas as warm as possible, and it was woven into my clothes.' Cautiously she reeled off a list of what she could do, making sure to leave out certain things she was sure she might need to protect herself. She did not mention that she could bring up mental shields to protect herself from manipulation, nor that she could place people under a deep sleep.

'You know how to connect your Source with someone else's,' Carlyle said it casually, but Alexandra could see he was trying to catch her out. She looked at him blankly unsure of what he meant. 'You did it that day, you sought me out with your Source and connected us. How else did you think you pulled me from the ocean?'

'Honestly I did not know what I was doing that day,' Alexandra shrugged. 'I think that was more my subconscious taking over than me actively doing anything. The same as the wind that swept through our chambers when you told me of Mathe's marriage...I think that was me at least.' Carlyle closed his eyes and rubbed his face as if he were exhausted.

'I never should have lied to you.' He said thickly.

'No, you should not have. But it is too late and you will get no sympathy from me. You knowingly decided to lie to me Carlyle, and it cost my mother her life...' *I am not completely blameless; perhaps if I had confronted Carlyle from the beginning then he would have taught me?* It was a thought that haunted her each day, but there was nothing Alexandra could do to change the past. Pushing her food around her plate thoughtfully Alexandra bit her lip. She loathed asking Carlyle for anything, but if he was serious about teaching her then what did she have to lose? 'Can you teach me to heal? I know the basics, healing minor burns and small wounds but I cannot heal larger ailments.'

'Unfortunately healing is not where I have focused my powers,' Carlyle replied gently. 'But I am sure Sorceress Rhonwyn would be more than pleased to tutor you in healing.' Alexandra wanted to ask if the Castle Sorcerers knew of her abilities but decided to leave it at that. What was the point in knowing? What could it change? 'Please Alexandra...you need me to tutor you, and I would like the opportunity to at least try and fix the mistakes I have made.'

'Very well,' Alexandra nodded. 'It would be foolish of me to refuse simply out of spite, and my mother did say that you would tutor me when we first married. I remember her mentioning you training me when we arrived back in Karstares.' A thought suddenly occurred to her, and she looked at Carlyle in shock. '*You* wanted to return immediately to Saphyre, but we ended up in Karstares – was that me?' Carlyle smiled wryly as he nodded.

'I am surprised you were not ill that took quite a lot of strength, but it had been moons since you'd used your Source. You probably had quite a lot of it stored up.' *Maybe I could be just as powerful as Carlyle,* Alexandra realised although the thought frightened her a little. Did she want to be that powerful? As their supper was cleared away, Carlyle stood behind Alexandra and rested his hands on her shoulders. She watched in fascination as a shimmering wall circled them curving over their heads, so they were enclosed in a shield of glittering gold and sapphire. Reaching out Alexandra brushed her fingertips across the smooth glass-like surface, pulling her hand back in shock at the numbness which spread up to her shoulder. 'Probe with your Source, carefully.' Carlyle warned her and Alexandra looked up at him nervously, her arm still numb. Closing her eyes she reached deep within herself and pulled a thread of her Source, but she did not need to touch it against the shield to feel the power resonating through it.

'I can put up a shield...but I could not numb someone with it.' She shook her head opening her eyes; she knew if she probed it with her Source it would give her a headache.

'You think too much when you gather your Source,' Carlyle replied. 'You should not need to close your eyes, your enemies will know what you are doing, and you would lose the element of surprise.' Alexandra blushed faintly at the light reprimand. 'Come, I have neglected my responsibilities long enough.' Offering his arm, Carlyle led Alexandra from the dining chamber. Thankful though she was to begin using her Source openly, Alexandra could not shake fear from her mind. Should she have remained silent?

# Chapter Twenty-three

Alexandra accepted the offered cup of warm buttermilk gratefully and gulped it down thirstily. Her head was pounding, and her mouth felt as if she had been drinking sand throughout the night. Beside her Carlyle slept deeply, his arm twisted behind the pillow and the blankets wrapped around his torso and legs. The previous night had seen the castle, and no doubt most of Saphyre, celebrating Carlyle's thirty-fourth life-day. Alexandra had overindulged and had been quite deep in her cups. Now she was left with regret and a disgustingly furry tongue. *I swear by the Goddess I will never drink again;* she thought slumping back against the pillows. Out of the corner of her eye, she could see Roisin watching Carlyle nervously as if waiting for him to awaken and begin barking a mixture of orders and abuse.

'He drank as much as I last night, perhaps more. He will probably sleep for a few more hours.' Alexandra was almost envious of the effect alcohol seem to have on Carlyle. It did not seem to sicken him as it did her, instead, he would merely sleep deeply for several hours. *The perfect time to strike him down,* Alexandra thought wryly but instantly regretted it. Did she really want him dead? *Stop it!* She scolded herself; there was no point thinking about what would happen with the resistance. It had been over a year since Caleb had departed Evany and she had, had no word from him as to how he was. Father Dóchas assured her that he was alive and well, but that was all she was entitled to know. 'I wish I could sleep until sunrise,' she murmured burrowing deeper within the blankets and pulling more to her side and away from Carlyle. It did not help that her limbs felt as if they were lined with lead, nor that the bed was just the right temperature.

'You know Krista will not forgive you if you sleep in.' Roisin smirked as she tugged Alexandra from the bed and ushered her into the dressing room. Helena was already pulling out a dress for her to wear later in the day but left it when she saw Alexandra yawning.

'Your Majesties certainly seemed to enjoy the celebration.' Helena forced a smile, but Alexandra could not muster up the energy to respond. Clothed in a pale green tunic over tan breeches and a white linen shirt Alexandra headed down to the barracks and indoor training grounds. For almost every day since Krista's arrival in Saphyre Alexandra had risen before dawn to train. As she half-stumbled into the training grounds, she was surprised, and a little annoyed, to see that Xander was already up and training with Krista. He stood behind her in what Alexandra deemed an unnecessarily close pose. Frowning she stood to the side and quietly observed the captain and her friend. Their heads were almost touching; Xander's chin resting on Krista's shoulder as he brought her hands forward in a sweeping movement. Alexandra yearned to confront Krista about her relationship with Xander. She was sure, and terrified, that the two were somehow involved together, but both were so careful to give no hint. *This is not a shared moment between friends,* Alexandra thought clenching her fists. She had never seen such a tender look in Krista's eyes. *Does she not realise he is dangerous?* Feeling ridiculous for spying Alexandra coughed, feeling a cold spark of satisfaction as they sprang apart. Xander was blushing furiously, and Krista was flustered, their reaction did little to alleviate Alexandra's nerves and suspicions. *I have to talk to her.*

'I am pleased to see Your Majesty is well enough to join us this morning. You were so deep in your cups I feared you might have drowned.' Krista grinned wickedly and took the training sword back from Xander.

'Very funny,' Alexandra picked up a training sword from the waiting barrel, wincing as her already stiff muscles protested at the extra weight. 'Dare I ask if I embarrassed myself much last night?'

'I am sure by now the citizens of Saphyre are used to seeing their queen deep in wine.' Xander shrugged, and Alexandra scowled at him. She was polite to him only for Krista's sake, but she was in no mood for his cutting remarks this morning.

'I did not realise you would be joining us today Captain.' Her voice dripped with cold dislike, and her eyes narrowed as she turned to face Xander.

'*Enough* Alexandra,' Krista warned and jealousy seeped through Alexandra. *Perhaps I am no better than Carlyle if I begrudge people their own happiness.* But she knew it was more than that. Of course, she wanted Krista to be happy. But not with him, not with the man who even Alexandra could not be sure who's side he was on. Did he leak information to Carlyle about Caleb's resistance? Or was he truly Caleb's man? 'Can both of you please stop acting like children?' For a few moments, Alexandra and Xander continued to glare at each other. Alexandra's hand gripped the hilt of her training sword so tightly her knuckles began to turn white.

'I actually came here to see you, *Your Majesty.*' Xander's tone dripped with sarcasm at the words and Alexandra straightened. Why would he want to see her? She had no business with the Castle Guards other than when they accompanied her to the temple. 'There is someone who wishes to see you. I know that you and Krista train together each morning and that this would be the best place to find you in relative privacy. In fact, he would like to meet you too, Krista.'

'No.' Immediately Alexandra knew of whom Xander spoke, who else could it be? 'Krista will have no part in *any* of this. Carlyle will not hesitate to execute her.' Krista was staring at Alexandra as if she had never seen her before.

'Krista understands the risks –'

'You *told* her?' Electricity sparked at Alexandra's fingertips at the sudden rush of fury, and she dropped the training sword in shock. 'You had no right!'

'You never told me that Alexandra was involved in this,' Krista's voice was quiet. 'I have been here over a year now and not once did you mention that the very Queen of Saphyre is involved in the resistance. Why did neither of you tell me?'

'We operate in discretion; it is not my place to inform you both who is a member of the resistance. Her Majesty knows of only me, our leader and a scarce handful of others. Given how close she is to our enemy I feel even that small number is too many.' Alexandra ignored the jibe focusing her energy on Krista. *I should have done more to protect her; I should have tried to keep her as far away from Xander as possible!* Of course, he would have recruited her. Krista would be perfect bait against Alexandra; he could threaten to reveal Krista's involvement at any moment.

'You can have no part in this resistance Krista! Carlyle would take any rumour of your involvement as a reason to execute you!'

'You have no right to tell me what I should or should not do.' Krista's argued.

'I am your Queen!' Alexandra hissed without thinking. 'I forbid you to join this resistance – to have any part in it! I shall not have your blood on my hands!' Throwing the training sword to the floor, Alexandra marched from the room. 'Tell him I want no part of this anymore – and *she* is forbidden to join!' Wanting to put as much space as she possibly could between herself and Krista, Alexandra returned to the chambers she shared with Carlyle. Krista would not dare confront her with Carlyle in the room; at least Alexandra prayed she would not. She was disheartened to find Carlyle awake; she had thought she would have an hour's solitude at least.

'I was surprised to find you gone this morning. I did not think you would have the energy to train.' Carlyle moved to kiss her in greeting, but Alexandra turned her head so his lips barely skimmed across her cheek. 'Where is Krista?'

'I was not feeling well,' Alexandra shrugged telling herself it was only a half-lie. 'I thought I would come back to bed for a bit before going to the temple this afternoon.' Carlyle's hands slipped on to her waist, pulling her close.

'Perhaps we should both retire for a bit longer. We both drank our fair share last night; I am sure no one would think anything of it. Nor, I am sure, would the citizens mind if you missed your pilgrimage just once.' Alexandra was never more conscious of the locket at her throat than when Carlyle was undressing her. His fingertips twitched at the hem of her tunic, reaching up for the bare skin of her stomach.

'I cannot do that to our people it would not be fair – they expect me to be there!'

'Alexandra! You must give me a son, we have been married for over two years –'

'That is hardly something I need reminding off,' Alexandra shot back bitterly. 'With you hovering over me every moon waiting for a sign of conception. I cannot go on like this Carlyle; I am *scared*. What if...' She trailed off and blinked back tears. She had never forgotten her daughter; how could she? Her daughter should have been walking and perhaps even talking a little by now. *I could be reading her bedtime stories at night.* She saw Carlyle's eyes darken as they did every time there was a hint of their daughter in the atmosphere. 'Perhaps you can forget, even deny what happened, but I cannot. Nor do I wish too. I carried her Carlyle; she was physically a part of me. If you were capable of the slightest human emotion then perhaps you would understand how I feel, maybe even share the grief with me? But you do not care about her, or even me, or you care about is your succession and pride. You care more about your reputation than your own *wife*.' She could see that her words struck a chord and she angrily wiped the back of her hand across her eyes to clear them of tears. When her eyes had finally cleared she was surprised to see a combination of disbelief, sadness, and even guilt etched across Carlyle's handsome features. *Think of all he has done*, she warned herself before she could begin to soften towards him. *Do not be swayed guilt. He is a master of manipulation.*

'I never realised you would be frightened...I know that I failed you last time. Both in protecting you and...after...'

'You will not be able to protect me next time either Carlyle.' Alexandra reasoned gently. 'Even Krista cannot be at my side constantly, even I cannot be aware of...' She shook her head, could she have prevented what had happened? 'I do not want to dwell on the past, but I will not live in fear of my future. We are both young; if the Goddess wishes it, I am sure she will bless us with children eventually.' Carlyle nodded thoughtfully as if he agreed with her.

'Perhaps I should accompany you when you distribute alms later. I could offer my own prayers to the Goddess.'

'I thought you did not believe in her, nor even tolerate religion? Surely this would be blasphemy?' Alexandra asked dryly, desperate to keep him away from the temple. It was the one place she knew she was safe from Carlyle. *What if Caleb is there? I refused to speak to him earlier; no doubt he knows I will be at the temple.* She could only pray that if he was at the temple he would not be foolish to make his presence known with Carlyle in the same place.

Changing into a warm gown Alexandra broke her fast with Carlyle and joined him for the morning's council meeting. Only Ywain and Jacen were present, the rest still recovering from their hangovers. Carlyle seemed pleased that people had spent much of the night celebrating and Alexandra prayed his good mood would last for the rest of the day. When the meeting finished Alexandra was startled to see Krista waiting outside the council chamber, bowing when she saw Carlyle emerging.

'I will see you at the stables.'

'You really do not have to trouble yourself coming to the temple,' Alexandra tried to dissuade him, but Carlyle waved her off. Nervously she turned to face Krista, hating the tension between them. 'You met with him?' She murmured as they walked up to the tower that Alexandra had claimed for her own study.

'Yes...he is rather shocking. His appearance I mean...I thought it was a trick at first.' Krista's eyes were distant. 'Xander -'

'Krista please you must stay away from him,' Alexandra blurted out without thinking. 'There is something about him – he is a *traitor* I am sure of it.'

'Of course he is a traitor, but then surely that would mean you are also one? Which is worse; a traitorous servant or a traitorous wife?' Alexandra felt as if Krista had slapped and she picked up the black ribbon which had sealed the scroll with news of her parents' fate. She had never been able to discard it, and now she found herself twisting it around her hands as she tried to keep her face passive. Of course, she had often questioned what she was and had turned the word traitor over in her mind countless times. She had questioned what kind of person it made her, but to hear someone else voicing the word – and to hear it from her oldest friend. Self-loathing coursed through Alexandra, but she fought to keep her face passive. *She thinks that Xander is a traitor to Carlyle; does she truly think he is loyal to Caleb?* Not once had Alexandra been able to secure firm proof for her suspicions, or any proof at all. But she could not shake her dislike for Xander. She blamed him for the death of her child, but how could she prove any of her suspicions? 'Alexandra...'

'No, you are right.' Alexandra whispered hoarsely. 'I am a traitor.' She knew Krista wanted to apologise, but she couldn't bring herself to hear it, let alone accept it. 'What did you and Caleb speak off?'

'His cause...how long it has been going on. How could you never have mentioned this to me?'

'Because I meant what I said earlier. I want you to have no part in it; I forbid you.'

'You cannot stop me, Your Majesty,' Krista emphasized the Alexandra's title, and she recoiled as if she had been slapped. Would Krista use it every time they disagreed as if it were a weapon? Was she really going to put such a barrier between them? *Am I not doing the same by giving her orders?* Alexandra sat at her desk. 'But while we are on the subject of participation I think you need to withdraw from Caleb. You have not seen him since he left, I think it is better that it remains that way. If he succeeds in his claim, then you will have plenty of time to see him.'

'Did Caleb inform you of my fate after the resistance? *If* he wins?' Alexandra's voice was surprisingly calm, far calmer than she felt given what Krista was saying to her. What right did she have forbidding Alexandra to work with Caleb? Saphyre was *her* kingdom; she had to work in the best interests of the citizens and protect them. Caleb's actions had a direct effect on her citizens; of course, she had to see him. She had to work with him to make sure he had their best interests at heart.

'Yes. You will marry him. It seems like the best solution, you are after all the True Queen and cannot return to Karstares.' Krista shrugged nonchalantly, and Alexandra realised that her friend did not understand her position and that she never would.

'I need to see Caleb, to speak with him. I barely know him. I do not know whether he is truly good if he is different from Carlyle. Or if I do even like him.' The last part was a lie; Krista did not have to know that Alexandra did in fact trust Caleb. That she would trust him with her life should it come to that. All she was focused on doing was making Krista understand that of course she as queen must be a part of the resistance, but then Krista should remain as far away from it all as possible.

'Did you ever like Carlyle? Does it truly matter whether or not you like Caleb? Or do you mean *love*?' She could see that Krista was losing her temper. 'Remember all those times you *flirted* with Carlyle just to get back at Mathe over some pathetic argument?' *Was I truly that petty?* Alexander wondered, but of course, she knew she had been. The first time she had met Carlyle she had all but thrown herself at him during the ball. Perhaps he had even taken that as encouragement that she would be pleased with a betrothal between them. 'Why should it matter how well you know Caleb? You knew what Carlyle was before you accepted the proposal and what good did it do you? You *had* a choice back then Alexandra. You could have protested against it – you could have said no. Yet you gave in to him.' Alexandra blinked furiously, how *dare* Krista talk to her like this? She had known that Carlyle had threatened her, that he had callously murdered her grandmother and would have likely murdered more had she kept refusing him. 'You have to be protected Alexandra; you have to be *innocent* of all accusations. Things are going to happen, Caleb cannot remain underground for much longer. You are the closest person to Carlyle and the one who has the most to lose. We *have* to protect you.'

Alexandra knew that Krista and Caleb wished to keep her safe, but did they both really expect her to sit back and do nothing while they risked their lives? Saphyre was her kingdom now. These people were her citizens, *Krista* was her citizen. She had every right to protect them from Carlyle just as much as the rest of them.

'There are spies everywhere, even close to Carlyle.' Krista continued to try and reason.

'Xander –'

'No. Xander is not the spy.' Krista's voice was firm. 'I admit that Caleb has a spy uncomfortably close to him, even he is aware of that. But it is not Xander.' Somehow Alexandra managed to stop herself from pressing the issue. They were already furious with each other, their friendship dangerously strained. *Do not say something that cannot be fixed. You need proof to make her see the truth.* A sensible voice in the back of her head gently admonished her.

'One day I will have to marry Caleb,' Alexandra said calmly. 'I will not sit back while he defends Saphyre. He may be the rightful king, *may*, but I *am* the True Queen, and these are my citizens. I will protect them no matter the cost, even if it is my life.'

The line for alms was subdued and uncomfortable. Carlyle stood at Alexandra's side scowling at those who accepted coins from her hand. Some people did not even make it as far to the top of the queue; upon hearing that Carlyle was present, many decided to flee instead. Alexandra felt ridiculous standing there in outlandish clothing wearing her crown. Carlyle had insisted that she dress to reflect her station, ignoring her protests that she preferred to dress simply and that it put the people at ease.

Having noticed that some people were choosing to flee Father Dóchas had discreetly moved to the front of the temple where he waited outside on top of the steps. There he would press coin upon people and reassure them that this was hopefully a rare occasion. *It should not be like this,* Alexandra thought as her mind turned to Caleb. *These people should not fear me or anyone in the castle.* Her mind wandered to the future that Caleb had planned. Would he still allow her to distribute alms each moon? Would he join her? She was sure she would have no protests if it was Caleb standing beside her. He would never have insisted on wearing a crown or these rich clothes. She could not imagine having much time for the pomp, and ceremony Carlyle insisted on. But thinking of Caleb soon only turned her mind sour. Marriage to Carlyle would mean she was widowed. She loathed Carlyle, but to help bring about his death…could she really do it? *There has to be another way;* she continuously tried to tell herself. Surely Carlyle could abdicate? The spell binding her to the kingdom was ancient and used by his ancestors to keep their queen's in place. Carlyle was not bound here like she was. Surely he would choose a fresh start over death? Deep down she knew she was fooling herself and that Carlyle would never willingly give up his crown.

'You have come a long way with the people Your Majesty.' Father Dóchas appeared at her side, a warm but uncertain smile on his face. She could see the fear in his spiralled eyes and Alexandra lowered her head in silent apology. Was the priest uneasy simply because Carlyle was present or had the greater reason to fear? *Please do not let Caleb appear!*

'Thank you, Father. I hope that one day my husband and I will travel throughout more of Saphyre. It is hard to believe that I have not yet seen more of our beautiful kingdom.' Alexandra was caught off-guard by the sound of murmuring breaking out towards the main doors of the temple. Raising her eyes,

Alexandra sought out the source of the unrest, but there was nothing evident. The queue was still quite long but she could see the end now as people were waiting inside the temple.

Glancing up at Carlyle she wondered if he could see what was happening but he seemed to have not realised something was out of the ordinary. He continued to glower down at those before them. It was clear to all in the temple that he thought the whole afternoon a waste. Turning back to focus on the people in front of her Alexandra smiled at small elderly woman. The murmuring soon broke into frenzied shouts and Alexandra was pulled backwards by Carlyle as a ball of fire erupted where they had been standing only moments before. Carlyle's hands gripped Alexandra protectively.

'Are you alright?' He asked, and Alexandra nodded uncertainly.

'The king is a usurper! He has made a whore of our beloved queen! Death to the usurper! *Long live King Caleb!*' Carlyle's grip tightened on Alexandra as chaos broke out within the temple, monks swarmed around Alexandra, Carlyle and Father Dóchas while Krista and Xander withdrew their swords looking for the voice. People turned to flee the temple, screaming and trampling each other in their frantic bid to escape. Carlyle's hands suddenly slackened and released Alexandra as he stepped away from her trying to break through the protective circle.

'Your Majesty *no!*' Alexandra cried reaching out to pull Carlyle back and forcing his concentration to break. His hands were glowing brightly, flames licking at his fingertips. 'There are children here – innocent people who have done no harm nor do they wish harm!' She was surprised and frightened at how hot his skin had become; she could feel the heat scolding her hands even through his shirt.

'Bring me the coward who dares to insult my wife and I!' Carlyle roared ignoring Alexandra as she tried to plead with him.

'I mean no disrespect to Her Majesty,' the voice was nasally as if the speaker had a cold. The monks pressed tighter around Alexandra and Carlyle while Krista and Xander stood scanning the crowd. Carlyle ordered the monks aside giving him a clearer view of the temple, but still, Alexandra clung to his arm desperate to prevent him using his Source. 'Queen Alexandra is our rightful Queen. The Light of the Goddess at her coronation proves that she is the one to lead us from the darkness. No more shall we bow down to you,' the speaker stepped forwards; a ragged man with unkempt hair and a limp. 'But you have sullied Her Majesty; you make a whore of her, not a Queen. No longer shall we bow down to you. The people of Saphyre deserve better! Death –' The man's words were cut short as he clasped his chest and fell to his knees; his face contorting and turning an awful shade of purple.

Using her Source Alexandra reached out to the man, desperate to try and help him. Her power brushed against an invisible grip; something was penetrating the man's chest. *His heart!* She suddenly realised what Carlyle was doing; he was crushing the man's heart from within, killing him. Desperately she wrapped her Source around Carlyle's, trying to pull him away from the man.

'Stop it!' She yelled looking up at Carlyle while still fighting his Source with her own. She could see her power was startling him, *frightening* him even, but he refused to release the man. Sweat broke out across Alexandra's body and she collapsed on to trembling knees as she poured more of her Source into the man, trying to build a protective barrier around his diminishing heart. 'You are a coward!' She gasped clutching her own heart as the man's pain pierced her Source. 'If you do not like how the people perceive you then *change*, stop this senseless murder!' Carlyle had paled dangerously, his skin was whiter than marble, and his nostrils flared angrily. Instantly Alexandra knew she had gone too far, but she refused to relax her Source, not until the man was safe.

'Arrest this man!' Alexandra fell backwards as Carlyle released the man. 'Take Her Majesty back to the castle and keep her in our chambers. She is permitted no visitors – not even her slaves!' Alexandra put up no resistance as Xander and Krista picked her up and marched her from the temple. 'You, *girl!*' Carlyle barked at Krista. 'You stay with me. The Captain will ensure Her Majesty reaches the castle safely.' Alexandra turned to plead with Krista, but what could she say?

Neither Alexandra nor Xander spoke as they rode back to the castle. Xander escorted her to her chambers and dismissed both Helena and Roisin. He locked the door behind him as he left but Alexandra had no intentions of leaving, nor did she see the point in locking the door. She could open it with her Source if she wished. Pacing back and forth she replayed the scene over and over in her mind. Her skin began to crackle with electricity, and she was annoyed to find sparks flashing between her fingertips. Sitting on the window seat she opened the shutters; a storm was beginning to rage but the wind cooled her face. Taking several deep breaths she tried to calm her temper but to no avail. Would Carlyle truly have killed that man? *You know he would have!* She scoffed at herself.

The heavy wooden door opened with a burst and Alexandra barely had a second to rise to her feet before she found herself flying through the air. She grunted as she slammed in to the bed, knocking her funny bone on one of the wooden posts. The angry retort died on her lips as she glared at Carlyle, her eyes taking in her crown which lay discarded on the floor as if it were no more than rubbish. Before she could get up Carlyle was on top of her, pinning her in place and holding her head so she had no choice but to look at his eyes. The black spirals against his sapphire irises began to swirl in a clockwise motion, keeping Alexandra in place and clouding her mind.

'Get off me!' At the sound of ripping seams she was able to free herself from the cloudy haze of his eyes. She tried to use her Source, her mind frantically scrabbling to concentrate but she could already feel his own Source encircling her, pressing down on her power. Crying out in pain Alexandra curled into a tight ball, fighting back an anguished cry as pressure bore down on her. She felt as if she were being crushed. 'Stop!' She gasped but her own Source was tightly bound, and she failed to free herself from beneath him.

'You do not use your Source against me,' Carlyle's eyes had turned almost black with rage. *He is going to kill me*, Alexandra thought loathing herself as tears spilled down her cheeks. She could barely breath as he took her, his Source bound her in place so tightly she could barely suck air into her lungs. She loathed herself for crying out, for allowing Carlyle to see the pain and terror he caused her. She squeezed her eyes tightly shut blocking out the scene.

When it was over Carlyle helped her to sit up, the pressure binding her in place evaporated, and her Source slowly flickered back to life. Carlyle's hands softly stroked her hair, his fingertips brushing through her auburn strands which were damp from a mixture of sweat and tears.

'You had best pray that you have conceived,' Carlyle's words were threatening, but his tone was tender and loving making Alexandra shudder in disgust. She thanked the Goddess for small blessings. He would not get an heir from her. *Caleb warned me he could bind my Source. I never believed he would stoop so low though.* Carlyle tossed her a robe, and she looked down at the remnants of her dress. Shakily she slipped the robe on and belted it shut tightly. She desperately wanted to bathe, to wash every trace of him from her skin. She tried to push the assault from her mind, to bury it deep within. But she could not shake off the feeling of the suffocating pressure, of his hands and lips on her skin.

A goblet of wine was pressed into her hands. Carlyle's fury had completely evaporated and in its place, he was the perfect example of a tender and loving husband. Alexandra stared down at the crimson liquid within the goblet. Had it really only been yesterday she had been deep in her cups? Laughing with Jacen as they celebrated their king's life-day? Had it only been a day since Carlyle was declaring her as a brilliant queen, rightfully beloved by their people? She choked back a sob blinking back a fresh wave of tears.

'Drink,' Carlyle soothed. 'It will make you feel better.' She was not even aware of her arm moving before she could register what was happening her goblet was empty, and Carlyle's face was dripping with wine. '*Whore!*'

'You would have killed a man earlier for calling me that.' She pointed out; her voice was empty.

'That was a common peasant – not even fit to breathe the same air as us. *I* am your husband, your *king*. I *own* you.' Anger sparked within flaring Alexandra's source into a hot ball of flame. 'You may not like to admit it, but your body, your mind, and your soul all belong to *me*.' Pushing his sopping hear from his eyes Carlyle stood up and pressed a cloth to his face. Reaching out he clasped Alexandra's hand and pulled her to her feet.

'No.' Alexandra wrenched herself free. 'You do not own me.' But despite her words, she found herself staring helplessly into the spiral patterned eyes once more. In the back of her mind, she could hear a tender voice beckoning her forwards and her feet carried her towards Carlyle. 'Stop it,' she whispered as she stood on tip-toe and her arms reached up to drape themselves across his shoulders.

'We are bound by blood, duty, and love.' Carlyle's voice was low and suggestive as his hand slipped beneath her robe and came to a rest against her thigh. 'Of course I own you.' Tilting his head down Alexandra brought her lips up to meet his, her hands pulling him closer, so there was less space between them. She longed to close her eyes, to block out the sickening image before her, but she her gaze was transfixed to his.

*'Why should it matter how well you know Caleb?'* Krista's words rang through her mind as Carlyle's kiss deepened, and he gathered her into his arms. She could put up no resistance as he carried her down to the bathing chamber, as she poured water over his head and washed the wine from his hair. *It matters greatly,* Alexandra wished she could tell her friend. She had to know what sort of man she was marrying. She could not take another marriage such as this. What if Caleb turned out to be as cruel as Carlyle? *He would not be able to use sorcery on me,* Alexandra thought as she fought against Carlyle's hold over her. *He would never humiliate me like this.*

# *Chapter Twenty-four*

Shortly before the celebrations to mark Alexandra's second year of being crowned it became clear that, despite Carlyle's hidden threat, she had not fallen pregnant. Her mood was short-tempered, and she was plagued with headaches, it was not long before she was crippled by the pains of her bleeding. As quietly as she could she slipped from the bed she shared with Carlyle and hobbled up the staircase to her private chamber. Roisin was quick to fetch a potion from Rhonwyn who accompanied her up to the chamber. Alexandra's fingers twisted the locket as she lay curled on her side while Rhonwyn's Source soothed the cramps.

'He is going to be furious,' Alexandra whispered to no one in particular. *He will always be furious, but the only other option is to fall pregnant. I cannot do that.*

'You are young Alexandra,' Rhonwyn soothed. 'Women older than His Majesty have sometimes been blessed with children by the Goddess. His Majesty will not be furious; he loves you.' Alexandra closed her eyes blocking out Carlyle's assault. She had confided in no one what had happened after she had distributed alms, not even Krista. She loathed Carlyle for what he had done to her, but she was ashamed that she had not been able to fight him off. That even with her Source he had still managed to overpower her. She wanted no one to know of her humiliation. 'Did you know that never before has a queen's ascension to the throne being celebrated over that of a king?'

'No…' Alexandra groaned in pain burying her face into the pillow and clutching her belly as she tried to press down on her cramp. She was yet to grasp using her Source to disperse the pain. She was too short-tempered to concentrate for long enough to wield her power.

'The people of Saphyre truly love you and that light…it was the Light of the Goddess – she has marked you as our True Queen. Something His Majesty cannot boast off,' Rhonwyn lowered her voice to a murmur as she spoke. 'His Majesty could have ignored this event, but he celebrates it – he celebrates having you as his queen. His father did not do that with any of his wives. I know you fear him…but His Majesty truly does love you.' She knew that Rhonwyn was trying to soothe her, but it had little effect. Carlyle could not love her. *How could you hurt someone so viciously if you love them?* She asked herself. 'Sleep for now. I am sure either Roisin or Helena will fetch you when His Majesty wishes to break his fast.'

Nervously Alexandra made her way down to the intimate dining chamber to break her fast with Carlyle. She had never been able to forget the threatening tone after Carlyle's assault; *'You had best pray that you have conceived.'* What would he do? Or had he not meant it? *Do not hold out hope for the latter;* she thought biting back a sigh as she curtsied in greeting. She sat opposite Carlyle wearily, waiting for the scathing remark about her inability to conceive.

'Your slaves inform me you are unwell.' Carlyle poured her a drink and slid it across the table. There was something menacing in his actions, although Alexandra couldn't be sure whether she was imagining it or not.

'I am sorry,' was the only reply she could muster.

'You have conceived once; I am sure you will do so again.' Carlyle smiled reassuringly, and Alexandra looked up from her drink in suspicion. 'Although two years of marriage and only one pregnancy, which ended in failure, one cannot help but wonder if there is some sorcery at hand.' *Stay calm,* Alexandra instantly warned herself. 'I certainly have plenty of enemies; I would not put it past someone to ensure you did not give me an heir. I doubt you would be so foolish as to prevent yourself conceiving.'

'Of course not,' Alexandra replied in what she hoped was a neutral tone. 'The only person other than you who has taught me how to use the Source was my mother – and by then I was already with child. I do not think she would have taught me such a spell even if she had known of one, as much as she loathed you.' Carlyle nodded thoughtfully.

'There is of course Sorceress Rhonwyn; you have been learning to heal with her.' Fear stabbed at Alexandra; he would not blame one of his own Castle Sorcerers surely? *I cannot go on like this for much longer,* she realised. *He is going to start laying blame upon innocent people.*

'Rhonwyn teaches me just that – healing.' Thankfully this was the truth, and Alexandra did not even have to try and look innocent as she spoke. 'Carlyle please I...' she trailed off and shrugged, what could she say? She knew why she wasn't falling pregnant, but she knew now that it could not go on for much longer.

'I know you are frightened about falling pregnant Alexandra. But I pray you are not letting your fears get in the way of your duty.' His tone was gentle but his deep eyes glimmered threateningly. Resisting the urge to tug at the locket Alexandra nodded.

'I am sure the Goddess will bless us with a child in time.' She hated taking the Goddess's name in vain, especially when she had no intentions of allowing herself to conceive Carlyle's child.

'A son.' Alexandra closed her eyes choking back tears; she had never forgotten his anger when it was revealed the child she had carried had been a daughter.

The council meeting seemed to last an eternity, Alexandra forced herself to sit upright and at least look as if she were interested in what was being discussed. *You wanted to be more involved in the ruling;* she chided herself. *What did you think that would entail?* She had never imagined there could be so much to discuss around crops and irrigation. She wished she had thought to take one of Rhonwyn's soothing potions before she had attended the meeting. Each time someone spoke their voice grated on her nerves, and she fought to keep a control on her shortened temper. Rhonwyn had taught her how to make the potion for herself, but hers never had the same effect as that of Rhonwyn's. As she left the council chamber it wasn't until she saw Krista lounging against a wall that she realised she had forgotten her training session that morning.

'I am sorry,' Alexandra sighed praying that Krista was in a forgiving mood.

'Roisin found me after she sent for Rhonwyn,' Krista waved her hand and Alexandra felt a sudden rush of affection for her lady.

'If you do not feel up to training with Krista perhaps you would like to practice your Source with me?' Carlyle offered resting a hand on her waist as he fell in to step beside the two women.

'I think I would just rather rest.' Alexandra smiled uncertainly. She had not sparred or practiced her Source with Carlyle since the day she had distributed alms. She could not shake off the feeling of the awful pressure with which he had bound her Source. She loathed herself for admitting it, but she was frightened of Carlyle and the power he held.

'Very well. Should you change your mind, I will be in the Sorcerers' Tower,' Carlyle kissed her cheek and departed. Neither Alexandra nor Krista spoke until they were sure they were alone in Alexandra's study. Holding out her hands against the door Alexandra sealed her tower, making sure her barrier spread across the window to protect them from eavesdroppers.

'You have been quiet recently,' Krista said wearily. 'Is everything alright?' Alexandra could only bring herself to nod.

'While Caleb has been away I have been thinking about whom of Carlyle's men might be persuaded to join Caleb's resistance.' Slumping into a chair Alexandra thought over Jacen and Lemuel. *If they do not want to join they could refuse...I do not think they would report to Carlyle what was happening.* She was sure the two could be trusted, even if they did not join Caleb.

'You have not approached anyone yourself I hope.' Krista's tone was warning, and Alexandra scowled at her. 'You must be free from suspicion. Approaching people will hardly keep you innocent, pass the names on to me and I will inform Caleb. We will go from there.'

'*We?*' Alexandra hissed unable to suppress the bitter jealousy. *How many times has Krista met with Caleb?* It irked her that Krista had probably met with Caleb more times than she had. *Stop being so childish!*

'Do you realise how much Caleb cares for you? All he can talk about is how you are the True Queen of Saphyre. He *needs* you to be able to hold the throne; he is not excluding you out of spite he is doing it for your own protection.' Alexandra rubbed her forehead and nodded wearily.

'I know, you are right and I apologise. I am just short-tempered,' Krista snorted but Alexandra refused to retaliate. 'There are two men who sit on the council. They do not share Carlyle's loathing for those who do not possess the Source; one of them is even married to a woman who does not hold it. I think he fears for her safety, Carlyle makes it clear that should anything happen to his wife then there are several more who would make a suitable replacement.'

'Their names?' Krista pressed.

'I...I am scared.' Alexandra whispered as she thought back to the man at the temple who had proclaimed Caleb, the rightful king. She had never heard anyone mention Caleb's name publicly, let alone in front of Carlyle. 'I do not want anyone to get hurt – if something should happen to them...'

'Caleb would not approach them unless he was certain it was safe to do so. But how do you expect us to get close to these people? Once Caleb is king things will be different – Saphyre will change!' *But will it?* Alexandra wanted to ask, could they really be sure Caleb would be a better king than Carlyle? *Does he even realise what he would be doing? What it means to be queen?* Carlyle had been raised to rule, whereas Caleb had been raised to try and claim the throne. Had anyone taught him what it meant to rule if he succeeded? The resistance had been going on for so long had anyone in his family even thought about that?

'Jacen and Lemuel – they are close, and they seem to oppose Ywain in everything he aims for. I am sure they would openly oppose Carlyle on some issues if it did not carry a death warrant.'

The eve before the second anniversary of Alexandra's coronation she sat with Carlyle for dinner. The atmosphere between the two was subdued although the castle itself buzzed with excitement for the impending celebrations. *I cannot go on like this for much longer,* Alexandra thought pushing her food around absently.

'A merchant ship arrived from Karstares with news today,' Carlyle said in an attempt to make conversation. He refilled Alexandra's goblet although she had no desire to drink. 'It seems your brother's wife has fulfilled her duty; twin boys.' Alexandra raised her goblet in a silent toast. She didn't begrudge Mariah or her brother their happiness, and it saddened her she would most likely never meet her nephews. She just wished Carlyle did not use them as a weapon against her.

'Mariah does not live her life in fear, cut off from her friends...' *And with a husband who lied to her throughout the first year of their marriage.* But she managed to stop herself from saying the final part.

'I have hardly cut you off from your friends – you have Krista. Nor have I forbidden you to write to King Giric,' even now it was strange hearing her brother referred to as 'king' and Alexandra winced at the familiar stab of grief. It was true Carlyle had encouraged her to write to Giric often, even Mariah. But Alexandra could not bring herself to write to them. What would she say? She was sure her letters would only carry bleak news. 'Surely you do not wish for us to live out the rest of our days in misery?'

'Of course not,' Alexandra whispered.

'Then please; set aside your loathing - at least for tomorrow. Allow us to enjoy the celebrations.' Fingertips brushed against the nape of her neck with a feather-light touch as Carlyle brushed her hair away from her skin. Softly he kissed the curve of her neck.

As Alexandra bathed in the sheet-lined wooden tub in her chamber, her mind wandered to Karstares. She no longer saw Karstares as her home, how different was it now that Giric ruled over the kingdom? She could not picture anyone but her father on the throne. Nevertheless, it still saddened her that she had lost contact with Giric and Mariah. *If Karstares is no longer home, does that mean Saphyre is?* She wondered sinking lower into the tub and leaning her head against the edge. It had certainly become more bearable with Krista's presence. She could speak honestly to her old companion without fear that her words would be leaked back to Carlyle. She had also discovered Krista had been crucial to regaining much of her memory back; her friend had described past-events which had awoken something in Alexandra. She would never regain her full memory, but she was thankful for what she did have. *Krista said things are going to change soon...how soon?* A knock at the door snapped her from her thoughts, and she quickly sat up trying to cover herself as best as possible as the door to her chamber opened.

'Why are none of your ladies with you?' Carlyle asked frowning as he closed the door behind him.

'I am capable of washing myself,' she shrugged but up no argument as Carlyle began to wash her hair. His fingers were surprisingly gentle as he massaged her scalp. 'Did you want something?'

'No,' Alexandra arched an eyebrow but realised he could not see her face. 'I actually just wanted to talk.' Settling back she closed her eyes and listened to Carlyle's rumbling voice.

Despite her apprehension, Alexandra was surprised to find herself enjoying the ball the following evening. Neither she nor Carlyle had slept the previous night; instead, they had talked and played several games of cards and discs. From the moment the sun had first broken over the horizon it had been a glorious day. Even the procession through the city and the blessing at the temple had gone smoothly. Alexandra and Carlyle had been draped in layers of gold with their crowns reflecting the dazzling sun. Crowds of people had lined the streets cheering as Alexandra rode past and a few had even broke out in cheers for Carlyle. For the first time since their marriage, Alexandra had found herself wondering if Carlyle was truly capable of change. He had smiled at the crowds; a gesture Alexandra had never witnessed in him before.

'You seem joyous today,' Carlyle kissed her hand and bowed as they began to dance in the middle of the great hall slowly. A sudden shadow flittered through Alexandra's memory; the last time she had been this happy had been the ball on the eve of her miscarriage.

'It has been a joyous day,' Alexandra smiled as she shoved the thought aside. She rested her free hand on his upper arm, not quite tall enough to reach his shoulder and dance. Gradually Carlyle closed the gap between them as they danced and Alexandra rested her head against his broad chest. *If he could change...maybe the resistance could end. There would be no need for bloodshed.* Perhaps she was caught up in the atmosphere, or perhaps she had drunk a bit too much of the wine, but Alexandra prayed this could be a sign of a new start for the kingdom.

As Carlyle stepped back and twirled Alexandra around him her eyes caught sight of Krista standing at the edge of the room with an almost dreamy look on her face. Alexandra's heart plummeted as she saw Krista was deep in conversation with Xander, her eyes animated in a way Alexandra had never seen before. *How can I make her see sense? How can she be sure that Xander is not the one betraying Caleb?* Lost in her thoughts Alexandra was unaware of the music abruptly stopping, nor that she was suddenly standing alone; her hand still raised as if resting on Carlyle's arm.

'Citizens,' Carlyle's deep voice filled the hall and a hushed silence descended. Accepting two goblets from a slave, he presented one to Alexandra with a flourish. 'Today we have celebrated two glorious years since the crowning of my beautiful wife; Queen Alexandra.' Alexandra's cheeks flared as people began to cheer and she smiled, almost grinning when she caught Krista clapping. 'She has been a kind and gracious queen, distributing alms and advising on the council. However,' Alexandra felt the smile on her face suddenly freeze at the drastic change in Carlyle's tone. No longer was it cheerful but rather it had turned sour. 'While she has shown to be kind of heart she has continuously failed me and as a result failed us all. What good is the distribution of alms when she fails to ensure that your own children are guaranteed a safe future and protected by the succession of my son?' The wine in Alexandra's mouth turned to ash, the hand holding her goblet suddenly slackened and dropped to the floor, splashing her in the crimson liquid. Quickly Krista moved to her side, her legs planted firmly apart and her hand twitching towards the hilt of her sword.

'No,' Alexandra murmured bowing her head so Carlyle could not see her speak. 'Do not thing foolish.' But Carlyle had not missed Krista's intentions and he turned to glare down at her.

'You have mistaken me; I wish my wife no harm. However, there are others who do wish her harm, who have dared to harm her in the past and plot to do so again. People in this very room.' The air thickened and Alexandra could hear the beginnings of panic as people began to murmur amongst themselves. *Why is he doing this?* Alexandra thought helplessly, the day had been so pleasant. Why had he felt the need to ruin it? 'I recently accompanied Her Majesty on a visit to the temple while she distributed alms to the peasants of our beautiful city.' Carlyle's arms rose into the air, his goblet of wine floating casually beside him. An earth shattering *bang* followed by a blinding white light tore through the air, Alexandra felt her breath knocked from her as Krista pushed her to the ground, remaining on top of her until the air had cleared. *Has he gone insane?* 'This fool insulted Her Majesty, denouncing her as a whore before the very people who she tirelessly works to protect. Not content with humiliating your queen the fool decided to throw false accusations upon me.' Alexandra looked up from beneath Krista and was surprised to see the man from the temple on his knees with his hands bound behind him. She was sickened to see that his face was a bloody mass of pulp, his eyes barely visible beneath the swelling. 'There is only one punishment for such heinous acts.'

'No!' Alexandra pushed herself out from beneath Krista and instinctively threw her Source around the man. He seemed resigned to his fate and did not react as he was encased beneath a shimmering globe. 'Your Majesty please you *must* show mercy!' She begged. *How could I have been so foolish as to think he was changing?*

'Mercy is weakness,' Carlyle laughed scornfully, and Alexandra winced as his Source penetrated her barrier. The man before them began to writhe on the floor in startling agony as his body twisted in to impossible possible. Krista's hands gripped Alexandra, helping to keep her upright as the pain the man felt tore through Alexandra. *Concentrate!* She could feel her Source draining dangerously, and she realised that she had made the mistake of connecting it with Carlyle's. He was siphoning off her own power from the barrier she had thrown around the man, using it to harm him. Carlyle stretched out his left hand, clasping his feet as if he were crushing an object. *Please, Goddess lend me strength to protect this man.* Alexandra did not expect an answer from the Goddess; she expected her prayer to go unheeded. A tickling in her right hand almost broke her concentration, and she looked down, expecting to see Krista's fingertips or some object pressing her palm; yet there was nothing there. *Someone is lending me their Source?* She looked around for who could possibly defy Carlyle, but there was no evidence of someone using their own power. 'I hear all that passes within my kingdom; I have heard whispers of a man who claims that *he* is the rightful king. Let this man's death show you that this is a grave falsehood.'

'Carlyle…' Alexandra whispered feeling her knees beginning to buckle. Whoever was lending her their Source was strong, but neither Alexandra nor her unknown friend were a match for Carlyle. 'Please – you cannot do this! Carlyle *stop*!' She knew the moment his name escaped her lips that she had made a grave mistake. Gathering the stranger's Source she tried her best to throw Carlyle's power off course and away from the man, but it was like trying to push cement. She sobbed as the man fell to the floor with a dull thud, his glassy eyes staring at her blankly and his mouth twisted open in a silent scream of agony. She saw then that his tongue had been callously ripped out and she turned her head to vomit before she could stop herself.

'I can do as I please *wife*,' Carlyle hissed pulling her to her feet and forcing her to look at the corpse before them. 'I will not tolerate any form of rebellion in my kingdom. This peasant foolishly chose to slander me in public, in the house of our beloved Goddess.' Lowering his voice so that only Alexandra could hear him, Carlyle pressed his lips to her ear. 'You had best start praying for a son. For every moon that you fail to conceive I will hunt down each and every one of these pathetic rebels and execute them publicly. They are only a threat for as long as we have no sons…if you care for our people, then you had best protect them the way the Goddess intended.'

# Chapter Twenty-five

Over a week had passed since the fatal ball, and Alexandra had taken to her chamber, locking the door against Carlyle. She didn't emerge to attend council meetings or to dine. Roisin brought her meals up each day and a set of clothing but informed her that Carlyle had ordered Alexandra to be left in isolation. If she was to act like a child and throw a tantrum, then he would punish her as such. *I am not throwing a tantrum;* Alexandra cried pacing around her small chamber. But what else could she do?

Sitting on the window ledge, she pushed open the shutters to observe the city below. What was Caleb doing at that moment? Had he left the city? Had he evacuated those who had joined the resistance to protect them? *Even if Carlyle had meant his threat he would not look for people who were truly working with Caleb – he will just execute people at random. Who would argue against him?* Twisting the locket at her throat Alexandra couldn't help but wonder what she had done. Was this the Goddess punishing her? Surely the Goddess could not truly be in favour of Carlyle ruling? He would have been marked as a True King if she had. *What if the Goddess is not real?* Alexandra asked herself, *what if there is no one there. No one listening to our prayers?* She wasn't sure which thought was less appealing; the thought that there was no one watching over them, or the thought that there was but the deity chose to ignore them. *Could I go to the temple and talk to Father Dóchas? But what could he say?*

She quickly dismissed the thought of leaving the castle, not only would it rouse Carlyle's fury but she was sure Father Dóchas would not be able to offer her any words of advice. He had spent his life serving the Goddess; he would not be pleased to hear Alexandra doubting her.

'Alexandra,' Carlyle's voice was gruff and she held her shield against the door. 'Let me in.' *Go away;* Alexandra pleaded focusing her eyes on the door and watching for any signs that Carlyle was trying to force his way in. 'How do you hope to conceive if you remain shut in your chamber?' *But I do not hope to conceive;* she thought bitterly, instantly regretting the thought. How many people would lose their lives because of her fear? She wished Caleb had decided they should not see each other, that she would be safer this way. She desperately needed to speak to him, to confide in what she had done since her miscarriage. Would he be furious? *If I conceive how long would it protect people? If I bore another daughter surely that would send him into a rage? But if I give him a son…where does that leave Caleb?*

Turning to look out the window once more Alexandra glanced down at the drop below. What if she chose to end it now? *That would end my suffering, not Saphyre's.* She berated herself for her selfishness. Krista risked her life daily just by associating with Caleb as did others who had aligned themselves with him.

Sleep would not come to her, and she lay in bed tossing and turning as the question swam around her mind. How many people would die because of her selfishness? Of her fear? *Rhonwyn said that Carlyle celebrates my crowning over his because the people love me more – yet how can they? I am nothing but danger to them, no matter what I do.* As sleep continued to evade her, Alexandra knew there was only one thing she could do. She had to return to Carlyle's bed. She would visit the temple as soon as she could and ask Father Dóchas to remove the spell from her locket. But until then she would return to Carlyle's bed; what else could she do? If she failed to conceive that moon, she would throw herself on his mercy. *Even without the spell, there is no guarantee I will conceive,* she thought fighting back the rising bile.

Throwing back the blankets she slipped a dressing robe over her chemise and tentatively made her way down to Carlyle's chamber. She paused outside the door wondering if she should knock but quickly decided against it. She was not deemed unpure at that moment to sleep in his bed, so why should she knock? Steeling her nerves Alexandra pushed the door open still trying to decide what she should say or do. He was probably asleep, should she just slip into the bed?

Her mind slammed to a halt at the sight before her as she stepped into the chamber. The hearth was ablaze, the flames filling the room with a flickering light. Shadows danced across the walls and Alexandra watched at them in horrified fascination as they writhed. From the bed came the moans of pleasure and Alexandra forced herself to look in horror to see Carlyle and Helena, a writing mass of limbs. Bile rose in Alexandra's stomach, and she doubled over as if punched, fighting back the urge to vomit. For a few seconds, all she could do was stare helplessly at Carlyle and Helena, trying to piece together what was happening. The locket at her throat felt as if it was beginning to burn, she could almost hear Carlyle's image taunting her from within the jewellery. Reaching up she tore the locket and hurled it towards the hearth, fleeing from the chambers before either of them registered her presence.

She glanced for a split second at the staircase to her chamber but instantly dismissed it. Did she really think she could just go to bed and act as if nothing had happened? *I need Caleb;* she realised sprinting through the castle and towards the barracks. She had no idea where he lived, but she knew Krista did, she would make her friend take her to him. She was dismayed to find Krista's door locked, she thought about using her Source to open it but knew that her friend would never forgive such a violation of her privacy. With no other option, she pounded on the wooden surface, crying out Krista's name. She did not care that she was making a foolish spectacle of herself, what did it matter?

'What is the matter with you?' Alexandra barely took in Krista's state of undress as the door opened, nor that she was purposefully trying to keep Alexandra from entering her chamber.

'Take me to him now, *please.*' Alexandra begged, 'I do not care about it being dangerous – that I need to be free from suspicion. I have to see him, *now.*' Krista looked as if she was about to refuse and Alexandra felt something within herself snap. 'I am not asking Krista, I am ordering you as your Queen.

I demand you take me to see him; he is plotting a disturbance in my kingdom. I have every right to speak with him, perhaps more so than you.' She was surprised at the coldness of her tone, but she was fed up with people deciding what was best for her. Krista's dark cheeks flushed with anger, and she glared at Alexandra.

'Wait here, Your Majesty.' Krista spat as she retreated into her chamber and shut the door firmly behind her. As Alexandra waited, she could feel her anger evaporating, but she could not apologise to Krista. Nor could she confide in the scene she had just discovered. *What can Caleb do?* She asked herself wondering if she had made the right decision, but she would not turn back. 'You are a fool Alexandra Saorsa.' Alexandra winced at her former name.

'I have not been a Saorsa in over two years,' Alexandra reminded her bitterly. 'I am Alexandra, Queen of Saphyre.' Krista paused and stopped Alexandra in her tracks, eyeing her up and down. The anger had disappeared from her eyes and instead were full of concern.

'What has happened to you? Do you have any idea of what you are asking me to do? You have been locked in your chamber for over a week, how will you explain this to Carlyle should he discover you have gone?' Tears stung Alexandra's eyes, and her throat closed painfully, but she remained silent. What could she say to her oldest friend to make her understand?

'He will not notice I am gone,' was all she could bring herself to say. 'Please Krista I have to speak with him…there are things we need to discuss.' She was careful not to say Caleb's name fearful that there may be someone who would overhear them, although the thought did not deter her from her mission.

'He is not going to be happy.'

'I am sorry, but I do not care. I am sick to death at doing what people deem best for me; I am sick of living in fear.' Alexandra strode past Krista intent on finding her own way to Caleb but knew it was a futile mission. 'Blindfold me if you must that is what he always did – but please just take me to him.' Krista held out her hands to show that she had nothing to blindfold her with. 'I will close my eyes if it makes you feel better.' Despite the sombre atmosphere Krista smiled wryly and held out her hand.

'Very well then, close your eyes.' Alexandra smiled slightly as she took Krista's hand and squeezed her own eyes shut. 'I need a small light to see the way.' Nodding Alexandra conjured a small ball of light; she had practiced the spell so much it was now second nature to her. As Krista pulled her forwards, she could feel the air steadily growing colder, but despite the drop in temperature Alexandra still felt as if she were in a furnace. Anger pulsed through her veins and she regretted saying she would close her eyes. The scene between Carlyle and Helena replayed itself behind her closed eyelids. How long had he been sleeping with her lady? She felt sickened as she remembered when Carlyle had blackened Helena's eye. Had he forced her into this union? *He is not beyond forcing women,* she thought darkly as his own assault on her sprang to mind. As Krista came to a halt, Alexandra kept her eyes firmly closed. 'It is not too late Alexandra...you could still return to your chamber.'

'No...I need to speak with him.' Opening her eyes, Alexandra found herself outside a camouflaged door. If it had not been for the small ball of light, she would not have noticed the cracks which outlined the doorway within the stone walls. Knocking on the door, she did not pause long for an answer, afraid that she would change her mind. *He will be sleeping;* she scolded herself as she pushed the door open – or would he? Surely she should have learnt her lesson from only a short while ago.

'Caleb I am sorry,' Krista spoke before Alexandra could even open her mouth as both women stepped into the cramped chamber. 'She was insistent upon seeing you; I could not dissuade her.' Alexandra glanced around the small room, taking in the makeshift bed of wooden crates under a straw-filled mattress, hardly the bedchamber of a man who claimed to be the rightful king. She took in Caleb's crumpled shirt lying on the floor and the bloodstained cloth that he held to his shoulder.

'It is fine Krista. I know Her Majesty has a mind of her own,' Caleb smiled from his seat on the bed and rose to bow to Alexandra wincing as he moved. 'Please do not stay on our account, I will see Her Majesty safely back to the castle.' Caleb said before Krista could question him on his injury. Looking torn but knowing she was dismissed Krista departed, throwing one more concerned look for both Alexandra and Caleb. 'Alexandra, what is the matter?' To hear him saying her name made Alexandra relax, she had feared he was furious with her when he spoke her title. She could tell that he was divided between anger and concern for her stupidity at visiting him, wondering what could have driven her to do so. Settling the bloodstained cloth on a barrel he pulled her away from the door, searching her face for traces of harm.

'What happened to you?' She asked looking at the grotesque wound oozing from his shoulder. Thoughts of Carlyle's betrayal flood her mind, replaced with concern for Caleb. 'Have you been fighting?'

'It was nothing. Just a mistake.'

'Let me heal you,' Alexandra held up glowing fingertips and blushed as Caleb shook his head in protest. His eyes widened in fear and beads of sweat broke out across his forehead. *He truly fears the Source? Even mine?* 'Caleb please that wound looks nasty – it could become infected.'

'I have had worse,' Caleb shrugged her off and hissed in pain as the movement tore the wound in his shoulder ever-so-slightly. Gesturing for him to sit back on the bed, Alexandra picked up a jug of water and tore a strip of fabric from the bottom of her dressing robe.

'Caleb this *needs* healing,' Alexandra argued as she began to wash the edges of the wound. 'Either that or stitching at the very least – but that could leave you with a scar.'

'Stitch it then,' Caleb hissed closing his eyes as she continued to gently dab at the wound. 'Promise me no sorcery!' Alexandra was shocked to see how frightened he was of the Source, the muscles in his neck bunching up as he tensed from the pain. *How can I marry this man when he fears part of me?* She did not allow herself to dwell on the thought; there were so many obstacles in their path she wasn't even certain if they ever would marry.

'Do you have a needle and thread?' She asked trying to keep her voice steady. She had observed Rhonwyn stitching wounds but had never done so herself, Carlyle had scoffed at the thought of his queen touching commoners and expressly forbidden her from practicing. Other than cloth she did not have much experience with a needle and thread, and she doubted skin would yield the same as cloth. She fetched the needle and thread at Caleb's directions, looking around for something that would numb the pain.

'I have been stitched more times than I care to count,' he reassured her as Alexandra sat down to work on his wound. She could feel the bile in her stomach rising once more, but she refused to show how faint the work made her feel. She worked in silence, intent on stitching the wound as neatly as possible and keeping an eye for any signs that there may be an infection. Only when she was finished did Caleb break the silence that had descended between them. 'Alexandra you know better than to seek me out, that we should not see each other. What has happened?' Alexandra wondered she could say, but her reason for seeking him out suddenly seemed foolish.

'I have not returned to Carlyle's bed since the ball…he threatened that he would kill someone each moon that I did not conceive. I locked myself in my own chamber; I did not want to see anyone – mostly him. I went to his chamber tonight – I…' She trailed off not wanting to go into detail with Caleb about what she had expected. 'When I went into his chamber I expected him to be asleep, it was late, but…he was bedding Helena.' She felt foolish for being upset, for the tears which blurred her vision. What did it matter to her if Carlyle slept with other women? She had no love for Carlyle, only loathing. So why did she feel devastated? 'I want to go home Caleb. There is no one I can trust,' she sobbed burying her face into her hands. 'I want to be away from all of this, I want out of this marriage!'

She realised as she spoke she did not mean home to Karstares, that after all was no longer her home. Instead, she wished to return to Bournemouth, she had begun a life there once. She could just as easily carve a new one out.

'Alexandra you can trust me, I promise.' Alexandra shook her head; how could he be so sure of that? She had trusted him once, two years ago she had trusted him to help her return to Karstares before her coronation. Yet he had never intended to help her flee; his goal had been for her to be crowned. 'I know I have let you down.' Caleb's voice was low and full of guilt as he spoke. 'I think perhaps I have been as bad as Carlyle. I have tried to use you for my own gain, but I promise you that is not how I want things to be between us.' Strong fingertips tilted Alexandra's head up and she found herself staring into Caleb's deep eyes. So similar to Carlyle's yet so different, soft and tender rather than cold and hard.

She was stunned as Caleb's head lowered, his lips seeking out her own. She didn't pause to think about what they were doing. All thoughts had vanished from her mind as his fingers deftly reached for the lacings of her chemise, pushing it back from her shoulders along with her robe. She slipped her arms free, allowing the chemise to pool around her waist and leaving her bare, shivering as Caleb's fingertips brushed against the sensitive skin along her back.

She had been a wife for two years and had known her duty as a wife entailed. But already she could see that life with Caleb would be different. Not once did Alexandra flinch away under his touch, instead her body responded to his touch. She yearned to explore every inch of Caleb, and as he picked her off the bed, she felt her legs wrapping around his waist and her eyes daring to meet his own as her back was pressed against the cold stone wall. His lips moulded against hers; warm, soft and full. Not once did she have to fight the urge to push him away, to tell him to stop. She didn't want him to stop. As their eyes met once more Alexandra could see the questioning look in Caleb's eyes as he sought her consent frightened that he was taking advantage of her; Was she sure of this? Without hesitating, Alexandra nodded and pressed her lips to his once more in answer. For once her mind was silent; there was no pleading for the ordeal to be over. She allowed herself to enjoy Caleb's touch, to lose herself in the moments of pleasure.

Curled up in the warmth of Caleb's arms Alexandra craned her neck slightly so that she could study him. His eyes were closed, his nostrils flaring with each breath he drew. She smiled and nestled against him as he began to snore lightly, his fingers twitching against her waist and drawing her closer. How could he and Carlyle look so similar yet be so different? Caleb reminded her of the summer, warm and tender. Whereas Carlyle was as cold and harsh as the winter moons, brutally uncaring about the wellbeing of others. Resting her head against Caleb's chest, Alexandra listened to the sound of his heart beating steadily. Never before had she felt content, but there was tugging at her heart.

'Caleb?' She spoke softly almost as if she did not want to wake him and spoil the moment. This was the first moment she had felt truly happy in Goddess only knew how long, why was she intent on spoiling it? Caleb's eyes opened a fraction to indicate he was listening, the fingers on her waist squeezing lightly. 'You do not love me, do you?' She felt her cheeks warm at the question; she sounded as if she were a love-struck teenager. But there was more to it than that. She was already trapped in one loveless marriage; did she really want to go through it all again? And what of Caleb? It was hardly fair on him to be trapped in that sort of marriage.

'No,' he answered truthfully but surprised her by following up with a question of his own. 'Do you love me?' It felt ridiculous to be discussing love when she was wrapped in his arms. She stared up at the low ceiling thinking over his question before shaking her head. 'Does it bother you?'

'I am already trapped in one loveless marriage,' she answered truthfully. 'I do not want you to be in that same position. You should be free to choose who you wish to marry – I will not stand in the way of you choosing your queen.'

'I am choosing Alexandra,' Caleb replied firmly tilting her head up to kiss her softly. 'I want to marry you, it is true we do not love each other, but we like each other at least. Other than Xander, and perhaps even Krista, I have very few people I can trust, but I count you amongst those people Alexandra. I trust you with my life; I wish to protect you – do you know how much I loathe not being able to protect you from that monster?' Alexandra blushed deeply. 'You are the queen I want to rule by my side; it is your right after all. The Goddess has chosen you. You will help me keep Saphyre stable, the people may not trust me but will trust you – they *love* you. Without you I could not take the throne, it would plunge Saphyre in to even more chaos, and I cannot bear to bring more suffering upon our people.'

'I always imagined I would marry for love. When I was in Karstares I was in love with a knight; I was sure that we would marry – that being a princess would not stop me from marrying who I chose.' For once there was no pain in confessing her past, nor was she embarrassed to admit her first love to Caleb. 'But perhaps marriage between friends is wiser.'

'Perhaps it is, we cannot afford to let passion rule our heads.' Caleb grinned, and Alexandra could not help sharing it with him as she thought back to their moments of passion. 'I do love you…perhaps not as a lover should, but I care for you deeply.' Alexandra closed her eyes and nestled against him, perhaps that was what love was? She felt safe and at ease with

Caleb. Surely that was what mattered? 'I promise you I will never harm you, not like I have done in the past. I never should have lied to you, and it has haunted me every day…nor will I harm you like *he* has done.'

'No!' Alexandra bolted upright and looked around the dark room. She had no idea how much time had passed nor was there anything present to signify the time. 'He will most likely be searching for me right now,' or would he? Had Carlyle even noticed her walking in on him and Helena? Was he still with her now? *I can hardly criticise him for bedding another woman when I am currently in another's bed.* She thought sarcastically, but she knew she could criticise him. What had passed between her and Caleb had not been intentional, she had not come here seeking out Caleb's arms. Not once had she berated Carlyle, made him feel inadequate or a useless failure. Nor did she love him or even like him. She was not his wife willingly. Jumping to her feet she snatched up chemise and robe, throwing them on clumsily.

'I will take you up; I know a shortcut to your chamber.' Caleb reassured her as he quickly dressed. Alexandra was too worried about how she could explain her disappearance to Carlyle that she missed the door to the cramped chamber opening and quickly closing. Her nose sniffed the air at the smell of porridge and honey, but when she glanced at the door, there was no one there. *Are we under the kitchens?* She wondered sniffing the air, but the scent had disappeared. As she looked at Caleb, she could see he was uncomfortable as he gestured to the blindfold in his hand. 'I know you did not wear one with Krista, but I want to take no chances. I want to keep you as safe as possible,' Caleb answered her unspoken questions. 'I will not have you harmed because of me.'

'Please do not shut me out,' Alexandra begged him as she turned around. 'I need to see you – I need to be a part of this resistance. At least let me see you when I distribute alms? Carlyle came with me just once; I am sure he does not wish to repeat it…' She couldn't explain to him why she needed to see him, but if she knew he was physically there then perhaps she could have some hope. Her answer was a tender kiss as Caleb slowly turned her around.

'I will do my best; I am sorry I ever suggested shutting you out of the resistance. I had no right…you are my Queen after all.' Alexandra smiled wryly at the thought; right now she had more of a right to rule Saphyre than Caleb.

# Chapter Twenty-six

Alexandra was relieved to see that the sun was only just beginning to rise when Caleb returned her to her study. She quickly made her way to her chamber and sorted through the clothes Roisin had brought her, relieved to discover a pair of breeches, shirt, and tunic.

Riding through the outskirts of the city Alexandra glanced towards the temple, considering whether she should go and pray. Deciding against it she made her way to the shore and down to the cave she had discovered shortly after learning of her parents' deaths. Leaving Solas in the cave, Alexandra moved to sit on the shore, remaining on the sand rather than risking the slippery rocks. The day Carlyle had slipped into the ocean was still fresh in her mind. Lying down on the sand Alexandra crossed her arms behind her head and watched as the sky lightened bringing with it the promise of a golden day. The sound of the ocean helped to soothe her, and she imagined herself being carried away on the current.

She was sick of feeling guilty, angry and frightened. Her mind turned to Caleb, and the night they had shared together. There had been no fear or awkwardness between them, just a tenderness she had never shared with Carlyle. She was surprised that of all the guilt she felt, her night with Caleb was not one of the reasons. Why should she? Not once had she felt love towards Carlyle, or even a bond of friendship. She had never wanted this marriage. *I did not intentionally seek out pleasure with Caleb,* she told herself. *Nor will I do so again...not unless we are married. Last night happened by accident, it cannot become a regular occurrence.*

Turning, so she lay on her side Alexandra looked out towards the horizon, spotting the sails of a ship. What was the ship's destination? Were the crew leaving Saphyre? Were they happy to be leaving? Or were they merchants from a far-off kingdom? *What do merchants say of Saphyre?* She wondered turning on to her back once more. Did they speak of the tyrannical king? What did they say of her? In Karstares they had known so little of Saphyre and the tyrannical family, the merchants had spoken so rarely of the kingdom.

Her mind turned to the man Carlyle had murdered during the celebrations of her coronation. She could still not work out what had been going through Carlyle's mind at the time. Had he planned the man's execution from the moment of his arrest? Or had it been a gradual idea that had formed? *He had made sure the day was so pleasant,* Alexandra thought remembering how they had ridden through the streets to the cheers of people. Had he decided to execute the man purely because she had bled? *He must have meant his threat, and even if he did not, he could just as quickly change his mind.* The image of Lemuel's wife came to fore of her mind; a plain and timid looking woman who had shown Alexandra nothing but kindness on the few occasions they had met. Would she be Carlyle's first victim? Two birds with one stone. In truth, no one would believe that she was a member of Caleb's resistance, but who would dare defy Carlyle? *Would he really murder the wife of his own councilmen just to wipe out those without the Source?* But she knew the answer to the question; of course, he would.

She was beginning to understand how Caleb and so many others perceived the Source as a crutch. Carlyle had not even bothered to execute the man with a sword. Instead, he had literally squeezed the life from the man's heart using his power. She thought of the own pressure which had squeezed her Source during the chaos at the temple. Would Carlyle really kill her? She had been warned that if her part in the resistance was discovered, then he would have grounds to execute her without fear of repercussion from Karstares. But would he? And even if he did have grounds, would Giric really stand for the death of his sister knowing that Carlyle was a tyrant?

Regardless of what Caleb and Xander believed though, Alexandra was not a fool. Taking away Carlyle's Source would not strip him of his power completely. He could wield a sword just as well as any other man, perhaps better. It was evident he was lazy and relied mostly on his Source, but that was more from snobbery than an inability at swordsmanship. The thought frightened her; even if Carlyle was stripped off his Source Alexandra would still be unable to defend herself in a battle against him. How could she ever hope to defeat him?

Her stomach began to rumble painfully, and Alexandra realised that she had not eaten since supper the previous evening. *I should return soon;* she thought sitting up and brushing the sand from her hair. What would she do when next she saw Helena? She wasn't sure if she could stand the thought of Helena being so close to her, dressing her and bathing her. But what other options did she have? She could not dismiss her. She knew that Helena had been a bed warmer before Carlyle had purchased her to be one of Alexandra's ladies. *Was this* why *he purchased her?* The thought was sickening and instantly Alexandra knew she could not dismiss Helena, what if she was forced back into that life? Deep down she knew that Helena would not have been free to refuse Carlyle, but she still did not feel as if she could be at ease in the woman's presence.

*If Caleb wins the throne both Helena and Roisin will be free to do as they please.* She had never spoken of the matter of slavery with Caleb but Alexandra was intent on abolishing it. Thoughts of Caleb tugged her mind back to the previous evening, and she couldn't help but smile wistfully. It was true neither of them loved each other in the passionate sense, but she had felt wonderfully safe and accepted in Caleb's arms. Their marriage would not be perfect, but there would be no threats overhanging her, and she was sure Caleb would not berate her every moon when she failed to conceive. The sound of approaching hoof beats pulled her back to the present, away from the memory of Caleb's lips grazing her neck and she fought to keep the blush from her face afraid it would betray her. She stood up expecting to see Carlyle storming towards her but was surprised instead to see Krista and Xander dismounting from their horses and approaching her.

'Alexandra you *must* come back – Carlyle is frantic!' Krista cried and her dark eyes were wide in panic. 'Everyone in the castle is panicking; he is going to go on a rampage if you are not found!'

'He could easily find me.' Alexandra shrugged dismissing their fears.

'Do you not think he has tried that? Both Carlyle and his Scryers have searched for you using their Source, but you have put a shield upon yourself. The whole city is looking for you; even Caleb has people searching – it is only a matter of time before their groups clash!' Xander looked furious with her and Alexandra glared at him determined to stand her ground.

'I just wanted –'

'Alexandra you know that you do not have the luxury to do what you want.' Krista cajoled her gently, 'I do not know what happened last night, but you must come to terms with it. You are a Queen; people look upon you for guidance.' *Perhaps I should have learnt this lesson the first time,* Alexandra thought back to the time she had first come to the cave.

'Has he hurt anyone?' She asked suddenly remembering how he had struck Helena.

'No. He has been with the Castle Sorcerers searching for you, but if you do not return soon then he will.'

'The citizens of Saphyre look up to you.' Xander's voice was soft as they followed Alexandra to the cave. 'They do not respect Carlyle, but for some reason they do you. They need to be reassured that they can rely upon you.' There was something in Xander's tone that suggested to Alexandra he had more of an idea of what had passed during the night than Krista. She looked at him but found he would not quite meet her eyes; blushing Alexandra looked away.

'You are right, both of you.' Alexandra nodded. 'I hope you get a reward for being the ones finding me.'

'Of course we do; our heads.' Krista's solemn reply was no joke and Alexandra shuddered as she mounted Solas and rode back to the castle. When they arrived Krista and Xander escorted her to Carlyle's study where she was surprised to find him in more of a state of panic than fury. He rushed forwards to embrace her, but Alexandra pushed him away coldly. Bowing Krista and Xander departed, closing the door quietly behind them.

'Why were you so worried? You know I cannot leave.' Alexandra's voice dripped with scorn, and she dropped into the chair opposite Carlyle's desk.

'There have been rumours about this *rebel* leader. This man they call Caleb, the name that peasant shouted in the temple.' Alexandra tried to keep her face as neutral as possible. 'I have messengers throughout Saphyre, apparently this *Caleb* has been trying to recruit *my* citizens – including you.'

'Me?' Alexandra's throat constricted so tightly she could barely breathe, let alone speak.

'He thinks he can use you to take the throne.' Alexandra's mouth was as dry as sandpaper, she tried to swallow, but it just made her throat constrict further. 'You are *not* to leave the castle without my permission. There are whispers this man plans to abduct you; I cannot bear to think what he would do to you in order to persuade you to join his cause.'

'We cannot disrupt our lives because of rumours, what would our people think? If they see you panic then surely, that will only cause fear amongst our people.'

'I am not panicking!' Carlyle hissed gripping the edge of his chair; there was loud cracking noise as the chair suddenly shattered into a thousand splinters beneath his grip. Alexandra arched an eyebrow as she leant back in her own chair. *He is truly worried; he has never lost control of his Source before.* 'Abducting me would do this man no good. He cannot be king with you alive...can he?' She blushed at the hopeful tone of her voice. Even now she could not stomach the thought of Carlyle's death, of her playing some sort of part in it. He had taken so many lives, but that did not give her the right to take his. 'What I mean is that surely you would be his target and not me. What could I do?' She wanted to ask why he took the rumours so seriously now and not when Xander had claimed the rebels planned to kidnap her two years ago. 'Perhaps if I were abducted then surely it would be better for you? You could claim they killed me. You would be free to choose a new wife, one who could perform her duty to you and provide you wish a son.'

'Alexandra –'

'I am just pointing out that this could be of great benefit to you.' *And me*, she added silently to herself. Why had she not thought of this before? If Caleb abducted her, then she could live underground with him. She could work with him closely.

*No,* she dismissed the idea. *Xander told me that the people of Saphyre rely on me. They need to know they can trust me. What message would it send out if I went missing, or if they believed me dead, only to reappear once the fighting is over?* 'These are just rumours Carlyle. I will be careful but I am not going to shut myself in the castle until you are satisfied it is safe. I am in control of my Source, I am sure I am almost as powerful as I was before I ran away – perhaps more so now. Nor am I defenceless without my power, Krista has been working hard to train me in combat.' Carlyle sighed as he realised he would not win the argument. 'May I go now?'

'No.' Picking something up from his desk Carlyle held out his hand. Alexandra's locket lay in his palm, and she looked at it uncertainly. 'I found this beside the hearth in our chamber…'

'I remember when I came to your bed for the first time, you *threatened* me. You said I had better be free from another's touch. Yet you had hardly been chaste before we married, I doubt you had not been short of bedfellows long before we even met.' She could see a spark of fear cross over Carlyle's handsome features as he took in her words. *Yet I never expected that you would take another to your bed once we were married.*

'You were not fulfilling your duty,' Carlyle shrugged trying to appear as if he had done nothing wrong. 'You chose to lock yourself in your chambers; to sulk and neglect your duties. What else was I to do?'

'How long?' Alexandra asked forcing herself to meet his eyes, 'how many?'

'I cannot remember how many,' he taunted coldly, and Alexandra closed her eyes in an effort to stop herself from rolling them. *What does it matter? Perhaps it is just Helena he has bedded – why else would he have purchased a bed warmer to be my lady? Had he always thought to take a mistress?*

'How long?' She forced herself to ask unsure of why she needed to know.

'Since your miscarriage.' Alexandra looked at him in pure disgust, had he really cared so little for her during that time? Rising to her feet, Alexandra straightened her tunic and turned to leave but Carlyle grasped her arm. 'Alexandra –'

'Do *not* touch me,' she seethed conjuring a wall of ice to appear between them. She was surprised to see that her cold fury had channelled itself into her Source and realised she would have to reign her temper in. She stared at the locket in his outstretched hand and snatched it, staring at it with unhidden loathing. Forcing herself to slip it on she tucked it beneath her tunic. 'I will take my supper with Krista, but I will return to your chambers tonight. *That* was why I came to you last night…to return to your bed, to fulfil my *duty.*'

Knowing that she owed Krista an apology for the way she had behaved Alexandra sought her out in the training grounds. Now that the queen had returned to the castle everyone seemed to have returned to their normal duties, and Krista was no exception. When she wasn't with Alexandra she helped to train the squires and those hoping to join the Castle Guards. Staying towards the back of the room Alexandra leant against the wall and observed Krista with a small smile. The boys looked at her in stunned awe as she moved fluidly with a broadsword, the heavy weapon hindering her not in the slightest. *It must infuriate her that she cannot have a place with the Castle Guards simply because she is a woman.* Alexandra thought sadly, perhaps that would be a way she could mend her friendship with Krista? Things had become strained recently, and she knew it was down to her. Caleb would not object to women joining the guards surely?

'Thank you for earlier. I – I am sorry for the trouble I undoubtedly caused.' Alexandra tentatively apologised when the room had cleared, and the two women were alone. She could feel the frosty wall between herself and Krista, almost as if her Source had summoned one similar to earlier. Only this one Alexandra was desperate to thaw.

'What in the name of the Goddess happened?' Had Xander truly not confided to Krista what had taken place last night? She did not doubt that he knew something of what had passed between them. She doubted Caleb would have gone into detail, but Xander would have no doubted pieced together his own conclusions if he knew that she had spent the night. 'Alexandra!' Krista's biting tone snapped her from her thoughts. 'I think you at least owe me an explanation.'

'Of course but not here. Please. I – I told His Majesty that I would take supper with you, I hope you do not mind.'

'I am but a humble servant. Who am I to question my Queen?' Krista's tone had thawed ever-so-slightly, and her body language relaxed. 'Go to my chamber; we can eat there and talk in private.' Opening a leather pouch fixed to the belt around her waist Krista pulled out an old and rather battered looking key. 'Go, I will fetch us some supper.'

Krista's chambers were small and sparse in comparison to the chambers that Alexandra shared with Carlyle, yet bigger than her own private chamber. There was a small privy connected but other than that she had just the one room. A simple bed, two chests and a desk with an uncomfortable looking chair were the only furnishings. Two maps decorated the walls; above her desk hung a map of Saphyre while a map of Karstares adorned the wall above her bed. Alexandra studied the second map feeling a twinge of nostalgia. Karstares was home no longer, but she had been happy there. *Until Carlyle,* she thought bitterly. Quickly Alexandra sent her Source into the corners, cracks, and crevices of the room. Concentrating on joining it all together until the walls seemed to have a watery sheen to them. Smiling she couldn't help but feel proud of her work, she had come a long way from passing out due to exhaustion as she had done all those years ago.

'Queen Ismenya would be proud,' Krista commented from the doorway, and Alexandra looked away sadly.

'I am not sure she would,' Alexandra shrugged and accepted a bowl of stew from her companion. She could not see Ismenya being proud of her daughter pulling rank over her friend. *I do it only to protect her – yet even then she ignores me!* Nor could she imagine her mother being pleased at her purposefully preventing herself from conceiving. 'Krista I truly am sorry for last night, I hope I have not landed you in trouble with Caleb.' She shredded the still-warm chunk of bread that Krista had given her, dropping the pieces into her stew as she thought over the previous night.

'Do you know what would have happened if we had been caught?' Krista slammed her wooden bowl on to the floor and leapt to her feet, rapidly pacing back and forth. Alexandra couldn't help but wonder how long she had been keeping her anger pent up, waiting to let it burst forth. 'Caleb could have been discovered. You could have destroyed *everything* he and his ancestors have worked towards for *centuries* and for *what*? What was so urgent that you could not wait until morning? Or that you could not allow a message to be brought to him?' Krista did not bother to keep her voice down, clearly trusting Alexandra's abilities in protecting them from eavesdroppers. Alexandra was so stunned, even a little frightened, at Krista's anger that it took her a few minutes to summon up the courage to speak.

'I went to Carlyle's chambers last night. I knew I had to return to his bed, but I was frightened.' She looked down at her stew finding that she no longer had an appetite. 'When I arrived I found he was not alone but bedding Helena. I cannot explain why it upset me – why I feel so betrayed. I do not love Carlyle, far from it – I loathe him. But to find him like that…' She trailed off and clenched her fists, 'Honestly I do not know what I expected from Caleb – why I had to seek him out. I think a small part of me hoped that he would help me run away although I knew he would not do that. I counted on his help once…' The memory of his betrayal was still bitter but she knew there was no point in dwelling on it. Caleb had done what he thought best, he had apologized for it, and he had meant it. She chose not to confess the night's events to Krista. She was not ashamed, but she did not want Krista to judge her further or even lecture her. Telling her that she had slept with Caleb would achieve nothing, and she wanted some privacy. She could not take back what had happened that night, nor did she want to. 'What can I do? I cannot dismiss Helena; I am not even sure if she was a willing bedfellow or not…'

'It is a man's right to seek a woman to warm his bed should his wife be absent. It is how things have always been. More importantly, this could be used to your advantage. At least you know that Helena will not be able to usurp your position, nor would she poison Carlyle against as other mistresses might. Think of the damage that could have been caused had Carlyle chosen a free woman. She could have decided she wanted a position higher than the king's mistress – and without an heir, your position is hardly secure.' *But if people believe that I am the True Queen then surely I am secure?*

'I did not think of it that way…' Alexandra sighed. 'What can I do though Krista? I hate her for what she has done. Even if it was not willing part of me resents her for this, she knows how I loathe him…'

'It is not in your nature to hate,' Krista reassured her. 'I am sure given time you will forgive her. But what will you do in the meantime? Carlyle meant his threat Alexandra, and I think you know that. So what will you do?'

'I have to return to his…I have to give him an heir.' She could see Krista was horrified at the thought. 'What else can I do Krista? You said it yourself; he *meant* that threat. I cannot be responsible for someone dying every moon…but I do not want to destroy Caleb's work. I meant to speak to him last night when you brought me to him but…I…' She trailed off and bowed her head in an attempt to hide the blush she was sure stained her cheeks.

'A son would not destroy Caleb's chances. It would be a hindrance of course, but he would find a solution.'

'It is not just that…what if I have a daughter again? Or what if the rebels –'

'None of us will harm your child. Caleb has known for a while that you could not prevent yourself conceiving forever. There are solutions; the child could return to Karstares.' Alexandra shook her head at this option, she could not stand the thought of sending her child away, but she also knew Carlyle would never agree to it. 'He could serve the Goddess. Men have turned down the throne for a religious path before, not in Carlyle's line but previously it has happened.' Alexandra found this suggestion far more comforting, but only slightly. Would her child begrudge her? Would he grow up to loathe that he was forced to give up the throne? What if he thought it was his right? Krista squeezed her shoulder gently. 'It is getting late; go to Carlyle…it will all be over soon.' *You keep saying soon, but how soon will it be?* Alexandra wanted to ask, but she knew Krista was right. Forcing herself to finish her supper she embraced Krista tightly and left her friend in peace.

Carlyle was sitting beside the hearth when Alexandra arrived. Her eyes rested on the dressing chamber door; was Helena in there? Was she with Roisin preparing for bed? *Does Roisin know?* Of course Roisin would have known about Helena's duties, she had told Alexandra she had been assigned work elsewhere. Was this what she had meant?

'Your slaves are fine. I have sent them to sleep with the rest of the slaves for the night; I wanted to have you to myself entirely.' *Or you were too cowardly to face a scene between Helena and I*, Alexandra thought but she nodded to Carlyle. 'You are returning to our bed then?'

'Do I have a choice?' Alexandra asked coldly. 'If I do not return to your bed then I shall never conceive. I will not be responsible for the deaths of our people. Just be warned that killing people will not enable me to conceive faster, what if your actions displease the Goddess?'

'The thought has certainly brought you back to our bed quicker.' Carlyle shrugged and Alexandra felt her blood boil. Flames burst to life in the hearth and a strong wind whipped through the room. Taking a deep breath, Alexandra fought to regain control of her Source not wanting to give Carlyle the satisfaction of seeing that his words had an effect on her.

'I am coming to your bed for one reason only Carlyle,' she could see his sapphire eyes darkening, but for once it wasn't in anger. 'I am doing my duty – nothing more. You cannot threaten me, betray me and think that things would remain the same between us.' Turning his back to her Carlyle ran a hand through his blonde hair. Discarding her boots and clothes Alexandra took the opportunity to slip beneath the blankets whilst he had his back turned.

'I could make you fall in love with me,' this Alexandra knew was not an empty threat. He certainly did have the power to manipulate her, but she knew he would not stoop so low. He might want too, but she knew he could not stomach the thought. *He does not want a fake love, but why?* She couldn't help but wonder it would certainly make his life easier.

'You tried to make me believe that I loved you when you found me in Bournemouth. I do not think you would dare to use your Source to manipulate me that far. It would be nothing but an illusion, deep down I would continue to loathe you and eventually I would remember the truth. You would spend each day living in fear that sooner or later the power you hold over me would fade – and what then?' Lying back Alexandra resisted tugging at the locket. *Take it off,* she told herself. *You cannot keep yourself conceiving.* She closed her eyes and waited for the mattress to sink under Carlyle's weight, for his hand to begin caressing her, but there was nothing. When she opened her eyes, Carlyle was standing over her, looking down at her sadly.

'I am not going to take you unwillingly.' He said simply, and Alexandra arched an eyebrow. She wanted to ask him why? To point out that she had hardly ever been willing to go to his bed, but she was too exhausted.

'I am willing to do my duty to our people.' She replied stonily.

'But not willing to love your husband?' At Alexandra's silence he lifted the blanket and lay down beside her, but he made no move to touch her. Surprised Alexandra stared at the ceiling, only daring to close her eyes when she was sure Carlyle had fallen asleep.

# *Chapter Twenty-seven*

Alexandra quickly resumed her daily pattern of waking before dawn to train with Krista. Rarely did she break her fast with Carlyle; instead she would join Krista in the great hall with the rest of the castle residents and sit amongst the Castle Guards. At first, people had been cautious of breaking their fast among their queen so casually, but soon she felt almost accepted.

In council she observed Jacen and Lemuel, looking for any signs that they may have been approached by one of Caleb's people. But if they had, they gave no signs of it. She had not seen Caleb since their encounter and had, had no chance of questioning him over whether he would approach them or not. Their plan to meet in the temple after she had distributed alms had been crushed by a sickness in the city. Even Krista had sided with Carlyle and forbade Alexandra for leaving the castle lest she fall ill herself.

On a glorious spring morning when she was due to distribute alms, Alexandra woke up feeling as if she stood on the deck of a violently rocking ship. The memory of her voyage from Karstares to Saphyre burst into her mind. She could hear the waves launching into the sides of the ship, almost crushing the vessel beneath their weight. Shaking her head, Alexandra tried to clear the image from her mind. She had no wish for memories of her past at that moment, especially one that made her feel as if she were being hurled to and fro. Shakily she stood up, being careful not to wake Carlyle. She was due to meet Krista for training, but she could not even stand up.

'I cannot,' she whispered to Helena unable to meet the woman's eyes. She had never mentioned the night she had discovered Carlyle's betrayal to Helena, but the woman knew that she had been caught. Their friendship had drastically altered, and Alexandra loathed herself for the petty jealousy she felt. She did not love Carlyle; she did not want this marriage. So why did she feel so hurt?

'I will let Krista know...do you still wish to distribute alms?'

'Of course, I could not go before due to the sickness. I do not want to let the people of Evany down a second time. I will be fine.'

When Helena returned, she helped Alexandra to dress, her fingers gently lacing up the fastenings of her gown. With each tug of the lacings, Alexandra felt her stomach threatening to revolt. She braced her palms against the wall, feeling as if she might pass out. *Get through today,* she told herself. *There will be plenty of time to be ill tomorrow.* Panic flared within her as she thought of the sickness which had swept through the city. Had it reached the castle? *No,* she reassured herself. *It is just an illness. I will see Rhonwyn tomorrow for a potion.*

'Your Majesty are you sure you are well enough?' Roisin asked dabbing a damp cloth to Alexandra's face.

'I am fine, really. The fresh air will do me good.' Neither Helena nor Roisin looked convinced, but Alexandra brushed them off. Knowing that Carlyle would insist upon her staying in bed and resting Alexandra decided to skip breaking her fast.

'You do not look well,' Xander greeted Alexandra in the stables, a fleeting look of concern on his face. As much as the two disliked each other Xander was always present when she journeyed to the temple to distribute alms. Whether it was on Carlyle's orders or Calebs, she had never bothered to ask him.

'I am fine –'

'No you are not,' Krista corrected. 'Otherwise you would not have sent Helena down to me before dawn claiming you are too ill to train.' Alexandra flushed and the warmth spreading through her cheeks did little to alleviate her discomfort. 'You are in no fit state to ride.'

'I will use my Source to keep me in the saddle then,' Alexandra smiled tightly. 'Now please can we go? I am not going to let my people down.' Seeing that they would only be arguing a losing battle Xander and Krista rode closely beside her, both ready to catch her should she fall.

Father Dóchas was furious with Alexandra as soon as he laid eyes upon her and berated her for her foolishness. How could she come so far from the castle when she was clearly too ill to stand? His tone softened only when Alexandra protested that she could not miss out on distributing alms for the second time in a row. Suitably chided she at least accepted his offer that she sit down while she handed out alms.

'Forgive me for my earlier scolding, Alexandra.' Father Dóchas apologised as she joined him in his personal chapel for lunch. 'I understand that you do not wish to let your people down. However, I do wish you had paused for at least a moment to think about their reaction to seeing you like this. It will frighten many of them. Your citizens look up to you for hope, should something happen to you then they will lose that hope.' Alexandra nodded guiltily and sipped the tea that Father Dóchas made her.

'I did not think of that,' she admitted. 'But what else could I do? I was not able to attend last moon…I could not let them down for a second time.'

'You could always send your ladies. The people look forward to seeing you, but if you were to send your ladies in your place, then it would show that the people are still in your thoughts.'

'That does seem like the more sensible option,' Alexandra smiled wryly. 'Although I have to admit I look forward to having a whole day away from His Majesty.' She paused as she drained the rest of the tea, closing her eyes as a fresh wave of dizziness swept over her. 'I assume Caleb told you of the events at the celebration?'

'He did…he was outraged.' Alexandra looked up at the statue of the Goddess; hundreds of questions were on her lips, but she dared not ask them. 'You would not be the first to question the Goddess,' Father Dóchas reassured her as he followed her gaze. 'His Majesty lost his faith shortly after his mother's death. The Light of the Goddess is a sign that those who rule are chosen by her. But people have been too frightened to find their rightful king.'

'What if it is not Caleb?' Alexandra asked, 'what if he is crowned and the Goddess does not show her favour upon him?' Father Dóchas could merely shrug.

'She has given you a hard path to walk Alexandra – no one could deny that. But she has given us free will; she could not intervene when things go wrong simply because we pray for it. She would be taking away the very gift she bestowed upon us.' Alexandra remained silent, not sure if she was satisfied with the answer.

'Is it her wish that I conceive for Carlyle?' She asked pulling the locket over her neck. 'I do not know if I can rightfully prevent myself conceiving…but even if I do not wear this, there is no guarantee I will fall pregnant.' Tears blurred her eyes as she held the locket out. 'I know I have already asked too much from you Father, but I do not know what else to do.' The locket hung in the air between them, and Father Dóchas observed it with a thoughtful expression.

'Have you worn this since returning to His Majesties bed?'

'On and off,' Alexandra admitted guiltily. 'Mostly on…all I can do is pray that if I have not conceived that I can throw myself upon His Majesty's mercy. I know I should have spoken with Caleb before taking it off, but what else could I do? Krista assured me that if I give Carlyle a son, there are options…perhaps he could even join the church?' Alexandra shared a wry smile with Father Dóchas.

'Nothing would give me greater pleasure than welcoming your son to the Goddess's Path but let us cross that bridge if it arises.' Father Dóchas took the locket and turned it over in his hands. 'Caleb does not wish to see if His Majesty's threat was serious any more than you do. Does anyone else know of this?' He asked indicating the locket, and Alexandra shook her head.

'Not Krista or even Caleb…I felt like it should remain between us, especially as the consequences would be severer for you.' Alexandra looked away guiltily, and Father Dóchas reached out to squeeze her hand reassuringly.

'I will take the spell off if you are sure this is what you want.'

'I am not sure what I want, but I do know I want to cause no more grief. His Majesty will not seek out actual people working for Caleb should he have meant his threat. He will use it as an excuse simply to dispose of those who oppose him.'

Feeling well rested Alexandra returned to the main temple smiling as greeted the citizens. When the temple had emptied of worshippers Father Dóchas invited Alexandra and her companions to take supper with him. Not feeling quite up to the return journey Alexandra gratefully accepted his offer. As she moved to stand up her legs buckled beneath her weight and she cried out as they gave out beneath her. With surprising speed the elderly priest caught her arms, keeping her upright as Alexandra turned her head to empty the contents of her lunch on to the marble floor.

'I – I am sorry,' she gasped crimson with embarrassment and horror as Father Dóchas slowly lowered her back into the chair. She tried to summon her Source to clear up the mess but blood roared through her ears, large black spots exploded across her vision, and her head lolled heavily to the side. Someone pressed a cup to her lips but even swallowing required more energy then she had.

'Someone contact His Majesty, he will have our heads if she returns to him in this state without prior warning.' Xander's calm voice sounded distant, Alexandra tried to focus on him, but she felt as she was being pulled down in water.

'I will contact His Majesty myself, but I think it would be best for Her Majesty to remain overnight at least. She will stay in my chambers.' Father Dóchas reassured the group, Alexandra tried to lift her head and respond that she was fine. She would go to the castle and sleep, by morning she would be fully recovered.

'I knew I should not have let her travel,' Krista's voice was high from worry, but Alexandra could say or do nothing to alleviate her fear. 'Will she be alright?' Strong arms lifted Alexandra, and she groaned at the sudden movement. She could not help but remember the feeling of a violently rocking ship.

'She will be fine. I think His Majesty will be more than pleased once I have spoken with him. I believe the Goddess has blessed Her Majesty with a child.'

# *Chapter Twenty-eight*

'Father Dóchas is correct Your Majesty. The Queen is indeed with child…but I fear it is not all good news. The child is not growing as it should, I can hear a heart, but it is weak – as is the Queen. I fear there is a possibility she may lose this child.'

'She had better pray for her sake that she does not.' Alexandra recognised Carlyle's growl, and she tried to move, to open her mouth, but her limbs were fixed in place.

'Do you not realise that *this* is why she loathes you? Why she has been so terrified of conceiving?' A bitter voice cried out in protest. 'Her Majesty not only has to worry about what other people will do to her, if her babe will be safe, but she has to worry about failing *you*. Do you care for her so little?'

'Need I remind you that I am your *king*? You will show me the respect I deserve!'

'A king who needs to demand respect is no king. Alexandra is my dearest friend and my Queen. I am here to protect her, and that if includes protecting her from you than I shall lay down my life to do so.'

'Krista…' Alexandra tried to protest but her voice caught in her throat and came out as a barely audible confused mumble. She could hear Carlyle yelling about treason and Krista's angry retort, but the words were growing dimmer.

'Please Your Majesty,' Rhonwyn protested. 'The Queen is awakening and you are both upsetting her.' She could feel a spark of energy at her fingertips, slowly weaving its way through her arm. *Take a little of my strength;* she heard Rhonwyn speak through her Source. *Try not to use your own.* A soft and feminine hand squeezed her own as Rhonwyn departed on Carlyle's orders. Alexandra forced her eyes to open and was surprised at her surroundings. She was lying on a small and hard bed in an unfurnished room. Carlyle sat beside her on a wooden crate. Stubble frames his jaw; there were deep circles beneath his eyes and lines at the corner of his mouth where previously there had been none.

'Where are we?' Nausea swept through her and pain gripped her stomach tightly as she fought to sit up. For a fleeting second, she feared she was in a dungeon until she remembered the horrifyingly cramped cells in the castle.

'Lie down,' Carlyle growled at her. 'We are at the temple. You passed out, and that useless priest thought it would be unwise to move you.' For once Alexandra chose to listen to Carlyle and settled back on the bed. Closing her eyes she tried to block out the spinning room, but although she could no longer see the room she could still feel everything violently spinning.

'I thought you would be happy at the news.' She whispered hoarsely wishing that he would at least give her some water.

'Did you not hear what Rhonwyn said? You may lose this child. Through your foolishness you almost *did.*'

'I apologise, I did not realise I was pregnant. Had I known I could assure you I would not have made the journey until I was better.' She yearned to ask him for water, her throat was painfully dry and scratched when she spoke but she was too frightened to ask him for anything.

'You truly did not know?'

'Of course not,' Alexandra rasped. 'With you threatening to kill innocent people I am hardly going to keep it a secret am I? Nor would I put the child in any danger.' How long had she been pregnant? 'Did Rhonwyn say when?'

'No…the child is weak.' Alexandra forced her eyes open to see that Carlyle was for once looking concerned. 'I think it would be best if you remained her for a few days until you have fully recovered. When you are well enough, you will ride back with me, until we can be sure our child is safe I do not want you visiting the temple.' Alexandra was saved from answering by a gentle knock at the door. Father Dóchas entered with a deep bow, carrying a tray with steaming food and water. Overjoyed to see the priest Alexandra allowed Carlyle to help her upright and gulped the water down greedily.

'Krista informed me that you had awoken, I thought perhaps you would be hungry.' Father Dóchas set the tray gently on Alexandra's lap and stood back. 'How do you feel?'

'Tired,' Alexandra replied truthfully. 'Like I am trapped on a ship during a storm. I fear that without your help I would have caused another grave tragedy for Saphyre. I apologise for any worry I may have caused you and your monks. And for...' She trailed off blushing as she remembered her illness.

'You should not apologise, it is an unseemly behaviour in a queen.' Carlyle scolded her lightly as he began to feed her the soup gently. *And this is not unseemly behaviour for a king?* She wanted to point out but remained silent.

'His Majesty is correct of course,' Father Dóchas's eyes crinkled at the edges and Alexandra could see that she was forgiven. 'I am your humble servant; there is no need for you to apologise.' Father Dóchas departed leaving Alexandra alone with Carlyle. Once he had finished feeding her, he stood up and kissed her cheek softly.

'I will return to the castle and let you rest. I will have Krista remain here to keep you safe. I would rather we not tell of our news just yet.' Alexandra nodded instantly regretting the movement although the soup in her belly did alleviate the sickness a little. She was not sure how long she was left alone for, she stared into space blankly and turned over the news in her head. She was pregnant. Would she at least carry this child to full term? *Please, Goddess...I know I purposefully tried to prevent this but do not punish the babe on my account.* The door opened once more, and Father Dóchas greeted her with a small smile.

'I truly am sorry,' Alexandra said. 'Not just for being ill but for the trouble I have no doubt caused you.' She touched the locket at her throat as Father Dóchas took up Carlyle's seat. 'You knew did you not? When I gave you the locket, you had such a strange look on your face.'

'I had my suspicions, and when you answered that you had worn the locket on and off, they were confirmed. I hope you can forgive me for informing His Majesty.'

'There is nothing to forgive,' Alexandra smiled knowing that she would not have been able to keep her pregnancy a secret even if she had wished it.

'Your Majesty,' Father Dóchas suddenly seemed uncomfortable as he reverted to Alexandra's title. 'Caleb visited me two moons ago…he had a sensitive matter to discuss.' Alexandra felt her cheeks flare with embarrassment as she knew what Father Dóchas spoke of.

'I –'

'I hold no judgement; it is not my place. But I must ask you to be honest with me. When you sought out, Caleb were you wearing the locket?'

'Of course!' Alexandra protested, 'I never…' She trailed off as she remembered that night. Had she not torn it off? She had not wanted anything of Carlyle's close to her. Swallowing a lump, Alexandra looked at the priest in a mixture of horror and uncertainty. 'I tore it off in anger – Father Dóchas I *never* intended what happened between Caleb and I to pass. I certainly did not plan on *this*,' she gestured to her belly. 'Do you think the child could be…' She trailed off too terrified to contemplate the question.

'There is of course the possibility.'

'I need to speak with him,' she whispered moving her legs from the bed and trying to stand but the priest firmly pressed against her shoulders.

'You must rest. When Sorceress Rhonwyn confirmed your condition, I thought perhaps that this was a sign from the Goddess. Caleb is here in the temple, he is safely hidden, but I think it best if you speak with him. He does after all have a right to know.' Father Dóchas squeezed Alexandra's shoulder once more, and she slowly obeyed him, withdrawing her legs back beneath the cover.

'What do I do?' She whispered, 'If the child is Caleb's then Carlyle will surely kill it!'

'Why should His Majesty ever discover the truth?' *How can I keep this from him?* 'Alexandra there is a way to determine who the child's father is, but not until the birth. Until then I implore you to not put yourself or the child at risk.' Alexandra nodded, she of course had no desire to bring harm upon her child. Whether it was Carlyle's or Caleb's did not matter, it was her child also. *I will protect you,* she promised it but instantly felt overwhelmed with guilt. She had not been able to protect her daughter. 'Do you feel up to speaking with Caleb now?' Alexandra nodded; she knew she would not sleep until she had spoken to him. Although what could she say?

Father Dóchas led a hooded monk into the room and Alexandra bit back laughter as the monk pushed back the hood. Towering over the priest, Caleb looked ridiculous dressed as a man of holy vows, and she could not help giggling as he scowled at her.

'You are well then?'

'Better for seeing you dressed like this,' she teased him. 'Perhaps this is a sign from the Goddess?' Father Dóchas frowned and Alexandra looked away chastised. 'I am sorry…I know the resistance is not something to laugh at, nor do I.' She quickly added, but she could see Caleb's own eyes were dancing with laughter. With a small sigh, Father Dóchas bowed from the room. Alexandra fell silent suddenly unsure of what to say, how could she break the news to Caleb? *What if the child is not his? How would that make him feel?* She did not yet know how far along she was; surely she should find that out first? *But when will I see Caleb next? He has a right to know about this before it is publicly announced.* 'Caleb…I do not think I can prevent myself conceiving any longer – but I do not want to be yet another obstacle in your path.'

'Alexandra you will *never* be an obstacle – even if you bore Carlyle a hundred sons.' Alexandra arched an eyebrow at his exaggeration. 'I will always protect you and your children, I pro –'

'No,' Alexandra cut him off sharply holding up her hand. 'You promised me once that you would protect us but you could not – *I* could not and nor could Carlyle. You cannot be close to me at the best of times, let alone when I am most vulnerable. Please Caleb do not make promises that you cannot keep.' Caleb looked sombre and ran a hand through his hair as he sat down beside her. Once again Alexandra could not help but think how similar to Carlyle he looked; it was terrifying at how similar their appearance was yet their personalities could not be more opposite. Studying his appearance, she noticed that like Carlyle, Caleb too had aged. He looked exhausted, and his face was thinning from his work. Both he and Carlyle were in their mid-thirties, how long did Caleb have before time was against him?

*He is hardly old;* she scolded herself but what if the resistance went on for another decade? What if he achieved what he wanted when Alexandra could no longer bear children? *Stop it!* She scolded herself resting a hand on her belly; she may already be carrying Caleb's son…would he succeeds his father to the throne if she was? Pulling her mind back to the present she focused on the state of Caleb's wrinkled and stained clothes as he shrugged off the monk's robe. *He has not bathed in days;* she thought wrinkling her nose slightly. 'Are things truly that bad at the moment?' She gestured to his appearance and Caleb grimaced in embarrassment.

'There is someone informing Carlyle of my whereabouts – I have to be constantly on the move.' He looked down at his shirt in disgust and Alexandra could see he was contemplating putting the robe back on despite the warmth of the room. She took the robe from him and folded it up decisively. 'I apologise I am hardly dressed for an audience with the queen.' She knew he was jesting, but Alexandra could not quite bring herself to smile. She longed to raise a conversation involving Xander. Who else was close enough to Caleb to know all of his movements? But she could not raise such an unpleasant discussion when she already had a sensitive issue to discuss. 'You are right of course though; I cannot protect you all the time. *But* I can and shall promise to do my best. Now…I must ask you a personal question that has given me great cause for worry. Have you been preventing yourself from conceiving?' Alexandra was stunned by the question and she drew in a sharp intake of breath. 'You cannot endanger yourself or our people Alexandra, if you are you *must* stop. Falling pregnant will not be the end of the world.' Tears streamed down Alexandra's cheeks and she bowed her head feeling ashamed.

'I was preventing myself, after the death of my daughter. I was too scared but…' She pulled the locket over her head and handed it to Caleb. 'I had a spell put on this, as long as I wore it while laying with Carlyle, with anyone,' she blushed, 'I would not fall pregnant. But on the night I discovered Carlyle…I tore it off in anger.' Caleb looked between the locket and Alexandra as if unsure of what she was saying. 'Caleb when I came to you that night I had not planned what happened – but even more foolishly I was not wearing that locket…I was not thinking.'

'I do not understand,' Caleb's voice was shaky and Alexandra could see he was frightened to voice aloud what she was trying to tell him.

'I am pregnant…' Caleb's eyes widened ever so slightly and he sat back almost toppling off the crate he'd sat upon.

'Have you worn that locket since we lay together?' Alexandra nodded and could feel the room growing even hotter as their conversation progressed.

'Not all of the time though – and I do not yet know how far along my pregnancy is. There is no guarantee this child is yours…but…'

'There is a chance.' Caleb seemed to lose himself in thought and a gradual smile crossed over his features. 'So, I could be a father? Possibly?' Alexandra arched an eyebrow; this had not been the reaction she was expecting.

'A small chance yes but Caleb…we lay together *once*. There is more chance that Carlyle could be the father – and what do we do then?' Silence descended upon them as both thought about the consequences of Alexandra's pregnancy. *Will I ever be able to celebrate without having to worry about causing misery?* She thought bleakly. Finally, Caleb reached over and took both of her hands in his, squeezing them tightly.

'Alexandra regardless of who the child's father is, I will not harm him. Even if he is Carlyle's, *you* will always be his mother. I cannot hold a child responsible for their parentage.' She nodded feeling slightly comforted at his words. Alexandra bit back a yawn and felt herself sink back down on to the pillow. Caleb kissed her forehead and squeezed her hand in a silent farewell.

Carlyle left Alexandra in peace for the next several days as she recovered in the temple. News of the Queen's temporary accommodation had been kept quiet, Alexandra was desperate to avoid disappointing people journeying to the temple only for her to be too weak to greet them. Instead, she kept to Father Dóchas's private chapel during the day, although she was unsuccessful in convincing him to take his chamber back.

'It would be inappropriate and where would you stay? I am quite content in the dormitory with the monks.' He had waved her off, and Alexandra had soon given up trying to convince him otherwise.

Unable to sleep one night Alexandra tiptoed from the sparsely furnished chamber and out into the main temple. Despite the late hour, the temple was still open to worshippers, and Alexandra slipped up the hood of her robe so that she would not be seen by anyone. The marble floor was shockingly cold against her bare feet, and she shivered as she walked across the floor and towards the altar. Kneeling before it she bowed her head and clasped her hands in prayer. The sound of approaching footsteps caught her off-guard, and she glanced up to see Father Dóchas approaching her.

'It is peaceful here,' she smiled wistfully as the priest joined her before the altar. 'Perhaps I could follow a different path and serve the Goddess more fully.'

'You are an anointed Queen and the Goddess has truly chosen you to rule over Saphyre. You can serve her in no better way than from your current position.' Alexandra nodded but could not help questioning whether she was a good choice for queen. 'Have faith Alexandra, Saphyre has endured for centuries. I am sure you are the Goddess's hope for the kingdom.'

# Chapter Twenty-nine

The pregnancy with her second child was far more difficult in comparison to her first. Not only did she leave every day in constant fear that harm would befall her child but she was plagued with a constant sickness. Seven moons into her pregnancy Alexandra was still finding herself battling morning sickness; only it seemed to last throughout the day. Unable to train with Krista each morning Rhonwyn had taken to visiting Alexandra at the beginning of each day, bringing with her a soothing potion. Not only did she have to battle the daily sickness but she had been horrified to discover early on in her pregnancy that the child was wreaking havoc with her Source.

'It is a sure sign you are carrying a strong son.' Carlyle soothed her gently rubbing her swollen belly as she gulped down Rhonwyn's potions.

'Because he is stealing my Source?' Alexandra sighed wearily, 'Regardless of whether it is a son or daughter I wish they would stop it.' She feared that if the child was using her Source, it was a sign that it was Carlyle's. She knew that the child could have inherited the Source from her side, but she could not listen to the rational voice in her head. When she had returned to the castle after she stay at the temple, Rhonwyn had taken great time to expect the child. She had guessed the conception to be around the time Alexandra had returned to Carlyle's bed.

Turning to look at Rhonwyn she smiled in thanks for the potion. 'Where is Krista? Will, she come and walk with me?'

'She begs your forgiveness Your Majesty, but she has been unwell. She came to see one of my healers this morning. It is nothing serious,' Rhonwyn quickly reassured her, 'but she does need to rest for a day or two.'

'She is meant to be looking after her queen – that is her duty as she continuously reminds me.' Carlyle growled, but Alexandra turned to glare at him.

'How do you expect her to look after me if she is unwell?' She snapped moving to stand up but glancing down in disgust at her protruding belly. *Can it really only be one more moon until this is over?* She asked herself, wincing as the child gave a sharp kick against her bladder. At the side of the room, Helena and Roisin stood awaiting orders. Try as she might Alexandra had still not forgiven Helena for what she saw as a betrayal. Every so often Carlyle would permit Alexandra to sleep in her own chamber, but she was under no illusion that he did it purely for her benefit or that he slept alone. She was torn between pity and anger for Helena. She had never asked if Helena was willing to perform the duties requested for her or if she endured it simply because she felt she had no choice. Alexandra knew she should speak to Helena, to try and console the woman, but she could never quite bring herself to speak to her. Especially now when she could barely control her emotions. 'Is Krista well enough for visitors?' She asked Rhonwyn as the sorceress grasped her arm and helped her to her feet.

'Of course,' Rhonwyn smiled. 'I am sure she would be glad of a visit from Your Majesty.'

'I do not think that would be wise,' Carlyle rebuffed. 'You should not be attending sickbeds in your condition, especially those of *servants*. You will rest.' Sighing Alexandra nodded knowing that she would not be able to win this argument. 'You may go Rhonwyn. Please ask Sorceress Neith to come attend to Her Majesty and I after supper, I have a task for her.' Rhonwyn curtsied and departed with the promise that she would deliver his request.

Without Krista, the day was agonisingly slow. Declining Carlyle's offer to sit in council Alexandra decided to go for a walk in the castle gardens. Sitting for long periods of time was too uncomfortable, but so was walking. *I cannot wait for this child to be born,* Alexandra thought wistfully as she rested a hand over the bump. Had her previous pregnancy been this uncomfortable and she had simply forgotten? *No, I would never have attended the ball if I had been this uncomfortable.* Carlyle was eager to throw a celebration for the birth of the upcoming child, but Alexandra was too frightened. It felt like they were mocking their daughter or even tempting someone to try and harm her child again.

The child was due shortly before their third anniversary, and Alexandra feared this was a sign from the Goddess. Had she conceived Carlyle's child just in time to celebrate third year of marriage? Was it a sign that the Goddess favoured him over Caleb? *Stop being so foolish!* She scolded herself returning to the warmth of the castle when she grew too cold to stay outside. She was cautious in using her Source frightened that she would overexert herself.

Caleb had visited her at the temple when she had given alms. Those short hours she had spent with him alleviated her fears. He had been fascinated by her gradually swelling belly and the way the child had kicked against his hand. She had laughed when he had knelt at her feet, crooning to the child within. He never mentioned whether he would prefer a son or daughter, he was more concerned over the wellbeing of both Alexandra and the child. The only time she had been disheartened had been when she'd mentioned in passing that the child wreaked havoc with her Source. Caleb had become almost fearful at the thought that a child of his would have the magical ability.

Carlyle was almost as attentive to Alexandra as Caleb had been. Each night he would rub her belly and sometimes even her feet if she was in pain. His temper had certainly calmed with the news of his impending fatherhood. When Alexandra had begun to develop cravings Carlyle had set about ensuring that the castle was well stocked with berries, quails eggs and whatever she desired. But still, he would only refer to the child as a son. There was the hidden threat of things to come should Alexandra bear him a daughter.

After supper, Alexandra sat on the window seat as she waited for Carlyle's newest Sorceress to arrive. She rested her cheek against the shutter, opening it a crack so that the air could cool her skin. She alternated between freezing one moment to being uncomfortably hot the next. Carlyle looked up from his small desk at as Helena rushed forward to open the door. A woman dressed in silver robes and with lilac hair curtsied as she stepped into the room and Alexandra smiled shyly at her. The woman had a gentle appearance; she gave the impression that she could put people at ease simply by being close.

'Alexandra this is Sorceress Neith from the kingdom of Dania.' Alexandra studied Neith curiously; there was something in the woman's pale eyes that suggested she had not come to Saphyre willingly.

'Dania…was there not a war between your kingdom and Saphyre?' She remembered how her father had spent countless moons locked up in his council chambers discussing tactics to help Dania. *And yet he had still permitted my marriage to Carlyle even when we had faced war against them?* Her mouth dropped open slightly as she remembered Carlyle had proposed marriage to form an unbreakable alliance between Karstares and Saphyre. She looked at him, but Carlyle just shrugged. *He knew my father would declare war on him – he used this alliance to prevent that?* Snapping herself back to the present Alexandra focused once more on Neith.

'There was Your Majesty thankfully that war ended four years ago. His Majesty has graciously permitted me to come to Saphyre in order to develop my Source. I am proud to call Saphyre my home now.' *She wants to be here less than I,* Alexandra thought sadly as she realised Neith was a political hostage. *She must be quite important in Dania to have been sent here…who is she?* Carlyle stood up and squeezed Alexandra's shoulder in warning to drop the subject. Neith set a silver bowl on Carlyle's desk and began lighting several candles that she pulled from her draped sleeves.

'Can you not light candles with your Source?' Alexandra blushed at the ignorance of her question.

'No,' Neith smiled. 'I am not as blessed as Your Majesties are. My Source allows me to Scry only.'

'That is not strictly true Neith. I have caught you levitating objects; you could have strengthened your Source further in Dania had you received the proper training. However, I admire your determination to master Scrying, and I am sure it will serve my kingdom well. I would not have elevated you to this position if I thought your Source to be inadequate.' Neith curtsied in a gesture of thanks, but Alexandra could see the stiffness to the gesture and the smile that did not quite reach the woman's eyes.

At Carlyle's gesture, Alexandra took his seat behind the desk. The bowl of water sat in front of her, and she looked down at her distorted reflection. 'I will need your Source for this, only a small amount.' Carlyle instructed her, it was not a question, and she knew she had no choice but to obey.

'But the baby…what if it hurts them?' She loathed using her Source at that moment; it made her feel sick and dizzy.

'Just a small amount,' Carlyle reassured her coming to stand beside her. 'I will be here should anything go awry with your Source, do not fear.' Nervously she held her hands over the bowl of water, they trembled slightly, and she fought to keep them still not wanting Carlyle to see that she was frightened. What was he planning? *Do not do it;* she tried to tell herself as she felt for her Source. *What if he is tricking you? What if he manipulates your Source to discover information on Caleb?* But she knew she would not refuse. Closing her eyes she drew in a shaky breath and coaxed her Source through her veins and out from her fingertips, stopping only when Carlyle squeezed her shoulder. Opening her eyes, she watched as Carlyle held his own hand over the bowl, adding his Source to the water.

'What are you hoping to See?' She asked looking between Carlyle and Neith.

'I want to make sure that no harm will befall our son,' Carlyle's voice was flat, and Alexandra felt her insides turn to ice. 'More and more I am hearing rumours of this man Caleb; I want to be sure that he will not harm my son.'

'*Our* son,' Alexandra hissed wincing at the possible lie. She saw no point in aggravating Carlyle further by pointing out she could have a daughter.

'Your Majesty knows of course that Scrying is a difficult branch of the Source to master,' Neith's voice betrayed the slightest waver and Alexandra watched as the woman began crushing herbs before adding them to the water. A look of deep concentration creased Neith's face as she levitated the bowl over the candles and bringing it to heat lightly. 'I can only See what the Goddess wishes me to See.'

'Then for your sake, I hope that the Goddess wishes you to See what I want to know.' Carlyle said calmly, Alexandra tried to smile reassuringly at Neith but could see the woman was lost in concentration. Stirring the mixture, Neith picked up the bowl and brought it to her lips and drank deeply. Alexandra recoiled when Neith's eyes opened, they had been a clear grey colour, but now the irises were completely white the only colour was the deep black of her spiral pattern, and at the centre even her pupils had turned a stark white giving her an eerie appearance. 'Sight for Sight.' Carlyle whispered seeing the horrified look on Alexandra's face.

'I only need to See what the Goddess wishes me too,' Neith's voice was distant and dreamy, but she turned her empty eyes upon Alexandra and smiled reassuringly. Standing up Alexandra gently guided Neith to the seat she had occupied only moments ago, terrified that the woman might topple over. Neith gazed blindly into the bowl where only a third of the mixture remained, Alexandra tried to peer over her shoulder, but she could see nothing but herbs lazily swirling around in the green and blue of her Source combined with Carlyle's. Gently Carlyle pulled her backwards and gestured for her not to get in the way. 'Death is coming,' Neith's voice was no longer distant and dreamy but had taken on a raspy quality, like gravel being thrown on the ground. 'Death will claim the babe, and with death, destruction shall follow. She will be betrayed, and life will be born into blood.'

'No!' Alexandra cried wrapping her arms over her large belly. Her head turned to face Carlyle fearfully as she felt her throat tighten. Did he know? *He would not hesitate to kill the child if he had the slightest of suspicions.* When she looked back at Neith the woman was coming out of her trance, her eyes blinking rapidly as she regained her sight.

'How dare you?' Carlyle's voice was dangerously low, and his sapphire eyes blazed with frozen fury. 'How dare you frighten Her Majesty?'

'Your Majesty –' Neith protested.

'*Silence*! Did I permit you to speak?' Holding out his hand a pale blue ball of light appeared. 'Guards! My chambers, *now*!'

'Carlyle,' Alexandra pleaded fighting back a wave of hysteria. 'The child may not be mine!' *Please, Goddess let this all be a mistake, do not let my child die! Do not take any child!* The grief of losing her daughter was still painful, and she did not wish that on anyone. 'Sorceress Neith said that she could only See what the Goddess wishes her too.' The door burst open as three Castle Guards stormed into the room. Alexandra looked pleadingly at Xander as the man bowed to Carlyle awaiting his orders. Not once did he look at Alexandra, in fact, he seemed to go to great lengths to avoid looking at her.

'Take Sorceress Neith to an execution cell.' Neith's face paled considerably, but she shakily rose to her feet.

'*No!*' Alexandra shook her head. 'Your Majesty thinks of the consequences – this may inflame Dania, they may attack us! What use is Sorceress Neith if she is dead? We need her to look into this. The Goddess may allow her to See further – whether the child at risk is even mine –'

'Alexandra *hush!*' Carlyle roared halting Alexandra's helpless babbling. Neith's eyes were wide as she looked at Carlyle waiting for him to decide her fate. 'Take the Sorceress to her chambers and make sure she remains there. She is permitted no visitors except Sorcerer Éibhear.' Carlyle took a threatening step towards Neith forcing her to keep her head up. 'Keep Scrying otherwise you will be praying to the Goddess for a lot more than the gift of Sight.' Xander and the two guards bowed deeply as they escorted Neith from the chambers. Carlyle rounded on Alexandra, directing his fury at her. '*What* were you thinking blurting out what she had Seen? I asked her to come to our chambers for a reason!'

'I – I was not thinking. I was frightened but what happened was not Neith's fault – you asked her to Scry for you. You cannot punish her because of what she Saw.' *Will Xander pass on what he heard to Caleb?* She wondered. Focusing on Carlyle, she could see her words were having the desired effect. Gradually his face relaxed, and expression softened. Quickly Alexandra poured him a goblet of wine but could not quite bring herself to meet his eyes as she gave it to him. She was frightened at how quickly he had turned on a Castle Sorcerer if ever she had needed proof that no one was safe from his anger then this was it. Sitting back down at his desk Alexandra buried her face into her hands, fighting back the urge to break down.

A few hours later Alexandra lay in bed beside Carlyle. He was lying on his side with his hand resting against her belly, his other hand resting on her pillow from where he had fallen asleep stroking her hair tenderly. Even in sleep Carlyle looked stressed; the lines around his eyes growing ever deeper, the corners of his mouth were turned downwards, and his skin was taking on a greyish tinge. Quietly Alexandra slipped from beneath the blankets and tiptoed over to the window seat. Despite the chill of the night and her thin nightgown she still felt hot and flushed. Opening one of the shutters she leant out the window slightly so that she could let the wind cool her.

Looking up at the sky she studied the moons; one was a sharp crescent while the second was almost full. Normally she found the two moons comforting; she enjoyed watching their reflections waver on the surface of the ocean. But tonight she found them both eerie and disturbing. *I cannot sit here all night fretting over what Sorceress Neith meant,* she told herself. Moving as silently as possible she closed the shutter and picked up her dressing robe, slipping it on only for the sake of decency. Turning towards Carlyle, she watched him for a few moments to make sure he was still asleep before picking up one of the candles from a wall sconce as she crept from the room. She was keen not overexert herself and did not relish the thought of using her Source; it often encouraged the child to begin playing with it. Biting her lip, she risked a quick spell to light the candle and flinched at the stinging sensation ringing through her arm. *At least when you are born I can have my Source back,* she thought to the child.

As she walked through the castle's cavernous hallways and spiralling staircases, she paused at each corner to make sure that there was no one nearby. *I should have brought something with a hood;* she scolded herself. She dreaded to think what someone would say to Carlyle if she was found creeping around the castle in the dead of night. She was surprised to see the training grounds deserted, many of the Castle Guards would practice late at night as they worked in varying shifts. Not wanting to push her luck Alexandra hurried through the hall and made her way towards the barracks. She was so close to her destination that she almost grew careless. At the sound of an opening door, she panicked and blew out her candle before she had even registered what she'd done. Rolling her eyes at herself she looked around for a place to hide, ducking behind a stack of crates. She was surprised to see Rhonwyn and Xander appear in Krista's doorway.

'She insists that Her Majesty should not train but will she listen to her own advice? What if I hurt them? Or if someone else does?' Xander's voice was a fearful tone that Alexandra had never heard from him before and she peered around the crates in curiosity.

'She is tough. From what I have learnt from her she was practically born on the battlefield with a sword in her hand. She will not stop fighting now, she would see it as a weakness. Just trust her Captain and protect her, that is all you can do. Although do not let her know that,' Alexandra could hear the smile in Rhonwyn's voice and she watched as the sorceress squeezed Xander's arm reassuringly. Alexandra tried to sink as low as possible behind the crates as the two drew closer, their features highlighted by the glowing ball of light levitating between them. Alexandra could see the beads of sweat lining Xander's forehead, a detail that Rhonwyn too had noted. 'After all this time you still fear the Source?'

'It is unnatural,' Xander's voice was tense, but Rhonwyn only laughed rather than take offence. 'If Caleb marries...*her*...she has bewitched him I am sure!'

'No Xander,' Rhonwyn sighed in exasperation. 'Both of them are doing their duty. What does she gain from marrying him? Her position would not be elevated; if that were all she cared for, then she would be better off staying as she is now.' A muscle in Xander's jaw twitched, and Alexandra realised they were talking about her.

'She is betraying her king – her *husband*. How can we trust her if she will betray the man whose bed she shares?' Alexandra fought back the urge to leap up and strike Xander. How *dare* he?

'And you are not?' Rhonwyn scolded him lightly. *No,* Alexandra wanted to answer, *he is betraying his closest friend!* 'And what of Krista? You cannot judge her for something we are all, in the eyes of the law, doing.' Knowing that they were on dangerous territory, Rhonwyn quickly changed the subject. 'Krista will be fine. She is nervous of course, but she is fine.' Finally, the two turned to leave but Alexandra waited until there was no sign of the light or voices before emerging from her hiding place. She stood outside of Krista's door, her hand poised to knock when she heard the sound of retreating footsteps at the end of the hallway. Her Source escaped from her in a spark, flooding the hallway in a bright light. She could just make out the rapidly retreating figure of a slender woman with dark hair. *Vanya?* Alexandra thought frowning; what was she doing so far from the kitchens? *It is probably just a slave;* she corrected herself. *It is too dark – and Vanya has no reason to be in the barracks.*

Pushing the thought from her mind, she knocked on Krista's door while simultaneously trying to regain control of her Source. She was not able to extinguish the light, but she had at least achieved dimming it somewhat. When Krista's door finally opened she let out a gasp of horrified surprised. There was a sickly green pallor beneath Krista's dark skin, her black hair hung limp and lifeless around her soft face, and her bloodshot eyes betrayed her sheer exhaustion.

'I – I cannot make the light go out,' Alexandra apologised sheepishly as Krista, blinking wildly, gestured for her to come in.

'The child is still controlling your Source?' For the first time since Alexandra had known Krista she could see fear in her friend's eyes.

'It did not happen last time; I do not understand why it should now.' Alexandra studied Krista closely and wondered if she should question her about her late night visitors. *She would tell you if she wanted too,* she told herself. Krista was entitled to privacy after all. 'I saw Rhonwyn this morning…she told me you were unwell.'

'It is nothing. Just a passing illness…a few of the Castle Guards have been struck down by it. I am sure it is nothing serious though so please do not worry yourself.' Krista shrugged and sat down on her bed, gesturing for Alexandra to sit beside her. As Alexandra sat, she could tell that Krista just wanted to curl up. She caught Krista's eyes looking at her swollen belly, and she self-consciously drew her robe tighter about herself. 'There is a rumour going around that one of the Castle Sorcerers has been arrested.' Alexandra almost asked how she had heard such a rumour before remembering that Xander had been present. She bit her lip wondering what she could say, had Xander repeated her frantic babbling? 'Scrying is unpredictable – you should pay it no heed.' Krista advised, and Alexandra forced herself to smile, but she could tell that neither of them believed this was nothing to worry about. Try as she might she could not shake the unhappy feeling that if it was not her child the prophecy spoke off, then it was someone's else's; but who? And what could she do to prevent the impending tragedy?

'It was the rebellion,' Alexandra muttered for the hundredth time. 'What else could it have been?' A moon has passed since the infamous Scrying incident but still Alexandra obsessed over it. She sipped at the herbal tea Father Dóchas had prepared for her and sat back in the seat piled with cushions in an attempt to get comfortable. She had finished distributing alms for the final time until the child was born and was sitting in his private chapel resting before making the journey back to the castle.

Setting the cup down with trembling hands her mind turned back to the castle. Carlyle had informed her shortly before she had departed that Krista was too ill to accompany her and had sent a random selection of Castle Guard's in Krista's place, even Xander had been absent from her entourage. She was terrified that one of the men would talk in to discover her sitting not just with the priest but with a man who looked remarkably like the king. She had learnt that not all of the Castle Guards were on the side of the resistance, in fact, a surprisingly large number were loyal to Carlyle – despite many of them not possessing the Source. *But equally quite a few of the Castle Sorcerers support Caleb…but then perhaps they have realised they are not safe after what happened to Neith.*

'It could have been a number of things. Please Alexandra try to put it to the back of your mind. Neith has been released from her imprisonment and is back working with Éibhear, surely that is a sign she is back in Carlyle's good graces.' Caleb tried to comfort her but to no avail. 'Please think of the child and what your fretting could do to them.' Caleb knelt beside her so that he could affectionately stroke her belly and Alexandra could not help but grin in response, resting her hand over his. While Caleb could not allay her fears completely he was able to offer her some form of comfort, even if he was not aware of it.

Recently Carlyle had begun to look at her in disgust, his lips curling in disdain as he looked at her ever-growing belly. He had even begun to let her bathe and dress in peace. While she was glad that he was no longer pestering her or taking ownership of her body she could not help but feel upset, and even a little betrayed, by his newfound disgust in her. *Am I that repulsive?* She wondered but quickly shoved the thoughts aside, did it matter?

'Caleb is right; there is no point in fretting.' Father Dóchas smiled at Alexandra in a fatherly gesture. 'Sorceress Rhonwyn has given your child the strongest protection possible. if there is a threat to your child, then those who wish harm upon them will have a difficult task.' There was a knock on the door, and

Alexandra froze as she looked down at Caleb in clear terror. Winking at her he ducked through a hidden tunnel, slipping the hidden partition back in place.

'Forgive me for intruding Your Majesty, Father,' a guard bowed to them politely. 'But it is growing late. Are you ready to return to the castle?' Alexandra gulped down the rest of her tea and nodded.

'Of course, thank you for the tea Father.' She held out her hand for the priest to take so that he could help her to her feet. Turning to follow the guard from the room she was re-joined by Helena and Roisin on top of the temple steps. She gripped Roisin's arm tightly as they began the long descent. She had never been able to shake the feeling of palms pressing into the small of her back as she had been pushed down the stairs all those years ago.

Too large to ride anymore there was a litter awaiting Alexandra and her two ladies at the bottom of the staircase, and they both helped Alexandra to settle within. The journey in the litter was heavy with silent tension; Helena peered out from beneath the heavy velvet curtains despite the dark hour while Roisin restlessly twisted her fingers. As they approached the castle the stiff silence was pierced by angry shouts.

'What is happening?' Alexandra asked pulling the curtains back and addressing one of the guards riding alongside them. She saw the smug look on the guard's face and instantly knew that something terrible was happening. *Caleb!* She thought pressing her hand to her mouth to stop herself being ill. Had he been discovered? *That would not be possible, he left the temple on foot, and I do not even know if the tunnel comes back to the castle.*

'That is a question you should ask His Majesty,' was the reply she received and Roisin gently pulled her back before she could strike the man.

'I am asking you,' Alexandra hissed trying to pull away from Roisin. 'I am your Queen, you will answer me!'

'Please Your Majesty,' Helena pleaded, and Alexandra turned to look at her surprised at how frightened her lady sounded. All around them were the sounds of shouting and the violent clash of metal upon metal. *They are terrified, do they know what is going on?* But she knew neither of her ladies would know what was happening any more than she did. Their eyes looked around in terror as the cries grew louder, harsher and more violent. *Helena must know something – surely Carlyle confides to her once he is done with her?* A voice in the back of her head cruelly persisted, building on the irrationalness that her fear was conjuring.

'What does my husband discuss after he is done with you?' She asked surprised at the bitterness in her voice as she addressed Helena. She had never acknowledges Carlyle's infidelity aloud to Helena. She could see the shock in Helena's eyes at Alexandra finally mentioning the tension between them, but she did not look ashamed.

'He discusses nothing with me. I am a *slave*. After His Majesty is done with me, I am dismissed. I have no choice when His Majesty commands me to his bed; he knew what I was when he picked me to be one of your ladies.' Alexandra felt a stab of pity at Helena brazenly acknowledging why she had been chosen to serve Alexandra. 'Do not dare feel sorry for me,' Helena snapped tossing her blonde hair defiantly.

'No one would ever tell us anything Your Majesty,' Roisin broke in, jumping at the sound of a dying scream. The litter was carefully placed on the ground, and the curtains wrenched backwards.

'Queen Alexandra, His Majesty has ordered for you to be confined to your chambers.' Strong hands grabbed Alexandra's arms and pulled her from the litter.

'Be careful she is with child you fool!' Helena cried as Alexandra was practically dragged towards the castle. White heat swept through Alexandra, and she fought back a surge of sickness as her child tried to take control of her Source. The guard gripping her arms dropped her with a shout of pain and Alexandra looked at him, shocked to find him nursing blistered and scorched palms. Her nose wrinkled at the stench of burning flesh and she turned her face away frightened that she was about to be violently ill. Rubbing her belly in an attempt to soothe the child she was surprised to feel the heat radiating through the layers of velvet fabric.

'I am more than capable of taking myself to my chambers,' she hissed at the guard as she shakily stood up. 'If you wish to escort me than so be it, but do not think to lay your hands upon me again.' Turning her back on the guard she swept through the castle doors. She wanted to run down to the barracks, to Krista's rooms, and to find out what was happening. Was Krista involved in the fighting? *No she cannot be, not if she was too ill to come to the temple. She would not be caught up in this chaos.* Thankful that her friend would at least be safe Alexandra allowed her feet to carry her to her chambers. *Do I go to mine or Carlyle's?* She wondered dumbly. As she walked through the castle, she saw that there was no evidence of sparring but there was an unusual heavy presence of Castle Guards and Sorcerers at each corner. 'What is going on?' Alexandra asked the nearest Castle Sorcerer who met her gaze uneasily. She was unnerved further to see that many of the Castle Sorcerer's wore the red robes signifying them as Foréignean's combative sorcerers.

'Please accept my apologies Your Majesty, but I am not permitted to say. For your own safety, you should do as His Majesty commands, go to your chambers.' Alexandra looked back towards Helena and Roisin; both were huddled together looking beyond terrified. Nodding at the sorcerer Alexandra took a deep breath and fought to take control of her Source once more. When she was sure her skin was no longer molten to the touch she held out her hands for each of her ladies to take. Guards were stationed at the bottom of the staircase to her private chambers, and Alexandra took this as a meaning that she should barricade herself there. Passing the guards she asked for water to be brought up and fresh blankets; she had no idea how long she would be confined and she wished to at least be comfortable along with her ladies. Helena went with the guard and Alexandra hoped the woman would bring news of what was happening with her.

'There are guards and sorcerers throughout the whole castle, Your Majesty,' Helena informed her as she returned. The door closed behind her with an ominous click and Alexandra stared at it in dismay. They were to be truly confined? *What is happening?* Alexandra wanted to cry out but fought her fear back. The child began to kick restlessly against her, and she slumped to the floor wishing she had at least been confined to Carlyle's chambers – at least he had a separate privy chamber.

'Perhaps we should play discs? I am sure His Majesty will come to you soon.' Roisin suggested weakly, but Alexandra shook her head. She knew Roisin was only trying to offer comfort, but she could not relax while she was left in the dark about the chaos outside.

'No thank you, but you two can play amongst yourselves if you wish. I assume we shall be sleeping here tonight...' She trailed off, why had the guard dragged her from her carriage? Had she been arrested? Sitting by the window, she rested her hands on her belly and stared out at the scene below. She could only look for a split second before the sight of the battle made her queasy. She should not have gone to the temple. She should have remained in the castle; she should have stayed with Krista. Out of the corner of her eye, she saw a flickering light, turning to look at the source of the light Alexandra could see a fire blazing below. *What is going on?* She thought swallowing a lump of fear as she realised the fire was close to the barracks and training grounds. The fear that something had happened to Krista, that her friend desperately needed her, intensified. Ignoring the sickness pulling at her stomach she held out her right hand and summoned a glowing ball, it was pale in colour and flickered weakly.

'Carlyle,' she called out bringing up his image in the centre of the ball. She was surprised to see him drenched in sweat, his face smeared with soot and even blood. 'What is happening?'

'Stay in your chambers!' He barked back, the ball of light diminishing and leaving Alexandra alone with her thoughts and ladies once more.

Several hours later Alexandra was curled up in her bed, her eyes fixated on the window. She had left the shutters open despite the cold weather, but neither Helena nor Roisin had complained of the cold. The sounds of fighting had long since faded, but the stench of burning was still strong, it smelt as if it had sunk in to every pore of her skin. Her ears pricked at the sound of shuffling from the floor and she bolted upright to see Helena watching her.

'What do you want?' She could not help the bitter tone in her voice, and she blushed, but Helena did not even flinch.

'To talk,' Helena replied simply and Alexandra lay back down closing her eyes. 'Your Majesty I am truly sorry for hurting you, but what can I do?'

'You could have said no,' Alexandra whispered but knew she was being unfair, unreasonable even.

'Can you?' Helena asked quietly, 'Are you always willing when His Majesty takes you?' Alexandra bit down on her tongue, squeezing her eyes tightly shut to stop the tears from falling.

'I am never willing,' she whispered thickly.

'Then how can I, a *slave*, refuse the king when even the queen cannot do such a thing?' Helena's voice was firm, and Alexandra forced herself to open her eyes and sit up so she could face the other woman. She was surprised at the emptiness in Helena's eyes and her guilt and self-loathing wash through her. *How could I have ever thought she wanted this?*

'It will not always be like this.' Alexandra tried to reassure Helena in compensation for her bitterness.

'Yes it *will*,' Helena replied bluntly. 'Your Majesty as soon as you accept that this is how we live in Saphyre, that this is how it will always be, then you will be happier.' Settling back into her blankets Helena closed her eyes and turned her back, leaving Alexandra alone with her thoughts once more. No sooner had Helena turned her back to Alexandra than the door to her chamber opened. Sitting up she looked to see Carlyle filling the doorway, surprised to see that in addition to the soothe now had a blackened eye and an angry gash across his right cheek.

'What has happened?' Alexandra cried jumping to her feet.

'Sit down,' Carlyle barked ribbing his face. The gesture smeared blood across his features, and Alexandra winced. Ignoring his command, Alexandra dipped a cloth into the jug of water so she could dab it lightly across his face. *Stay on his good side,* she told herself. 'Shortly before you returned from the temple there was a disturbance.'

'Is Krista safe?' Alexandra burst, 'I saw the fire by the barracks.'

'Never mind your husband and sovereign lord,' Carlyle growled. 'Who do you think is responsible for this disturbance Alexandra?'

'It could not have been Krista; she was too ill to accompany me to the temple. If she could not do that then how do you expect me to believe she caused all this?' Alexandra protested dropping the cloth on to the floor.

'Open your eyes you fool. She *lied*. She is not ill nor has she ever been. She has been working with the rebels since she stepped foot in *my kingdom*.' But she can't have been, Alexandra protested. *I saw her – she is ill!* Blood roared through Alexandra's ears as she realised what Carlyle was saying. Shaking her head she tried to look at him, but her vision was spinning, and she slumped against the wall.

'Where is she?' She murmured, 'where?'

'Where do you think? Krista has been arrested. For treason.'

# Chapter Thirty

Alexandra was confined to Carlyle's chambers the morning after he had broken news of Krista's arrest. The door was pointlessly locked as Carlyle kept her in place with the same spell he had used upon her arrival in Saphyre; she could not even stick her arm out of the window. Each day Carlyle rose early and departed, leaving Alexandra alone with Helena and Krista.

Whenever he returned to his chambers his attitude to Alexandra would drastically change. He constantly flitted between suspicion and tenderness, as if he could not make up his mind about whether to trust Alexandra or not. Once moment he would look as if he was prepared to sign her death warrant, the next he was trying to draw her close to offer her comfort. Alexandra would push him away each time he tried to touch her. She passed much of her days in confinement sitting on the window seat and staring blankly at the city below.

*What happened?* The question was on a continuous loop in her head, driving her to the brink of insanity. Not for a second did Alexandra believe Carlyle's events of the evening. He claimed to have gone down to the indoor training grounds only to discover Krista training several Castle Guards, squires and slaves on Carlyle's vulnerable spots. Where the best place to catch him off-guard would be, or even attacking Alexandra herself to make him react.

'How can he think that I would believe such foolishness?' Alexandra asked Rhonwyn, the only person permitted to visit her, as the woman handed her a potion to soothe the child.

'Of course he does not, but he is growing desperate,' Rhonwyn's lips barely moved, and she spoke in a whisper. Alexandra decided to risk using her Source to prevent them from being overhead, letting her power fill the room and protecting them. She set the goblet on Carlyle's desk and sat down wearily. Rhonwyn looked as if she wanted to scold Alexandra but instead took her hand, sending a bolt of her own Source through Alexandra's arm.

'Is that not dangerous?' She asked it was the second time Rhonwyn had given her power.

'In large doses yes, I am just making sure the child does not sap you of strength completely.' Sitting opposite Alexandra Rhonwyn stared at the doorway as if she expected to Carlyle to burst through at any moment. 'Alexandra please you *must* be careful. Caleb is now in a precarious position; His Majesty knows that the resistance is a true threat. He has discovered that some of the Castle Guards have sworn fealty to another, he is suspicious of everyone. I am sure it is only a matter of time before he turns his suspicions on us…' Alexandra frowned.

'I did not realise you…'

'Then I have at least played my part well,' Rhonwyn smiled wryly. 'You know some of us in the Castle Sorcerers were a part of this; you truly did not suspect me as one of them?' Alexandra thought back to the night where she had seen Rhonwyn and Xander coming out of Krista's room. How had she not pieced it together then?

'How many of you are there?' Alexandra asked suddenly feeling a small light of hope. 'If there is enough perhaps we could combine our power – we could help Krista!' Rhonwyn looked grave as she reached over to grasp Alexandra's hand.

'I know what I am about to say is terrible, even cruel, and I loathe myself for it, but you must listen. You cannot help Krista. She knew the price she could end up paying when she joined Caleb. If you try to help her, if you try to set her free, then her situation will be far worse. Caleb is trying for everything; he has dispatched several messengers all tasked with finding Captain Xander and bringing him back…but he is unlikely to arrive in time.'

'In time for what?' Alexandra asked feeling the dread fall in her stomach like hard rocks. 'He is accusing her of treason; surely he would not believe such a thing. I have to speak with Carlyle – make him see sense. I cannot let her…in time for what Rhonwyn?' Alexandra pleaded, she knew the answer, but she could not bring herself to admit it.

'You can hardly protest her innocence; he would be able to test if you are lying. Alexandra please,' Rhonwyn begged. 'We all know the penalty if we are caught but we accept that all of us would willingly lay down our lives knowing that if we do not things will never change.' *But Krista is not even Saphyrian – this is not her battle! She is here only because of me!* Alexandra wanted to protest but knew it was useless. *I should have done more to protect her; I should have sent her straight back to Karstares the moment I found out.* Wiping her eyes, Rhonwyn stood up. 'Forgive me, but I should not be here for too long.' Alexandra watched Rhonwyn retreat, glimpsing the two Castle Sorcerers who were stationed outside. *Does he really think I will try to break free?* She asked herself; she was hardly in a state to flee at that moment. Grabbing one of the furs from the bed she burrowed beneath it and sat on the floor beside the hearth.

Helena and Roisin were confined to Alexandra's personal chamber, and she feared what was happening to them. *Please, Goddess protect them,* Alexandra bowed her head. *Please protect Helena and Roisin; please protect Krista – I need her! I need them all!* She had no doubt that Carlyle would put Krista on trial and find her guilty. She ignored that he was right, that Krista was guilty. To Alexandra, Krista had done nothing wrong, nor was it fair for her to be punished while Alexandra was not. *Why is he doing this?* She knew why of course, but she could not get her head around that he could be this cruel. He had no real proof that Krista was acted against him; he had arrested her on falsehoods. *He surely does not know she is really aligned with Caleb.* When Carlyle returned, Alexandra was pacing around the room, still wrapped within layers of fur blankets.

'You should be resting!' He scolded, and Alexandra shot him a look of loathing.

'How can I rest when I am locked away from everyone? When my dearest friend is in the dungeons and ridiculously accused of treason?'

'Ridiculously?'

'Krista is no more guilty of treason than I am!' Alexandra cried not caring that it was a grave error to make. She matched Carlyle's glare as he looked at her in silence. *He knows,* she realised refusing to show her fear. *How much? How?* Caleb had told her that someone was betraying his whereabouts, was that same person also betraying those aligned with him now? *It has to be Xander – Rhonwyn said he is not here, that Caleb has dispatched messengers. Has he left so he can claim innocence in all this?* Alexandra had not been aware that Xander was not in the castle, no reason had been given for his absence the day she had distributed alms.

'I suggest you think *very* carefully before you speak. Just because you are a queen does not mean you are protected from our laws. If I find you have played a part in all this...' Carlyle let the threat hang in the air between them, and Alexandra took a step backwards. He would truly execute her? 'Women in your condition often make silly decisions; they are not capable of rational thought at the best of times.' Her hand itched to reach up and slap his face, her Source yearned to strike out against him, but somehow Alexandra resisted. She recoiled as Carlyle stepped towards her, one hand cupping her chin and the other resting atop her large belly.

'I know what you are thinking – should I deliver a daughter then it will prove I am guilty of treason. If I have a son, then I am innocent for surely the Goddess would not bless a son upon a wife who had plotted against her own husband.' Alexandra tried to shake her head, but Carlyle's grip on her chin was firm. 'Why are you doing this?' She whispered, 'if you truly think I am guilty then imprison me with Krista! You cannot suspect us of the same crimes and punish only one!'

'Think what you like,' Carlyle's voice was soft. 'You are confined for your own protection, or have you forgotten Sorceress Neith's prophecy?' *Death will claim the babe,* Neith's words were forever haunting Alexandra, and she looked down at Carlyle's hand resting against her. *She will be betrayed. Who though? Krista? By who?* Alexandra blinked back tears.

'Of course not,' she replied in defeat. 'But Krista would never harm my child nor me. Please, Carlyle let me talk to her.'

'No. Her execution is tomorrow, put her from your mind.' Alexandra's head snapped up, had there even been a trial? *He would argue a trial is not needed; she is a traitor – he claims to have caught her in the act even though we both know it is a lie.*

'You signed her death warrant the moment she stepped foot in this kingdom.' Alexandra whispered in disbelief. *How could I have been so foolish?* She had been overjoyed at Krista journeying to Saphyre, to joining Alexandra in her new home. Her selfishness had cost her oldest friend her life. *It is my fault she was caught up in this; I never should have let her come here.* 'If you execute Krista for treason then you would have to do the same to me.'

'What do you know of this rebellion?' Carlyle asked sharply.

'Nothing!' The protest was out of Alexandra's mouth involuntarily. 'How could I know anything when you watch me so closely? This rebellion is just as bad for me as it is for you!' *These words are not mine!* Alexandra protested in her head angrily, but she could not get the words from her mouth. Her eyes rested on the empty goblet on Carlyle's desk, and she swore at Rhonwyn silently, her mouth still talking involuntarily. 'I want nothing to do with this rebellion Carlyle. I want simply to live my life as your Queen, to raise our sons.' *Too far Rhonwyn,* at that moment she was furious with the sorceress. She could not believe that Rhonwyn had spiked her drink, that she was preventing Alexandra from protecting Krista. But each time she opened her mouth to admit about Caleb, that she *agreed* with him, her tongue grew numb, and she could only utter fierce denials. *How can I help Krista if I cannot admit the truth?* 'Please, Carlyle – if you have even the smallest amount of love for me then you will not execute Krista.'

'Alexandra it is because I love you, and our son, that she must be executed. She is a rebel; she is plotting against us. How can we trust her with our son? We have lost one child already,' Alexandra's eyes narrowed to slits at the mention of her daughter. How dare he acknowledge her now, when it suited him? 'She must be made an example of. I truly am sorry.' He moved both his hands to her face, smoothing her hair back gently. 'You must not worry, nor think about this traitor – think about the wellbeing of our son.'

'It is *you* who should think upon the safety of our child.' Alexandra hissed shaking her head free from his hands and stepping back. 'You cannot execute my friend and think that I will go on as if nothing has happened.' A strong wind was beginning to sweep through the room, the fire in the hearth began to splutter, and Alexandra fought to keep her power under control. Whether her child sensed her anger or whether they had picked up on the events unfolding she could not easily grasp her power. 'Get out, just leave me in peace and send me *both* of my ladies.' She held out her arm, and the main door to the chamber burst open. Carlyle looked at her with a mixture of concern and fury etched upon his features.

Abruptly he nodded and left, looking over his shoulder he paused as if he was about to speak but thought better of it. As the door slammed shut behind him, a sharp pain stabbed Alexandra in her lower abdomen. Biting back a cry she leant against the wall, doubling up as the pain continued. *Not now,* she pleaded. *It is too soon – I still have another moon!* She could not go into labour, not before she had seen Krista released. Falling on to her knees she pressed her forehead against the floor as she pains grew thick and fast.

'Your Majesty!' Two pairs of hands helped Alexandra to her feet and guided her towards the bed. 'What is wrong?'

'The baby,' Alexandra cried tears streaming down her face. 'It *hurts!*'

'Ssh,' Helena soothed her gently, 'lie down and I will fetch Sorceress Rhonwyn.'

'No,' Alexandra cried not wanting Rhonwyn nearing her. What if she slipped something else into her drink? Had she done it on Carlyle's orders? *No...whatever she put in my drink stopped m from confessing about Caleb...I almost betrayed him to protect Krista.* Screams tore her throat as the agonising pain continued.

'You need Sorceress Rhonwyn,' Roisin argued and fled before Alexandra could stop her.

'I cannot lose my child, not again!' Alexandra desperately clinging to Helena.

'You will not Alexandra, hush,' Helena brushed her hair back from her forehead and pressed a damp cloth against her skin. 'The child is telling you to rest; you are both upset.' Alexandra curled up as the stabbing persisted, surely it was too soon?

'His Majesty is on his way,' Rhonwyn said the words in a comforting tone but Alexandra knew it was a warning. 'He was with me in the Sorcerers' Tower; it is not Roisin's fault.' Alexandra shook her head; she didn't care, all she cared about was stopping the pain. 'Take a deep breath,' Rhonwyn instructed her as she gestured for Helena and Roisin to step back.

'What is happening? My son, is he safe? Alexandra?' Alexandra gritted her teeth to stop herself from screaming. Carlyle's hand rested against her forehead, a coolness washing through her body at the soft touch. As Rhonwyn continued to hold her stomach, she felt the pain beginning to subside to a dull throb, and she turned her head trying to clear her head.

'The baby is trying to tell us that they are ready,' Rhonwyn's voice was strained. 'I can soothe the child, but Your Majesty you *must* rest otherwise you will go into early labour. Once your child decides it is time for them to be born I cannot stop it.'

'I do not need rest,' Alexandra gasped, 'I have to speak with Krista!'

'No.' Carlyle's voice was firm, 'I will not allow you to risk the life of our son so you can foolishly speak with a traitor.' Alexandra tried to argue, but she could feel her body growing heavy. She looked at Rhonwyn; the sorceress's hands were glowing, and Alexandra could not help but watch in fascination as the glowing light moved from Rhonwyn's hands and into her belly. *I'm sorry,* Rhonwyn spoke through her Source as it wrapped around Alexandra's own power. She felt darkness pulling her down into a deep abyss, she tried to fight it but could feel Carlyle's own Source lulling her into a deep sleep.

Carlyle was not in bed when Alexandra woke up several hours later. Carefully she sat up, the stabbing in her abdomen was still present, but it had subsided considerably to a dull throbbing. Helena and Roisin were asleep at the foot of the bed and Alexandra could tell they had been told to sleep there in case she awoke. *He has sorcerers at the door and his own Source keeping me in place,* Alexandra thought bitterly. Carlyle's determination to keep Alexandra confined just made her even more determined to break free. *He is going to execute her tomorrow; I cannot sit around any longer.* Alexandra hoped that Rhonwyn's spell had soothed her child enough to leave her to use her own Source in peace. Tentatively she pressed her fingers against Helena and Roisin's temples, using her Source to push them into a deeper sleep.

Breaking through Carlyle's Source was a difficult task; she knelt on the floor and concentrated on finding a crack in the barrier on the door. Working her own Source through it, she smiled in cold satisfaction as she managed to tear the barrier apart, as if she were ripping linen apart. The effort almost exhausted her but Alexandra clung on, focusing next on turning her Source upon the two Castle Sorcerers.

Not caring that she was barefoot Alexandra grabbed her hooded travelling cloak and pulled the hood up so that she could conceal her face. She paused at the threshold of the chamber door before a sudden voice commanded her to turn around. She had no idea if she would find Krista, or even what state she would be in, and so she grabbed the jug of water that was kept close to the bedside.

She had avoided the dungeons since the first time Carlyle had shown her the castle. Pausing at the winding staircase, she used a small ball of her Source to light her way down. She rubbed her belly as she walked down the stairs trying to keep her child from stirring within. She winced at a fresh stabbing pain but pushed it from her mind.

'Please do not steal my Source now,' she pleaded with the child as she walked ever deeper down the staircase. The air in the dungeons was damp and rank with filth. Alexandra forced herself to try and breath through her mouth in an attempt to avoid the rancid stench. As she finally reached the bottom of the steps, she peered helplessly into the darkness. How would she know which cell Krista was in? *How can I even open them?* She thought remembering of the stone cells which Carlyle had used his Source to open. Was he the only one who could open the cells? *Blood magic,* she thought to herself staring down at her hands. If it was blood magic how could she possibly hope to open the cells?

Sickness crashed through her, and she leant her arm against the wall to stop herself from collapsing, clinging to the water jug with her free hand to stop it falling to the ground. How long did she have? She had no idea where Carlyle had chosen to sleep but what if he had simply worked late in his study? There would be hell to pay if he returned to their chambers to discover her gone, especially when he had gone to such great lengths at keeping her imprisoned. The ball of light in front of her flickered wildly, bouncing backwards and forwards as if trying to grab her attention. *Please stop it;* she begged sensing that her child was beginning to stir once more. *Please behave!* She could not afford to be discovered just because her unborn child did not know the severity of events unfolding. The light came to a halt further down the narrow corridor, and Alexandra forced herself to follow it. Closing her eyes, she held her breath as she listened for any sounds that would reveal Krista's whereabouts.

Pressing her palms to the stone wall, Alexandra gritted her teeth and pulled her Source, forcing it into the wall. *I am Queen Alexandra;* she thought as she focused on her power. *True Queen of Saphyre, I order you to reveal my friend.* Green light flared across the wall outlining several cell doors, slowly one door disappeared, and Alexandra rushed forth to catch Krista as the woman stumbled from the cramped cell.

'Oh Krista,' she gasped stroking her friends face in horror. Her right eye was swollen shut, she bore several cuts and bruises along her face and arms, and her skin had turned an almost ash grey colour. As Krista sat up, Alexandra pressed the jug into her friend's hand and she gulped it down greedily. 'What happened? I returned from the temple to find the castle in utter chaos, Carlyle said he had found you training people to attack him.' She tried to help Krista to her feet, but the woman had spent the past several days in the cramped cell, unable to sit or stand and her muscles were slack.

'Is everyone alright? Xander?' Alexandra had never heard Krista sounding so desperate, even frightened, in all the time they had known each other.

'I – I do not know where Xander is, he did not come to the temple with me. Rhonwyn said that he was sent away, Caleb has sent messengers after him.' Anger flared, and Alexandra gripped Krista's shoulders. 'Krista do you not see? It was Xander who betrayed you, who else could it have been?'

'No.' Krista shook her head and doubled over as a hacking cough tore through her. 'I promise you whoever is betraying Caleb it is not Xander.' Alexandra opened her mouth to argue, but Krista cut her off. 'Alexandra you *must listen to me.* It is not Xander; you both need to put your differences aside. You both want the same thing but if you do not work together and trust each other, then how can you hope to achieve it?'

'It does not matter, come we need to get you out of here.' Alexandra had not thought about where they could go, but all she cared about was getting Krista as far away from the dungeons as possible. She tried to help Krista to stand, but the woman refused her help, shaking her head.

'I cannot Alexandra – where would we go? You will not get me out of the castle, let alone out of the dungeons, without us being discovered.' Krista leant against the wall, but Alexandra refused to let her just sit there.

'Krista please…you cannot give up –'

'I am not giving up,' Krista snapped, '*look* at me, Alexandra. Do I look as if I am in a fit state to journey? I have accepted my fate; please do not make this harder.'

'There is still time…' Alexandra trailed off, but she knew there wasn't.

'I know I am to die today Alexandra. Carlyle did not need evidence for a trial; he is lying – when the fighting broke out I was in bed. One of the Castle Sorcerer's – Carlyle's second, stormed into my room and began yelling treason. He dragged me out…when I saw Carlyle I snapped and just…went for him.' Krista smiled weakly, but Alexandra could not share the smile. 'He was not quick enough to use his Source on me; I managed to get a nice hit in.'

'Krista…' Alexandra lowered hear head and brushed away tears. 'I cannot lose you…I will talk to Carlyle, I will plead with him…anything –'

'Do not *dare*,' Krista hissed at her. '*fight* him Alexandra. You must bring him down and make him suffer for all the crimes he has committed.' In the distance, she could hear footsteps and her head snapped up; had Carlyle discovered she was missing? 'Promise me you will trust Xander, you do not have to like him although you should! You will see soon enough he is not the one.'

'I cannot…'

'Alexandra I *love* him. If you do not trust Xander, then please trust me. I had hoped once this was over…'

'Krista *please* let me get you out from here,' Alexandra sobbed.

'There is nothing you can do. You should go before you are found here it will only make your situation worse.'

'No,' Alexandra moved closer to Krista and drew her companion close. 'Besides I could not just leave you out the cell – and I will not lock you back up.' Krista choked back a sob and the two clung to each other.

'It has been an honour serving you, Your Majesty.' She whispered, 'Your parents would truly be proud of you – they always were.' Alexandra looked up at the dark ceiling as she fought back fresh sobs. The approaching footsteps grew louder, and she clung to Krista tightly.

'How can they be when I cannot even protect those closest to me?'

'Alexandra!' Carlyle's voice, ripe with fury, echoed through the tunnel but Alexandra did not answer. He would find her soon enough.

Rhonwyn advised against Alexandra attending the execution but Carlyle firmly dismissed her, and for once Alexandra found herself agreeing with him. She could not abandon her friend in her final moments. *There may still be a chance at saving her;* she thought as she followed Carlyle down to the throne room. Both were draped in black velvet, their crowns glittering in what Alexandra felt was a mocking manner. She longed to rip the crown from her head, to throw it across the room and denounce Carlyle as king.

She could tell he had been concerned when he had found her last night; he had been unsuccessful in hiding his shock at seeing Krista freed from her cell. Whatever magic that controlled the cells Carlyle had not expected her to possess it.

Sitting on her throne Alexandra stonily stared ahead, refusing to look at Carlyle or any of his men who stood close by. Xander was still missing, and Alexandra wondered where he was. Had Carlyle sent him away so that he could carry out this farce? Krista was led into throne room with her hands shackled behind her back. She wore a coarsely woven dress; her hair was matted and her feet bare. Her face had been cleaned bringing out cuts and bruises. Krista stood before the two monarchs, brazenly staring at Carlyle and refusing to look away. Alexandra felt a rush of love for her friend, even now she was defiant. She would not give Carlyle the spectacle he craved. No doubt he wanted Krista to plead for her life, to promise information in exchange for her life. As she studied her friend Alexandra wished she could be just as brave; her own eyes were raw from crying and her skin was blotchy. Behind her Helena and Roisin, each held her shoulders, keeping her from jumping up.

'You have been found guilty of treason,' Carlyle rose to his feet and walked slowly down to Krista; clearly relishing each step. His blonde hair shone brilliantly against the sombre black velvet. 'The penalty for which can only be death.' The hands gripping Alexandra's shoulders tightened as she flinched. *He cannot do it.*

'You cannot stop this,' Roisin whispered. 'If you try to prevent His Majesty then he will only make Krista's suffering worse.' Alexandra knew Roisin was speaking the truth, but she could not sit back and watch her friend die.

'No!' She cried out as Carlyle held out his right hand. 'You cannot do this! She did nothing wrong!' No one even glanced at the distressed queen; all eyes were upon Carlyle as he clenched his right fist tightly as if squeezing juice from an orange. Krista dropped to her knees, clenching her jaw to stop herself from screaming. *He cannot kill her with the Source! She does not deserve death but she does not deserve that!* Biting back a scream as a knife-like pain tore through her lower abdomen Alexandra summoned her Source and threw it at Carlyle, using it to try and bind his own power.

'Alexandra!' Carlyle turned to glare at her as his fist dropped to his side. Alexandra ignored him and focused on binding his power, wrapping her Source around his own and squeezing it tightly. *You are being foolish!* He hissed at her as their powers connected.

'You cannot even kill me like a real man,' Krista taunted as she straightened her shoulders to glare at him. She tried to stand up, but a guard pressed her roughly back down to her knees.

'Krista please,' Alexandra said through gritted teeth. Carlyle was fighting her Source, sweat had broken out across her body making the velvet cling to her. She managed to shake Helena and Roisin from her shoulders and ran down the steps towards Carlyle. She did not care how foolish she looked trying to run with her extended belly; she had to put a stop to the foolishness. From nowhere a Castle Sorcerer grabbed her arm and pulled her backwards, holding her tightly against them. Alexandra glared up to find herself staring into the menacing eyes of Foréignean.

'Foréignean watch how you handle Her Majesty. Should any harm come to her then this pathetic woman will not be the only death of the day.' Alexandra tried to pull free but cried out as she was overwhelmed by a sharp pain starting in her lower back and moving to between her legs. She feel to her knees, fighting to keep her Source under Control. Foréignean knelt beside her, holding her shoulders but the threat from his king had obviously struck a chord and he slackened his group. 'Bring me my sword!' Alexandra flinched at the ringing sound that echoed through the throne room at the sound of a sword being unsheathed. She felt the baby moving in protest, and she cried out in pain.

'Carlyle!' She cried not caring that she risked enraging him further. 'The baby – *please stop*!' She clasped her belly fighting back the urge to scream as the gaps between the pain grew lesser and lesser. She looked up helplessly as Krista raised her chin stubbornly, glaring at Carlyle as she awaited death. Not once did the woman break eye contact with her murderer. Blood roared in Alexandra's ears and dark spots began to explode across her vision.

'Your Majesty you are draining your Source – you will use your life's force if you do not cease your foolishness!' Foréignean scolded shaking her in an attempt to break her concentrate.

'Stop it you fool!' Rhonwyn hissed rushing to Alexandra's side, 'can you not see Her Majesty is going into labour?' Rhonwyn began barking orders, but Alexandra was oblivious to what was happening around her. She focused on the sword in Carlyle's hand, it was glowing cherry read, and she could see it was taking all of his self-control to grip it. 'Your Majesty you must stop using your Source!'

'That is not me,' Alexandra gasped feeling pressure gripping her head. She could feel the child moving within her and she cried out and scrambled for Rhonwyn's hand.

'Your Majesty you must *stop*!' Rhonwyn called out desperately, '*please*! Her Majesty – the babe is coming!' Whether Carlyle was truly deaf to what was happening or if he chose to ignore them Alexandra was unsure. She could hear the people filling the room murmuring in fear, questioning the unfolding events, but it still did not deter Carlyle from his mission. A chilling *swoosh* filled the air followed by a dull thud. The murmuring ceased, the room was filled with a deathly silence broken only by Alexandra's sobbing and cries of pain as the babe fought to free itself.

A burst of light filled the room blinding everyone in attendance and Alexandra was reminded of the white heat from her coronation. As her vision cleared she was horrified to see that all traces of Krista had disappeared, there was no sign of her friend anywhere except for a grotesque pool of blood. A small sparrow like bird flittered around the room before coming to a rest in front of Alexandra. She stared at the beautiful multi-coloured feathers, but as another wave of pain ripped through her, she fell into darkness.

# *Chapter Thirty-one*

'She cannot be in labour – it is too soon surely?'

'Your Majesty with respect I told you that the queen should not have attended the execution. It is an incredibly stressful situation without being close to the person, but Her Majesty was extremely close to Krista – how did you think she would react?' From the depths of her dark prison, Alexandra was surprised at the coldness to Rhonwyn's tone as she addressed Carlyle. 'All we can do now is try to help her deliver the child, but she is extremely weak – she may not make it.' Alexandra did not register the words; all she was aware of was the agonising pain splitting her body asunder.

'Do not let her die, do not let *either* of them die.' Carlyle's voice was low but through the pain, Alexandra caught his wavering tone.

'This is your fault,' she mumbled. 'You have killed my child.'

'Hush you need your strength,' gentle pressure was applied to Alexandra's hands. 'It would be best if you left us, Your Majesty. I will send one of my healers should there be any news.' Alexandra screamed as the pain grew insistent and Rhonwyn had to shout over her. 'You cannot be here it is unseemly, men have no place in the birthing chamber!'

'Get out!' Alexandra managed to scream through the pain. 'I do not want my child born in the presence of a murderous tyrant!'

'Hush now,' Rhonwyn scolded, 'do you think yourself better? What were you thinking using your Source when you were in such a state?' Alexandra shook her head choking back a sob.

'Krista –'

'Alexandra I am sorry to sound cruel, but you will have time to grieve, *later.*' A jolt of energy shot through Alexandra as Rhonwyn began weaving her Source. Biting down on her tongue Alexandra slumped further back on the bed unaware of what was happening around her, barely able to hear the voices as they spoke in hushed tones. 'Alexandra you need to push,' Rhonwyn half-urged, half-pleaded. 'Think what will happen if you allow yourself to die; think of your people. We need you.' But she was too weak to absorb Rhonwyn's words and could barely make sense of them. Pain throbbed in her abdomen and between her leg; resonating throughout her whole body and tearing her apart. 'I want everyone out,' Rhonwyn commanded. '*Now.* Go to your chambers, the great hall – the temple, just *go* and pray for Her Majesty. No one is to disturb us until I send word, *no one.*'

'Just let me be,' Alexandra pleaded wearily as she finally managed to force her eyes open. Her vision was blurred, and she could not even make out Rhonwyn standing beside her. 'I cannot do this Rhonwyn; I am not strong enough.' Something cool touched her burning face, and Alexandra turned away.

'You *are* strong enough Alexandra.' *But if my child will not live, then I do not want to live, not anymore. Caleb will do better without me; Saphyre would do better without me!*

'Neither said my child would not make it.'

'It was not your child Neither Saw,' Rhonwyn tried to offer her comfort. 'Your child, *Caleb's* child, must live.' *This child cannot be Caleb's – not if they have been wreaking so much havoc with my Source!* Alexandra shook her head; exhaustion was pulling at her. It offered her a sweet release from the pain; a warm blanket to envelop her in. 'Please Alexandra if you will not do this for yourself then do it for Caleb; he has so looked forward to becoming a father! I have worked with him since before your arrival to Saphyre and never before have I seen him so full of life and hope. Your pregnancy, the fact he could soon be a father, has given him a new lease on life. He almost conceded defeat – but he knows the child will need him. Need *both* of you.'

'I cannot –'

'You *can*!' Alexandra screamed as Rhonwyn literally *shoved* her Source into Alexandra's body and commanded her to push. She had never before felt a pain so severe, and the blanket of exhaustion was torn away with her, snatching her only hope for relief. She was too weak to fight against the pain, let alone obey its command and push. Blood rushed through hear ears blocking out Rhonwyn's words, all she could hear was the sound of her blood like a river about to burst its banks. Darkness consumed her yet mercilessly the pain would not relent. She was aware of her screams, she couldn't hear herself over the rush of her blood but she could feel her throat growing raw.

*'You cannot die,'* Krista's stern voice broke through the deafening pain and filled the chamber with a calming silence. Through the darkness she could see a golden light, she could feel it reaching out to embrace her, pulling her away from the cold of the darkness. Krista's musky scent brought her back into the abyss of pain, but she had something new to focus on. *'You are better than this Alexandra!'* Alexandra shook her head pleading to be left in peace, why could they not just let her die? *'Do as Rhonwyn says, I promise you it will all be over soon.'* Fighting back the urge to tumble once more into the darkness Alexandra forced herself to listen over the roaring blood, to pick out Rhonwyn's voice. She was dismayed to find that the pain only grew worse.

'Alexandra your child is almost here, one more push.' Rhonwyn encouraged but Alexandra picked up the tense undertone, the slight panic. She tried to bear down, to push the child, but she had no strength.

'I cannot, please no more.' Alexandra begged as he body screamed at her to push, but she had no energy even to lift her eyelid an inch. Her muscles had slackened, her limns were limp and lay uselessly on the bed. Her Source was no more than a flicker; she had used a dangerous amount of her power and almost drained her life into it. *I could use the rest of it…I could use my life's energy to make sure my child is born.* She knew if she gave up completely then they would both die. Limply she reached out for Rhonwyn's hand; the sorceress had used a dangerous amount of her own Source bringing Alexandra this far.

'Send for the king,' Rhonwyn commanded one of her healers who she had summoned back in.

'*No!*' Alexandra mumbled struggling to light her Source one final time. 'He will harm my child, what if…' she could not bring herself to ask what if he somehow guessed he was not the father, or what would happen if the child she bore was a girl? 'Please...'

'We have both drained our powers; you need more to keep alive – to keep your child alive. His Majesty will ensure you live. I give you my word that I will not let him harm the child. Please, trust me.' Alexandra had no energy to nod or even speak. She was too weak to do anything and could barely muster a breath as she continued to fight against the pain.

*Keep fighting Alexandra. I will stay with you.*' Krista's golden light enveloped her, growing brighter as Alexandra felt herself begin to fade. She could hear Rhonwyn and Carlyle speaking in the background.

'Please Your Majesty I have done all that I can, both Her Majesty's Source and my own are almost depleted. If Her Majesty and the child are to have any chance at surviving you must give her some of your Source.' Alexandra half-hoped that he would refuse, that he would just allow her to die and be at peace.

*What of your child Alexandra? Regardless of whether Caleb or Carlyle is the father your child deserves a chance at life. Please do not give up.*'

'Alexandra please,' Carlyle echoed Krista's words, his hands were scalding hot as he clasped her right hand. Dimly she was aware of his Source threading through her fingertips, down her arm and throughout the rest of her body. 'Please do not let our child suffer because of my foolishness.' *Child*, the word reverberated through Alexandra's mind. Not once throughout her pregnancy had Carlyle referred to the child as just that, he had only referred to her child as his 'son'. *Is he that concerned?*

*Even Carlyle wants you to fight Alexandra,*' Krista's light grew stronger and warmer. *They need you. Please, I know it is hard, but you must keep fighting, it will all work out in the end I promise you. Live, promise me you will do that.*' Somewhere deep within she found the final piece of strength she had to push. Letting out a feral scream she was aware of Rhonwyn and Carlyle gripping both her hands. She tried to focus on what was happening but she felt empty, she could not even must the energy to acknowledge the deathly silence. The roaring of her blood had ceased, replaced with a deafening silence.

'What?' She gasped fighting to breath, 'what is happening? Rhonwyn?' Surely her child should be crying? Surely there should be some noise?

'Your Majesties…he…' through large dark spots Alexandra could see Rhonwyn holding a fragile bundle washing the blood from the shockingly blue skin.

'No,' Alexandra cried, 'no…she cannot do this!' *You told me it would be alright Krista! I fought and for what?* She looked at the shockingly still form in Rhonwyn's arms, unaware of Carlyle sitting beside her. Forcing herself upright she held out her arms, ignoring that she swayed to and fro even while sitting. 'Give him to me. She cannot take him; the Goddess cannot take *everyone* that I love!'

'The Goddess can take those of us who she chooses Your Majesty. I – I am truly sorry.' Tears spilled form Rhonwyn's eyes as she looked between Alexandra and Carlyle.

'Give him to me Rhonwyn, *please.*' Out of the corner of her eye she could see Carlyle nodding slowly, she turned to look at him, but his face was blank. His eyes empty of any emotion, not even a flicker of anger. Hesitantly Rhonwyn places the still bundle in Alexandra's waiting arms, tears blurring her vision as she looked down at the delicate features of her son. 'Death will claim the babe,' she whispered stroking her index finger along the soft cheek, the soft downy hair and the fine eyelashes. She wasn't aware she was crying until a tear splashed against her son's soft golden hair, turning the small patch a dark brown almost black colour. 'This is *your* fault,' she hissed looking up at Carlyle. 'You are a foolish and cruel tyrant. Your cruelty has cost the life of *my* son.' Choking back a sob she lowered her head closer to that of her son. 'I am sorry,' she whispered kissing his cheek. 'I should have done more to protect you…'

Her Source was almost completely extinguished, yet as she brushed her lips against her son's cheek, she felt her power momentarily flare to life. A warm breeze filtered into the room and Alexandra watched in fascination as her son's skin went from a bluish-pale tinge to a golden colour, sniffing the air she felt fresh tears spill over her cheeks.

*'I told you it would all work out. Have faith, Alexandra.'*

'Alexandra!' Rhonwyn was so shocked she forgot Carlyle was present in the room, 'how?' Alexandra shook her head. Her Source was completely extinguished and as Rhonwyn took hold of the baby boy just as Alexandra collapsed back on to the pillows, swallowed by the darkness completely.

Alexandra slept deeply for days; she was unaware of anything happening around her. She felt safe in her cocoon of darkness. No one could harm her where she was; she was just surrounded by nothing. Gradually the sounds of someone cooing permeated her cocoon, and groggily she opened her eyes. Too exhausted to life her head she could barely make out Carlyle standing in front of the window in her chamber, bathed in the soft glow of the green moon. She was surprised to see there was only one moon in the sky. In Carlyle's arms was a small bundle, his face hidden in the shadows.

She tried to sit up, to move so she could see her son. Had it all been an awful dream? Had her son truly been born dead? Had she even given birth? *Maybe this is a dream?* She wondered but quickly dismissed the thought. Her body still felt raw from the ordeal, each cell that made her screamed in agony.

'He is perfect,' Carlyle said as he turned to see Alexandra awake. As he sat beside her, Alexandra studied him intently unsure if she was looking at Carlyle or Caleb. Studying his eyes, she saw out the warmth and tenderness she was so accustomed to seeing in Caleb's eyes. When she was met with a coldness, she was satisfied she was with Carlyle. As he moved to kiss her, she weakly turned her head away. 'Alexandra I had no choice but to execute Krista, she was guilty of treason.'

'No she was not,' Alexandra was surprised at the calmness of her words. 'Krista was loyal to me Carlyle; she would never have harmed me. I am the True Queen of Saphyre, how many people witnessed the Light of the Goddess at my coronation? How many people witnessed it at yours?' She met Carlyle's eyes unflinchingly, whether it was the exhaustion and trauma of the birth of her son or the grief for Krista she was unsure, but her fear for Carlyle had evaporated. 'Lie to yourself all you like if it makes you feel better that Krista was a traitor, but do not waste your falsehoods on me.' She smiled down at the babe in her arms, love washing throughout her as he opened bleary eyes. They were a deep blue, wide with curiosity as he studied the new face in front of him.

*Thank you, Goddess,* Alexandra bit back tears as she cuddled her son. Had she really almost lost him? Her thoughts turned to her first child, had she been smaller than this? What colour had her eyes been? *She is safe with the Goddess,* she was sure she heard Krista's voice, and a tear slipped down her cheek. The babe grasped her index finger, curling his tiny fingers around her slender one and gripping it softly. *I will never let any harm befall you again!* She silently vowed pressing her lips to the crown of his head.

'What do you wish to name him?' Alexandra had forgotten Carlyle was beside her and was stunned that he would ask her opinion. She stared down at the small bundle, was it right for her to choose the name alone? *What if he is Caleb's son? Surely he should have a say?* But she knew that it was a foolish thought, how could she delay naming the child just to consult with Caleb? *He would understand I am sure.* Had anyone told Caleb of the child's birth? *I am sure Rhonwyn would have informed him,* she hoped someone had told him they were both well.

'Bréanainn,' she whispered after a moment's thought. She saw something flicker in Carlyle's eyes, and she wondered if he had expected her to name the child after him. *He helped me give birth;* she thought as she stroked Bréanainn's soft hair. She had still not recovered from the birth, the overwhelming exhaustion which had brought to the brink of death still tugged at her. She thought how Carlyle had gripped her hand, giving her his Source so that she could find the strength to finally deliver her child. *It was his fault I had gone into labour early,* she thought flinching away from Carlyle as he rested a hand on her shoulder. She was consumed by a frightening sense of loathing for this man. She opened her mouth instinctively asking for Krista to come up but closed it quickly. How could her dearest friend be dead?

'Very well, Prince Bréanainn.' Carlyle rested his hand on the baby's head and smiled in a tender way Alexandra had never seen before. 'I would like to speak with Rhonwyn,' Alexandra said. She wanted to thank the woman for saving her life, but Carlyle shook his head.

'Sorceress Rhonwyn is confined to her chambers, *resting.*' Carlyle sighed as Alexandra looked panic-stricken. 'Like you, she drained much of her Source, she is recovering. I will let her know that you are awake, I am sure she will be eager to visit you and our Prince when she is strong enough. I will send your slaves up.' Alexandra focused her attention on the small prince as Carlyle departed. He appeared to bear no signs of the trauma of his birth; he seemed full of energy and waved his arms as he tried to grasp Alexandra's hair.

'Your Majesty he is beautiful!' Roisin gushed as she curtsied; she sat beside her mistress and cooed over the small bundle. Helena stood uncertainly in the doorway of the small chamber and Alexandra could see the woman was unsure of entering. Alexandra smiled at her and bowed her head.

'Have you named him?' Helena asked as she closed the door behind her and hesitantly took a seat on Alexandra's other side.

'Bréanainn,' Alexandra managed to croak.

'You should rest Your Majesty – you almost died.' Helena chided her gently, 'shall I put the Prince to bed?'

'No,' Alexandra's grip tightened protectively on her son. 'Please leave him with me; I am sure I will rest better knowing he is close by.' She wanted to correct Helena, to tell her to call her by her name. But she was too exhausted. She settled back on the pillows cradling Bréanainn close to her as she lay on her side. She was just beginning to drift off to sleep when he began to squirm beside her and began to let out a shrieking cry. 'What is wrong with him?' Alexandra cried frightened that something terrible was happening. She picked up him and bounced him lightly, although he felt as if he were made of lead as she tried to lift him with her weak arms.

'He is just hungry,' Roisin reassured her. 'I shall fetch for the wet nurse.'

'No,' Alexandra protested shaking her head. 'I do not want someone else feeding my child.' Carlyle had told her it was inappropriate for a queen to nurse her child as if she were no more than a cow, but Alexandra did not care. Pulling at the strings of her chemise she smiled as Bréanainn latched on to her, drinking greedily. She felt a powerful surge of love for her son, mesmerised by his presence. Had she really carried him for eight moons? *The same time I carried his sister,* she thought sadly closing her eyes to stem the tears from flowing. She had failed his sister two years ago, and now she had almost failed him. 'How long have I slept? What has – His Majesty been doing?' She cut herself off from enquiring about Caleb and studied her two ladies curiously. Did they know of Caleb and his resistance? She had never thought about it before, but then she had never suspect Rhonwyn.

'His Majesty has not left your bed in over a week Alexandra. Sorceress Rhonwyn collapsed the day after your birth, and he has ordered her care to be of top priority – after you and the Prince of course. He has not even left your room to take meals, we have brought them to him here…he has slept on the *floor*.' Alexandra arched an eyebrow surprised at his devotion, but her heart did not thaw towards him. 'The kingdom has been waiting to hear of your recovery. They rejoiced at the news of the Prince's birth but when news soon leaked out that you had fallen ill…it as if the city went into mourning.' Alexandra was surprised to hear of the drastic reaction. 'His Majesty feared you would not awaken…he has been stricken with grief.'

'It is too late for His Majesty to think he can repair the damage of our marriage,' Alexandra pulled her chemise up and rubbed Bréanainn's back instinctively as he finished feeding. 'Krista was no less guilty of treason than I. He should not have punished her, not without punishing me.' Roisin and Helena eyed her wearily, and Alexandra realised she needed to be careful. What if Carlyle decided that she was becoming too bold and that he would be better off without her? *I need to stay alive;* she realised as she thought over Krista's words. *I have to fight…I must protect my people and my son.* 'I cannot forgive Carlyle for what he did; Krista did not deserve her death. Nor can I forgive myself for failing to protect her.'

For over a week Alexandra remained in the confinement of her chambers, but for once she was happy to be isolated from the rest of the world. Now that she was awake she adamantly refused to allow Carlyle into her chamber, but she realised she had no way of physically stopping him. Her Source was completely extinguished, she could not even sense the flickering of light. *Have I drained it completely?* She wondered ashamed at the feeling of loss; what would she do without her power? She had become so accustomed to using it once more; the thought that she no longer possessed it…she felt helpless. *Caleb and Xander are right – it is a crutch.* But that did not lessen her loss in the slightest.

Thankfully Carlyle seemed to respect her wishes. Helena and Roisin remained with her at all times in case she should fall ill. Her only visitors were Rhonwyn who had recovered from her own draining and on occasion Neith. The sorceress had been guilt stricken at the trouble her prophecy had caused, how she had been able to do nothing to stop the events from unfolding. Alexandra had quickly dismissed her guilt, what else could any of them have done?

Rhonwyn checked Alexandra each day when she came to visit and praised Bréanainn each time she saw him. Alexandra had confided in the sorceress about her missing power but Rhonwyn had been quick to try and reassure her that it was nothing serious.

'His Highness was wreaking havoc with your Source throughout much of your pregnancy and of course there was very little strength left when you delivered him. You have not extinguished it, it is simply recuperating. Trust me, in time your Source will return.' Neither woman broached the subject of Bréanainn and the Source, since his birth he had shown no signs of possessing the power. Did he simply not have it? Or had he used up his own somehow? Alexandra cared little for whether or not he possessed the Source, but she feared Carlyle's reaction when the feeling of elation at his son subsided. It was only a matter of time before he turned his attention to Bréanainn's power, or lack off.

'When can Caleb see him?' She dared to mention the subject to Rhonwyn when she was finally left alone with the woman for a brief moment. She did not feel right that she had not only named Bréanainn with consulting Caleb but that it had been down to Rhonwyn to recount the trauma of the birth. What must he be thinking? *It is not right, Bréanainn is possibly his son – he deserves to see him!* Each time she picked up her son she would gaze adoringly into his deep blue eyes, intent on trying to see if she could see either Carlyle or Caleb staring back at her. The way the child smiled at made Alexandra determined to believe that it was Caleb's son she had borne, but she still could not be sure.

'When you are well enough I will ask assure His Majesty that you are well enough to journey to the temple. We will take the Prince Bréanainn with us; Caleb can meet him then and Father Dóchas…' *We can learn the truth;* fear pierced Alexandra's heart as she looked down Bréanainn sleeping in Rhonwyn's arms. She thought how whenever Helena and Roisin would take turns in bouncing Bréanainn he would laugh with glee. Often Alexandra had overheard Roisin singing to him in her native tongue, it would stop his cries instantly and he would fall in to a deep sleep. He was completely free of prejudice. Surely a child of

Carlyle's would show some sign of cruelty? *I am being unfair;* she scolded herself. *We had a daughter together; do I really think she would have been incapable of cruelty? I do our daughter an injustice; I do my son an injustice…no child can be held responsible for their parentage.*

As much as she wanted too, Alexandra knew that she could not avoid Carlyle forever. Half a moon had passed since Bréanainn's birth, and Carlyle began sending her requests to dine with him in their intimate dining chamber. Alexandra was cautious, and even a little fearful, at leaving her chamber. She had not stepped outside her chamber since Krista's execution, part of it was her weakness after the traumatic events, but she also dreaded leaving the safety of her chamber.

'You cannot avoid him forever,' Rhonwyn scolded her one evening. 'I think you should see him. The sooner you dine with him then you can prove you are on the mend, he will allow you to go to the temple once he is sure you are healed.' Alexandra closed her eyes and bit back a sigh, Rhonwyn was right.

On the eve she was to join Carlyle for supper Helena dressed her in a velvet gown with full sleeves and a flowing skirt to hide the slackness of her belly. Once she was dressed, Roisin took her turn at trying to bring Alexandra's pale features back to life. There were lines around her face where only half a moon ago there had been none, and vainly Alexandra fretted over the strands of grey hairs which had appeared in her auburn locks.

'I am awful!' Alexandra cried in disgust, 'Bréanainn almost died and Krista…' she choked back a sob frightened that she would smudge Roisin's handiwork. 'Why do I care so much about how I look?'

'You are thinking like a queen,' Roisin comforted her. 'It is good for you to worry over something you *can* control. Your appearance is important to the people if you walk around looking as if you are a corpse they will worry greatly. You and your child are their hope.'

'You are sure Bréanainn will be safe?' She trusted Helena and Roisin to look after Bréanainn, but after almost losing him to the Goddess she could not stand the thought of being separated from him.

'I give you my word we will watch over him,' Helena reassured her. 'His Majesty has asked for him to be brought down after your supper – you will not be without him for long.'

Alexandra bit her lip nervously, part of her wanted to keep Carlyle as far away from her son as possible frightened that if he held him for too long, he might grow suspicious of the child's parentage. 'Alexandra, His Majesty *is* Prince Bréanainn's father and both of you could have died had the king not given you his Source.' Alexandra felt a pinch of betrayal at Helena's defence of Carlyle, but she knew the woman could not help it. She did believe Carlyle was the father after all. As she looked at Helena, she could not help wondering how often the woman had been summoned to Carlyle's bed and the woman blushed sensing what Alexandra thought. 'He has not requested a bed warmer,' Helena said softly as she knelt beside Alexandra. 'I truly think the events that have come to pass have changed – you and Prince Bréanainn have been his only concern.'

'I am sorry,' Alexandra sighed. 'I know it is not your fault…' She trailed off, and Helena shrugged with a small smile. 'But it was because of Carlyle that Bréanainn and I nearly died.' She could hear the awful of *thud* of Krista's head hitting the floor of the throne room, would she ever be able to go back into that room? Did the blood still stain the floor? 'I wish that I did not have to see him let alone speak with him.' Helena squeezed Alexandra's hand and stood up, pulling her mistress with her.

'That is hardly an option, especially with the Welcoming celebrations to organise. These may even overshadow your own anniversary.' Alexandra had forgotten that in less than a week it would mark the occasion of her third year of marriage to Carlyle. *Thank the Goddess for small blessings*, she thought smiling wryly. The thought of the Welcoming did not excite her as she thought it should do. There would be a procession through the city and Father Dóchas would bless Bréanainn into the Goddess's family. But while it was a joyous occasion to celebrate the child's birth Alexandra could not help but feel saddened. What if Caleb was not the father? He would be forced to the back, to observe his son's Welcoming afar while Carlyle paraded around, usurping him once more. If Caleb was Bréanainn's father then what would it be like for him to witness another man, his greatest enemy, raising his son? Mercifully she was pulled from her chain of thoughts by a knocking at the door.

'Captain,' Alexandra greeted, kissing Bréanainn before finally forcing herself to hand him back to Helena. She felt her body grow tense as Xander remained in the doorway as he bowed to her. She had not been prepared for the sight of him, and his appearance startled her. His grey eyes were red-rimmed and bloodshot, his dark hair unkempt and had a greasy appearance and his face was dotted with stubble where had clearly missed areas while shaving carelessly.

'Your Majesty. Congratulations on the birth of the prince, you must be overjoyed.' His voice was hoarse yet strangely devoid of emotion. Alexandra remembered her final conversation with Krista; how the woman had been adamant of Xander's innocence at the fate which had befallen her. Alexandra had not believed Krista, even as she had declared her love for the Castle Guard's captain. But seeing him in such a state forced herself to re-evaluate her opinion of the man. Surely he would not be in such a wretched state if he had been the one to betray Krista? How could someone so callously betray their friend and yet be so obviously torn at their death? *He loved her...they loved each other.* A lump the size of an apple rose in Alexandra's throat and quickly swallowed it.

'Would you like to meet him?' She asked in a strained voice. Did he think her overjoyed? Did she appear to be so? She was of course thankful for the birth of her son that he had eventually lived. But she knew her joy was overshadowed. She gestured to the cradle Helena and Roisin stood beside, but Xander shook his head refusing to look in their direction. Alexandra was startled to see his eyes shining brightly and desperately wished she could offer some form of comfort. *Krista wanted us to get along, to settle our peace and trust each other...but how? For three years we have hated each other, not trusting one another. How can we put that behind us?*

'Perhaps another time Your Majesty,' Xander replied stepping backwards. 'I have simply come to bring you to the king's dining chamber. He is waiting for you there now, he did not feel it safe for you to wander alone but did not want to intrude upon you...' Alexandra nodded, turning she walked over to the cradle and looked down at Bréanainn. Could she really leave him? what if something happened?

'Go,' Helena and Roisin whispered in unison. 'He is sleeping, and we will bring him down soon.' It was the most difficult thing she had ever done leaving Bréanainn for the first time. She could feel her heart tearing, but she forced herself to follow Xander from her chamber. As the stepped into the well-lit hall, she bit back a gasp as Xander's features were illuminated in the torchlight. His skin was swallowed, blotchy and he looked like he had lost a dangerous amount of weight in the past half moon.

'Captain –'

'Please do not mention her,' Xander's voice was thick, and Alexandra found herself yearning to comfort him, but unsure of how. 'I was sent away. I heard what was to happen and turned around but…by the time I arrived it was too late. I was such a fool to turn my back on her, to leave her in pursuit of what I thought my duty…I should have *known*.' Alexandra felt tears trickling down her cheeks at the unjust cruelty; she had at least been able to say goodbye.

'I will not let him get away with what he has done.' Alexandra vowed. Resting her hand on Xander's arm, she drew him to a halt and glanced around before speaking. 'I know that it is dangerous but…I *must* see Caleb.' She lowered her voice. 'Please, can you ask him to meet me outside?' She felt naked without her Source; she could have asked for Caleb to be brought to her study and protected them with a spell. She felt useless without it, how had she managed on Earth? How had she coped during her first several moons in Saphyre? She was desperate to see Caleb, but she was frightened she could not protect them without her Source. She expected Xander to refuse, to ask her how she could possibly think to be so foolish at such a time but finally, he nodded.

'I will not take you to him,' he said quietly. 'But not outside. I will come to your study at the first hour of the morning; I will take you to him from there.' They resumed their silent walk, neither quite sure of what to say to the other. Alexandra tried not to think of Krista, but been so close to the man her friend had claimed to love made it difficult. She thought of the throne room several floors below and the pool of blood which had stained the floor. She frowned as she thought back to that awful day; the pool of blood, the blinding light and the disappearance of Krista's body. Finally, Alexandra could keep silent no more.

'Captain I am sorry but I must ask you something.' She looked up at Xander for some sign that he had heard her, but his face remained impassive. 'When…after it happened there was a flash of light and heat…similar to what had happened at my coronation. When it disappeared she – she was no longer there,' she could not bring herself to say Krista's name to him. 'I remember there was a small multi-coloured bird in her place…what does it mean? What happened?'

'Have you noticed that those birds are quite common?' Xander asked as if he was trying to change the subject.

'I had one nest in my chambers a few years ago,' Alexandra nodded. 'They had birds of a similar size on Earth; they were called sparrows. I just assumed it was a common bird like those.'

'They are actually quite rare,' Xander's voice took on a bitter tone. 'Beautiful birds but they are rare, except here in Saphyre. But then our kingdom has lived under tyranny for such a long time…'

'I do not understand.' Alexandra asked, 'What are these birds?'

'When the blood of someone pure is spilt that bird appears, it is believed they are the soul of the innocent making its way to the Goddess. The bird is the incarnate of an innocent's soul given a brief chance at life; many make their way straight to the Goddess – a few, such as the one who nested with you, will remain with us for a short while. Perhaps to come to terms with what has happened, or to watch over their loved ones.' Alexandra thought back to the bird which Carlyle had crushed. She had always put down its miraculous recovering down to his Source, but was it in fact because the bird could not be killed? *It is already dead…was it a cruel trick Carlyle played on me to over emphasise his power?* She would not put it past Carlyle. 'She…Krista,' Xander's voice choked on her name, and Alexandra reached out to squeeze his hand tightly. 'She never revealed to you the true cause of her illness, did she?'

'She – she said it was a bug,' Alexandra said as she began to dread what Xander was saying. How could she have been so foolish to miss the signs? She had been experiencing them…she should have noticed them. 'She told me it would pass…'

'She swore Rhonwyn and I to secrecy. She did not want you to know until your child was born, she thought the truth would worry you and cause harm to your child…never mind her own.' Her final conversation with Krista burst to the fore of her mind, and she remembered her words. *'I love him. If you do not trust Xander then please trust me. I had hoped once this was over…'*

'She was pregnant,' Alexandra whispered in horror. 'Y – You?'

'She was terrified people would discover our secret. I tried to convince her that we could marry before she began to show, but she knew Carlyle would never have given his blessing on the marriage. As his Captain, I must seek his permission to marry...'

'I would have given you my blessing, why did you not come to me?'

'I mean no disrespect but would you have honestly consented to a marriage between Krista, your closest friend, and I? It is no secret that there is no love lost between us, that neither of us has been able to trust the other. If Krista had sought your blessing, you would have tried to talk her out of it...I do not wish to think how you would have reacted if I had come to you.' Alexandra looked away feeling ashamed of herself. 'I do not blame you; I have often tried to convince Caleb that he should not marry you...' Xander trailed off as he realised where they were and the subject they spoke off. 'Even if you would have given us your blessing it would have counted for nought. His Majesty would have dismissed it instantly, no matter how much you argued for us.'

'Captain I truly am sorry,' Alexandra tried her best to fight back her tears but eventually she let them fall. What did she care if the paint upon her face smudged? 'I owe you several apologies. Ever since we have met I have not trusted you – I even thought you were responsible for the death of my daughter...' She decided to be bluntly honest. Why should they lie to each other? 'Saphyre is more your kingdom than mine; it is your home. I never had reason to doubt you...'

'What makes you think you should not doubt me now? That I was not the one who gave the order to harm your daughter? Or that I even did it myself.'

'I warned Krista to stay away from you. The night before...her murder...I broke her out of her cell, but she could not leave with me, she refused. We talked...' Alexandra took a deep breath as she forced herself to return to that awful night. 'She told me I was wrong about you, that she loved you. She told me I would one day finally believe her, that you are true and loyal.' Clutching the locket at her throat, she resisted the urge to tear it off. 'I know of only one man callous enough to harm a mother and child. You are not that man.' Xander nodded, his mouth set in a straight and grim line. Alexandra was surprised when Xander dropped to one knee, bowing his head deeply.

'What are you doing?'

'I swear fealty to you, Queen Alexandra.' She blushed at the formal tone in his voice. 'I have done you a great dishonour – even after the Goddess made it clear that you are our True Queen I refused to acknowledge you as thus. I promise to lay my life down to protect you, Prince Bréanainn and of course our future king.' Xander's voice lowered to a whisper and Alexandra gave him her hand to kiss.

'I gladly accept your fealty.' Alexandra said formally, 'and I offer you my friendship…if you will accept it?' She was relieved when Xander rose to his feet, a small smile on his lips.

'Nothing would give me greater pleasure than calling Her Majesty, my friend. But if we are to be friends perhaps in private, we should not be so formal. Please, from now onwards call me Xander.'

'Then no more calling me Your Majesty,' Alexandra begged smiling. 'Truth be told I long for the days on Earth when I was just plain old Alexandra…I was happy then.' The air between them felt clear for the first time, and Alexandra was sure that Krista was with them, mocking them both for their stupidity.

Realising that they had been keeping Carlyle waiting for long enough the two picked up their pace. As they drew closer to the dining chamber, Alexandra felt her blood beginning to boil at the evening's revelation. Had Carlyle known? Murdering her closest friend was unforgivable enough, but to kill a child? One who had not even had a chance at life? Alexandra doubled over as if she had been struck in the stomach, Neith's prophecy ringing clearly through her mind. *Death will claim the babe and with death destruction shall follow. She will be betrayed, and life will be born into blood.*

*The prophecy had never been about my child,* Alexandra realised in horror. Only the last part had applied to Bréanainn, for had he not been borne through blood? She had gone into labour when Krista had been murdered when her child had been murdered alongside her. Xander was at her side, talking to her, but she could not make out his words through her anger. Straightening up she marched towards the dining chamber. Briefly, she thought it was just as well she did not have her Source at that moment as she would surely kill Carlyle if she could.

'You murdering, treacherous, cold-hearted *bastard!*' She flung the dining chamber door open, ignoring the startled looks of the slaves serving their supper. At a glance from Carlyle, the slaves fled the chamber, closing the door behind them. Alexandra nodded at Xander to leave, determined to speak with Carlyle alone. She did not want Xander in the same room as the man who had murdered his child. 'Did you know?'

'Know what?' Carlyle thundered rising to his feet. He glared down at Alexandra but for once she was not in the least bit intimidated by his towering frame of over six feet. 'What is wrong with you?'

'The child in Sorceress Neith's prophecy was never about Bréanainn.' Alexandra fought back the urge to throw herself at Carlyle, to strike him and cause as much as possible. 'Only the last part applied to him 'life will be born into blood', blood that *you* spilled from the murder of an innocent!'

'That *female* was not innocent –'

'Krista was pregnant.' Carlyle stepped backwards his hand scrabbling behind him for a chair. His expression was one of disbelief and the colour drained from his face. *He truly did not know; did he also think she was just ill?* Alexandra realised, but it did nothing to alleviate her anger or hatred towards him. 'Surely you must have known something was wrong Carlyle...the Goddess herself showed her displeasure at the execution.'

'How could she have been pregnant? She was not married...' Alexandra rolled her eyes at his stupidity. *That is what he chooses to cling to? That the woman he murdered had conceived outside of marriage?*

'Death will claim the babe and with death, destruction shall follow. She will be betrayed, and life will be born into blood.' Alexandra recounted the prophecy in a deadpan voice. 'You are a fool Carlyle and one day you shall be held accountable for *every single crime* you have committed against our people. I will see to it myself that you are brought to justice. I would advise you to perhaps pray for forgiveness but I doubt even the Goddess could forgive someone as evil as you.' Turning her back on him Alexandra left the dining chamber; surprised to find Xander waiting for her on the other side of the door.

# Willow Woods

# *Chapter Thirty-two*

'*No,*' Both Caleb and Xander shouted and Alexandra looked about nervously; had someone overheard them? *We are too far underground;* she scolded herself. 'Alexandra I have put you through too much already. I will *not* make a murderer out of; killing has consequences. Especially if you were to use your Source, it would darken your soul and turn your Source sour. I sometimes think one of the reasons Carlyle is so cruel is that his bloodline has become tainted, their Source completely soured.' Alexandra looked down at her feet, what if Bréanainn was Carlyle's son, did that mean he was already darkened by Carlyle's sins? *He has shown no signs of the Source since his birth;* she tried to comfort herself. *And I will raise him to know he cannot kill those who oppose me.* 'It would end things quickly if you were to undertake the task but I do not want to tarnish you. Nor would Krista want you responsible for his death, however, justified we feel it may be it is still murder.'

'It would be a small price to pay for the protection of our people, to put an end to all of this.' She tried to argue but it was weak. Of course, she did not want to kill Carlyle, but she was desperate for Saphyre's suffering to end. She wanted peace and the chance for her people to live safely. 'If it is souring my Source you are worried about you should not fear...I do not seem to possess it. I used it all giving birth to Bréanainn.'

'Will it come back?' Xander asked curiously, but Alexandra shrugged helplessly. 'I am sorry...' She smiled at the genuine tone of his voice.

'Rhonwyn is sure it will return, but I cannot even feel a spark of it. Please Caleb, my Source cannot sour if I do not have it. Let me help...'

'I want your help of course I do,' Caleb reached out to take her hand. 'But we must do this properly. I want you and Bréanainn, regardless of whose son he is, kept safe and out of danger as much as possible. This is my battle; I am the one claiming to be the rightful king. I cannot have someone doing my dirty work.'

'The Welcoming Ceremony...' Xander murmured thoughtfully as if he had only been half-listening to Caleb's speech.

'What about it?' Alexandra sighed rubbing her forehead wearily; she had forgotten that was the reason she was to have dined with Carlyle that evening. They would need to begin planning the event soon. She loathed the idea of planning the event with Carlyle; she was sure it would be a more joyous event if she could share it with Caleb. She looked at Caleb as Xander remained silent but he only shrugged, clearly as lost as she was at Xander's murmurings.

'It would be the perfect time for us to strike, Carlyle will feel at his securest knowing that he has a son in the cradle.'

'No.' Caleb cut in sharply. 'I will not have Bréanainn put in any danger. If we were to strike at the ceremony there would be rioting, he and innocent people could get caught up in the battle.' Xander clenched his jaw and Alexandra could see him casting an uneasy glance at her. It was true they had called a truce, but it was difficult completely erasing four years of distrust and hatred.

'Your – Alexandra,' Xander quickly corrected himself. 'Forgive me I have to ask, of course, I want no harm to come to Bréanainn for he is just a babe but...what if he *is* Carlyle's son?'

'There is a chance of course...Caleb and I...we only...' She blushed furiously and looked away. 'But regardless of who is father is he is still *my* son, I will not put him at risk just because he is the son of a tyrant. He is not a threat to Caleb if that is what you fear,' she tried to console Xander. 'Regardless of who his father is I think it best if Bréanainn was not put on the throne...when the time comes. I think we should raise him for the expectation that he joins the church, or perhaps let him choose a different path – one away from the throne.' Alexandra could only hope that if she bore more children, more sons, then Bréanainn would not begrudge them what he may have seen as his birthright. *We will raise him to know of what happened, the circumstances of his conception and birth...I will not hide anything from him lest he be ashamed!*

'When will you next be at the temple?' Caleb asked pouring more wine for them, Alexandra shook her head not wanting to return to her chamber drunk. Already she was growing conscious of the time; what if Bréanainn needed feeding?

'I will be distributing alms in a few days, and of course I will be bringing Bréanainn with me to the temple. Carlyle has apparently already given his permission, although he will be left alone with one of my ladies while I distribute alms...perhaps I could ask Sorceress Rhonwyn to attend to him that day. Who better to watch the Prince than a healer?' Caleb smiled at Alexandra and nodded in thanks.

'I still think we should strike at the Welcoming Ceremony,' Xander looked ashamed as he spoke and Alexandra resisted the urge from striking him. She knew he was torn at the grief of losing his own child, but to put hers at risk? A sudden thought struck her, and she looked between the two men with a spark of determination.

'*After* the ceremony,' she emphasised. 'There will be a celebration. Carlyle will of course put on a grand feast, a ball...it would go on late into the night, well past Bréanainn's bedtime. We could give him to Helena and Roisin to take to bed long before any fighting begins. Sorcerers who are aligned with you could put spells on my chamber...' She hated the thought of Bréanainn being near any fighting, but surely this was better than him being in the same room. 'I want Helena and Roisin protected along with as many slaves as possible. It is not fair they should be caught up in this.'

'She...Krista...said you were kind and smart. It is refreshing to hear someone talk as if the slaves are people.' Xander's voice became strained at the mention of Krista, and he took a deep drink from his goblet.

'They *are* people,' Alexandra pointed out. 'Caleb you must promise me that when you come to the throne, there will be no more slavery in this kingdom.'

'Do you know how many slaves are involved in the resistance?' Caleb smiled at her, 'of course I will end it. But we must go about abolishing it carefully; many would rather have their slaves slaughtered before seeing them go free. We are already working on protecting those who would be most at risk.

Those who do not wish to stay we will evacuate from the city. When I left Evany, I sought out communities who would be willing to help slaves readjust to freedom. I give you my word Alexandra that slavery will be abolished under my rule, but it will take time – it is not something I can accomplish in a week.' Alexandra bit the inside of her cheek to stop herself from pelting him with useless questions. Why? Why could it not be accomplished even quicker? But she knew it would be a length process, people would be changing their lives, and some may have to start with nothing. *We will help them, all of them.* She silently vowed.

Alexandra lay on the grass holding Bréanainn in the air above her with outstretched arms. Bringing him close she would kiss his cheek before raising him upwards once more. She could not help laughing with Bréanainn as he waved his plump little limbs around. Beside her Helena and Roisin watched, both bundled up in thick cloaks and furs just as Alexandra and Bréanainn were. *I should not keep him out for too long;* she gently chided herself as overhead the clouds turned to an ominous shade of grey, threatening to bring the first snow of the winter upon them.

Sitting up she cradled Bréanainn close, tucking his hood firmly around his head and wrapping him in her own cloak. A Castle Sorcerer had infused Bréanainn's clothes with heat to ensure he would be protected from the cold, but still, Alexandra worried that he might grow ill if she kept him out for too long. As she and her ladies rose, she saw Carlyle approaching them from the corner of her.

'Can you please take Bréanainn inside?' Helena took hold of the young prince, wrapping him up beneath her cloak, so he was almost hidden beneath the layers of fabric. Alexandra began walking at a slow pace so that Carlyle could catch up to her. 'I do not want a lecture; I am not keeping Bréanainn inside until the winter is over. He is perfectly warm.' Alexandra wished she could say the same for herself. She still had no trace of her Source and could not shake the feeling that maybe she had lost it forever. Her mother had died from using her Source up, she had never heard of someone draining themselves completely and surviving, but it did not seem impossible.

'I came to ask if you would join me for a walk,' Carlyle was dressed in a thick velvet jacket lined with fur, but Alexandra could feel the heat from his Source emanating. She could not help looking at him wistfully, missing her own ability to keep warm. 'Your Source will return, most likely stronger than ever. You should not worry.'

'And Bréanainn?' Alexandra could not help herself asking, she was still nervous how Carlyle would react if it turned out her son did not possess their power. Carlyle was still enamoured with the prince, but how long would it last if he failed to have the Source?

'He will have it,' Carlyle shrugged her fears off casually. 'No child could have survived the ordeal he underwent without it. You must remember that he too is recovering.' They walked along the stony path, both ignoring the fat snowflakes which had begun drifting from the sky. 'We should begin organising his Welcoming Ceremony, but it should be more than just that. Bréanainn's birth signifies a fresh start. For Saphyre, our citizens...for us.' Carlyle tried to take Alexandra's hand, but she crossed her arms tightly over her chest. Did he realise how ironic his words were? *Is he suspicious?* She could not help wondering but shoved the thought aside; she was just jumpy.

'You *murdered* my dearest friend *and* her unborn child.' Alexandra said quietly. 'Of course I want a fresh start for our kingdom but I cannot forgive you for what you have done.'

'We are *married* -'

'After all that has come to pass in the last three years Carlyle you hardly have to remind me of that. But our marriage is political. I have never loved you; I do not think I have even *liked* you. I cannot deny that when first we met I was attracted to you, but I was young and naïve.' Alexandra shrugged. 'Tomorrow I am going to the temple to distribute alms and pray I think Sorceress Rhonwyn should attend me on this occasion. It would be good to have one of the Castle Sorcerers close by, and she has taken to Bréanainn.'

'We have a temple in the castle, why do you insist on making this foolish journey?'

'Would you open the castle to the citizens so they could receive their alms here?' Carlyle remained stubbornly silent, and Alexandra rolled her eyes in reply. 'Father Dóchas married us, crowned me queen and cleansed me after the birth of our daughter. He knows me well, and I can trust that he is devoted to the Goddess.'

'Very well. I have spoken with Father Dóchas about your visit to the temple tomorrow; he will join you on your return to the castle. We should discuss the ceremony with him, and I think it is time you are cleansed.' Alexandra bit back a lump of fear; she was not ready to return to his chambers, she never would be. But it was more than just a fear that she might conceive again, what would happen if the rebellion failed? Once Caleb moved out into the open she would not be able to hide her involvement, nor did she wish too. How would Carlyle react knowing his own wife had betrayed him? *Do not dwell on what ifs,* she ordered herself but she could not prevent the flicker of fear crossing her face. 'What is wrong?'

'I...I am frightened of returning to your bed, at conceiving. I almost died Carlyle and Bréanainn...he was...' She choked back a sob, 'I do not want to be pleading with the Goddess to spare another child, nor do I wish to abandon Bréanainn.' Carlyle was silent but paused in his footsteps, drawing Alexandra close.

'Return to our chambers at least...we will see where things go from there.' Alexandra closed her eyes knowing she could not argue with him.

'Very well,' she whispered knowing full well where the evening would lead too.

Father Dóchas was smiling as Alexandra placed Bréanainn into his awaiting arms. The little prince studied the priest with wide and piercing ocean blue eyes before giggling happily. Exhausted from her early morning and the journey to the temple Alexandra almost slumped into the seat in the priest's private prayer chamber.

'We have prayed for both you and the prince since news of your labour reached us. Caleb blamed himself, even now I dread to think of what he might have done had things turned out differently.'

'Thankfully the Goddess decided to spare us. Although I still have nightmares...' Alexandra confessed. Each night she had woken up drenched in a cold sweat and would refuse to go back to bed until she had Bréanainn tucked up safely beside her. She no longer put him to bed in his cradle but would instead fall asleep with him cradled in her arms. Nervously she watched the wall of the chamber where she knew Caleb would soon emerge.

'She will always test us. Unfortunately, those born to lead must endure the harshest of tests.' Father Dóchas tried to comfort her and Alexandra managed a small smile; her eyes still focused on the wall. 'He will be here soon.' *He was meant to be here earlier,* Alexandra had planned on leaving Caleb to bond with Bréanainn while she had distributed alms, she had brought Rhonwyn with her to ensure both were given privacy. But she had been disheartened to find he had been held up at the castle.

When the hidden partition to the wall opened Alexandra felt relief flood through her and it took all of her self-control not to jump up and embrace Caleb tightly. He smiled at her sensing her fear and tweaked her nose playfully as he kissed her hand in greeting. As he turned to greet Father Dóchas, his eyes came to rest on the small bundle in the priest's arms.

'Is this...' He trailed off awestruck as the priest carefully set the bundle in his arms. 'Alexandra he is beautiful,' Caleb whispered sitting down slowly and looking at the child in wonder. Bréanainn too seemed to share Caleb's fascination as he stared up at him, his blue eyes frowning in curiosity and his face puckering. For a split second Alexandra feared he would cry, but almost instantly he seemed to relax and stretched his arm out, almost as if he was trying to touch Caleb's face.

'Should we begin?' Father Dóchas waited a few minutes before broaching the subject of their visit. Alexandra looked at Caleb and Bréanainn torn between what needed to be done. Did they need to know? It seemed so cruel. Caleb looked so happy, so fascinated, at the small bundle in his arms. What did it matter if Carlyle was the father? *We need to know;* she chided herself. *We have to know for his own protection.* She could see that Caleb was sharing the same thoughts as her as his eyes deepened. Slowly he nodded and passed Bréanainn back to Alexandra, kissing his head as he relinquished the child.

'What do you need to do?' Alexandra asked trying to shush Bréanainn as he began to squirm against her. She smiled at Caleb as the babe continued to thrash, reaching out for Caleb. 'I think he likes you better.' She laughed at the hopeful look in Caleb's eyes, was it a sign he was the father?

'I need a small amount of blood from both Caleb and the young prince – just a drop.' Father Dóchas reassured her as he pulled out two needles. He passed one to Caleb, but Alexandra was hesitant in accepting the second. 'It will cause him a moment of discomfort, but only for a moment. It is unfortunately the only way we can be sure.' Seeing that Alexandra was still unwilling Father Dóchas smiled and left the chamber, returning instantly with Rhonwyn. The sorceress smiled reassuringly at Alexandra as she knelt beside her, gripping Alexandra's knee gently.

'Would you like me to do it?'

'No,' Alexandra smiled. 'I am sorry I know I am being silly – he will not even remember it is just...' She shook her head and forced herself to look down at Bréanainn. Rhonwyn took the needle from her hand, the slender object glowed brightly, and she repeated the same process on Caleb's.

'They are both safe,' she reassured them. Biting back a sigh Alexandra readjusted her hold on Bréanainn and watched as Caleb swiftly pressed the tip of the needle into the skin of his index finger. He did not even gasp and smiled brightly as he turned to look up at Alexandra, holding out his finger to Father Dóchas and letting a drop of blood fall on to a piece of linen. Holding her breath she quickly pressed the needle to Bréanainn's own finger, feeling her heart squeeze painfully as he let out a wail. She held out Bréanainn's finger to the linen, almost unable to watch as his blood fell.

As soon as the two drops met on the linen, there was a flash of green light, and the air above the cloth shimmered. Rhonwyn's hand gripping Alexandra's knee tightened, and she looked at Father Dóchas desperate for confirmation.

'Is this good?' She asked tightening her grip on Bréanainn without even realising.

'Yes,' Father Dóchas smiled between Alexandra and Caleb. 'Congratulations,' Caleb whooped in delight and Alexandra looked at him in shock.

'Very dignified,' she laughed at him and pressed Bréanainn back into his arms. She was overjoyed at the news but the impending Welcoming Ceremony now tugged at her mind. It was not right that Caleb would be excluded, forced to watch from the background and only then if he could do so safely. She met Caleb's eyes and smiled shakily, unable to hide the twinges of guilt.

'There will be other events in his life,' Caleb tried to console her although she could see it irked him that he would not be there. 'Rhonwyn would you mind asking Xander to join us? I believe there may be another worshipper who may wish to join us.' Rhonwyn nodded and slipped from the room. 'Alexandra...' Caleb trailed off as he looked back down at Bréanainn, a grin breaking out on his face. 'He truly is a blessing from the Goddess; this is proof that I should rule, that I am the True King.' Alexandra smiled, but she could not bring herself to share his joy completely in that, they still had so many obstacles blocking their path. When Rhonwyn returned, she brought with her Xander and Neith. Alexandra was surprised to see the second sorceress and rose to her feet to greet her.

'What are you doing here?'

'Worshipping of course, what else?' Neith teased her as she sat on the floor. Alexandra wished she could join them; she felt uncomfortable seated while others knelt before her. The small chamber was soon filled with laughter and gentle croons as Bréanainn was passed around to each person. When it was finally Xander's turn to hold Bréanainn it was clear he was overwhelmed.

'Xander I am truly sorry,' she whispered thickly. 'I know the pain at losing a child at never even having the chance to hold them.' Xander managed a small and watery smile as he passed the babe back to her.

'At least my child did not suffer,' silence descended upon the room, and Caleb inched closer to Alexandra, almost protectively.

'Do you have it?' Caleb looked towards Rhonwyn who nodded and pulled a small pouch from the inside of her robes.

'What is that?' Alexandra asked holding her hand out for the pouch. Rhonwyn passed it to her with a sheepish expression on her face.

'I am afraid I owe you an apology,' the sorceress murmured. 'While you were still carrying the young prince I often spiked the soothing potion that I brought down for you. It was more a precaution, but it became necessary after Krista's arrest. We were frightened that you would jeopardise yourself in order to protect Krista.' Alexandra remembered the day where she had tried to tell Carlyle that she too was guilty of the same crime he had arrested Krista for. 'These herbs are a spell to stop you from speaking of the resistance. Unfortunately, these have found their way into the castle's water supply, and wine of course.'

'Of course,' Alexandra murmured dryly.

'We are still no closer to finding out who is betraying us, in the meantime, this should give us some protection. If the person goes to Carlyle, or anyone, with our plans, then they will find themselves suddenly forgetful. Should anyone be questioned, they will deny all knowledge of our cause.' Rhonwyn poured the herbs into a jug and sloshed it gently to try and mix them in.

'We are all to drink it?' Alexandra asked as she was handed a goblet.

'I do of course trust everyone in this chamber, but I would like to lead by example.' Caleb raised his own goblet. 'To Prince Bréanainn and his beautiful mother, Queen Alexandra.' Alexandra blushed raising her own goblet.

'To Caleb, our future King of Saphyre.' The atmosphere grew sombre as each person drained their goblet. Now that they were beginning to form a plan, that a deadline for Caleb to reveal himself had been set, the stakes felt increasingly high. Alexandra looked down at Bréanainn now sleeping in her arms. *I will protect you, no matter what I will make sure no harm befalls you.* She silently vowed.

Alexandra joined Carlyle for supper later that evening, the day had worn her out, and she longed to return to her chamber and sleep. Father Dóchas had returned with her to the castle and talked through the Welcome Ceremony with both he and Carlyle before performing the cleansing ritual upon Alexandra. She dreaded Carlyle would command her to his chambers that night.

'Is something wrong?' Alexandra asked as she sat opposite Carlyle. 'You were quiet all the time Father Dóchas was here; I thought you would be overjoyed that the Welcoming Ceremony is almost upon us.' *Half a moon,* she thought feeling frightened. *In half a moon one way or another this will all be over.*

'I am just concerned about the rumours I am hearing. Disturbing rumours which concern you.' Carlyle set his cutlery down and paced around the table so that he stood at Alexandra's side. Taking her chin in his hand, he firmly forced her to look up at him. 'Alexandra, you do realise that you are not untouchable do you not? If I suspect your loyalty —'

'What reason have I given you to suspect my loyalty?' Alexandra snapped too exhausted to try and act submissive, to bend herself to his will as he so obviously craved. 'I am not going to live my life under constant suspicion.'

'I fear these rebels will seek you out, to either recruit you or bring harm upon you – to *use* you against me.' Carlyle's voice became hoarse, and the hand gripping her chin tightened ever so slightly. 'Your words before Krista's execution – that she was no less guilty than you...Alexandra whatever these people have told you, they are *all* lies. This man they call Caleb will not bring peace to Saphyre, he merely means to usurp me. What do you think will happen to you if they claim the throne? Who will want the wife of a usurped king?' Alexandra glared at Carlyle.

'No one has told me anything,' she did not even have to try and lie for the herbs were beginning their work. She was thankful to Caleb and Rhonwyn for their quick thinking. 'I am the True Queen of Saphyre. You, or even rumoured Caleb, would be a fool to harm me.' Keeping a firm grip on her chin Carlyle leant down to kiss her on the mouth, forcing her eyes to remain looking at his.

'Tell me one thing Alexandra; with who do your loyalties lie?'

'With the True King, Your Majesty.' She answered obediently and honestly, thankful that her answer seemed to satisfy him.

# *Chapter Thirty-three*

As the day of the Welcoming Ceremony drew ever closer Alexandra could do little to stop the rising tension growing bit by bit in the bottom of her belly each day. It had been agreed that she would not seek out either Caleb or Xander unless absolutely necessary, and that for appearances sake she and Xander must resume their hostile relationship. She knew it was for the best, but it still did not make her feel any less cut off from everyone. It was hard not to think of Caleb when she stared down into Bréanainn's face.

She resumed joining council meetings, leaving Bréanainn with Helena and Roisin. When she was not in council, she began joining the Castle Sorcerers in their tower in hopes that her Source would return if she was in the right environment. She also began to force herself to spend more time with Carlyle in an attempt to try and relieve any linger suspicions he may have still carried.

'What if I *have* lost my Source?' She burst out rising from behind his desk and pacing the length and breadth of his study. She paused beside the window to look at the city below and the flickering lights. Snow had fallen constantly over the past two days and covered the city and castle grounds in a thick white blanket. 'I...' She trailed off, she had almost admitted that she *needed* her Source, but did she?

'I have told you Alexandra, both you and Bréanainn will regain your powers. Please just give it time.'

'You do not seem upset that my Source has not returned, nor that Bréanainn shows no signs of it. Especially as you were convinced he would be a powerful sorcerer before he was even born...you gave the impression that he would not be worth having if he did not possess it.' Alexandra could not help the suspicious feeling creeping up her spine, was there more to her missing Source than Carlyle was letting on? She had never forgotten the night he had bound her Source, let alone that he had lied to her about even possessing it.

'Our son was drawing on your Source while you carried him if he was powerless he would not have been able to do that.' Alexandra tried not to flinch as Carlyle referred to Bréanainn as 'their son'. She was relieved to know that Caleb was her child's father, but her relief was short-lived as now she was terrified Carlyle would discover the truth. Sitting down at his desk she glared at the solitary candle that she had been trying to light with her non-existent powers for much of the evening. 'Alexandra you almost *died*. You drained your Source and almost all of Rhonwyn's, do you realise you could have potentially killed her? Not to mention the amount of my own power that I had to give you.'

Alexandra looked up in surprise, had she really almost brought Rhonwyn to the brink of death? She remembered how Rhonwyn had been bedridden for several days after the ordeal but had she really almost died? *This has to stop;* she thought shuddering at the memories of that awful day. She had always thought the birth of her child would be a joyous occasion, the memories of which would fill her with warmth and happiness each time she looked back on them. Instead, all she could feel was a cold emptiness and overwhelming sense of grief when she thought back to the day of Bréanainn's birth and the events which had led up to it. She had never been able to forget the sight of him laying cold and blue in her arms, never had she seen anything so still as he had been during his first few moments of life.

'Let us finish the preparations for Bréanainn's Welcoming Ceremony, once that is over with we will both have the time to focus on regaining your Source and looking into it.' Carlyle kissed the top of her head and leant over her shoulder. The wick of the candle began to smoulder before igniting with a bright orange flame.

'I cannot wait that long!' She protested and felt ashamed at the pleading tone in her voice. *My Source has made me weak,* she thought to herself in disgust. *Krista spent so much time training me in hand-to-hand combat, but what good will a sword do in battle with Carlyle?* Carlyle sat on the opposite side of his desk, leaning back in his chair he studied Alexandra quietly; his hands folded neatly in his lap as he suddenly leant forwards.

'Why Alexandra? Why do you need your Source? You have managed without it before. In Bournemouth, you lived perfectly fine without it, and even your first several moons in Saphyre – you were not troubled at all by it.' Even after three years to hear Carlyle refer to Bournemouth felt strange. 'Why can you not wait less than a week?' As he continued to study her, Alexandra could feel his gaze pulling her in. *What does he know?* She asked herself; she was sure he could not know of Caleb's plans. Rhonwyn's potion worked well, she had experienced it for herself, but still, Carlyle held his suspicions.

'It is true I coped before but remember I only did not know of my powers because *you* kept them from me – and look where that led. My mother *died* helping me when it should have been you helping me to learn my powers.' She bit back a satisfied smirk at the look of guilt on Carlyle's face. 'I know what I am capable of Carlyle and truthfully I need my Source because I am frightened. I do not feel safe; I would like to be sure that I can protect myself – that I can protect Bréanainn.' This at least was not a lie, and Carlyle did seem satisfied with her answer.

'No one will harm you or our son; I give you my word. I will keep this rebel Caleb and his followers at bay.' Alexandra mulled over his words, blowing out the candle she focused on the burnt wick once more.

'You cannot always protect us Carlyle. These rebels got to me once before, remember?'

'As long as you are by my side these rebels would not dare harm you. They would be too frightened to incur my wrath, the cowards.' Something within Alexandra snapped, and she glared at Carlyle, offended on behalf of Caleb and those working with him.

'How stupid do you believe me to be? I understand my position; I am the True Queen of Saphyre. If the rebels wanted to take the throne, to rule Saphyre, then surely they would need me?' She could see worry flickering in Carlyle's eyes. 'Surely you need me just as much as they do? What would happen if you executed me? The citizens feel at ease with me on the throne; they are terrified of you but not me. I am not a fool Carlyle; I am worth more to you, and the rebels, alive.' *When did we start acknowledging the rebels so openly? When did he realise that Caleb is a true threat?* A small wisp of smoke emanated from the candle wick, and Alexandra glanced down grinning. Was her Source finally

returning? Her elation was short lived as the wick burst into
golden life, only for the flame to consume the candle within a
split second, leaving nothing but a puddle of wax on the
polished oak desk.

'Alexandra I have warned you, you are *not* untouchable.
You are certainly not above the laws of our kingdom.'

'I am bound to the laws of Saphyre,' Alexandra replied
calmly refusing to let Carlyle frighten her. 'As are *you*.' An urgent
knocking on the door put an end to their conversation. Roisin
opened the door at Carlyle's bark, a thrashing Bréanainn
struggling against her hold.

'Forgive me Your Majesties, but we cannot soothe His
Highness,' Carlyle took the screaming babe from Roisin before
Alexandra could reach him. She could not help feeling smug as
Bréanainn refused to quieten in Carlyle's arms, his shrieks
seemed to intensify.

'He needs feeding,' she said taking her child from Carlyle
and turning her back on him so that Roisin could unfasten her
dress. As she sat down to feed Bréanainn, she caught the look of
disdain twisted across Carlyle's normally handsome features.

'We will be getting a wet nurse for the next child, as is
appropriate for your status.' His voice was calm, but his eyes
warned Alexandra against arguing. A warning she chose to
ignore.

'We will do no such thing,' she replied primly but keeping
her voice low so as not to frighten Bréanainn. As he continued
to feed, she stroked his hair, smiling as he reached up to grasp
one of her fingers. 'Carlyle, Bréanainn is *my* child and I know
what is best for him. Why should I not feed himself? Surely the
milk of a queen is better for him than the milk of a wet nurse?'
She hated herself for saying the words but knew her strongest
allay lay in Carlyle's passion for social status. As Bréanainn
yawned lazily, she readjusted her gown and her son so that his
chin rested on his shoulder. Gently she rubbed his back,
grimacing when she remembered too late that she had not
thought to cover her back with the cloth which was now
outstretched in Roisin's hands. She could see the woman fighting
back laughter as she took Bréanainn back into her arms.
'Perhaps you could have a bath prepared for me?'

'Of course Your Majesty,' Roisin curtsied and happily
departed, clear relieved that her young charge was no longer

thrashing but instead fast asleep. When Alexandra turned to face Carlyle once more, she found herself confronted with a thunderous expression.

'I will not tolerate you disobeying me in front of a *slave*,' Alexandra rolled her eyes but managed to somehow bit back a retort. Rather than placating Carlyle, her silence seemed to infuriate him further. 'How can I not suspect you are plotting against me when you so brazenly disrespect me?'

'It is not disrespect Carlyle,' his face began to redden and Alexandra squared her shoulders, oblivious to the mess trickling down her back. 'Carlyle you can accuse me of any crime you wish, but we all know you be a fool to condemn me to death. After Krista's execution people already have their doubts about. The Goddess has shown you that she is displeased – even you cannot deny the omen from that day.' Her throat closed painfully as she mentioned Krista, with each day it just felt harder to realise that her friend was no longer with her. 'I am not naïve; I do think I am safe. I am perfectly aware that while you may not kill me, you would certainly make my life a misery; perhaps even make me beg for a death that will not come. I do not care.' This was only a half-truth. She had nothing yet to lose, yet at the same time, she had possibly everything to lose. If she died, then she left Bréanainn alone, and she was not prepared to endanger her son. She was determined that Caleb would finally succeed in claiming the throne. She had been brought to Saphyre for a reason; perhaps this was it. Leaving Carlyle alone with her words she turned and left for her chamber.

'You should be careful about angering His Majesty over the rebellion. The more he believes there is a plot against him then the more paranoid he will become.' Helena warned as she rinsed soap from Alexandra's hair. Helena sat on the bed holding Bréanainn, engrossed in keeping the prince entertained.

'What do you know of the rebellion?' Alexandra asked looking between the two of her ladies in surprise. She had never really considered the possibility that either Helena or Roisin would know of the rebellion, nor be involved in any way.

'We know nothing,' Roisin answered firmly, and Alexandra fought back the question her further. 'All I know is that His Majesty would be greatly reassured if he could believe his wife was not plotting his downfall.' Alexandra closed her eyes as more water sluiced over her head. She could sense Roisin wanted to say more, but something held the woman back. 'His Majesty would be less suspicious...if only he could believe you truly cared for him.' The woman finally said as she offered Alexandra a sheet to dry herself in.

'Thank you,' Alexandra murmured clasping the sheet loosely. She had barely dressed in her chemise for the night when Carlyle strode into the room, not even bothering to knock. *He would not have been able to do that if I had my Source,* she thought glaring at the intrusion.

'I would like you to return to our chambers enough,' the request was said kindly, but beneath his tone Alexandra could sense it was an order. 'Why should we wait any longer? You have been cleansed, and our chamber is too empty, I have missed you Alexandra.'

'What of Bréanainn?' Alexandra asked weakly, 'he will need feeding throughout the night. I need to be close by.' Carlyle gestured to a woman plump woman behind him, she was on her knees and leaning forwards with her forehead pressed to the floor. The woman glanced up at Alexandra for a second and she could see the woman had a kindly face although it was a mask of terror at that moment.

'Your slaves seem to have done an adequate job watching over him so far,' he gestured to Roisin and Helena. '*She* will provide him with nourishment should he need it during the night.' He gestured to the woman who was still on her knees. 'Bréanainn should not be an only child Alexandra; we should give him brothers to play with. I do not want him to grow up alone as I did.'

'I –'

'I am your husband Alexandra, is it wrong for me to want to lie with my wife?' Alexandra could only look at Carlyle helplessly, her mouth paper-dry. She was terrified to return to his bed. It was only a few days until Bréanainn's Welcoming Ceremony, what if she fell pregnant with Carlyle's child? She could not even reassure herself that it was just one night, he would expect her to join him in his chambers each night. *It only took one night with Caleb;* she thought glancing towards Bréanainn. 'Stop putting the inevitable off,' Carlyle stroked her cheek fondly and tilted her head up with his thumb.' Feeling as if she was in some sort of sordid nightmare Alexandra nodded slowly and turned to kiss Bréanainn's forehead goodnight before following Carlyle down to his chambers.

Carlyle had barely closed the door to his chambers before he was crushing his lips upon Alexandra's, his hands working to disrobe her. He tried to force her to meet his eyes, but she had never forgotten how he had hypnotised her on their wedding night. She still had no memory of her first time, and although she was not sure if she wanted to remember that night she still felt robbed.

She put up no resistance as Carlyle scooped her up into his arms and carried her to the bed. As he laid her upon the cloud-like mattress, she quickly slipped beneath the covers, desperate to cover her bareness. As Carlyle joined her she could not help flinching away as his hand reached out to stroke her thigh.

'Alexandra...' She forced herself to look at Carlyle, but she quickly looked away at the sorrow in his sapphire eyes. The spiral pattern was moving slowly in a clockwise position and she warned herself not to fall for his trick again. 'Please,' he leant closer to her trying to tilt her face towards him. 'Just once can you not bring yourself to love me as a wife should?' She had never heard the tone in his voice before; so heavy with grief, sorry and something else...guilt? Alexandra tried to answer him but her throat was too constricted and she remained silent, staring ahead. 'Please, all I ask is for you to love me.'

'You know I cannot,' she whispered truthfully. 'Carlyle you have done too much. You have lied to me – you have *murdered* in cold blood not only our citizens but people I have loved and known. My grandmother, Krista...her unborn child.' She forgot her warning and turned to look at him, horrified that he could truly think to ask her for her love.

'Just this once, that is all I ask of you.' He whispered leaning closer so that his body pressed against hers. His lips sought out her own and she realised her mistake too late, no longer could she tear her gaze free and she lost herself in the depths of his eyes mesmerised by the hypnotic pattern.

*Sitting in the middle of the throne room Alexandra shivered as she looked around, loathing being back there. She had avoided the throne room since Krista's execution; if she could have sealed it off from everyone, she would have done so. It did not feel right using the room when it felt as if it was a tomb now.*

*She wore a sleeveless gown with a full skirt but as she looked down to admire its elegance and beading she felt sickness wash through her. The gown was crimson in colour and shimmered like water beneath the torchlight reminding her strongly of blood.* This is where it happened, *she realised jumping to her feet and crying out when she saw the hem of the skirt pool around her like a puddle.*

*A strong breeze filled the room, and Alexandra's hair whipped around her face; stinging her eyes and blinding her. When her vision finally cleared she realised she was no longer alone in the hated throne room. A slender woman with dark skin and ebony hair stood before her, grinning widely. Behind her stood a slightly taller woman her skin just a fraction of a shade lighter and with the same ebony hair. She was muscular yet slender and held a graceful air about herself.*

*'Krista!' Alexandra moved to embrace her friend but her arms simply past straight through. She could see Krista was unsurprised by this revelation, she smiled sadly at Alexandra and simply shrugged. Forcing herself to put her grief aside Alexandra stepped back and stared at the young woman.*

*'My daughter...the woman she was never able to become.' Xander's steely grey eyes shone brightly in the woman's oval face. Her ebony hair hung in ringlets down past her shoulders, and she curtsied gracefully to Alexandra. Krista was smiling proudly, but her smile was tinged with sadness. 'She cannot speak...the Goddess was kind enough to bless her with her form.'*

*'She is beautiful Krista...what is her name?'*

*'Maithiúnas, Mai for short.' Alexandra frowned as she tried to place the vaguely familiar word. 'It is ancient Saphyrian meaning forgiveness. Xander does not quite approve.'*

*'I hardly blame him,' Alexandra replied hiding her shock that Xander had not mentioned Krista had visited him.* It is rather personal, *she thought still trying to get over her shock at the dream. 'You can hardly expect him to be full of forgiveness after all this...'*

*'Alexandra you* must *find it in your heart to forgive Carlyle, as must Xander.'*

*'He murdered you and your child!'*

*'I am fully aware of that,' Krista snapped and Alexandra looked away feeling ashamed of herself. She missed Krista terribly; she did not want to fight with her! 'The Goddess was kind in giving Mai a form, but I died with hatred in my heart and hatred is a terrible burden to carry. Mai cannot speak, that is my punishment...' Krista's voice softened, and she reached out, her fingertips hovering millimetres from Alexandra. 'Carlyle will be judged*

*Alexandra. He will pay for all the crimes he has committed, but please do not make yourself suffer alongside him.'*

*'How can I forgive him after all that he has done? Why should I?'*

*'For yourself, you must. If you send him to his grave with hatred in your heart then it will never pass – it will only turn sour during your mortal life.' Alexandra did not miss Krista's choice of words. She remembered how Caleb and Xander had protested at the thought of her killing Carlyle, that Caleb needed to be the one to perform the loathsome deed to prove he was the rightful king.*

I've known all along that it would have to be, *she thought feeling frightened. It had to be her. She was the queen; she could not leave the murder of the king to someone who was technically a subject.* At least my Source will not darken, *but how could she possibly defeat Carlyle without her Source? Even if Carlyle did not use his own power, he would just as easily overpower Alexandra physically. He was rarely seen with a sword but that did not mean he could not use one.* What happened to thinking that we would not have to kill Carlyle? *She loathed the man it was true, but the thought of murder still sickened her. But she knew there could be no other way. Carlyle would not agree to step down from the throne to exile himself from Saphyre. Even if they managed to banish him, they would spend the rest of their lives fearing he would seek revenge.*

*'I cannot,' Alexandra swallowed an apple-sized lump in her throat as her eyes slowly came to rest upon Mai. 'Krista, why did you never tell me? I could have helped you; I could have* protected *you...'*

*'I was frightened,' Alexandra was lost for words. She had never imagined Krista as someone who could be frightened. Krista, the woman who had left her home kingdom just to come and protect Alexandra.* And I failed in protecting her. *Alexandra felt as if she had failed all those she loved. 'Everyone gets frightened Alexandra. Do you know what Carlyle fears?'*

*'I do not want to know!'*

*'His greatest fear is losing you,' Krista carried on as if she had not heard Alexandra's reply. The temperature in the already frigid room seemed to plummet as Alexandra glared at Krista, her bare arms breaking out in goose pimples. 'He fears losing his throne of course, but above all else he fears losing you. He loves you...in his own twisted way.'*

*'Please stop.' Alexandra begged wanting to cover her ears with her hands but knowing it was a childish thing to do.*

*'Kindness does not come easily to Carlyle; it rarely comes at all. But this is* why *you must forgive him. He* loves *you –'*

*'No!' Alexandra shook her head desperate to block out Krista's voice. How could she kill someone,* murder *them, when they supposedly loved her?*

*'You* must *forgive him Alexandra.'*

'Stop!' Alexandra cried bolting upright. She looked around in shock startled to find herself in Carlyle's chambers. The shutters were closed against the howling wind outside, the hearth was the only source of light, but even the embers were beginning to fade. Beside her Carlyle reached out to draw her close, mumbling words of comfort as he nestled against her hair. The dream was fresh in Alexandra's mind, and she recoiled against Carlyle's touch. *Am I capable of murder?* She thought blinking back tears, but she knew there was no question about it. She had no choice if she wanted to set Saphyre free.

# Chapter Thirty-four

Eating her supper alone on the eve before Bréanainn's Welcoming Ceremony Alexandra could not help but contemplate the past three years. How differently would things have been had she not fled her home world? If she had never lost her memory? Would her parents still be alive? Would she have been able to help Caleb's resistance succeed quicker? Would Krista have left Karstares and joined her in Saphyre? So many questions that she knew she would never get the answers too swarmed around her mind, bringing with them the heavy pounding of a headache.

The food on her plate had long since grown cold and all she could do was push it around aimlessly, finding that she no longer held an appetite. Beside her was an untouched goblet of wine. Every so often she would pick up the goblet, but all she could do was stare into the shimmering liquid. She was desperate to speak with Caleb, or at least Xander, to seek some kind of reassurance that the next day would be a success. But they had shut her out in order to protect her; even Rhonwyn was careful around her. *What reassurance can anyone give you?* A bitter voice in her head scorned.

If everything went to plan then by the end of the next day, Alexandra would be a widow. A murderer. How could that be a success? A victory? Dropping her cutlery to the table Alexandra dug the heel of her palms into her eyes, grinding them into the sockets in a feeble attempt to stem the flow of tears. *I cannot do this!* She thought as her stomach filled with butterflies. Bile began to rise, burning the back of her throat and leaving a revolting acidic taste.

Perhaps she could convince Carlyle to give up his claim to the throne? If he stepped down then why should he die? She felt sick at her weakness; he had murdered her grandmother, her closest friend, an unborn child and countless others. Yet she was too much of a coward to take his life in retribution. *You know he cannot be exiled or jailed,* she thought to herself. She had spent countless hours telling herself why there was only one option, yet she could not bring herself to accept it. Closing her eyes she prayed to the Goddess for forgiveness for the crime she would commit, and for the strength to carry it out.

The day of the Welcoming Ceremony passed agonisingly for Alexandra. Pulling the blankets over her head, she burrowed deeper into the feather filled matters. Would this really be the last day of waking up beside a tyrant? *If I do not kill him, then we have failed – and he will make us all suffer.* The thought did little to soothe her conscience and she felt bile rising.

As Carlyle rose and dressed, he was oddly quiet, looking at Alexandra solemnly every so often. *He knows,* she thought as chills swept down her spine. How could he know? Surely if he had heard news of the day's events, then he would have put a cruel stop to it. He had shown he had no qualms spilling blood, so why hesitate now? He opened the shutters to the chamber and Alexandra could see the reason for his sombre mood. A blizzard had swept across the city; the snow was falling so thickly she could not even see the city below.

'Oh no...' Alexandra cried blushing as Carlyle looked down at her. 'The Welcoming Ceremony – we cannot have Bréanainn travelling in this. Even with the Source, it would be foolish...' Carlyle nodded in agreement and Alexandra wrapped herself in a fur blanket as she joined him at the window. What would they do now? She had no idea how Caleb had been over the past several days, what would he think of this blow? *Perhaps this is the Goddess's way of saying Carlyle is the rightful king?* Alexandra quickly squashed that thought; she had been told the light at her coronation had not been seen in centuries. He could not be. *Perhaps it is a test;* she thought biting back a wry smile.

'We could perhaps hold the ceremony in the castle temple. I am sure Father Dóchas is on his way now, you know there are tunnels leading from the temple to here.' Alexandra fought to keep her face neutral; did Carlyle know those were the tunnels Caleb used? 'The purifying chamber is between both castle and temple.'

'Oh...' Alexandra nodded slowly. 'I try not to think of that place.' She mumbled truthfully.

'Alexandra please try to put your hatred for me aside. For today at least, for our son.'

'Of course,' Alexandra murmured, she looked towards the door waiting for Helena and Roisin to bring Bréanainn down to her. Carlyle had insisted she return to his bed, she slept uneasily loathing the thought that Bréanainn was not close by. She had, had no choice but to relent to the wet nurse, but she only permitted it during the night as Carlyle would not tolerate her ladies coming in to disturb them. *They will bring him down when he wants his morning feed;* she tried to console herself.

Carlyle led her to the dressing chamber where he had a simple yet elegant shoulderless gown waiting for her. The skirt flowed gracefully from her waist and the train appeared to flat as she moved. The sleeves were fitted to her elbows but flared out and draped around her wrists. Alexandra held still as Carlyle rested his hands on her hips, weaving his Source into the fabric so that she would stay warm.

'At least we will not have to journey into the city; you should be warm enough in the castle.' He reassured her.

'What of the people though? They were so looking forward to meeting Bréanainn, only those who reside in the castle will be able to attend. It does not seem fair those who cannot live in the castle are excluded from the celebrations; Bréanainn is their prince after all.' Carlyle looked thoughtful as he took a seat at his desk.

'We will arrange a grand occasion for the spring. I do not think it fair to those who are here to cancel the celebrations, especially if Father Dóchas is on his way.' There was a knock on the door, and Alexandra jumped up to open it, smiling widely as she took hold of Bréanainn and cuddled him. Roisin bustled around her attaching a slender gold belt emblazoned with sapphires around her waist and began fussing with her hair.

'Are you well Your Majesty?' Roisin asked as Alexandra sat down so that Roisin could work on her hair. Carlyle joined them pacing around as Roisin worked, rocking Bréanainn gently in his arms.

'Yes.' Alexandra lied and forced herself to smile.

'You are beautiful,' Roisin smiled at her as she pulled Alexandra's thick auburn locks back to expose her slender shoulders. Like her dress, her hair was kept simple but Roisin did work some diamonds and sapphires into her hair.

'Father Dóchas has arrived Your Majesties,' Helena appeared in the dressing chamber doorway. 'He is in the great hall warming up and will be in the castle temple before the tenth hour.' Alexandra felt fear almost paralyse her. *Get a hold of yourself,* she scolded. *Caleb will not move until tonight when Bréanainn is far away from trouble.* But still, she could not relax. The celebrations for her two years as queen were fresh in her mind; the day had gone so well.

She studied Carlyle's own clothes, like her he was dressed in a deep royal blue, and she noticed he wore the tunic she had sewn for him several years ago. Beneath it, he wore a black shirt with full sleeves. Her eyes came to rest on the scabbard buckled around his waist and at the lethal looking sword with a jewelled hilt.

'It is ceremonial,' Carlyle's voice was reassuring, but Alexandra did not feel in the least bit reassured. Had he worn that sword at their wedding? At her coronation? *He must have done;* she tried to soothe herself. She glanced at Helena and Roisin, but neither lady seemed disturbed by the weapon. Taking Bréanainn into her arms Alexandra pressed her lips to his head, stroking his back gently. She bowed her head as Carlyle placed her golden crown on her, she could feel his eyes watching her intently 'Alexandra we could have been happy...when we first met, you did not fear me. You admired me...we could still be happy together.' He rested his hand on her bare shoulder, squeezing it gently. His tone was soft and Alexandra longed to believe his words, but after all that had come to pass she knew it could not be. 'I do not want Bréanainn to grow up as I did; I want him to be happy. To play with his brothers and to know his parents love each other.'

'That is all I ever wanted,' Alexandra said as they walked from the chambers, Helena and Roisin following close behind.

'I have only wanted the same thing Carlyle,' Alexandra lowered her voice as they walked through the castle. 'I want Bréanainn and his siblings to be proud of their father, to know they are *all* loved and safe. But I know I cannot guarantee that. You say Bréanainn will have the Source, yet what happens if at the age of five he has still shown no sign of his powers? Will you still love him? Or will you begin calling me a whore and saying he is not your son, that no son of yours could ever be so weak and powerless?'

'Bréanainn is my son, regardless of whether he possesses the Source or not I shall always love him.' Alexandra managed to suppress a snort of disbelief. As they approached the castle temple, Carlyle reached out to stop her, gesturing for Xander and her ladies to remain back. 'Tonight we shall start over; tomorrow will be a fresh beginning for Saphyre.' In her arms Bréanainn reached up to play with the Alexandra's hair, his eyes wide in fascination at the glittering sapphires and diamonds. Carlyle smiled and leant down to kiss his forehead. As he moved Alexandra forced herself not to step back, to try and remain neutral. 'Come, let us welcome our son.'

As they approached the great hall, Alexandra resettled Bréanainn into her arms. She had been overwhelmed by a tender proudness towards him during the Welcoming Ceremony. Not once had he cried, instead he had looked upon Father Dóchas and the monks with wide-eyed fascination. Alexandra had looked around the small temple at the people who had gathered; they had looked at Bréanainn with equal fascination. As her eyes had scanned over the faces of those in the temple she had been shocked to see Caleb standing in the back amongst a cluster of monks. She had quickly turned away caught between fury at his stupidity and relief that he had at least been able to witness the ceremony.

The calmness Alexandra had felt during the ceremony began to shatter almost as soon as they stepped within the great hall. Music was playing, and many people had begun dancing, several tables were laden with food and people stood beneath fountains which poured wine. Bréanainn began to murmur and wriggle against her shoulder at the loud noises.

'Shush little one,' she tried to comfort him. 'Just a little longer.' She berated herself for her selfishness. So far Bréanainn had been kept away from large crowds, the ceremony had been his first experience of large groups of people, and it was clearly overwhelming him.

'Carlyle I think perhaps we should let him go to bed,' Alexandra said nervously suddenly desperate for Bréanainn to be tucked away safely, far away from the great hall. 'He is frightened.' Carlyle acted as If he had not heard her, resting his hand on her lower back he gently pushed Alexandra into the great hall.

Abruptly the music drew to a halt and the revellers dropped to their knees. Carlyle reached out to take Bréanainn from Alexandra's arms, a dark shadow crossing his face as Bréanainn started to cry.

'Citizens,' Carlyle's voice boomed through the great hall drowning out even Bréanainn's shrieking. He tried to soothe the prince, rubbing his back and rocking him lightly but to no avail. Seeing that nothing would soothe him, Carlyle carried on as if the babe were asleep in his arms. 'The Goddess has blessed my kingdom. Our Queen has given us a prince; she has bestowed upon me a successor to my throne.' Alexandra felt indignant on Bréanainn's behalf; Carlyle spoke as if he were nothing more than a possession. *But does he think any more of me?* She thought bitterly. *Just get through tonight, it will all be over soon.*

Slowly the crowd began to rise to their feet as applause rang through the cavernous room. The new noise frightened Bréanainn even more who began to bawl in earnest and thrashed violently in Carlyle's arms. Terrified that Carlyle would drop the child, Alexandra reached out and hurriedly took him back, cradling the back of his head and making cooing noises.

'The noise is too frightening for him,' she tried to console Carlyle who nodded abruptly. Resting his hand on her lower back once more he guided her to the dais where their thrones had been set up. Alexandra halted in her footsteps not quite able to bring herself to approach her throne. She had not sat upon it since the day of Krista's execution, nor had she stepped foot in the throne room. She clutched Bréanainn tightly and squeezed her eyes tightly shut.

'Give Bréanainn to your slaves, dance with me.' Carlyle said with a sigh. Knowing she would be unwise to anger him Alexandra nodded and kissed Bréanainn's cheek as she gave him to Helena. She was thankful for his offer to dance, anything to keep her away from the thrones. 'I have been thinking of my mother recently...' Alexandra was startled to hear Carlyle speak of his mother and she looked at him curiously as they danced. 'I truly want Bréanainn to have a happier childhood than I; one that includes his mother.'

'I want the same for him too Carlyle; I want him to grow up with both his parents loving them...and knowing he is loved back.' As Carlyle gently twirled Alexandra her eyes swept the great hall trying to see who was present from the resistance.

Rhonwyn stood to the side talking with Neith and a group of Castle Sorcerers while Xander stood beside the doors looking alert. As she was brought closer into Carlyle's arms, she could not shake the burning sensation that she was being watched. Vanya stood over one of the trestle tables, her dark eyes blazing as she alternated between looking at Alexandra and Carlyle and ordering a group of slaves. 'I also want Bréanainn to grow up respecting people, and for people to respect him out of love – not fear.'

'Alexandra do not think to spoil this evening,' Carlyle's voice was gentle, but the hand gripping the back of her head was anything but. To an onlooker, the embrace would no doubt look tender and protective, but they could not feel the threatening pressure squeezing against her skull. 'And do not think to fill Bréanainn's with these weak ideas. He is *my* son; he will learn to rule from *me*.'

'He is *my* son,' Alexandra reminded him before changing the subject of his parentage. She did not want to give Carlyle the slightest reason to be suspicious. As she grew tired from dancing she was grateful when Carlyle relieved her to sit down, only to replace her with a simpering woman. Biting back the urge to roll her eyes Alexandra walked towards the dais, hesitantly sitting upon her throne. Helena gently passed her Bréanainn and a grin broke out across Alexandra's face as he reached up once more to play with the glittering jewels fixed in her hair. As she gently disentangled Bréanainn's fingers from her hair, she looked up to see Lemuel approaching the dais and bowing low as he stopped just before her.

'Your Majesty you look as radiant as ever,' Lemuel greeted her. 'And your son is quite the handsome prince.' Bréanainn seemed to smile almost smugly as if he had understood Lemuel and Alexandra bit back laughter.

'Thank you Councilmen Lemuel,' she smiled.

'I could not help but overhear you speaking to His Majesty whilst dancing,' Lemuel lowered his voice. 'I hope that we grow to respect the prince from love and not fear...I share your belief that Saphyre deserves a fresh start.' Alexandra felt her smile tighten, worrying that Carlyle would somehow overhear.

'Councilmen,' she murmured. 'I pray that Saphyre one day can live peacefully and happily...' She trailed off unsure of what she could say without endangering them both.

'My wife is pregnant once more…we both long for the day where we can stop living in fear; both for her safety and our children.' *He is with us,* Alexandra realised her eyes widening slightly.

'Councilmen should you ever need support you have only to ask. I will do my utmost to ensure your family can live without fear.' She held out her hand for Lemuel to kiss.

'Thank you, Your Majesty. The Goddess truly blessed our kingdom when she delivered you to us.' Alexandra blinked back tears; she still felt as if she were an imposter when people praised her so. Would she ever feel like she was really the True Queen? As Lemuel bowed and departed she turned her attentions once more to Bréanainn who was beginning to grow sleepy. She rocked him in her arms wondering how much longer Carlyle would insist on keeping him up for. *Am I really eager for him to be sent to bed?* She asked herself. *Once Bréanainn is put to bed it will begin.* She swallowed her fear and wondered if she should tell Carlyle Bréanainn needed to be put to bed. It was already well past his bedtime, the longer he stayed up, the fussier he would grow, and she desperately wanted to avoid Carlyle losing his temper.

As if he could sense what she thought Carlyle joined her on the dais, taking a seat on his throne as he reached for the infant prince. Exhausted Bréanainn put up no resistance and even seemed to doze in Carlyle's arms. The baby suddenly looked much smaller, and Alexandra found it hard to imagine him ever growing as tall as Carlyle. *When he grows older will I see Carlyle in him?* She thought suddenly. Carlyle and Caleb looked so similar…was this to be her punishment? *Will I see Carlyle every time I look Caleb in the eye? Whenever he takes me to bed?* The thought made her shudder, but she quashed it instantly. She had not thought of Carlyle that time she had ended up in Caleb's bed, why should the future be any different? *Regardless of whether Bréanainn looks like Carlyle or not, he is Caleb's son, and I will not love him less for reminding me of a tyrant.* She silently vowed.

'I believe it is time for our prince to retire for the evening,' Carlyle clicked his fingers and Helena took Bréanainn from him. Alexandra tried to smile as she bid her son goodnight, pressing her lips to the crown of his soft head. Her mouth was suddenly dry and her stomach rolled sickeningly.

'Be careful,' Alexandra murmured to her ladies as she straightened up, her hand Bréanainn's head. A guardsman accompanied from the room and Alexandra wished she could tell if it was one of Caleb's men who were with them. *As long as Carlyle believed he truly is the father then no matter what happens tonight Bréanainn should be safe.* But she could do little to comfort herself.

Out of the corner of her eye, she caught a flash of golden hair. Tensing Alexandra fought back the urge to turn and look to see if it was Caleb. She desperately wanted to join him, for the resistance to be out in the open but she knew it was not the right moment.

'A toast to our gracious queen – my beautiful wife!' Carlyle accepted the two goblets that Ywain offered him with a flourish and passed one to Alexandra. Clasping her free hand Carlyle brushed his lips against her skin, his eyes glittering as he looked at her. 'To Queen Alexandra of Saphyre.' Goblets were raised into the air as people cheered her name. Alexandra smiled and tried to resist the urge to look downwards. *Please Caleb,* she silently begged. *Do not hold off for too long.* A sudden burst of wind tore through the great hall; Alexandra's dress whipped around her legs and several of the jewels were sent scattering from her hair. The torches along the wall guttered before plunging the room into darkness. 'Alexandra!' Carlyle growled in warning, and he gripped her hand painfully.

'It is not me; I do not have my Source.' Alexandra truthfully looking around as her eyes began to adjust to the darkness. A ball of light appeared before Carlyle, and he tried to pull Alexandra closer, but there was someone pulling on her arm. Surprised Alexandra dropped her goblet sending wine splashing across her and Carlyle. The ball of light flickered dangerously, threatening to plunge them into darkness once more. 'What is going on?' Carlyle roared as he released Alexandra's arm. *He is having trouble with his Source;* she realised as she watched the flickering light. Was it one of the Castle Sorcerers? *More likely several if they are trying to bind his power.* The hand on her arm tugged her backwards once more, and Alexandra quickly followed the unseen figure from the dais, creeping into the thick of the crowd. A cluster of people moved aside as a tall figure swept down the middle of the great hall, coming to stand several feet away from Carlyle.

'Citizens of Saphyre!' Caleb's voice boomed just as powerfully as Carlyle's and Alexandra heard the people around him murmuring in surprise. She fought back a burst of hysterical laughter as she looked at the confusion on peoples' faces. There was little difference between Carlyle and Caleb physically, one could easily pass for the other, and many seemed to fear this was a trick. 'For centuries we have lived under the tyranny of this imposter and his ancestors! Five hundred years ago our rightful king was murdered and with his murder came the rumours that his son had died alongside him. Since then we have lived in fear under the Tioranach house.'

Alexandra tried to look over the towering shoulders of those who surrounded her protectively, trying to keep her from Carlyle's sight. It was impossible for her to see anything, she was sure even if she knelt on the floor and tried to peer through their legs she would see nothing but those in the resistance. The thought eased her nerves slightly; perhaps they would at least be evenly matched against those loyal to Carlyle. In the centre of the great hall Caleb continued his speech.

'Tonight we will end these five hundred years of suffering and bring a fresh start to Saphyre! With the blessing of our True Queen, I will found a new ruling house – the house of Saoirse!' Despite the battle ahead, Alexandra could not help a small smile at Caleb's choice of name. Over the years as she had pieced together her memory she had found through studying Saphyrian books that ancient Karstarian and Saphyrian were similar. Caleb had chosen to found his new house with a word similar to that of Alexandra's; freedom. Her spark of happiness was short-lived, and she was abruptly brought back to the present.

'How dare you?' Carlyle's voice thundered and held out his arm towards Caleb. A loud *bang* roared through the air and Alexandra fell to her knees as the floor began to shake violently. Caleb seemed to hold his ground and even managed to keep his balance. 'Alexandra!' Her breath caught in her throat at Carlyle's roar and shakily she stood up accepting the help of the person beside her. 'Where is Alexandra?' Those encircling her grew tighter, but she gently nudged them aside.

'Here,' her voice was stronger than she felt and she calmly walked towards Caleb, coming to a stop at his side. She was frightened by the stares of pure hatred of some of the people in the crowd but reassured by the spark of hope in others. 'Carlyle I have constantly pleaded with you to change, but each time you refuse. I can no longer live under a tyrant; I cannot live every day in fear wondering if I have conceived – and whether that child is a prince or princess. Nor should my citizens live in fear. No one should be judged on whether they possess the Source or not, nor should they be denied their very freedom. My citizens have the right to choose to live their lives as they please, they should not be forced in to slavery because they are seen as lesser beings. They should not be forced into starvation because they are thought unworthy because they do not have the power we possess. Those who wield the Source have a duty to care and protect those who do not wield it. Just as those who are skilled with a sword have the same duty and care to those, who cannot wield one.' She forced herself to meet Carlyle's blazing eyes and forced her legs to remain upright. From the hatred blazing in his eyes, she was no longer certain that he would not execute her should they lose. 'You are consumed by hatred, by *fear*, you no longer think rationally when making decisions. You are driven purely by greed and power. You murdered an innocent *child* – someone who had not even taken their first breath simply because of your hatred!'

'You lying, traitorous *whore*!' Alexandra was surprised to hear the words not come from Carlyle but from a woman in the crowd. She turned to seek out who had spoken, and her eyes landed on Vanya. 'The child of whom you speak was conceived by traitors who plotted the downfall of our king! As was –'

Vanya began to choke, and she held her throat as she fought to keep speaking. In horror, Alexandra realised that it had been Vanya all along who had betrayed Caleb. She found herself suddenly in the indoor training ground on the night she had sought out Krista, crouched behind crates as she overheard Rhonwyn and Xander talking about Krista. *Vanya...she overheard them both; it was her I saw running away.* She felt as if she had been punched in the stomach and she gripped Caleb's arm. Turning to look up at him she could see that he too had come to the same sickening realisation.

'I will not deny Krista aligned herself with Caleb, but she was not a traitor. I told you all along that Krista was no more guilty than I – but never have we been guilty of treason. We fight for Saphyre, not against her.' Alexandra raised her chin as she looked back at Carlyle, refusing to let him see that she was frightened. 'I am the True Queen of Saphyre. Unfortunately for you Carlyle you cannot claim that you are the True King. Can anyone in this room claim that they witnessed the Goddess's Blessing at Carlyle's coronation as they did at mine? Her blessing has been witnessed in centuries.' She used Carlyle's name intentionally, hoping to show the people that he was not a symbol of fear. Despite her trembling legs.

'And you are willing to throw the kingdom into chaos, just to see if this imposter can make the claim?'

'Caleb will not let our people starve. He believes, as do I, that the Source does not make you better or that people are mere possessions. I stand alongside Caleb, and I am confident the Goddess will bestow her Blessing upon him.' Fresh murmurs broke out through the crowd.

'Silence!' He roared. 'Alexandra *enough* of this foolishness! How can you believe that this man has any claim to the throne?'

'Look at us Carlyle,' Caleb spoke up, 'as loathe as I am to admit it, we share ancestral blood. There is no denying this; however, I can claim to be descended from the *rightful* king who was murdered in cold blood for his crown.'

'Alexandra, you realise that by publicly aligning yourself with this traitor I could have you executed here and now?' Carlyle continued as if he had not heard Caleb. Alexandra could see that Caleb's words had struck a chord with many in the crowd as they observed their king and the newcomer.

'Then do it,' Alexandra spoke defiantly and stared at Carlyle with an expression far braver than she felt. 'I would rather die a traitor than as the cowering wife and queen of a tyrant.' She had not realised that Caleb wore two swords until he unsheathed one and passed it to Alexandra. She dared not glance down at her long skirt, frightened it would betray the flicker of fear in her eyes. 'We are not afraid to fight you Carlyle, your reign ends tonight.' She turned to survey the sea of faces many of whom look terrified. 'If anyone does not wish to fight then, please leave now, we will not hold it against anyone. We want those who fight to do so because they *choose* too.'

In a split second the atmosphere had changed, no longer were people standing in a hushed silence. Chaos rang through the great hall as those loyal to Carlyle moved towards the exit, trying to imprison those who tried to escape. The clang of metal upon rang through the air making Alexandra's ears ring painfully. Caleb moved towards Carlyle and Alexandra grabbed his arm, bringing him to a halt.

'Be careful of his Source,' she warned him and felt little reassurance as he winked at her before plunging into the thick crowd. She knew that the Castle Sorcerers who were on Caleb's side were working to bind Carlyle's Source, but how long could they hold out? Gripping the sword Caleb had handed her, Alexandra scanned the crowd searching for Vanya. She spotted the cat-like woman standing over someone who looked horribly still, a smug smile upon her almost feline features. Alexandra sprinted across the great hall, ducking and waving between those who fought in her desperation to confront the woman. 'How could you? Caleb *trusted* you!' She spat raising a sword and parrying a strike from Vanya.

'And his Majesty did not trust you?' Vanya spat. 'You have bewitched and weakened Caleb. He is not fit to rule. I had hopes that he was our True King. He never realised that I worked for His Majesty, but the closer I got to him the more I *hoped*. Perhaps I should thank you for that at least. I knew from the moment I caught the two of you together that he was not worthy to rule us and neither are you. You betrayed your husband, you have plotted his downfall while all the time sharing his bed. And the child…well, we both know that is *not* a prince.' The blood in Alexandra's veins turned to ice as Vanya lazily stepped into the hallway. She ran forwards to follow but found her path blocked by a familiar invisible glass-like wall.

'*No!*' She cried slapping her free hand against the invisible barrier. 'Vanya –'

'You never appreciated His Majesty; you have no idea what he has done for this kingdom. I regret taking him for granted, for doubting his leadership and thinking that Caleb could rule in his place. All he wanted from you was a son and you could not even give him that.'

'Please you cannot harm Bréanainn, he is just a baby!' Alexandra pleaded casting a look over her shoulder for help. She had to find someone who could leave. *Bréanainn was meant to be safe! No harm was to come to him! Please, Goddess protect him!* When Alexandra turned back to the doorway, she was horrified to see Vanya had fled. Desperately Alexandra flung herself back into the crowd, her eyes seeking out Caleb.

She found him towards the back of the great hall, close to the dais and battling Carlyle. Both men moved in a blur, too fast for her eyes to focus on them, their swords thrusting with lethal determination. *If I distract Caleb now, he will die.* A scream to Alexandra's right tore her from her panic. A Castle Guard had pinned Rhonwyn to the wall and was holding his sword against her throat. A second Castle Sorcerer was close by and tried to rush to Rhonwyn's help, but they were thwarted by Foréignean.

Without hesitation Alexandra sprinted towards the Castle Guard; holding her sword by the hilt, she swung the flat of the blade up and into the guard's skull. As he stumbled backwards Rhonwyn took advantage and brought him to his knees with a well-aimed kick.

'Your Source?' Alexandra gasped pulling her friend away from the wall and scanning her for injuries. Rhonwyn nodded towards Carlyle, too exhausted to speak. Her face was drenched in sweat, and her breathing came out in ragged gasps. 'Vanya has gone after Bréanainn, but Carlyle has bound me to this room.' She could see Rhonwyn was dangerously close to using her Source up and Alexandra cursed herself for still not having her own power.

'I will distract Carlyle – you alert Caleb.' Rhonwyn gasped bracing herself against the wall and closing her eyes so she could concentrate. As Alexandra sprinted towards Caleb, she could see that Rhonwyn was not wasting any time. She watched as Carlyle seemed to trip over his own feet, stumbling backwards into a group of sorcerers. Alexandra grabbed Caleb's arm, pulling him backwards into the crowd and away from Carlyle.

'Vanya has gone after Bréanainn; she knows that Carlyle is not the father!' She was thankful that Caleb did not pause to think upon what to do; he turned and bolted from the ballroom. Alexandra prepared herself to take his place, turning to face Carlyle she was frightened to see his filled with hatred and betrayal but disturbed to see the look of longing still lingering within.

'I have given you *everything*.' He growled.

'You have given me nothing but sorrow,' Alexandra hissed. 'You have done nothing but lie to me from the moment you found me in Bournemouth – and let us not forget that you *blackmailed* me into marrying you! That you murdered my grandmother simply because I dared to refuse you!' She cried out in surprise as Carlyle lunged at her with his sword, managing to bring her own up to parry him with only a split second to spare. 'Carlyle *please* if you give up the throne we can spare your life! I do not want to kill you!' Even now she loathed the thought at committing murder; if she could reason with him then surely he would go peacefully?

'Nor do I wish to harm you,' Carlyle's voice was soft but he swung his sword at her once more. Alexandra was not as quick to block his strike, and she bit down on a cry of pain as his blade slashed her from shoulder to elbow, slicing through the fabric of her dress and the skin of her arm. Blood poured from the wound, and she knew she had made a fatal error the moment she stepped backwards, trying to press the fabric of her dress to the wound in an attempt to staunch the flow of blood all the while frantically trying to block his strikes.

All around her she could hear the clashing of steel upon steel and feel the rushing of air as sorcerers used various spells throughout the room. But it was the cries of those who lay dying that would haunt her for the rest of her life. She longed to close her eyes, to block it all from her mind. Unable to hold her sword anymore in her right hand she switched it, almost slipping in a puddle of her blood as she tried to evade Carlyle.

'This is entirely your fault,' Carlyle's voice was tauntingly soft. 'Our people are crying out in pain, *dying* because of you.' *Stop it!* Alexandra wanted to plead and choked back a sob. She continued blocking his strikes, but it was half-heartedly, almost as if she were already defeated.

'Long live Queen Alexandra!' Xander's cry surprised both Alexandra and Carlyle, but it gave her a new burst of energy. Using the distraction to gain even ground she began attacking Carlyle in earnest once more. Her sword work was clumsy, and she fought to maintain control of the weapon with her left hand, it felt unnatural and awkward, but she tried to ignore her mind telling her to switch hands. Somehow she managed to keep the sword moving without dropping it, slicing it through the air but not matter how hard she tried Carlyle managed to counter each of her strikes.

'When this is over I will make you and that traitor watch each and *every* execution.' Carlyle hissed. The hilt of the sword in Alexandra's hand began to grow slippery with sweat but she refused to slacken her grip for even a split second so she could readjust her hold on it.

'When this is over you will not be the king,' her breath was coming out in ragged gasps, and her lungs felt as if they were on fire. She grew desperate as she continued to block Carlyle's strikes and she knew he could see she was weakening. *Just hold him until Caleb returns,* her mind flew to Bréanainn and she prayed that Caleb had reached him in time. *Please, Goddess let no harm come to Bréanainn, Helena or Roisin – they had no part in this!* She was snapped back to attention as the flat of Carlyle's sword struck her hand, and she almost dropped her sword in pain.

'Alexandra, you have been misled, can you not see that? This imposter has taken advantage of your sweet nature, of your naivety.' As Carlyle spoke Alexandra could feel her body grow heavy and stiff as if she were turning to stone. The sword in her hand was too heavy to lift, and she looked at Carlyle furiously, unable to move. 'Think of what you are doing to our son, do you want him to grow up thinking that his mother is a liar? A *traitor?* That she would put his own birthright at jeopardy?' A surge of anger burst through Alexandra, releasing her from Carlyle's spell and freeing her limbs. Thrusting her sword, she almost succeeded in striking Carlyle but at the last second, he managed to block her and force her backwards.

'I *am* thinking of Bréanainn. I am not prepared for him to live his life in fear!' Out of the corner of her eye, she could see Rhonwyn fighting a group of sorcerers, her robes were singed and bloody, but there was a look of determined concentration upon her face. Several feet away Foréignean was slumped, but Alexandra was unable to tell if he was dead or alive. As she glanced around she was horrified to see that the Castle Sorcerers who had aligned with Caleb were exhausting themselves and that they were so embroiled in the battle that they were struggling to keep Carlyle's Source bound.

Fighting back waves of panic Alexandra focused on trying to keep her balance. Krista had trained her for this very reason; in case she needed to defend herself without her Source. But never for a second had Alexandra really thought that it would be with Carlyle she fought against. *Every moment spent here is a moment where I am not protecting Bréanainn.* She prayed that Caleb was safe, that they were all safe and he was on his way back down. How much longer could she hold Carlyle off? *I cannot wait for Caleb to return,* she argued. *This has to end now!*

She saw Carlyle's left foot slip on a puddle of blood and seizing the opportunity she brought her sword up and slashed it across Carlyle's chest. The tunic she had spent weeks stitching was soaked with blood as she managed to strike him from chest to midriff, but she could see it wasn't a mortal wound. Unrelenting she continued to strike at him. Using his loss of balance against him, she dared to get closer to him, slipping her leg behind his knee and driving her elbow into his stomach. Carlyle's sword was sent flying from his hand as he fell backwards, the wind clearly knocked from his lungs. Quickly Alexandra kicked his sword aside, pressing the tip of her own into the hollow of his throat. *I cannot do this;* she thought in horror as she watched his skin dip beneath the pressure of the blade. *I am not a killer.* But she forced herself to not betray her feelings.

'I do not want to kill you; I have never truly wished you dead.' Her voice cracked and she felt her cheeks flame. 'I loathe you Carlyle, but I do not want to be a murderer such as yourself. *Please* see sense, accept your defeat and let us live in peace.'

'You cannot kill me,' Carlyle laughed seemingly unaware of the sword pressed to his throat. A gust of wind swept Alexandra through the air, sending her flying backwards and crashing into the wall with a heavy *smack*. Landing on her knees, Alexandra doubled over as she fought to fill her lungs with the oxygen she was desperately lacking. Her sword lay a foot away, completely forgotten and useless to her.

A hushed silence descended upon the room as everyone seemed in frozen place, their eyes upon Alexandra and Carlyle. For a split second, Alexandra had thought the fighting had ceased, that the battle had been miraculously won. But as she took in the stillness of all those around her she realised that it was not because they had won the battle that the fighting had stopped, it was quite the opposite. Carlyle was in full control of his powers and was keeping everyone pinned in place to stop them from interfering.

A cry escaped from her lips as Carlyle seized her by her arms and pulled her to her feet, squeezing her injured ne with a bone brushing pressure. His hands were searing hot and she could feel her own skin scorching beneath his hands, blistering from the intense contact. *He is using too much of his Source;* she realise as she took in his sweat-drenched appearance and sickly pale skin.

'You are weak Alexandra,' Carlyle's sapphire eyes blazed with anger, and the spiral pattern began to twirl at a sickening speed. But despite the anger in his eyes, his voice was soft and tender; he brought up one hand to cup her face and stroked her cheek gently. 'You cannot kill me. You have no power of your own; did you think a sword would really be enough to defeat me?'

'No,' Alexandra whispered shaking her head. She forced herself to avoid looking at his eyes; if she fell under his power now, then she would be truly finished. The hands gripping her arms tightened and with their vice-like grip came a fresh pain. She could feel his Source gripping her heart, squeezing it tightly as if he hoped to squeeze the life from her. 'Carlyle...' Alexandra choked as black spots burst across her vision, threatening to plunge her into a suffocating darkness she was sure she would not want to take from.

'When this is over you will understand that I am the rightful king, Alexandra. I can forgive you this time, you will be punished of course, but I will show you some leniency. But do not think to cross me again. I will not tolerate the slightest of defiance; no speaking against me nor refusing my company. You will understand that my wishes are yours. Your duty will be to beget me heirs, *only* sons!' Alexandra gasped as she continued to fight for her breathe. Molten hatred flared through her, filling her veins and very core. She tried to kick out but her brain was too starved of oxygen for her to even lift her foot a millimetre and she found even blinking had become a struggle.

*Forgive him, Alexandra.* Krista's voice filled the thick darkness, bringing warmth and comfort to Alexandra. She tried to shake her head but found she was completely frozen in place. She could feel Krista's hands squeezing her shoulders protectively, she longed to turn her head but she was fixated in place.

*I cannot!* Alexandra pleaded as she felt tears skim down her cheeks, perhaps she should just give up? *Please Krista do not ask me to do this, I cannot forgive him for all that he has done. I* loathe *him!*

*You do not understand the fate that awaits Carlyle. He will die unloved, and there will be no one to defend him against the Goddess's judgment.* Krista squeezed Alexandra's shoulders tightly, but she could no longer focus on her friend's words. The comfort Krista had brought was drowned out by blind panic. All she could focus on was the burning sensation of her lungs pleading for air and that of her heart being crushed beneath a boulder. Fighting back the panic Alexandra fought against her darkening vision and tried to focus on Carlyle. His face was contorted into a mixture of grief and anger, but his eyes were empty almost as if he was completely lost.

'Carlyle,' Alexandra choked. *'please -'*

'I love you Alexandra. I have tried to give you everything; a kingdom, love...all I have wanted is your happiness.' *He is genuine,* Alexandra realised as pity flared throughout her. He truly believed that he had been acting in her best interests. She found she believed that he did love her, but they had different concepts of what love was. Carlyle's idea of love was warped, twisted and even poisonous.

*Forgive him!* Krista insisted as deep within Alexandra felt a light begin to flare and her hands began to crackle with electricity. Alexandra's Source returned to her as a sudden rush of energy. It filled her starved lungs with oxygen and broke up the black spots which had blinded her vision. Meeting Carlyle's eyes she found that his spiral pattern was still twisting hypnotically, but his power held no effect over her. *Please Alexandra, for your own sake you must forgive him!*

Inwardly Alexandra nodded, and she felt sadness as she looked at Carlyle, lost for words. Before he could react, she reached out to grasp the front of his tunic, pulling him close so that she could press her lips to his. She felt his stunned surprise; the hands on her arms slackened their grip and moved to caress her shoulders. Carefully, as if she was approaching an enraged animal, Alexandra rested the palms of her hands flat against the blood soaked tunic. Closing her eyes so Carlyle would not see her tears Alexandra gathered her Source and shoved it through her hands and into Carlyle's chest, wrapping it around his own heart. She clenched her fists, clutching at the ripped fabric of Carlyle's tunic. Forcing herself to open her eyes she pulled her head back ever so slightly and looked into Carlyle's own eyes. They were wide with shock, his mouth opening and closing as he fought to speak.

'Alexandra *no*!' Rhonwyn's voice broke through the silence and Alexandra realised that she had completely forgotten they were not alone. The room was full of people who stood watching in horrified silence. 'You cannot kill him, not like this! Your Source will go sour!' Alexandra's concentration almost broke, but she forced herself to focus on her task. She prayed her Source would not go sour, that she would not tread the same dark path that Carlyle had taken. As Carlyle fell to his knees, Alexandra knelt beside him, her pity for him growing stronger. He had caused so much fear, grief and pain yet in his final moments he looked so weak and helpless.

'Alexandra...' Carlyle's lips took on an unpleasant shade of blue and Alexandra almost relaxed her Source but held on at the last second. He raised his right hand, seeking out her own and Alexandra seized it with a tight grip. 'Bréanainn...'

'Will be safe, I promise.' It was strange; Alexandra had spent years loathing this man for all he had done to her. For the pain and suffering, he had brought upon her and those closest to her. Yet even as his life gradually left him, she found her hatred evaporating. It was as if a great weight had been lifted from her. It never crossed her mind to confess to him the truth of Bréanainn's parentage. What was the point of adding to his suffering?

'I...I am sorry,' he fell backwards on to the floor so that he lay gazing up at the ceiling. Around them, people slowly began to regain control of their limbs, and the sound of weapons dropping to the floor rang through the air. Alexandra ignored the shouts as those who had fought for Carlyle fled the room, the sound of pursuing footsteps close behind them. Her attention was focused solely on Carlyle and let the tears flow freely as she took his life, all the while loathing herself for carrying out such a deed. Carlyle's eyes met her own, and she realised there was no longer hatred within the sapphire depths. 'Please...forgive...me...' His voice was hoarse and struggled to hear him.

When Krista had told her she needed to forgive Carlyle, it seemed like an impossible task. That her friend was asking too much of her. But as he lay on the floor, dying, she was overwhelmed by pity for the man who had ruled a kingdom through fear. Gone was the loathsome tyrant, instead, Alexandra found herself staring at the lost young prince who desperately grieved for his mother. Leaning down Alexandra brushed her lips lightly against his own, they were surprisingly cold, but she didn't recoil.

'Of course Carlyle,' she whispered squeezing his hand. 'I forgive you.' A fleeting smile crossed his lips, slowly his eyes glassed over and he chest ceased to rise and fall.

Alexandra was unsure of how long she sat beside Carlyle's lifeless body. She reached out to brush her fingertips against his eyelids, drawing them to a close so that he looked peaceful. A hand squeezing her shoulder pulled her from her thoughts, and she looked to her side, surprised to see Rhonwyn kneeling beside her. The great hall was surprisingly empty. Several castle guards stood around prisoners who had been bound with the Source, all looking glum and frightened. She could see Ywain sitting at the head of the prisoners, his face pale and his eyes sweeping from side to side as he sought an escape.

Xander leant beside the doors to the great hall; he was favouring one leg over the other and Alexandra was disturbed to see it bent at a dangerous angle. He met Alexandra's eyes, and she realised that Caleb had not yet returned. *It is not over,* she realised jumping to her feet and sprinting for her chamber. No longer was she imprisoned within the great hall, Carlyle's hold over her had completely dispersed.

'Bréanainn!' She cried out as she found the door to her chamber shattered on the staircase and the chaos that lay within. Vanya's body sat half-propped, half-slumped against the wall; a dagger embedded in her neck. Roisin sat on the floor, cradling something in her lap. 'No...' Alexandra felt her knees buckle as she reached Roisin, kneeling beside her.

'She had no part in this...she knew nothing of it...' Roisin's voice was thick, and her eyes were swollen from crying. 'That woman...she came from nowhere. We locked the door and refused to open it, but she would not leave, she broke it down...the guards who were meant to protect us were nowhere to be found. Alexandra clasped Roisin's hands and found them slick with blood. 'Helena...she refused to let her near Bréanainn.' Alexandra looked down at her lady; Helena's face was calm and [peaceful. Her eyes were shut as if she slept but when Alexandra reached out to touch her; she found Helena's skin unnaturally cold. Blood stained her golden hair, matting it in several places. 'She protected us...'

'Helena, please wake up,' Alexandra whispered and turned pleading eyes towards Roisin. 'You were both meant to be safe, all three of you – no harm was to come to you!' *I should have done more;* she wept to herself. *I should have protected them better.* Why had she not arranged for them to go underground? To reside in Caleb's chamber until the battle was over? But she knew it would have taken too long for them to get down there, and that Vanya would have found them just as easily. *My foolishness cost Helena her life,* fresh tears streamed down Alexandra's face, and she wept bitterly. 'Rhonwyn – she could heal Helena, I will get her...'

'Alexandra no,' Rhonwyn's voice was soft from the doorway and Alexandra felt the last flare of hope gutter out. She watched as Rhonwyn took a blanket from her bed and spread it over Helena. 'Let her rest; she has earned her peace.'

'She would not wish you to grieve.' Roisin murmured and quickly wiped her eyes, ignoring the bloody streak she left across her face.

'W – Where is Bréanainn?' Alexandra asked her eyes darting around the small chamber.

'With Caleb, he took him down to Carlyle's chambers. He did not want to leave us, but I hardly thought it appropriate to be here...and I did not want to leave Helena.' Alexandra leant forwards to embrace Roisin, burying her face into the woman's shoulder.

'I am sorry I failed you both.'

'Caleb is downstairs,' Rhonwyn helped Alexandra to her feet. 'Go to him, you both have a lot to discuss. I will ensure Helena is brought down and well looked after.' Alexandra looked down at the covered woman, unable to see through the tears. Forcing herself to turn around she hugged the wall as she walked down to Carlyle's chambers. She found Caleb sitting cross-legged on the floor, cradling a sleeping Bréanainn.

'Carlyle?' He asked rising to his feet and pressing Bréanainn into her arms.

'Dead,' Alexandra's voice was hoarse. 'I had no choice Caleb...I...' She shook her head and flung her arm to the side, sending a ball of fire to light the hearth. When she turned back to look at him once more, she could see he was nodding in understanding.

'I never meant for you to be the one,' he whispered drawing her close. 'I wanted to protect you from this.' He kissed the top of her head and wrapped both arms around her shoulders, being careful so as not to crush Bréanainn between them. Alexandra focused on Bréanainn, but her mind was on Helena who lay lifeless upstairs. How many countless others had fallen because of them? Squeezing her eyes tightly shut she pressed her face into Caleb's front and broke down into sobs, allowing them to rack through her body freely.

# *Epilogue*
# *One Year Later*

Alexandra leapt down from Solas's back and patted the mare's neck affectionately. The first snow of the winter had begun to fall and was softly blanketing the city and northern part of the kingdom. Yet in the clearing it was lush and green, the air not yet frozen from the winter chill. Kneeling down Alexandra checked over the pieces of cloth infused with her Source that she had wrapped around Solas's legs to keep her warm. Satisfied that they had survived the journey, she straightened up and relieved the mare of her saddlebag.

As she opened the saddlebag, her mind wandered to the first time Carlyle had brought her to the clearing on her twenty-second life-day. Only a short while ago she had celebrated her twenty-sixth and had decided the time was right to do what she had long been putting off. As she looks around surveying the lush greenery and warm spring she could not help but admire had despite all that had gone on this small haven had stayed the same; untouched by misery enveloping the kingdom.

Pulling herself away from the past Alexandra concentrated on the task at hand. She had told Caleb what she was doing, but not where she was going. As peaceful and serene as she found this small clearing she had decided this would be the last time she would visit it. She had no right to disturb the peace. She had seen no reason to reveal the location to Caleb, and she had been thankful that he had understood her need to be alone. Not once had he tried to talk her out of her decision, nor to put it off even longer.

It was remarkable the difference between her first and second husbands, although she could still not shake the unease at their strong physical similarities. When she had first met Caleb, it had not disturbed her, but then she had not been a murderer. Now each time she looked into Caleb's eyes, she found herself staring into those of Carlyle and would often wake up drenched in a cold sweat reliving the horror of that evening in the great hall.

Reaching into the saddle bag Alexandra pulled out a battered urn and stared at the object sadly. It did little to ease her conscience knowing that if Carlyle had won the battle than those who had fought for Caleb would have died horrible deaths. In an attempt to atone for her crime, and to prevent her Source from souring, Alexandra had thrown herself into learning the art of healing from Rhonwyn who had been freshly promoted to the Commander of the Castle Sorcerers.

Saphyre had entered into a moon of mourning after the battle, but discreet preparations had been made for Caleb's coronation. Even now Alexandra could not forget the tension of that day. She had sat on a throne beside Caleb, holding the golden cloak in trembling hands. She, along with many others, had been unable to breathe as Father Dóchas lowered the crown on to Caleb's head. What if the Goddess did not bestow her blessing upon him? But their fears were allayed almost instantly. The Light of the Goddess had been just as blinding and scorching as when Alexandra herself had been crowned. She had never seen Caleb looking so relieved, nor the onlookers so overjoyed, and the applause had been deafening.

Many of those who had been loyal to Carlyle had been pardoned, neither Alexandra nor Caleb wanting to start Saphyre's new beginning with more deaths on their hands. Foréignean had been one such follower who had maintained his position as the head of the Combat Sorcerers, although he begrudgingly answered to Rhonwyn as the overall leader. Alexandra still did not trust the man, but she had learnt to value his experience. He gained nothing from displeasing either her or Caleb and so had seemingly settled into the new reign. She had learnt that Éibhear had been one of the first to fall in battle as he had tried to flee the great hall, not wanting to be caught up in the bloodshed. But it was the disappearance of Ywain which even now Alexandra feared. *He would gain nothing by returning and trying to cause upset.* Those who were not pardoned had been imprisoned in the new dungeons, cells where people could stand and sit rather than being trapped in the walls.

Caleb had been true to his word, and his first act as the True King of Saphyre had been to end slavery. Alexandra had been grief stricken that Helena had not been there to celebrate, to enjoy her long deserved freedom. She and Roisin had spent Roisin's first official evening as a free woman together, talking of Helena and sharing their grief. She had expected that Roisin would soon depart Saphyre and return to her home kingdom to start her life afresh. She had been overwhelmed with joy when Roisin had point blank refused to leave Saphyre, stating that she would much rather support the new reign. She had not chosen to come to Saphyre, but it was her home. Her determination to stay in the kingdom was clearer when Alexandra discovered that Jacen had begun courting her lady. Alexandra had teased Roisin mercilessly but had given her blessing to the two, happy that at least Roisin was able to live happily.

Jacen and Lemuel were the only people left who served from Carlyle's council. Both seemed relaxed, especially Lemuel who no longer had to fear his wife passing from a mysterious illness. She had borne him a daughter and Alexandra had been touched that the child not only carried her name but that Alexandra had been chosen to be the young girl's godmother.

Opening the urn Alexandra tilted it an angle and began to pace around the clearing, letting the ashes scatter in the breeze. People had been so fearful of Carlyle, afraid that his Source would resurrect him, that Caleb had decided to build a funeral pyre in the city. Alexandra had feared the crowds would riot but she had been surprised by the subdued atmosphere. Any skirmishes which had broken out had been peacefully quashed by Xander and his Castle Guards. Scattering Carlyle's ashes where his mother rested had been Alexandra's hope that he would find some sort of peace. She had never forgotten Krista's words that he would face judgement alone and she truly pitied him for it, even shedding tears on several occasions for him.

*I loathed this man;* she thought wiping her eyes. *Yet I cry freely for him, why?* From inside her tunic, she pulled out the locket that Carlyle had given her on their voyage to Saphyre. It had never crossed her mind to keep the locket or even to melt the golden metal down. It had never truly belonged to her. She would never forget her first marriage, and she would be surrounded by plenty of reminders. Placing the locket into the urn Alexandra knelt at the water's edge and gently eased the urn beneath the warm surface.

Sitting down she tugged off her boots and stockings to allow her feet to dangle in the water. Her mind on her first visit to the clearing, had it been here that she had conceived her first child? The thought of her daughter still tugged at her heart, but at least now she was able to grieve and acknowledge to the tragedy openly. A small smile tugged at her lips as she rested her hand on her stomach. She and Caleb had been married for seven moons, and she was fairly certain that she had recently conceived. They had waited before marrying, both wanting to ensure that there was no question as to the child's parentage and Alexandra not quite ready to step straight into her second marriage.

Her marriage to Caleb was certainly different. She had accepted that there was no passionate love between them; but there had been friendship, and over time it had developed into a form of love. She had not even shared friendship with Carlyle and had been grateful just to have that with Caleb. She did not find sharing his bed an enduring experience, nor did he insist on their coupling every night. He had offered to switch chambers with her, taking the tower for himself but Alexandra had refused. Even on nights where they did not couple she found it peaceful just to be close to Caleb, to listen to his soft breathing and the gentle beat of his heart.

Bréanainn would sleep in his cot at the end of their bed, but Alexandra knew they would have to prepare his own chambers soon enough. Bréanainn was showing signs of saying his first words any day and both Alexandra and Caleb waited with bated breath, teasing each other on what he would most likely say first. It had been made clear that Bréanainn was prince in name only, that he was not destined to be king. Many believed that he would one day join the church but Alexandra was adamant he would have the one thing she had been denied throughout her marriage to Carlyle; choice. They would of course encourage him to join the church as thanks to the Goddess, but neither she nor Caleb were prepared to force him too. If he felt he could serve Saphyre, and the Goddess, in better ways then they would support him.

Carefully climbing to her feet, Alexandra returned to Solas. She would seek out Rhonwyn before she had supper with Caleb, perhaps she would even be able to give him good news before they retired for the day. Swinging up into the saddle Alexandra surveyed the beautiful clearing one final time, brushing aside tears as she turned Solas and trotted away.

# ABOUT THE AUTHOR

Willow currently lives in London with her husband and cat Nora. An animal lover she fosters whenever possible. During her free-time she enjoys reading, gaming, going to comic cons, sewing and of course writing.